LE DIVORCE

Diane Johnson was born in Illinois and educated at the universities of Utah and California. She is the author of several acclaimed novels, including *Le Marriage*, *Persian Nights* and *The Shadow Knows*, two collections of essays, and biographies of Mary Ellen Peacock and Dashiell Hammett. She has also written screenplays and collaborated with Stanley Kubrick on *The Shining*. She lives in Paris and San Francisco with her husband.

ALSO BY DIANE JOHNSON

Fiction

Fair Game
Loving Hands at Home
Burning
The Shadow Knows
Lying Low
Persian Nights
Health and Happiness
Le Marriage

Non-Fiction

Lesser Lives
Dashiell Hammett
Terrorists and Novelists
Natural Opium

Diane Johnson

Le Divorce

VINTAGE

Published by Vintage 1998

8 10 9 7

First published in Great Britain by
Chatto & Windus 1997

Vintage
Random House, 20 Vauxhall Bridge Road,
London SW1V 2SA

Random House Australia (Pty) Limited
20 Alfred Street, Milsons Point, Sydney
New South Wales 2061, Australia

Random House New Zealand Limited
18 Poland Road, Glenfield,
Auckland 10, New Zealand

Random House (Pty) Limited
Endulini, 5a Jubilee Road, Parktown 2193,
South Africa

The Random House Group Limited Reg. No. 954009
www.randomhouse.co.uk

A CIP catalogue record for this book
is available from the British Library

ISBN 0 09 975391 X

Papers used by Random House are natural, recyclable products made from wood grown in sustainable forests. The manufacturing processes conform to the environmental regulations of the country of origin

Printed and bound in Great Britain by
Cox & Wyman Ltd, Reading, Berkshire

To our French friends
Colette and Paul,
Marie-Claude,
Hélène, and Mireille,
who've told me things,
and Linda and Michelle –
Américaines in Paris

Man isn't at all one, after all – it takes so much of him to be American, to be French, etc.

– Henry James to William Dean Howells,
May 1, 1890

PROLOGUE

I am the doubter and the doubt,
And I the hymn the Brahmin sings.
– *Ralph Waldo Emerson*

I SUPPOSE BECAUSE I WENT TO FILM SCHOOL, I THINK OF MY story as a sort of film. In a film, this part would be under the credits, opening with an establishing shot from a high angle, perhaps the Eiffel Tower, panning tiny scenes far below of the foreign city, life as watched from the wrong end of a telescope. Closer up, the place is identified by clichés of Frenchness – people carrying long baguettes of bread, old men wearing berets, women walking poodles, buses, flower stalls, those Art Nouveau entrances to the metro that seem to beckon to a nether region of vice and art but actually lead to an efficient transportation system, this contradiction perhaps a clue to the French themselves.

Then, in a series of close shots we become aware that some of the people we are seeing are not French, that among all the Gallic bustle are many Americans. Far from their native land, their flavor changes ever so slightly as they absorb the new perfumes, just as the slightly toxic chemistry of Americans abroad erodes, just a little, the new place in which they find themselves.

Some closeups of individual Americans:

People hanging around American Express (one of them me,

Isabel Walker, trying to get money from the wall machine).

Two young women in jeans drinking coffee at a café. They glare at a man smoking, get up and move to a table farther away, disgust on their blandly pretty California faces. (These are Roxy, my sister, and me, Isabel.)

A well-dressed couple with a camera, having a drink in the Ritz bar, reading maps, swaying with jet lag. These might also be Germans. Germans are the only nationality that can sometimes be mistaken for Americans, even quite close up.

An elegant man reading the *Herald Tribune* at a sidewalk café. He too might be mistaken for European until he carefully removes the butter from the toasted tartine he has ordered, exposed by his pathological American fear of cholesterol.

A handsome, rather stout woman in a mink coat buying oranges at a sidewalk fruit stall. She is speaking French but with a strong American accent. Her brilliant smile does not leave her face, though she is saying, "I was disappointed, Monsieur Jadot, with the fraises."

Charles de Gaulle Airport. A sort of space-age place with people arriving via moving conveyor belts in long tubes, pulling out their blue American passports, irritated at being asked to submit to the ritual of identifying themselves. They know who they are.

In fact these are not generic Americans but some of the actual people in my story. The cast of characters. My sister Roxy and I are the two young women who move away from the smoker, the tourists in the Ritz bar are our parents, Chester and Margeeve Walker, newly arrived in Paris to support Roxy in her time of crisis. (Her French husband has left her, she is about to give birth, and we have at stake a large sum of money.) The man in the café removing butter from his toast is Ames Everett, one of my employers, but he might be any one of a number of American expatriates living in Paris, elegant and independent and detached, bearing some pentimento of past shame or failure like five o'clock shadow along the jaw. The stout woman is the venerated American writer

Olivia Pace. The people arriving at the airport are our brother, Roger; his wife, Jane; another lawyer from his firm; and the other lawyer's wife.

There are, also, certain ghosts of Hemingway and Gertrude Stein, Janet Flanner, Fitzgerald, Edith Wharton, James Baldwin, James Jones – all of them here for something they could not find back home, possessed of an idea about culture and their intellectual heritage, conscious of a connection to Europe. Europe, repository of something they wish to know, and feel they are entitled by ancestry to know.

All of us are wearing the same expression every American wears here, of wonderment mixed with self-satisfaction at having cleverly removed ourselves from the quotidian discomforts and dangers of life in America while at the same time bravely exposing ourselves to the exigencies of foreign money, a difficult language, and curious food, for instance tripe or *andouillette*.

Everyone respectful of Roxy's condition, and of her grief. Or disappointment might be a better word. Everyone respectful of her bravery in sustaining her great disappointment in life, a *chagrin d'amour* that lasts forever.

ONE

If we do not find anything pleasant, at least we shall find something new.

– Voltaire

I THINK OF LIFE AS BEING LIKE FILM BECAUSE OF WHAT I learned at the film school at USC. Film, with its fitful changefulness, its arbitrary notions of coherence, contrasting with the static solemnity of painting, might also be a more appropriate medium for rendering what seems to be happening, and emblematic too perhaps of our natures, Roxy's and mine, and the nature of the two societies, American and French. The New World and the Old, however, is too facile a juxtaposition, and I do not draw the conclusions I began with. If you can begin with conclusions. But I suppose we all do.

I am, as I said, Isabel Walker, a young woman abroad who, in several months in Paris, has learned enough to be considerably changed – and is this not in fact the purpose of young Americans going abroad? To make them think of things they never thought of? I should explain who I *was*.

I had come to France planning to spend some months babysitting my pregnant sister Roxeanne's three-year-old, Geneviève (Gennie), reading books in French that I didn't expect to like much (had read a bit of Rabelais in school and thought it was disgusting, with its talk of farts and twats), and under the cover of being a help to Roxy, hoping to get some of my rough California edges buffed off that the University of Southern California had failed to efface. Leaving college (I had not actually graduated) ordinarily points one to the future, whereas France was not the future, it was only temporizing and staving off the day I would have to make real decisions. When I dropped out of college I became aware that the people in my world, usually so understanding and fond of me, had now a certain hardness of expression when asking me what I planned to do, as if they expected a serious and detailed answer, and my friends, as they awaited the results of their MCATs and LSATs, tended to avoid my eyes. I'll be working on my screenplay, I would tell them, and I'll be helping Roxy with her new baby, and I want to investigate the European film scene. But these statements only earned me a moment of silent scrutiny from my inquisitors before they changed the subject.

I arrived in Paris as scheduled – it is now six months ago – by coincidence the day after Roxy's French husband, Charles-Henri, walked out on her. I took a taxi from the airport, Roxy having explained that she didn't drive a car in France because she didn't want to take the time to go to traffic school. That seemed strange to me, since Roxy as a true Californian has been driving since she was sixteen. I couldn't even imagine a society where a young housewife wouldn't drive.

I had never before been abroad, unless you count Tijuana. Stumbling off the plane, I was too excited to be tired from the long flight. I felt an almost unpleasant thrill of apprehensiveness when the man stamped my passport, sort of as if I had been asked to jump the space between two roofs. Would I make it?

Everyone was speaking French. I had known they would be, of course, but had failed to anticipate my dismay. "Don't get too Frenchy," my father had told me when they took me to the plane. "Remember 'jus plain English's good enough for a 'Merican.' " This was a literary allusion to Kipling's "Why the Leopard Changed His Spots." ("Jus plain black's good enough for a———" – a word Margeeve had carefully whited out of our copy, and naturally we had never pronounced.) No chance of me changing my spots, though – I would never understand French, so I was now cut off from human communication.

My wits were in a turmoil of concern about the correct pronunciation of "Maître-Albert," Roxy's street, lest the taxi man take me somewhere else altogether, and whether he would be surly, the way they are reputed to be, and, more generally, was coming to France a mistake and false detour in life? Roxy must have been watching from her window when I got there, or heard the rattle of the taxi in the street, and came out the big green wooden doors to meet me. She paid the taxi and kissed me. The taxi man leered amiably at both of us.

I was a little shocked by the stairwell of Roxy's apartment building, the peeling walls, the drab, sinking oaken treads. By now I have learned the beauty and value of seventeenth-century staircases and Louis Quinze furniture, but that first day, after the endless trip, I admit I had the feeling Roxy had come down in the world, from a California perspective, into a patch of bad luck. Or rather, I could imagine that our parents, especially Margeeve, would feel that way. I felt subtly co-opted by the secret that Roxy was living in reduced circumstances, here in this foreign place, and I wasn't to tell.

My sister Roxy – my stepsister really – is a poet. This is not an avocation but a vocation she trained for at the University of California at Irvine, and later at the University of Iowa. She has had a volume of poetry published by Illinois Wesleyan, and many poems in magazines. To tell the truth, I have always slightly resented the way our parents have encouraged her in this frivolous, totally unremunerative occupation, while urging me toward various careers such as accounting and personnel management – which means learning to interview people and assign them jobs – and computer service representative, to name only three of the peculiarly repellant occupations they, having heard of them for the first time in their lives, were willing to consecrate me to, so desperate were they to find something for which I might be fitted.

But I admire Roxy's poems, I don't mean otherwise. I wish I could find two screwy words and put them together so that they fizz, like she can. It always surprises me to read Roxy's poems, because in person, the way she talks, she just sounds like a normal person, you wouldn't have thought her thoughts would be odd and complicated.

There are people whose lives progress like one of those charts of heart attack, serrated peaks and valleys like shark's teeth, and my sister Roxeanne is such a person. I loved her from the moment we met, at the marriage of my father to her mother when I was twelve and she seventeen. As we grew up, I adored the way she rushed home from school, slammed the door of her room and wept histrionically. Later there were her school prizes and being the valedictorian, her causes and theses, her poetry and passionate seriousness – and then the surprising glamour of her romantic marriage to the charming Frenchman, and now the surprising drama of their breakup.

We are so different, my stepsister and I, that people don't compare us, and that has kept us friends. Hence my mission, for so it could be called, to come to Paris to help her with the new baby soon to arrive, and now, it seemed, to support her in this crisis. Ordinarily I would not be someone very good at babysitting. But I have always been good at helping Roxy; it was always I who picked up both our clothes and straightened our closets.

Roxy looked well, I thought, and only a little stouter than when I'd seen her last summer, not really showing yet. Her hair was cut to shoulder length, straight across the bottom, like pictures of Joan of Arc. Her hair and eyes are exactly the same light brown as a lovely forest animal's, and her skin was lit from within like a rosy parchment lampshade. I had never seen her look so well, but there was something distracted about her manner.

"Charles-Henri is in the country," she told me immediately. At first, that was all she told me about his absence. But I was too jet-lagged to take in much. A heavy hemlockian sleepiness was already seeping in on me.

"You look wonderful, Izzy," she said. "Don't you love Paris? I know you will. Give me that bag. Is that all you brought? Good thing – your room hasn't got a closet. I forgot to tell you, no closets in France. Gennie's at her day care." And so on.

Her apartment was small, white-painted, with an antique chest of drawers missing some sections of its inlaid wood, and a leather sofa, and several of Charles-Henri's large abstracts. There was a stone fireplace with our family's painting of Saint Ursula over it, her dreamy smile seeming to welcome me, a familiar face from my own past, like a family photograph. I had always thought the woman in the painting was a princess accepting the rich tributes of a wealthy wooer, but Roxeanne has always said she is Saint Ursula, the virgin/warrior saint. I suppose this shows Roxy's nature, exigent and chaste, despite her pregnancy and the romantic nature of her predicament. Saint Ursula was a ninth-century virgin who was massacred eventually, but in this painting, in a contemplative moment in her chamber, she reposes, a book on her lap, disdaining a heap of gifts from the king who wishes to marry her. Two handmaidens standing behind her seem sternly supportive. The room is dark except for a candle on the table at her elbow, and it is the glow of this candle, softly illuminating her face and incidentally the gold and jewels behind her, that has brought up the name of Georges de La Tour.

I believe Roxy loved this picture better when we did not know the girl was Saint Ursula, nor the painter La Tour (if it was) – before it had value, before it became the center and symbol of acrimony.

TWO

I was welcomed at this court with the curiosity naturally inspired by any stranger who comes and breaks into the restricted circle of monotonous etiquette.

– *Benjamin Constant,* Adolphe

I WOULD LIVE IN A SMALL ROOM IN THE ATTIC OF ROXY'S building, like Sara Crewe. Roxy took me up there, two further flights of stairs from her apartment. The last flight narrowed and the wooden treads were unvarnished. We had to squeeze ourselves against the wall to make way for a man in a white gown, his skin so black it was almost purple. Roxy must have felt my involuntary startle, for she said, when he had gone by, "You don't have to be afraid of them here, you know." There was a tinge of mockery in her voice, not against me but against an America where you are afraid.

There were other rooms up there, former maids' rooms under the slanted roof, and a single toilet, in the hall, and no bathroom at all. Roxy assured me that the other rooms were just used for storage or as studios, no one living there except the African family, hence they and I would be the only ones using the toilet, and I could bathe down in her apartment. Of course I was mad at her for not revealing these sordid conditions before I came, but she truly seemed to have no sense of adversity, and the room itself wasn't so bad, though small. You could look out the dormer window into the picturesque little crooked street. But as she had said, there was no closet.

Though it was only ten in the morning, she told me to go to sleep for a couple of hours, so I could make it through till night. But I couldn't sleep, I was speeded up as if on diet pills or No-Doz. I could feel my heart beating as I lay there, sun piercing in the window, thinking it had been a mistake to come, and also that what I really wanted to do was go out and look around the streets. Roxy had said I shouldn't get up until noon, so I tried to endure lying there. Then I got up instead and snuck down the four flights of stairs and out into the street, feeling illicit, as I had always done with Roxy, already disobeying her, thirty minutes after getting here.

I walked down the rue Maître-Albert to the end where I had seen the cathedral of Notre Dame, recognizable from some coasters Margeeve had always had, and sat on a little wall by the river admiring it, thinking I wouldn't go any farther on account of the probability of getting lost. It wouldn't actually matter if you got lost, it was all so magical, with strangers going by speaking their strange tongue, and a little shop with feathered headdresses from the Amazon, and one with old toys, balconied buildings and Citroëns – these were my idea of French. Those big-leafed trees, and bookstalls along the Seine, and guys in berets on scooters, as in old Audrey Hepburn movies. Notre Dame sat on its island across a little bridge; more bridges arched in the distance up and down the river, and boats came by, their loudspeakers announcing the names of this *pont* or that. People waved at me from the decks, as if I were a Parisian. There were pink tablecloths on tables spread out in the street, where people drank coffee, reading newspapers strangely called *Figaro* and *Libération,* their dogs at their feet glaring at each other. Liberation, I thought. Liberation!

I changed my watch. Nine hours later than California. A waking day. I had missed a day of my life. At noon I went back to Roxy's apartment for a bath and some lunch, and after that I did feel better. We sat in her living room. She embraced me again.

"Oh, Iz, I'm so happy you're here. What do you think?" she asked. "Isn't it beautiful?"

I thought she meant her rather dark little apartment. "I like the beams in your ceilings," I said politely. They were in truth quite Santa Barbaran, brown heavy beams. *'Poutres apparantes,"* she said. "Ours are the real, bearing ones. So many apartments these days just have fake ones, for show." This was the first of the cultural mysteries I would encounter. Why would they have fake beams in seventeenth-century buildings?

In the afternoon we walked across the river to pick up Gennie at her day-care place. She didn't remember me, but she had only been one year old when Roxy had brought her to California. Now she was three, and she seemed like a nice little kid, only intermittently bratty, with Charles-Henri's curly hair. The hard thing about her was, she spoke both French and baby talk, so I couldn't exactly talk with her. She understood English, though. Roxy always speaks it to her. I don't know why Gennie had chosen French to speak.

That same night, Madame Lemomja, the African mother, came down to babysit, and Roxy took me to a party at the home of Olivia and Robert Pace. Olivia Pace was the writer and reigning American intellectual in Paris, senior in this hierarchy even to Ames Everett, and Robert Pace was the leading wealthy person of the earnest trust-fund type, not counting some supremely rich notables that hobnob with the French couturiers and Eurotrash from Monaco, whom we were not in a position to know. I was to sense among all the rest of the Americans in Paris a certain camaraderie, even a certain affection, a clinging together in the face of a foreign culture – one that we all had chosen, however temporarily, but felt to be alien all the same.

This was a fateful dinner for me, in that I met several of my future employers – Mrs. Pace herself, Mr. Pace (always smoothly in the background passing drinks), Ames Everett, and the art historian Stuart Barbee. When we walked in, I was conscious of the collective scrutiny, and of being compared to

Roxy. It was then I began to realize that she was different in Paris, a popular person with an independent status – an attractive young American poet, sociable and sweet, the husband a French painter, expecting their second child. I mean, she was more of a personage in Paris than in Santa Barbara where she'd grown up, as no one thinks anything of you where you grow up.

The Paces have a top-floor apartment in one of those grand buildings on the rue Bonaparte. Everybody in the American community hopes to be asked here. Olivia Pace is interested in the abstraction Beauty, and her rooms are self-consciously beautiful. Charming paintings and flowers, but in the English or American fashion, no French furniture at all. The food is always luxurious, but not too French. Mrs. Pace considers it pretentious of someone not French to go too far in that direction. (This night we had asparagus, salmon hollandaise, and strawberries with thick sourish cream.) Apart from a few French spouses, almost all her guests are English or American, so there is no question of what language will be spoken (though when Nathalie Sarraute comes, everybody speaks French). There is always some new American academic couple on sabbatical, or new American writer, to lend variety and be a subject of gossip. There is the grand English anthropologist with his double-barreled name, and the famous English literary widow with her sweater out at the elbows to symbolize the evil days that have brought her to the pass of living in France, where, however, she appears very cheerful. There was even me.

These days, I help the maid Yolande pass the hors d'oeuvres, and am entitled by my intimacy with Mrs. Pace to answer familiar questions put by the guests ("It's through the door off the hall at the right."). But that night, all was strange to me, a blur of jet lag and new faces.

First among my new acquaintances was Ames Everett. He is the translator whose name is on many English versions of the great works of French scholarship and philosophy. His cleverness at unraveling the most baffling intricacies of the

French subjunctive and reknitting them into bright English phrases while – he swears – preserving perfectly the French nuances, has brought him a huge income as well as reputation. Deserved, I believe. I have sometimes sneaked a peek into his English version of something I'm supposed to read in French before certain occasions – more of this later – and no one has ever accused me of getting it wrong. He looked me over rather boldly (him being gay, though, obviously), as if assessing the strength of my limbs. Looking at him, I saw a young middle-sized plumpish man wearing a Nehru jacket and a monocle on a ribbon around his neck. I imagined him inspecting me through it minutely, like a butterfly collector.

"Roxeanne has talked about you. The little sister. She said I might speak to you about offering you a job. You'll be wanting jobs?"

"Sure, part time," I said, warily I suppose.

"Meet me at the Flore tomorrow at three. Roxy will explain where the Flore is."

"Well . . ."

"Forgive me!" he said. "Abrupt and task-oriented as I am, I should have welcomed you to Paris at least, and I can confide that all of Roxy's friends are glad to think she'll have her sister here to help her. Another baby! It seems so odd, all this reproduction. One had almost forgotten about reproduction, artifact of a simpler age."

Another person I met then was Janet Hollingsworth, a ruined-looking American beauty who told me she was writing a book about French women. She had a certain weary air of disapproval that suggested she had suffered at their hands. I must watch them, she said, and garner their secrets, though some of these were so profound as to defy discovery by mere Americans, little tendencies passed along from mother to daughter, assumptions so natural they might not even be able to articulate them. I gathered she meant things about fascination, sex, arts of seduction, but she did not say so, may have been talking about culinary secrets, or perhaps all of the above. There was a competitive edge to her tone, as if she herself had vied with them in rivalrous dramas for the fortune of a department-store heir or cabinet minister. To tell the truth, I was sorry to see an Anglo-Saxon so convinced that women need wiles and arts, and that the only quarry worth hunting was men. I told myself that she had spent too much time on the Continent, and had thus missed the modern mood of self-sufficiency and of being loved for yourself, or not – of being in any case without duplicity. But she was a lesson in herself, rather like the old courtesan grandmother in *Gigi*, a reminder of former days when American girls with money or style came over here and hunted for European husbands, counts or Rothschilds, as in novels by Henry James. It made you glad not to be living in an earlier day.

"Just their scarves alone, an entire chapter," Janet said. It is true they are never seen without scarves, I had noticed that already. "Knot in front, one end in front, other end over the shoulder; looped around double, ends tucked in; over the shoulders outside the coat, like a shawl; tied in back. *Châle, foulard, écharpe* – only think of the number of words they have, and in a language with a very sparse vocabulary."

"Do they tell their secrets?" I asked.

"Bulimia." She leaned closer. "Bulimia is one. Oh, we can learn from them. One I know, I heard from a tender friend, a man, is that they pay great attention to *les petits soins*. Someone should talk to Roxy about that. She always looks so awful."

"Roxy is beautiful," I objected.

"Of course, but her nails! And no scarf. She goes around in jeans, like an American, or in those awful flower-child clothes." She grinned. Maybe she was kidding.

After dinner Mrs. Pace, like the others, seemed to make a point of talking to me. I eventually realized this was not a tribute to me so much as to my novelty, my dilution of the small American pond. One drop in a bucket of Americans makes much more difference than a drop in the sea of French people.

"These cups are the old Meissen – that is, notice that the saucers have no indentations," Mrs. Pace said, handing me a demitasse of frightening fragility. "Do you plan to stay long in Paris?"

"At least until after the birth of Roxy's baby," I said.

"You must come over some morning next week and let me talk to you about a project I'm involved in, organizing my papers and so on. Roxy says you might be good at something like that."

"Does she?" That surprised me very much. But it is true that I know the alphabet. We agreed I'd go on Monday.

That night, when people asked where Charles-Henri was, Roxy would say "in the country" with every appearance of cheerfulness, but as we were walking home she uttered heavy sighs. I was impressed that you could walk home alone at eleven, no problems or menace. Jet-lagged as I was, I would have liked to stop in one of the myriad of bistros and bars we saw, full of people eating and smoking and laughing. But seeing the happiness and animation of others affected Roxy badly. Tears stood in her eyes, and she suddenly said, "Charles-Henri has left me," in a voice of tragedy I knew very well. I knew it so well, I discounted it a little.

She told me the story. It was a few weeks before my arrival in Paris. She'd been at her French doctor's clinic, waiting for the *sage-femme,* a sort of helpful midwife and adviser-to-the-pregnant that they have here. She was looking at the chart of gestation, thinking she didn't want to know if it was a boy or girl. She was three months along, and had just told us about this second pregnancy. Charles-Henri was not pleased. Gennie had just turned three.

Then coming home on the 24 bus, in the unseasonably sultry weather, she felt a little funny. She had waited at the stop on the Place de la Concorde. In front of the American consulate she saw the usual assortment of people – young ones in khaki she took to be American, some stouter, surlier ones, apparently eastern European, some hollow-eyed Middle Easterners, some Africans in dashikis – milling around with signs for disparate causes, protesting the American bombing of Baghdad, the decision of the FDA to allow a French abortion pill to be tested in the U.S., the repatriation of Haitians, action and inaction in Bosnia. The consulate guards stood with general vigilance without really paying attention to these people, who are just part of the atmosphere of protest and unrest surrounding America. Roxy didn't think she looked American anymore.

She was both happy and troubled, oppressed by a sense of the fragility of happiness, a sense (she says now) of something impending that could take it away. Was it the new child, a new hostage to fortune? On the bus, a young man – a boy really, in a workman's blue coat – got up to give Roxy his seat. At first she was surprised, not pleased, thought she had been taken for an old woman; it couldn't be that her pregnancy was beginning to show. Perhaps it was a force field of trouble gathering. She was thinking that happiness is by its nature fragile, friable, defying biological determinance, like a bacterium that can live outside the body only so long.

She let herself in the front door of number 12 rue Maître-Albert by punching in the code. In the hall she fished out her key and opened the glass door to the stairs. She waited till the door was closed, then climbed the two flights, slowly, trying to focus on thoughts of how hard it would be later with baby strollers and diaper bags, they should have an elevator – she tried to distract herself with mundane thoughts like this but she had a powerful feeling that something was wrong. When she opened the door, Charles-Henri was standing in the entry. She saw that he had two of his suitcases. An emanation surrounded him of turmoil, a hot atmosphere of passion and dismay, his expression so stricken and flushed and guilty and shocked to see her that she knew everything, or rather nothing. She said it was as if a sword had severed her head from her body, and all she had before known or felt, all sensation, bled into the ground. His suitcases packed, he had been about to leave.

At first she tried to tell herself that Charles-Henri's departure was just one of his periodic fits vital to artists, or from some uniquely French crisis or set of priorities she didn't need to understand. Certain political developments sent him into unreason, certain harmless encounters rendered irascible his usually sweet nature. She loved these mysteries of his temperament.

But now she sensed that he wouldn't be back.

"Where are you going?" she asked.

"I don't know. I don't know, Roxeanne. I will call you. I am sorry." Then he took his suitcases down the stairs without looking back.

The next few days passed as if nothing had happened. Charles-Henri didn't call her, wherever he was, and she couldn't call him. I could partly understand her shock, her simple stupefaction. You take for granted that your life will work out. When something calls that into question, then the entire world begins to seem like those films of demolition, silent fragments of roof and window flying through air with carefree velocity. I understood.

But she might have expected that if you do something odd, like marry a foreigner and live somewhere that is not America, people take for granted that your life will not work out. I was not surprised.

To be honest, I didn't quite get why she was so upset. "Do you think he's having an affair or something? Why would he leave?" I asked. "Haven't you been getting along? Have you been having trouble?"

"I didn't think so," she said. "I thought everything was so perfect. Oh, I know I'm not French, but except for that."

What exactly did that mean? Of course she wasn't French. I felt defensive of her American imperfections, for they were mine too. Janet Hollingsworth had made me think about them.

Of course I had to say something soothing. "You need to talk to him."

"Never," she said. From that response (really un-American) I decided that she must be unnaturally depressed, in a mood to extrapolate from a simple misunderstanding the end of her marriage. All that had happened, it seemed to me, was that Charles-Henri had gone to the country and had only been gone a couple of days, perhaps had not even thought of calling. To me his departure seemed to be only the beginning of a crisis, if that, not its resolution. It seemed typical of Roxy to overstate a case. At first I found myself berating her, trying to stiffen her up, but it was no use.

She continued to refuse to tell anyone that Charles-Henri had walked out. "But if I *were* to tell, say tell my friend Anne-Chantal Lartigue, that Charles-Henri was having an affair or that he has left me, she would say 'of course,' " said Roxy. "She's French. It's the French nature to say 'of course,' as if all perfidy were to be expected, even planned by grand design. Am I especially American in some way? I can never say 'of course.' "

"It isn't you, he's just going through something, you ought to talk to him," I would say. We would be sitting at a sidewalk table at the Brasserie Espoir, with three-year-old Gennie climbing along the little straw chairs and tormenting the brasserie dog, and smiling at the retarded boy who was always there.

"There you are, foolish American optimism," said Roxy. "You have no information and no evidence to say that, it's just a mind-set. American mind-set."

"I don't understand you. He came home and said he was going to the country, and you're saying, oh, okay then, that's the end of my marriage?" Surely there were scenes and tears and recriminations to come? I couldn't understand her docility, her submission to Charles-Henri's odd behavior, the almost beatified radiance of her resignation, when they hadn't even had an argument! I just hoped that things would right themselves between them, the way a boat poises on the angle between capsize and upright for a long moment before it comes down on one side or the other.

THREE

The heart has its reasons, that reason will never know.

– Blaise Pascal, Pensées

ONE MORE WORD ABOUT ROXY'S CHARACTER, HER NATURE, and mine. People say, have always said, she is too romantic, she is bound to be hurt. As for me, I am practical, I am analytical, and thus "strong," or so they believe. This has often been confusing to them, for I am also the designated Pretty One, and so am assumed to be kind of dumb, and Roxy, though she is beautiful now, had a long adolescence of plainness and indifference to her looks, and preferred reading and writing to washing her hair, and so has secured the reputation of being smart. I suppose we are both intelligent, actually, but only Roxy gets credit for it.

At first I wondered if this was to be the time, in this crisis, that Roxy's sentimentality, some defect of softness and illusion, would weigh against her. In the same spot, others (I) would leap from the lifeboat and swim strongly away, but she weakly drifts, confused, out to the fatal sea. It is true that she believed in Charles-Henri and he had hurt her, bewildered her, it was not what she expected, with the second baby due, its room ready, with a little chest for changing it, a blanket folded on top, strange garments ordained in the clinic instructions (belly bands?) readied, and a bright-colored mobile to suspend over its crib.

She had wanted her whole life to live in France. I never understood why. Some instinct, some non-fit, had caused her from childhood to disapprove of the land and city of her birth. The way children believe they are changelings and not the children of their parents, so she believed herself displaced, sprung from another race. Besides the painting of Saint Ursula in her bedroom, she had a photographic poster advertising some costume film, *Jules le Grand,* of the Place de la Concorde in lamplight, with horse-drawn carriages on a rainy pavement. A romantic, rather banal scene, taken perhaps by someone upstairs in the Meurice Hotel. She also had a little metal Eiffel Tower a junior-high-school friend had brought back from summer travels, symbol of cultural blandishments I the little sister didn't understand at all.

It goes without saying that she had her junior year abroad, though not in Paris, in Aix-en-Provence. She loved it, though there were so many Americans there that she didn't make much progress speaking French. All the same, she came home with a pleased, slightly secret look, as if she dared not share with us her new experiences of goose liver and *escargots*, and sex, which is what I imagined gave her this worldly, satisfied air; but it wasn't sex, it was her new ability to distinguish between Gothic and Romanesque and to read *Paris Match* that pleased her. Now she couldn't find food to suit her in Santa Barbara.

Roxy had met Charles-Henri while hiking with other girls in the Pyrenees. He seemed the ideal Frenchman, thin, curly-haired, and fair, always with a sweater or cravat picturesquely knotted around his shoulders or neck, and that resolute insouciance they all have. They corresponded for two years after her return to California; then, when Roxy was in graduate school, he came to visit and charmed all of us – such a good tennis player, taller than a lot of them (as Margeeve observed), and with perfect English. At the time, none of us had ever met a French person. Thus did our dreams for Roxy collude with our general ignorance of the French to approve him uncritically. Yet we were not wrong, he is very, very nice, and not a bad painter, and has behaved, given his initial crime, very well, or if not well at least with a courteous detachment. It is this detachment Roxy finds hardest to bear. Behaved well given the fact that it was he who did the running off, with a married Czech sociologist (which is how we always refer to her, though that is a bit unfair in several ways).

This cultural disloyalty of Roxy's – where did it come from? Nothing bad had happened to her in America. Why was she more charmed by the idea of *Toussaint,* for example, than of Halloween? Aren't they the same? I don't share her unqualified admiration for all things European. I see plenty that's wrong. But that's the curse of my nature. Even as a little girl, I lacked that endearing property of female credulousness.

FOUR

I speak of that dread which seizes her when she sees herself abandoned by him who swore to protect her.

– *Benjamin Constant,* Adolphe

As far as I knew, Roxy did not hear from Charles-Henri the rest of the week. For several days she refused to speak of the situation and adopted an artificially serene manner, visiting friends and introducing me into the life of Paris. She had not told Charles-Henri's family that anything was wrong between them, but she would have to mention it the Sunday after I got there, when we were expected at lunch at the Persands' and he would not be there with them.

Roxy's mother-in-law, Madame de Persand – Suzanne – is a vivacious matriarch close to seventy who expects her five children and their families to lunch every possible Sunday, including me during my stay in Paris. Suzanne is small, blonde, and worldly (most Frenchwomen over forty are blonde); her offspring are tall and good at sports: Frédéric, Antoine, Charlotte, Yvonne, and Charles-Henri, the youngest. Each is handsome and beautifully dressed and emanates the smell of cigarettes. Monsieur de Persand, I believe, managed a factory, manufacturing some item or substance, but I don't know what. He is now retired and spends his time in Poland or Rumania with other retired Frenchmen directing the resurrection of factories and things that have fallen into disrepair. I have never met him. He did not come to Charles-Henri's wedding, as if this rite, involving only the youngest of his sons, were too insignificant to cross the water for; or perhaps he disapproved of Americans – we never knew.

During the week, Suzanne lives in a big nineteenth-century apartment on the Avenue Wagram, with dark Santa Barbara-ish oil paintings, an inherited tapestry, an array of faience plates on the walls, and correct Louis Quinze furniture covered in faded brocade or fraying needlepoint. The furniture, with its curves and chipped gilding, so like the former grandeur of a rundown Westwood motel, looks very odd and pretentious to the American eye when you first come to France, until you remember that this is their normal furniture, the Louis were their kings.

Suzanne also has a small château with a tennis court, near Chartres, where the family would gather on weekends. So far, every French person I have met comes with three pieces of real estate – two in the country (one from each side of the family) and the Paris apartment. This place near Chartres did not descend from Charlemagne, however, but had been bought in the 1950s, following a successful business venture by Monsieur de Persand. Roxy and Geneviève and I took the Chartres train on Sunday, with Gennie dressed in her proper little dark blue dress and white stockings, and Roxy wearing rouge, me with my tennis bag, according to Roxy's instructions. I still remember Roxy's rouge, it was as if she felt she needed some symbol of brightness, an external antidote to the pallor and terror in her soul.

Her French family still call Roxy *l'américaine,* by which they seem to mean that her qualities are typical of us, each with its positive and negative aspect: frank/tactless, impetuous/heedless, fresh/gauche, generous/spendthrift. She got a lot of points in their view from buckling down to the French language with fair success, and secured their hearts by deciding to convert to Catholicism. "You are Protestant, I suppose," Madame de Persand had asked, at their first meeting. "But nothing peculiar, not Quaker or anything like that?"

Roxy will not brook loose cultural insults.

"President Herbert Hoover was a Quaker," she said.

"Oh, of course, one of your most notable presidents," Madame de Persand agreed with hasty politeness, as if she treasured this important fact. The question remained.

"My parents are Congregationalists," said Roxeanne, and Madame de Persand had still looked mystified. Then she must have concluded she would rather not know the peculiarities of a cult she'd never heard of, and the subject was dropped. The Persands did Roxy the credit of imagining her conversion was done from wifeliness and that, going against the grain of a stout Protestant nature, it represented a spiritual sacrifice. But in fact Catholicism suited Roxy all along – especially the music and priestly raiment. Chester and Margeeve, needless to say, were horrified.

We siblings were all surprised when the issue of Charles-Henri's Catholicism seemed to weigh on the minds of our liberal and nonreligious parents, especially Chester. Some unarticulated Protestant aversion, deeply submerged, now surfaced, invoking an imaginary destiny for Roxy of ceaseless childbearing, daily mass. They vividly pictured her dressed in rusty black, clutching a rosary, waddling on her knees across the forecourt of Lourdes.

"But I'm not becoming a Catholic," Roxy objected. "Anyway, I think you're thinking of Ireland. It's Ireland that's priest-ridden, not France. In France they invented the morning-after pill."

"I remember the Catholic kids, growing up," said Margeeve, supporting Chester. "When it became five minutes after midnight Friday night, they stuffed themselves with hamburgers."

We were wholly baffled by this seeming non sequitur. She tried to explain. "They weren't supposed to eat meat on Fridays, so they could hardly wait. It seemed so hypocritical. Why belong to a religion you don't feel wholehearted about?"

"Charles-Henri is not religious," Roxy reassured them. This turned out to be true; he was indifferent to where he was married. They were married in the Congregational Church, with a reception afterward in our parents' garden, and then celebrated in France at an elegant reception (according to Roxy) at the Persand country house. Charles-Henri's mother and one sister, Yvonne, came out for the wedding in California but none of us went to the party in France. So when Roxy eventually converted to Catholicism, it was not at any urging from Charles-Henri. It was her love of liturgy and form.

The day we went to Chartres, Roxeanne was almost as frantic at the prospect of having to tell Suzanne about Charles-Henri's leaving her as at the event itself. She knew that Charles-Henri would not have said anything, would not have wanted to confront his mother with unpleasant news, or ruin Sunday lunch, or have discussions. Of course Suzanne immediately saw that Charles-Henri was not with us, and from Roxy's expression divined her concern, and said during the air kisses, "*Alors,* where is *mon enfant?*" and Geneviève said, "I'm here, *grandmère,*" but of course Suzanne meant Charles-Henri, her youngest son.

"Are we the first? I had wanted to have a little word with you," Roxeanne said.

"No, Antoine is here with the children. Trudi is still in the country." Trudi is the German wife of Antoine. Antoine is quite attractive, tall and slightly balding. "And of course here is your sister Isabel," she said, turning to embrace me, for Roxy had forgotten me, I guess.

Charlotte and her family arrived. Charlotte is an impatient beauty in her late thirties, upper lip slightly protruding over the lower (orthodontia relatively unimportant here, compared to Santa Barbara), fair hair in a pony tail, a habit of pulling on it, tossing her head like a horse. Her children are rather pale and subdued in comparison to her, with strings of names: Paul-Louis, Jean-Fernand, Marie-Odile – if I have strung them together rightly. The other siblings of Charles-Henri were not there. At the far end of the garden, in a canvas chair, sat an elderly man wearing a straw hat as wide as a milkmaid's, who waved pacifically from afar and was explained to be l'oncle Edgar, Suzanne's brother.

They all treated me with great kindness, speaking English slowly, with the stately vowels of British television commentators. Taking me over the house, Charlotte showed me a large book that was said to date from, as she called him in her careful English for my benefit, Lewis the Fourteenth. "Righto," said Charlotte's husband, Bob, using chipper Brit slang. Despite his name, Bob is French. When they spoke to Roxy, they spoke in French, and I have to admit it sounded funny to hear her speak in this foreign and unintelligible way, and rather affected, as in the joke: "Pretentious? *Moi*?"

In the hot June weather, tennis was decreed. Antoine played Charlotte's husband, Bob; then Charlotte and I played with Antoine and Bob, with Bob as my partner. They were good players, and somehow this took me by surprise. Why should it have? I suspect they were surprised that I am a good player. (Tennis champion was another of my family's hopes for me, blighted by my hate of practicing.) L'oncle Edgar applauded from his vantage under the trees. Roxy seemed pleased by my victory. She doesn't play at all, even when not pregnant. She sat at a little table on the flagstones outside French doors leading to the dining room, talking to Suzanne, wearing the fixed smile of elaborate graciousness that she seemed to imagine rendered invisible her feelings of panic and despair.

Whatever her emotions, Roxeanne was obliged to dissimulate with civility and calm, through the *kir vermouth* that was served before lunch, through the *soupe aux moules*, the leg of lamb with white beans, the salad, the cheese, the *tarte aux fraises*. Suzanne had nodded to the girl who was helping to remove Charles-Henri's place, and no one so much as asked about him. Had they any reason to wonder? Might he not just be away on business, or tied up somewhere?

L'oncle Edgar, it turned out, was not unimaginably old, but a burly, imposing man in his late sixties, maybe seventy, tall and white-haired, with deep-set eyes and the nose of a Vichy general, very handsome in a way. When we went in to lunch, he limped slowly toward the house. Then I could see he had an ankle in a cast, but what had happened to him was not explained.

By now I was embarrassed that they were all making this polite effort to speak English, all of them compelled to use a language not their own because of one person's inability to speak theirs. "*Oui*" and "*non*" I tried to say through my nose when l'oncle Edgar, beside whom I was sitting, would ask me if I wanted more cheese or meat. I was imitating French in hopes they would think I understood it and could lapse back into speaking it.

"Eet ees very amusing about your senator," said Oncle Edgar. I did not at first know what he meant.

"The chap who kept the diaries," said Antoine.

"Detailing how he patted the knees of young women, detailing his erotic hopes, perhaps, and now he has to turn these private musings over to the public court," said l'oncle Edgar.

They all laughed. "No, no," said Charlotte, "he turns them over to the other senators, I believe." It was not clear whether comment was expected from Roxy or me.

"Yes, extraordinary," agreed Suzanne, "and it is supposed he'll have something to say about his friends." They all laughed, a merriment somewhat mysterious to me at that time. I would learn it had to do with our reputation for native prudishness and their native toleration of certain things of this world, like old senators with young women.

"*Zut,* I would hate for my colleagues to read what I thought of them," added Oncle Edgar.

The Persands were so pleasant, laughed so charmingly, they were so uniformly good-looking in their fancy wood-paneled room – yet I did not feel entirely welcomed. I felt young. I felt that a nurse would be sent in to take me out of the room when my sayings had ceased to amuse them. It was with relief that I saw their resolution about speaking English drain away with the second bottle of red wine. "Eleanor of Angoulême was not, as is often thought, the niece of . . ." said l'oncle Edgar, and that was the last thing I understood, as they all began to discuss some episode of French history, with violent gesticulations, in French.

After lunch, we had coffee on the terrace. Charlotte smoked incessantly. That seemed strange, keen as she was on tennis. She was telling me about her sojourn in England, when she was fourteen, and how the English cheated at tennis. I did not believe that. "Their line calls were very dubious," she was saying severely. By now I know that the things that French people say about the English are probably like what they say about Americans when we aren't around.

Antoine smoked in the garden while tossing a ball to his little boy. Roxeanne was evidently planning to stay at the end of the afternoon, in order to have a private word with Suzanne. When someone proposed a walk to the antiques fair in the town, I took Geneviève and went off with the others, Roxy insisting she preferred to stay behind to help with cleaning up. In the Persand family, such offers are accepted. The day had assumed a cast of normality, no sense of a looming catastrophe, and it even took on, at the antiques fair, an air of propitiousness, because Antoine found a sort of cabinet he had been hoping to find.

But when we got back and were walking into the courtyard, we were met by none other than Charles-Henri himself, looking pale and thunderous, not like the blithe and slightly distracted man I had met. He seemed astonished to see us. Perhaps he had hoped to see his mother alone, but he might have expected we would all be there. I thought at first maybe he had come to see Roxy and tell her it had all been a mistake. I hoped this, but my hopes were useless. He kissed his mother in a perfunctory way, greeting the rest of us, and drove off immediately in his Range Rover. It was days before Roxy heard from him, her husband, the love of her life.

In the train, riding back to Paris, Roxy burst into tears, like a person in a movie, and wailed into her scarf. We were surrounded by French families, whose children toddled in the aisles and stared at her.

"I'm sorry," she said, "it's dumb, I know. It never occurred to me that he might turn up there today, it took me aback, I handled it so badly."

"What did he say?"

"Nothing. Nothing. Nothing," was all she would say. I had the feeling that he had said something. Then she said, in a bitter, concentrated tone, "He told me the one thing I can never forgive." But she wouldn't say what it was.

FIVE

I am too American myself, and lack juices.
– Henry Adams

EXCEPT FOR THIS PROBLEM OF ROXY'S, PARIS WAS KIND OF promising. Then, I had no premonitions, no glimpse of the future. Looking back, it must have been at about this same time – when Roxeanne's troubles began, and when I arrived in Paris to help her – that our mother, Margeeve Walker back in Santa Barbara, got a letter from a Julia Manchevering, resident art historian at the Getty Museum.

Santa Barbara is a city of mythological dimension in the minds of the French because of a soap opera called *Santa Barbara,* which airs on French television, dubbed in French, involving the lurid social complications usual in soap operas, among uniformly blond, rich Californians, set against scenes of sunny surf and Washingtonia palm and bougainvillea-bright patios. A place not Los Angeles, not northern, quasi-Spanish, old Californian, bland. I actually spent most of my childhood in the Midwest, where my father taught political science at a small college, but we moved to California when I was twelve when he married Margeeve. I loved our new home better.

My father, now a professor at UC-Santa Barbara, and stepmother, with her odd name Margeeve, live in a California-style, that is to say modest forties bungalow in a valuable location on Miramar Avenue, with an ocean view and access to the beach, amid houses that are worth a lot more. Or I should say: our house, because of its situation, is worth a lot more than it's really worth. Margeeve and Chester had the good fortune or vision to buy during one of the periodic declines in the value of real estate near the beach that follow a particularly destructive storm, and they were aided by a loan from an uncle of my father's, William Eshrick, a Santa Barbara dealer in moldy European art – paintings dark and indistinct enough to look ancestral in the palatial haciendas of Montecito (a section of Santa Barbara lived in by those movie folk who think themselves too refined to live in L.A.). Tortured saints, especially Saint Sebastian, the one pierced by arrows, and heavily varnished landscapes are favored. Uncle William, now dead, had acquired a warehouse of indifferent Spanish and Italian examples of these gloomy subjects during the thirties, when more brilliant collectors were buying Impressionists and Expressionists, and he knew his market for art that was neither too distressingly religious nor too sentimental, and sufficiently crazed and cracked to look valuable. One of these was Roxy's favorite painting, of Saint Ursula, the virgin martyr.

Julia Manchevering was asking about one of Uncle William's paintings (most of which had been sold at his death). In the course of writing a book about the iconography of Saint Ursula, she had been tracking the provenance of a certain painting, perhaps representing Saint Ursula, sold in the thirties by a dealer on the rue du Bac to, possibly, our uncle William Eshrick and still apparently in the inventory of his estate at the time of his death.

> Approximately 100 cm by 140 cm, representing a young woman, her hand upraised, sitting at a table. (Saint Ursula 889-891?) The saint (?) is looking to her right, toward the lighted candle, and behind her a treasure, including a royal symbol signification unknown, is barely illuminated in the candlelight.

At this same time, coincidentally, in Margeeve's art history class they had taken up the study of French seventeenth-century painting – cursorily, for it is not considered to be of much interest, though of more interest lately because the Getty Museum buys French painting, which it seems American museums didn't used to do. I suppose the gloomy religiosity of Italian painting went better with the neo-Gothic mansions of the nineteenth-century American millionaires, or else the French emphasis on nymphs and people in swings having fun offended our ideas of seriousness, back then. But French painting is in fashion now.

Armed with this new interest in French painting, Margeeve replied to the Getty that their description did indeed sound like the picture Roxeanne had taken to Paris with her, and presumably still had. She noted parenthetically to Dr. Manchevering that they had always thought her daughter Roxeanne resembled the woman in the painting. Daughter Roxeanne had given it to her French husband as a wedding present. A correspondence (unbeknown to Roxy in Paris) had developed, in which the Getty lady hoped to borrow Saint Ursula, or at least to see it. She mentioned the possibility it was by a student of the French painter Georges de La Tour, and the Getty was planning an exhibition of his works.

The painting was hanging over the fireplace in Roxy's apartment on the rue Maître-Albert, and before that had hung for years in Roxy's room at home in Santa Barbara, but now has been crated and sent to Drouot, the auction house, for sale, breaking Roxy's heart, for she loves this saint and used to tell her her secrets. Inside an ornate gold frame, Saint Ursula regards a dark future of proposed matrimony. She would rather be massacred. The painting is listed in the catalogue as "Sainte Ursule(?)" by "un élève de La Tour."

In physics class (dumbbell physics) I learned about how the displacement of atoms means that the existence of anything affects the existence of everything, and that's how I imagine the painting of Saint Ursula, dislodging matter, making waves since the unknown seventeenth-century artist painted it.

SIX

The affairs of ordinary life cannot be forced to fit in with all our desires. It was sometimes awkward to have my every step marked out for me in advance and all my moments counted.
– Benjamin Constant, Adolphe

IT IS A TRUTH UNIVERSALLY ACKNOWLEDGED THAT A YOUNG American person not fully matriculated must be in want of a job; Americans in Paris fell upon my neck like swains, with a plethora of paying tasks.

The Café Flore: I am keeping my rendezvous with Ames Everett. That was Ames Everett de-buttering his toast in the prologue, for I see him doing this as I approach. An elegant, rich, fattish gay person was how I had categorized him.

"Good," he says. "What will you have? *Menthe à l'eau?* Perrier? A drink? Coffee?"

Having never had it, I choose *menthe,* which proved to be mint-flavored green mouthwash.

Ames explains that he would like someone to walk his dog Scamp every afternoon. People have never told me why they don't just hire French people to do things like this, though Stuart Barbee told me how much a Frenchman would have charged to paint his dining room – six thousand francs, more than a thousand dollars, amazing indeed. I paid myself twenty-five dollars an hour and it cost him $250.00. So one explanation is that it's cheaper to hire Americans; also, I had an idea that language counted, even among those who speak perfectly good French. Of course language would count when it came to sorting literary papers, as I do for Mrs. Pace; she on the other hand complains that I am too young. When I had to ask what a Trotskyite was, she looked at me for a long moment, turning over in her mind, I could see, whether to fire me or educate me.

But I think that language counts in a more important way when it comes to choosing, for instance, someone you trust with your dog. I think Ames Everett trusts me with his dog more than he would have someone who thought of Scamp as a mere *chien*.

"There are circles within circles here in Paris," Ames observes over our *menthe*. "American circles, I am not even speaking of the French. There are the businessmen Americans, they keep to themselves, unless they have French connections. Banks. EuroDisney. The lawyer Americans, having of necessity to have something to do with the French. The Franco-Americans, couples of whom one is one and one the other, usually American wives, French husbands. These women tend to have an annoying veneer of Frenchiness, a kind of inside manner I myself find irritating. The journalists and writers. That's my set, and the art historians, and the trust-fund socialites, living elegantly. The French love them the best, of course.

"You must tell me what you are running away from. Every American in Paris is running away from something," Ames said, at this first rendezvous, with the slight sneer that seems permanent in his voice, a querulous lightness. "Usually I never bother figuring out what in particular. The reasons, when you learn them, are usually too boring. Behind the immediate reasons, though, is another reality."

"What's that?" I asked.

"That's what you eventually find out. That is the fun of it. You would be surprised, sometimes." He smiled at me. They all, even Roxy, like to treat me like the naive, the ingenue, the overconfident newcomer for whom big, shattering lessons are in store. I, in any case, am not running away from anything, I hadn't especially wanted to be here. I said so.

"What is *your* reason, then, if not your reality?" I insisted.

He said, "I came to get away from AIDS. You can't imagine what New York was like in the early eighties, a death a week among your friends; you couldn't bear for the phone to ring. I hoped it wouldn't come here. It has, of course."

"Drugs are coming here too," I said. "You can buy crack at metro Saint-Michel."

"It isn't easy being an American," he said. "That is the final reality. It is hard. It is a moral obligation we come here to escape. We are too sensitive – I speak of us expatriates, though I hate to use that word. When we do go back, we see what we see, and it is hard on us." He sighed.

The Flore is right on the Boulevard Saint-Germain, amid tourists drinking espresso and regulars reading *Libération,* a smell of coffee and newsprint. The pavement was still wet from an afternoon rain, the sky was its characteristic Parisian gray, the air hung diesely and damp, slightly redolent of dogshit. I could see the beauty, which might be reason enough to come here. But I wondered what Ames's reality under his reason was, and why the special rancor he bore America, for he never failed to badmouth it, though he's famous there, even revered, in his coterie.

"How is Roxeanne?" Ames asked. "I thought she looked tired. I must introduce you to Stuart Barbee, I think he needs some work done around his place. Do you read French? Have you seen *Libération* today?"

Am I running away from something in America, as Ames suggests? I didn't think so. I supposed I was a prototypical American, not down on it like Ames and Roxy; but I will admit I began to be happy, these months in France, despite my mistrust of the whole society. Soon I had, besides the dog-walking job for Ames, the task of helping Olivia Pace sort her papers; I house-sat for some CIA types who were away in Provence, and arranged apartments for friends of Roxeanne (usually American divorcees over here to attend the Cordon Bleu and change their lives). I've been writing a little advice column for the American Church *Weekly Messenger* – where to find what – and occasionally I teach an aerobics class at the American Center as a substitute instructor.

I thought then how I would hate it if Roxeanne just packed up and left before I was ready.

And now I think I have met the love of my life, but it is a grotesque and doomed situation. I did not plan for anything like this to happen.

SEVEN

Virtue shuns ease as a companion. It demands a rough and thorny path.

– Montaigne

SUZANNE DE PERSAND HAD COME TO SEE ROXY DIRECTLY ON the Monday. She came solemnly dressed in a navy linen suit, with her decorations in the lapel, as if she were going to some high state occasion, and spoke in English, because I was there.

"I have talked to my son," she said, accepting an herbal tea. "I am very unhappy about his behavior. Add to this, the behavior of Charlotte. I don't know where it comes from. From their father perhaps."

"What about Charlotte?" Roxy roused herself from her lethargic mood.

"What indeed? She has a liaison – it is too stupid. And with an Englishman! What I want to say to you, Roxeanne, is just to be sensible. You are aware that when the wife is pregnant, sometimes the husband – the nine months gets to seem long to him. He thinks it will never end, and some young and slender woman makes him think of happier times. He supposes he is thinking with his emotion, but it is really biological, his male need."

"If you mean about making love, you can do it up until the last two weeks," said Roxy irritably.

"Really? *Tiens!* That is surely unwise. In my day the

doctors did not permit it. In any case, the *forme,* great ugly belly. Yes, sugar please. *Hein! Original!* Georges's cousin Hortense also uses grains of sugar instead of cubes."

"It's not up to me, it's Charles-Henri's deal," said Roxy.

"That is what I am trying to say. Expect nothing until the baby is born, then you can see. Maybe it will be a boy."

"A boy? An heir? I can't believe this, I'm in a novel by Balzac," snapped Roxy. Suzanne had the grace to laugh a little and finished her cup.

"This has happened to other women, often, and by far the best course, they would most of them tell you, is to just go on with life as it unrolls," she said.

"I ask myself, is it wise to have this baby," said Roxy suddenly, with a savage canniness. "It's early. Maybe I shouldn't go through with it. It's stupid to bring a baby into an unstable home." I recognized the wildness under her tone as being the real Roxy, dramatic and hysterical, but there was also an instant of calculation in her voice as she looked to see how this implied threat would affect Suzanne.

Suzanne did seem startled, began to speak, stopped, gauging, I could see, the best way to handle a distraught foreign girl.

"I'm thinking of not going through with it," Roxy repeated.

"Luckily you have weeks to decide something so large," Suzanne said slowly, watching Roxy as she might a skittish wild animal. "You wouldn't want to make that decision quickly."

I saw how smart Suzanne is, how she sensed Roxy's panic and her stubborn streak, and wanted to avoid animating it with preaching or argument. But she had turned pale. Roxy had scared her. Her eyes met mine for an instant, and I could see that she would have liked to ask me if Roxy would do something like that. But of course, she did not know me, or how I would stand. How did she stand, for that matter?

"I'll call you tomorrow, *ma chérie,*" she said. "*Bon courage.* These things arrive, with men, and then pass."

"Frenchmen are spoiled by their mothers," observed Roxy, when Suzanne had gone. "Charles-Henri can just do no wrong in her eyes."

"He'll come back," I predicted to Roxy. "You'll have to decide whether you want to forgive him. And of course you will."

"It isn't a question of forgiving him," she said. "I don't own him. He has his heart and I have mine, and it's mine I have to live with." With that she dumped the sugar into the sink.

"What on earth are you doing?"

"Didn't you hear her? '*Hein.* Granular sugar, how original.' Meaning, bizarre American ways. Meaning, why don't you have sugar cubes like a French girl?"

When Roxy says her first months of marriage were hard, she didn't mean anything negative about the French or Charles-Henri. She thought him the perfect husband, polite, helpful, and ardent. "The Anglo-Saxon male style is entirely different, all those obligatory football games and beer, their lack of interest in household matters, their notion that it would be somehow unmanly to take an interest in the dishes or tablecloths," she said. "Charles-Henri is capable of appreciating a soup tureen. His uncle Edgar collects seventeenth-century faience."

She is right that French men seem to have a pleasant air of collaboration with women, an air of being in the business of life together – marriage, society. It is quite unlike the atmosphere of strained toleration or active dislike between the sexes we seem to have at home. But when I said this once to Roxy's friend Anne-Chantal Lartigue, who lives near us across the Place Maubert, she sniffed.

"Don't be deceived," she said. "They are cads, like other men, spoiled by their mothers, unfaithful and evasive." Of course, being French she ought to know, but possibly she doesn't understand what other men are like – the non-French ones, like Americans, or the Muslims, say, who are said to seem nice until they get you back to Turkey or Algeria. The

French love reading about the disastrous adventures of young Frenchwomen who marry Algerians, make the mistake of returning to the native villages, and are then locked up with the goats in purdah and abused by their mothers-in-law, who take away their shoes and their passports.

Of their intimate life, Roxy and Charles-Henri's, I have no idea. Roxy was discreet and solemn about that.

She says when she was first married, she threw herself into French life, French housekeeping, French cooking, puzzling over the literal translations of recipes – how to decorticate a nut, make an onion sweat. Measures that she had thought an affectation of American foodies, M. F. K. Fisher groupies and people moving on beyond Julia Child, she now discovered to be the actual household standard in many French homes, and moreover seemingly done without effort. Women doctors came home late from the hospital and whipped up *potage aux moules, pigeon rôti, salade, fromage, dessert.* Did they really follow from scratch the recipe that directed them to *plumer, vider, flamber les pigeons?*

Actually it was not foodiness, or competitiveness, that made her obsessed with the cooking. What charmed her and drove her was the existence of a standard. There was no such thing as, hey, do it your way, though the recipes *à ma façon* implied individuality – along with expertise and authority. She liked the idea of things being long and difficult. Sometimes, having bought, opened, cooked the *oursins* and passed them through a sieve and added them to a *pâté de poissons,* she was disappointed, but only at her own inability to discern the difference they made. It was Mrs. Pace who pointed out to me the attraction of things rigorous and demanding. "The ballet is the only métier that requires discipline from women," she said, "or was in my day. Now you could run the marathon. In my day, after you won the Latin prize, there was nothing left for you."

Roxy became an accomplished cook, but tact and diffidence prevented her from seeming too accomplished when feeding French people. (In this she followed the example of

Mrs. Pace. I remain a little skeptical about the French. They pretend to love food so much, but why do they go to McDonald's?) Roxy could never find out what they really ate when at home, unobserved by Americans like her. She watched them in the supermarkets. From there, it appeared they ate the same on weeknights at home alone as when she and Charles-Henri were invited to dinner: *hors-d'oeuvre, entrée, plat, salade, fromage, dessert.* "But they do buy a lot of things frozen," she revealed, satisfied.

Charles-Henri was the most undemanding and encouraging of husbands, appreciating all her efforts, but also happy to eat sandwiches and frozen pizza, helpful with setting the table and making mayonnaise. "For heaven's sake," he reassured her, "it doesn't matter what you serve. Serve American dishes. People are interested in them. Serve pizza." (Looking back, she now mistrusts his blithe detachment.)

"There are no American dishes," Roxy stormed. "Pizza is Italian."

"Apple pie," he said. "*Trente-et-un* flavors. Pumpkin pie."

"I hate pumpkin pie. We all do."

Like a spy she sought other secrets of French culture. Yet she was always being taken unawares. When the first dinner guest appeared with a bunch of flowers she realized she had never taken flowers to her hostesses. When an American guest brought them a bottle of wine, Charles-Henri said, offended, afterward, "Perhaps he thought he wasn't going to get anything to drink."

("The end of *la civilisation française*?" says l'oncle Edgar. "I suppose when it became '*fromage ou dessert*' instead of *fromage et dessert.*' ")

She never unraveled the mysteries of all the cheeses, dozens in the market, round and reeking, leaking, swelling, dusted with pepper, wrapped in vine leaves, made from the milk of goats, cows, sheep, cooked or raw, hard or soft, each with a name that bore no relation to the names in her recipe books.

And the cuts of meat. What on earth was *gîte-gîte* or *macreuse?*

She thought French women were wonderfully chic. To me it appeared they all went around in drab beige raincoats, wearing identical plain scarves – English, Roxy said, from Burberrys. It's funny, this fashion, considering that they think of the English as treacherous, hypocritical, and unwashed – exactly what the English think of them. Businesswomen, for instance Charlotte, who does public relations, wear little suits with short skirts and jackets, red or plaid, with lots of gold jewelry. The women my age are pretty, though, with very little makeup and great assurance.

"Their bras are hopeless," Roxy had written to me in Santa Barbara. "They are so small-breasted, it's impossible for me, they have no tits at all, please send me four Olga 'Vanity' 34Cs, one ecru, two white, and one black."

With all this cultural progress Roxy had been making, what had gone wrong?

If she thought any more about "not keeping" the baby, as she put it, she said nothing to me. It had been perhaps an empty threat, made in the hope that Suzanne would be so shocked in her Catholic soul that she would compel Charles-Henri to come home. When that did not happen, Roxy's resentment of Suzanne began to grow, though it seemed to me that Suzanne had been sympathy itself.

She telephoned regularly, and took us to lunch at Récamier. Even by now I'd been in France long enough to understand French views about the consoling properties of food. During the lunches Suzanne would rail not at Charles-Henri but at Charlotte, whom I took to be an avatar of Charles-Henri for the purpose of this conversation, another troublesome offspring with an underdeveloped sense of duty. Unlike the blatant Charles-Henri, Charlotte was making an attempt to conceal her doings from her husband, poor Bob, who (I guessed) must have some skeletons in his own closet, for Charlotte to be so open.

It was surprising to me that Charlotte had taken up with an Englishman, given her views about their sportsmanship.

"I don't say a thing," Suzanne said. "Charlotte has always been headstrong. Criticizing her is a mistake." But what criticism would drive Charlotte to was left unsaid. I admired Suzanne's self-control. In the same situation, Margeeve would have said plenty. I wondered when Roxy was going to tell Margeeve and Chester about her marital crisis. I ventured no opinion about what she should do, not wanting to drive her the wrong way, whatever way that was, and not believing it to be my business, nor myself equipped to know about marriage, or love, for that matter.

The financial implications did occur to me. I wasn't sure how Roxy was fixed. Would having a new baby require Charles-Henri to give her more money, or, with another mouth to feed, would she be harder up? In our family we can talk about money, since Chester is not in the business of chasing after it. He has all the purity of the academic and none of the temptations of academic scientists, so money is a neutral topic for us, like social policy or what's for lunch. But Roxy had adopted something of the French reticence. Any mention of money seems to shock them; it is almost as bad as, and maybe worse than, asking someone's age.

She still had not told me the real problem, whatever it was, between them. Was it sex, was it some odd cultural misfit – her Americanness, her cooking – did he philander or gamble? I did not know, but once, coming down in the night for something from the refrigerator, I could hear Roxy quarreling in French and crying on the telephone, and who else could it have been but Charles-Henri?

EIGHT

All we know about foreign cultures – and those closest to us are in a way the most inaccessible – is their surface glitter and misleading details.
– Régis Debray, Charles de Gaulle

DAYS WORE ON, BUSY FOR ME, SLOW FOR ROXY, I GUESS. HER pregnancy wasn't showing yet, though she was more than four months along. For me, even walking on the street was a kind of social adventure. Conversations with bus drivers and old women. Me explaining that I don't speak French; cheerful laughter, pointing, sign language. Beautiful, famous touristic sights like Notre Dame and the Arc de Triomphe. Great dogs. I met a lot of dogs, walking Scamp. But frankly there is a huge dogshit problem in Paris. In all, I tried to see what made Roxy so crazy about the place, and only partly succeeded. I could see that it was pretty, with lots of movie theaters and good food. But I hated the traffic, the way you had to look where you were stepping, the way they all smoked their brains out, and the way it rained even in summer, which seemed totally strange to me.

I don't know if I was much help to Roxy at first. It's not so easy to be newly arrived in a country whose language you don't know and whose customs you either mistrust or fear. For instance, I feared the famous Parisian rudeness, though this never materialized. And it took time getting myself settled in Roxy's really uncomfortable, hot, low-ceilinged maid's room in the attic. In my heart, my situation was a bit too much like a maid's. Every day I helped Roxy get Gennie ready for her day-care center, and after they'd gone I did the breakfast dishes, afternoons I picked her up from this day-care center (called a *crèche),* and was very conscientious about helping. Truly, I didn't mind – but I sort of did.

Roxy in turn had been conscientious about introducing me to her friends and neighbors in and around the place, trying to make me feel at home, and making me register in a French class, held three afternoons a week at the town hall of the fifth Arrondissement. She was exerting herself to be nice to me in a way I had hardly expected, and that I appreciated, for I found more daunting than I expected the rapid French phrases, the forms I had to fill out, written in a bureaucratese inscrutable in any language. I even dreaded walking into the class where I would ostensibly learn to understand, in time. I had never thought of myself as shy, but when I had to say *bonjour* something sealed up my throat, as if people would catch on that I was only pretending to speak French.

I know I am dumb about speaking French, but the French aren't so great at English. Our words have no significance for them. For instance, all the proper French ladies at the gym do their aerobics to American music, but they don't hear it. There's a rap song that goes "He's a sexy motherfucker," and this doesn't cause them to miss a beat. These are words they don't know.

Talking of gyms, Roxy's view is that the style of exercise is an indication of national character: in California, high-impact aerobics, that is, mindless pounding to loud rock music drowning out thought ("Happy Nation/Livin' in a Happy Nation"); in France, narcissistic perfecting of the *Fesses-Ab-Cuisses,* or the *Bras-Buste-Epaules* class, or jazz dancing but with no regard for the beat.

I appreciated Roxy's niceness, liked it that after years of being the irritating little sister I was suddenly for her an object of gratitude and solicitude (she couldn't do without me). For this reason I didn't too much mind the faint superiority with which she now discoursed in a foreign tongue I would never master, or the proprietary air with which she explained which merchants came on which day to the market in the Place Maubert.

Roxy and Charles-Henri lived – Roxy lives – just off the Place Maubert in the fifth Arrondissement. On Tuesdays, Thursdays, and Saturdays, it is the scene of an open market. Long tables under awnings are set up, stout merchants behind them with food and flowers, a man selling *porcelaine blanche*, another offering to mend chairs. Across the Boulevard Saint-Germain is a little fountain and some benches, and the Brasserie Espoir, romping dogs, *clochards*. In former days, a statue of Etienne Dolet (whoever that was) stood there, melted down or removed in the Revolution or some war. I found an old print of it in a book by André Breton which was too difficult to read.

Her Place Maubert friends are Anne-Chantal Lartigue, a Frenchwoman, and Tammy de Bretteville, an American married to a French lawyer. When I arrived, they were both, so far as I could see, happily married women. I tried to look at them through the eyes of Janet Hollingsworth, to divine their tricks, their special Frenchness, but they seemed like regular women to me, though they did wear more beautiful shoes than us Americans in our tennies.

The days wore on with Roxy in her strange state of denial, neither trying to communicate with Charles-Henri, to reproach or persuade him, nor taking any other action, and refusing to disclose her state of affairs to her friends. To them, Roxy must have seemed calm, as if nothing were wrong. If you are calm when something is wrong, people think you are cold and unfeeling. But of course Roxy was crying, and feeling awful, however cheerful she was looking with her market basket and slowly swelling belly in the Place Maubert, meeting Anne-Chantal or Tammy de Bretteville as usual. As Roxy's waistbands slowly wouldn't fit, the Charles-Henri situation continued in her mind to have the same inevitability as her pregnancy, the same sense of a foregone conclusion, of there being no way back, no way of not going through with it; and where most women would have fought for their marriage, whatever that may mean, she continued to behave with bitter apathy.

"I'm just not ready to tell anyone," Roxy said, for days running. "How can I? All the implied I-told-you-so's. I couldn't stand it." (Our sister Judith, who had always referred to Charles-Henri as "the frog prince," would surely say I told you so.) She didn't phone anyone. I worried about her. I felt that she ought to tell her friends, so they could give her advice on how these matters are handled in France.

One night, when Roxy and Gennie and I were having supper in the Brasserie Espoir, Roxy said, "Iz, I apologize for sweeping you into my marital problems. I know you aren't having a good time, but you are being incredibly sweet. I know I'm just being a bitch and a drip."

"Well, I wish you'd cheer up, Roxy. Fuck Charles-Henri. Go back to California. Get a boyfriend."

"Sure, four months pregnant."

"That will end."

"I know. I know I'll get it together, but right now, I don't actually care what happens, and I'm sick of thinking about it. Are you having any fun at all?"

I was having some fun. I'd met some men. Conversations with men cannot, apparently, be avoided even should you want to. Men talk to us and we can't stop them. But the type of man is somewhat in my control. For instance, if I wear my hair – it is black, long, and frizzy – down to the middle of my back, and stride along in jeans and hiking boots, certain kinds of men will speak to me. North African boys try to pick me up. Loose American Girl, goes their thinking; maybe she will. "Adventure?" they whisper in the metro. "If you don't do things when you are young you will have a lifetime of regret," explained a lonely young Moroccan.

"Je ne regrette rien," I say, laughing, for it is my most secure French phrase, from the old Edith Piaf tapes Roxy used to play. But they don't understand the reference.

If I do up my hair and wear my glasses, the men will be subtly more prosperous looking – smooth businessmen and visiting Germans. If I wear a scarf around my neck, I will be taken for a French girl. Scarf, no scarf, hair up or down. Thus, controlling my destiny, I made the acquaintance of two attractive men, a wiry economist named Michel Breaux (hair up) and a student, very black-turtleneck, Yves Dupain, whom I met in line at a movie (hair down). I would spend a free afternoon now and again going to the movies with Yves, or go to supper with Michel – and sometimes more, with either of them – afterward feeling a little guilty about Roxy, as though I were betraying her. I couldn't bring myself to discuss love or sex with her. Perhaps I imagined these topics would unnerve her. I could imagine her standing before me, widening waistline and eyes in tears, a living illustration of the perils of sex and love.

Making it with Yves the first time, I wondered if I would notice anything different about a French person in bed. What I was remembering was once, I think it was after Roxy and Charles-Henri were engaged, when Chester had said at dinner, "The French they are a funny race," and he and Margeeve laughed and laughed, so that we demanded to know why, and finally Chester said: "The French they are a funny race / They fight with their feet and fuck with their face."

I remember that Roxy and I were sort of embarrassed and shocked, not by the rhyme but by Chester saying it, in front of us. Even as worldly as we both were, Roxy and I, we didn't think Chester should be.

"All the girls in France / Wear tissue paper pants . . ." added Margeeve.

"I see London, I see France . . ." said Roxy.

But with Yves and Michel nothing unusually French had happened, except that afterward Yves once had asked solicitously, "*As-tu pris ton pied?*" – which I understood, with my limited language skills, as "had I taken my foot?"

I guess it means, was it fun? It was, and I was having

enough fun generally – the occasional date with Yves or Michel, the occasional movie, the challenge of getting along here. Sometimes I felt as if I actually belonged in France. For instance, one night, as I was flipping the TV dial, looking for someone speaking slow French (my hope was that I could learn it as a child learns language, by soaking it up, though I knew in my heart this would not work and was a way of justifying not going to the class), I saw a familiar face, a large, white-haired old man in a suit, sitting with other men at a table, some sort of moderator speaking to them each in turn and now saying, *"Et alors, M. Cosset?"* and the large man began to speak in a familiar voice, and he was l'oncle Edgar, Charles-Henri's uncle! He began a vigorous discourse, thunderous of brow, which of course I understood not a word of.

"What's he saying?"

"He's talking about Bosnia," said Roxy. "He's very interested in Bosnia." I listened. Even if you couldn't understand it, what he was saying rang with indignation and authority.

"What does he do?"

"He's a kind of warmonger. He used to be an engineer. Then he was in the Chamber of Deputies," she said, drifting through the room.

"But what does he say?"

"He says France has betrayed the UN resolutions, its own promises, and the Helsinki treaty," Roxy said.

"What does he want?"

"War," said Roxy. "If it were up to Uncle Edgar, he'd have the French bombing Belgrade."

Of course we didn't approve of war, Roxy and I. Children of a California professor, we had never even met anyone who had approved of the Vietnam war. Yet – it is hard to explain – I found it thrilling to think that someone connected to us was in a position to comment publicly on national policy, even in a bellicose way. In California, we just live in our backwater, far from councils of government, so that knowing Oncle Edgar brought us closer to French national policy than we could ever come to American, and this gave me a vicarious feeling of influence and involvement. (Once, in college, I did go to hear the congressman from Santa Barbara, a balding young man who smiled all the time and sweated. But I didn't meet him, exactly.)

From the first I had found Roxy's state of mind unnerving, but I think it was only when I heard her talk of abortion pills that I took seriously her belief that her marriage was over. Before that it had been easy to see a gap between her emotions and the facts of her case; this was a marital tiff exaggerated by the hormones of pregnancy or by the resentful fatigue of an overworked young mother. I knew Roxy well enough to know she was impulsive and in some views spoiled. (It was part of the lore of our family that Margeeve's girls were spoiled, while Roger and I were little soldiers, and there is some truth in this.) But Roxy's storms were really her nature, not products of maternal indulgence. She had impossible ideals of conduct, and she had thought that knights and princes existed and that Charles-Henri was one of the latter. And now she knew otherwise, and was acting as if all were decided, divorce, life over – it was as if she were relieved to get through the biggest crisis of her life so lightly and quickly. But I could see she had trouble saying the actual, fateful words: Charles-Henri has left me.

I tried to stiffen her myself, and I tried to think how to tell our parents. Finally, one day when Roxy was out, I called them. They heard my report of Roxy's troubles without surprise, and Margeeve even said, "I knew something like that would happen," exactly as Roxy had predicted. They evidently *had* believed something like this would happen. Their own lives, their divorces, the lives and divorces of people they knew, had taught them not only to expect marital troubles for their offspring but to believe them inevitable, and even a positive good, leading to eventual happiness with a predestined mate you would not have been ready for the first time around. This had been their experience. My father with Roger's and my difficult mother, and Margeeve with her irascible, practically criminal, alcoholic husband, Roxy's and Judith's father – both had become tempered and wise from these bad experiences and, from the time they met, got along with each other as God had intended couples to do. We four children were therefore more the products not of broken homes but of a happy one, and if the psychologists were right, that should predispose us to happy marriages in turn. Thus did certain facts of social nature – divorce – dispute with the home-healing benefits of our nurture, a contradiction that was resolved if you accepted the first divorce as a boon. It is only if you view divorce as catastrophe that it is so.

I am trying to explain that Chester and Margeeve were somewhat detached about Roxy's plight and didn't react with the dismay she herself felt. I'm sure they also had a wish, conscious or unconscious, to see her back home in America where God intended Americans to be and where they always ended up, think of F. Scott Fitzgerald, Hemingway, Gerald Murphy, and a whole lot of others who came to France but went home again.

Eventually of course when Roxy did call Dad and Margeeve to say that she and Charles-Henri were "having trouble," they put on airs of suitable dismay and commiseration. But Roxy found their unsurprise galling, since she herself had not got over her surprise, would never get over it, that just when she had thought everything was perfect, it turned out not to be.

Roxy, not knowing how much I had discussed with Chester and Margeeve about her situation, was surprised too to get a call from Margeeve one day saying, "Roxy, don't let Charles-Henri take the picture."

"The picture?"

"Saint Ursula. In case he comes to move out his stuff, he shouldn't get the idea it's his."

Roxy, who had expressly given it to him, was dumbfounded and puzzled. "He wouldn't do that, it's right here, in the apartment. You've never liked him, have you?"

NINE

There are good marriages, but no delightful ones.
– La Rochefoucauld

ROXY HAD CLUNG LIKE AN OLD REACTIONARY TO HER view that their life had been perfect, but through chinks in her stories I began to see certain things that explained the trouble – from my outsider's view of marriage nothing unusual, just the regular things. Her descriptions of past events would include the mention of "the weekend Charles-Henri was in Nice" and things of that sort, from which it appeared to me that Charles-Henri had too often been away painting or visiting family members. It seemed to me that Roxy had been left alone a lot with Gennie, and I knew her well enough to imagine the petulance in her tone when he came home. She hinted once that Charles-Henri had not wanted kids. Also, they had money problems, and Roxy, devoting herself relentlessly to poetry, would never do anything so obvious and useful as to get a job. Having kids is a good excuse not to earn money, I can see that; to mantle yourself in motherhood, especially in France, is to be very snug – motherhood a cloak under which to write, just as when we were younger she used to write by flashlight under the covers. And perhaps two artists always compete, for time to work and for the right to be the pampered one. Why must human relationships have these binary tensions built into them, the pretty versus the plain, the smart and the dumb, the child and the grownup?

On the other hand, to take Roxy's part, it was selfish of Charles-Henri not to want a child. What did people do before they had these hard choices to make, when babies just arrived?

By September she had fallen into a quieter, even more depressed mood, but instead of focusing on her own problems, now it was the war in Bosnia that mesmerized her. French television and Euronews carried daily coverage of Slavs in headscarves weeping along roadsides, and ruins, and corpses in ditches. Roxy was especially fascinated with one recurrent image, one that had become for the television people a kind of emblem of the stupid war. She was captured by the Romeo and Juliet story that accompanied the grisly image, of a Serb boy and Muslim girl or vice versa, lovers, shot by one side or the other in a no-man's-land as they tried to flee across a foreground of rubble and barbed wire, their bodies photographed lying there (in jeans and tennis shoes), and their families afraid to crawl out to get them.

"The hypocrisy of America, going to war to protect a bunch of Arabs who mutilate women, and then refusing to help these poor Bosnians," Roxy would rave. "Letting the Serbs go on raping the women. Uncle Edgar is right, the cowardice of the French is incredible. Don't they remember World War I? Don't they remember Chamberlain? How can they let this go on?"

Of course this line of thinking was influenced by the public pronouncements of Oncle Edgar. He was always denouncing his country's policy in the pages of *Le Figaro* or on TV. Suzanne would call us whenever he was going to be on. Even without speaking French, I could easily grasp the essentials of his discourse: *horreur, scandale, honneur, honte.*

I could see that Roxy, ordinarily not a pretentious person, thought of her situation as something doomed on the Bosnian scale, and I could see that her self-pitying mood was mixed with malice, the imagined satisfaction of seeing Charles-Henri's lifeless abandoned corpse in a no-man's-land.

Still she didn't confront him or confide in me. I thought she must be preparing her moves, or else it was some lethargy of pregnancy. Once there was a scare when her ankles began to swell. I can still see her, sitting on the sofa *(canapé)* sobbing, "These are not my legs, these are piano posts, I can't even feel them." The doctors worried that it could presage a condition called eclampsia, and made her stop eating salt and go every two weeks for a checkup. When she was put into elastic stockings she felt better, but even when it seemed her condition could be grave, she would not let anyone tell Charles-Henri.

Eventually, I resolved to talk to Charles-Henri myself. I had found out where he was, because I had run into Charlotte de Persand Saxe, Charles-Henri's sister. Mrs. Pace had suggested I go to an "exposition" of the painters who called themselves Nabis. These turned out to be Vuillard and Bonnard, and some others I'd never heard of. My favorite was the one named Vallottan, because each of his gray street scenes and rainy landscapes featured a bright spot of red, in a scarf or umbrella, for me symbolizing the arrival of unexpected and sometimes felicitous events in life. And just as I was thinking this, there, felicitously at the same exhibition was Charlotte, wearing a red dress and smelling delightful. Charlotte is one of those Frenchwomen who are permeated with perfume from head to toe. I made a mental note to ask Roxy's friend Janet, the one who is writing a book about French women, how they do this.

She was with an Englishman she introduced as Giles Wheating, a name I had vaguely heard. British journalist? The "liaison" her mother had mentioned? But there was nothing of embarrassment or furtive surprise in their manner. I simply asked her where Charles-Henri was and she told me, and gave me a phone number in the country near Illiers. There's a sort of trailer there belonging to the Persand family, where he painted and gardened. "We will have to have a coffee sometime soon and talk more about it," she added.

Later the same day, I called up Charles-Henri, who was perfectly civil on the phone, with only the slightest apprehensiveness in his tone, and he seemed delighted to make a rendezvous for the following day.

Though the Café Vues de Notre Dame is near their apartment, it is so big and touristy that it could be considered neutral and safe to meet in, not unduly Roxy's turf or provocative of memories. I sat at the back of the sidewalk terrace, a little sheltered but still open against the smoke. Charles-Henri turned up a second after I had got there and ordered myself a coffee. He had a new scar on his chin, but was otherwise unchanged from the attractive man I had met in California, rather pale, a slight blue undertone to his skin, as if his beard, if it grew out, would be black, at odds with his fair eyelashes. He had the same engaging smile, replaced instantly with a frown of sincerity, and gave me three cheek kisses, familially.

"La petite Isabel! Ça va?" I am tall, but in France anything is petite if you want it to seem negligible, like a petit problem, or a petite invoice. "It's so nice of you to meet. I know how angry you are at me, my mother is too, and you can imagine how I feel about all this."

"I'm just meddling, really. I'm in the dark," I said. "Roxy doesn't tell me anything. I just thought maybe there's something I could do."

"How's my dear little Gennie? I hope to see her soon, I just haven't known how to work it out with Roxy, when I can visit and so on. I miss her so much."

"She misses you," I said, regretting the accusing tone as this slipped out. "She's fine. She asks for you, but then she forgets. She's only three."

Charles-Henri: "Oh, *mon Dieu.* Are you having something?"

Me (not understanding): "Huh?"

Charles-Henri: "I might have a sandwich, I didn't have lunch." Having been a number of weeks in France, I should have been aware of how at any awkward point in a conversation, the subject reverts to food. He waved at the waiter and ordered. "Sandwich *rillettes.*"

"Your family is being really nice, really supportive," I said. "The point is, no one seems to know what's the matter, between you and Roxy, I mean." I was being as direct as possible.

"Ah. There's nothing wrong between us," he said, and seeing my surprise, added a protestation about how much he loved Roxy and Gennie.

"Maybe I'll have a sandwich," I said. "*Jambon fromage.*" He waved for the waiter. There was a silence, the transition, the waiter again. How can you ask pointed questions without asking them pointedly? Like, why are you being such an asshole, if you love them so much?

"I feel absolutely in the wrong. I am the culpable one, there's no question," he said. Why is it men love to confess to badness? They have learned that women love to forgive – or so they think. In reality, no one ever forgives anything, that I can see.

"Couldn't you, you know, seek counseling? Don't they have marriage counseling here?"

"Isabel, there's nothing I can do about this. I – I've met the woman of my life, the love of my life, it's an inevitability. I want to be only with her. That would be hard for any woman to understand, and I know that Roxy doesn't understand."

I felt a big relief at this. It was as Charles-Henri's mother had diagnosed, he'd got a crush on someone, a temporary effect of Roxy's pregnancy, and all Roxy would have to do, if she could forgive him, was to have the baby and wait it out.

He could not forbear to talk about his new love. "Magda Tellman. She was formerly a teacher of sociology in Nantes. She's very brilliant. Married to an American, isn't that comic, in a way? A coincidence, each of us married to an American. The Tellmans are separated, we're separated. So symmetrical a situation."

He went on, tensely, trying to convince me, I wasn't sure of what. "I know it sounds unnecessary, extreme, romantic in the bad sense, it's just that there's nothing I can do. Believe me, there's a certain relief in that. To arrive for once in life at a certainty. Certitude?"

"Either," I said. I pitied him his romantic heart, as I pitied Roxeanne hers. At that moment I was glad I hadn't got one.

He did not seem to lose interest in being there talking to me. He continued to ask questions about Roxy, but I think he really wanted to talk to someone about Magda, about this wonderful thing (despite the complications) love. About how it removed all element of choice, and about how well he was painting. About how good could come out of bad. Eventually, we said goodbye.

My questions remained. Had Charles-Henri told Roxy about his passion in these same exorbitant terms? Was it a shame so humiliating to her that she didn't want even me to know? Could I mention to her that I had seen him, and that I knew about Magda (what a name!)?

Something odd happened as I was walking over to get Gennie at the crèche. I was crossing the esplanade in front of Notre Dame. This windswept stretch, crowded with tourists gawking up, knotted around, strangled with cameras, is always best avoided. After a month or so, I no longer got the religious shiver I had at first (though I am not religious), and so I usually walk on the other end to miss the people, but on this day I did walk on the near side, just outside the little fence that designates the forecourt, and I paused a second to meet the eyes of the angular stone apostles that line the façade.

A beggar always stands right here, and it is always the same beggar (or "homeless person"). Dark-skinned, he appears to be an Indian or Pakistani, or Gypsy, and blind. Always there, his cup stretched out, leaning on a cane, wearing a hooded sweatshirt, like someone in the Bible, his apparently unseeing eyes without pupils, as white as moons.

I have always noticed him because, regarding the exit to Notre Dame Cathedral, I have thought, is this not the preeminent, the reigning begging-place in Paris, if not the world?

Wouldn't there be competition for this lucrative slot, with the whole world's sinners guiltily stealing by him, traipsing in and out of the great building, feeling penitence? Is there a sociology of beggars, in which rank and seniority promote you to such precincts? Or are beggars like, say, pigeons, condemned to grow up where they hatch, indifferently assigned by fate to the pickings of barren, seedless alleys or abundant parks? This beggar, in any case, by whatever right or tolerance, has Notre Dame to himself.

And, as I walked by and glanced up, and then inadvertently at him (for I hate his white eyes), he said, "Isabel." This frightened me so much that I quickened my step and walked on toward the Hôtel de Ville, my fear and fascination growing, searching for explanation – coincidence, someone else speaking. This event has not yet been explained.

I came into Roxy's apartment quietly, thinking about what it could mean. Roxy was on the phone, speaking in English, therefore to an American friend or, as it proved, to someone in our family, either Chester or Margeeve. I heard her mention Roscoe, their cat, and Ralphie the dog. I wasn't listening especially, until I heard my own name. Hearing your name cuts through thoughts like a bullet through a cloud.

"She's doing better," Roxy was saying. "She's had some dates. She has about ten odd jobs – but I think she's trying to use them as a way of getting out of babysitting. And she still won't say a word of French."

This was unfair, since I had babysat every single time I was asked, and I said *bonjour* almost promiscuously. As they went on talking, it became clear that they had been conspiring all along, discussing my doings, my progress, my state of mind. "Olivia Pace thinks highly of her, apparently she's a real help," Roxy was saying. "She walks my friend Ames's dog, stuff like that. I think she's doing fine."

Of course I should have seen it before. In their minds, *I* was the problem, not Roxy, *I* was the subject they'd been putting their heads together about. I hadn't been sent to help Roxy, Roxy had been enlisted to look after me, the ne'er-do-well little sister with her aimless attitude to the future. I'm sure they were hoping I'd meet a nice European count, or maybe I'd become interested in teaching English as a Second Language. At worst, I'd learn to speak French. I was aghast. I felt a sort of angry and embarrassed flush in my cheeks, as if I'd found a bloodstain on the back of my dress and realized it had been there all afternoon.

My character had always been a subject that could flare up into a quarrel between Chester and Margeeve, once dramatically at the dinner table – a rare quarrel, I should add, for Chester and Margeeve are solid, but Margeeve thinks I have been raised to be too indifferent to my future, which she says betrays Chester's covert sexism. My brother Roger was steered toward the law since grade school, but my future would look after itself. "You never took Isabel seriously, that is the truth, because she is a girl," snapped Margeeve on this occasion. My father said, "I have always taken Isabel seriously," with a kind of sigh, "but I have never understood her," and I remember saying, "That's for sure."

But I did understand, and they understood, that Roxy has a true literary talent and love for poetry, and would probably not be that great at anything else, plus being a poet allows you a lot of time to raise a family, teach a class, or (as I have noticed) *flâner* in the streets of Paris, which means mess around, with no guilty sense of being unoccupied. Lucky Roxy. And now she had a reason, her pregnancy, never to skip meals. From my point of view, her life should have been complete, except for the marital problem, which I continued to view as a temporary aberration.

So I pretended I hadn't overheard anything.

"I saw Charles-Henri," I said, when she had put down the phone. "I talked to him. I thought I should talk to him myself, maybe you were exaggerating things."

"He came in to Paris? How was he?" She was newly alert.

"He says he's fallen in love with someone. Did he tell you that?"

She didn't answer.

"For me it was a big relief to hear that," I said. "Oh, is that all, I thought."

"All? All?" A rush of hysteria in her voice.

"Men get over that. People do. I always do."

"Yes, he'll get over it, the way he got over me, but it won't have never happened, it can't be undone. Yes, he told me he had met the love of his life. There's nothing you can say to that." So she had known all along. This was the one thing she could not forgive.

TEN

I was younger, and I cultivated the habit of keeping all my experiences and plans to myself, relying upon myself alone.

– *Benjamin Constant,* Adolphe

IT SHOULDN'T HAVE SURPRISED ME THAT MY PARENTS WERE worried about my life plans. I admit I was baffled myself. I'd write a screenplay, I'd decided in film school. I'd direct. Perhaps I was meant to be an actress, or the girl who gets the coffee – this is what I was ending up as, after all. But of course Paris wasn't "ending up" (I'd remind myself, lying in Roxy's *chambre de bonne),* this was a beginning, or, properly speaking, Time Out. But I hadn't realized that our folks were worried about me, and it made me sort of mad to think that other people looking at me saw things that worried them and then didn't tell me so that I could reassure them, or deal with their fears. *I* knew I would be all right, but they didn't. Crazy people must feel this gap between themselves and others, and the terminally ill must feel it. It's horrible to have people worry about you, and it's insulting besides. Or am I politically incorrect to think so?

Roxy was truly not so sure she would be all right. "Maybe I should get a divorce," she began to say every day. I urged her at least to talk to Charles-Henri before taking such a step as that, and to talk to others. I was not sure how often they had actually spoken in the time since my arrival – it was now more than three months. But she continued to refuse. "What's there to discuss? There's no point in protracting things. Infidelity will just happen again. The pattern of an unfaithful French husband, I know it all from my reading of Colette, Balzac, Zola. Pretty soon he'd have not this woman but another, a mistress permanently installed in another street, perhaps even a child, children, or he would chase the au pair girls, they would get younger and more gullible as he got older and older, or waitresses at McDonald's or the girl in the market. I can't bear to think of seeing him go through all that. And he would despise me more and more each time."

Though she wouldn't discuss it with him, she began to discuss it with other people, in my view a healthy development. The women of the Place Maubert, Tammy de Bretteville and Anne-Chantal Lartigue in particular, agreed with Roxy's take on it. A pattern of infidelity once begun is never abandoned. But they also did not believe Roxy should divorce. In France you just put up with the way men are.

This was also part of Suzanne de Persand's pitch. "*Le divorce* is always a mistake. Now you are hurt, you are wounded and *enceinte*, it is not a time to make a decision." French husbands – like men everywhere – just always philander, she explained. "Why ruin your life and lose your social position over it?" Roxy condemned this attitude as Victorian, a vestige of a time when women were powerless and lacking in self-respect.

"That is so American," sighed Suzanne impatiently. "Think of the children, their need for a father. Think of the inconveniences of single motherhood." Suzanne thought Roxy was being impetuous and self-indulgent, but I knew it was just that her feelings were hurt with a mortal hurt.

Mrs. Pace also counseled patience. Roxy came to lunch one day when I was working for Mrs. Pace, and we all discussed it.

"I have myself been divorced," Mrs. Pace observed, "and I'm not sure it solves a great deal. Though it does permit you to marry someone else. In my experience the soundest procedure is to have the someone else lined up beforehand."

I was the only one of Roxy's confidantes who wasn't so sure she was wrong. What about love? How can you stay married to someone who loves another better than you? What about the future, perhaps with another mate? She had her whole life in front of her, in the phrase. I tried to slow her down, we all did, but part of me thought she just ought to bag this marriage and get on with her life.

I was working for Olivia Pace three times a week. Mrs. Pace became a famous writer when she was very young, in the 1940s, and hence had by now outlived many of the important literary figures whom she had known and slept with back then. Judging from the number of letters she got, the world was looking forward to her memoirs, and she was starting to pull things together to write them. My job was to organize papers and facts, in folders marked by date, year by year. A folder might contain letters, any newspaper clippings she happened to have saved, copies of what she wrote at the time, and a list of things she had bought, if she remembered, like "blue silk Cardin suit, 1972," or "first Dior, 1959," or "Sheraton sideboard, Bristol, 1948," or a review article from any of several little magazines she wrote for.

What I liked best about my days at Mrs. Pace's was that we had a sort of working lunch at which she identified objects and people's names that I couldn't identify on my own. It was then I heard her stories. The reason she liked me, I think, was because I had known the name of a character in Conrad's *Victory*. I knew and she didn't; therefore she respected me and looked at me thereafter with new eyes, as someone more promising than she had thought. She considered me educable. In fact, we had used Conrad's *Victory* in a film class on adaptation, but I had never actually read it.

For my part, I fell under the spell of her encouragement, for she was a woman who had not been caught in the character traps I considered that other women I knew had fallen into, for instance Margeeve, who had never really used her brains that I could see, and hence has a certain restless troublemaking quality of dissatisfaction even though I think she is happy. Even Roxy, with her trustful, romantic view of men, was sort of an underachiever, except for the occasional poem, and poems are short. It only just comes to me now that Roxy's starry-eyed view of men probably originated in my father's gallant rescue of her mother, Margeeve, from the cold rigors of single motherhood and battered wifedom.

Mrs. Pace, it appeared, had had all the perks of female life – rich husbands, children, Givenchy dresses, lots of Haviland china. She had also had the perks of male life – the pleasures of sexual misdeeds (or call them exploits, like a man) as well as the intellectual pleasures of writing, of having opinions, of having her opinions listened to – the masculine pleasures of independent thought and judgment on general subjects, not including the Woman's Lot, which didn't interest her. Her example made me understand what, perhaps, I had been looking for in film school: autonomy, though that was not the place to find it. In my case, I had been already too far gone down the road of conventional female socialization to relish the technical side of film – the lighting, the questions of Steadicam or handheld camera, the dub, the cut, the mix.

This left me with, precisely, a kind of blank spot when it came to what to do with my life. Mrs. Pace did not worry about me but felt confidence in me, and so she became my idol, for I suppose that is the right word, overwrought though it may be, for someone who makes you want to please them and be liked by them, whose regard you care for. What I felt for Mrs. Pace I didn't feel for Chester and Margeeve or my siblings; on them, I bestowed affection, in varying degrees, without caring much what they thought of me.

But Mrs. Pace was a mighty person. She said what people were. And if she said someone was a fool, that didn't necessarily mean that she held it against them. It depended on what kind of fool. She was the first person I had met who told the absolute, even if politically incorrect, truth, and it was usually a truth I felt in my heart already. She would not be afraid to say that we do not really like, say, the handicapped people taking up all the parking places. But she was a moral force too, and she would also say we ought not to act on our feelings. She taught me that it is not abnormal to have bitter or illiberal reactions to things, but it is just wrong to act on them, and that people get no moral credit for the hypocritical way they conceal such things as racism even from themselves. Only when you confront your racism can you expunge it, she would say. "The truth I don't say will make you free," she said, "but it is better than piety, because you know where you stand with it."

Through Mrs. Pace I got a number of jobs. One was house-sitting for the Randolphs, Cleve and Peg, a couple in their sixties who I thought fit into what Ames Everett calls trust-funders, but Mrs. Pace said, "Spooks, actually." When I was horrified, she added, "They're very nice, of course." And the Randolphs were nice. Retired CIA – or do you ever retire? – *plus* a trust fund, judging from the splendor of their apartment on the Place des Vosges. Mrs. Pace quite liked them. "We were all CIA," Mrs. Pace reminded me. "The CIA came to Wellesley at our graduation and offered each girl a job and a camera and the sense of doing her patriotic duty. I accepted, of course, but my post was to have been Guatemala City, so I backed out."

For someone so associated with leftwing causes in her youth (I was learning about Trotsky, Stalin, Wobblies, etc.), she now seemed comfortable with a wide political spectrum. (As long as the people were rich, I am tempted to add – but then, in a sense, all the Americans I saw were rich. Even the backpackers, sandaled and out of funds, were standing in the American Express line to tap some affluent stateside source of money. I soon learned that I didn't really understand what comprised wealth. The symbols reliable in Santa Barbara, cars for example, were unreliable or missing here, and all the apartments looked small to my eyes. In the beginning I would assume people were hard up, and Roxy would laugh and say, "Are you kidding?")

It was not the CIA Randolphs but another client, employer, whatever I am calling them, Stuart Barbee, who most surprised me. I had supposed that all the Americans living in Paris were there because they preferred it, and so had contrived their lives to be there. But there were a certain number who seemed to hate France and wistfully to long for America, as if from some cruel exile. So it was with Stuart Barbee, the art historian whose dining room I painted. A rangy man in his fifties, slight southern accent. I think he used to be Ames Everett's boyfriend, but now he's with an English hairdresser named Conrad, or Con, whose name is a huge joke because *con* means something rude in French. Stuart seemed always to be testing my attitudes. "This rainy weather in late summer must make you long for California, Isabel. September is so beautiful there. I spent a month at the Getty once. So beautiful, and the ocean – I'm mad for the ocean. Are you? I can imagine you surfing in a bikini. (Unconvincing leer.) Or, "My God, these people, the way they sabotage the lowly hamburger." Or, "It isn't easy sitting by while your country falls into the hands of a redneck draft dodger. It almost makes me want to go back and get involved in precinct work, or maybe work for Ross Perot."

I recounted this last conversation to Mrs. Pace at lunch. She sniffed. "Draft dodger? This revisionist sanctimoniousness about Vietnam does astonish me. Why it should be coming up now I don't know. Imagine resurrecting the term 'draft dodger,' an expression not even used in the Vietnam period, as I remember. A Second World War term, maybe even First World War. Look in the OED. I think it's being used now by men who are no longer attractive, to get at a younger president. Would I have allowed my son Drew to go to Vietnam? Of course not. Luckily his number was a safe one." She warmed to this subject, laying her napkin next to her plate and touching her pearls.

"You wouldn't remember, you were too young, Isabel, but people could see with their own eyes that those little Vietnamese children were not a threat to the free world. And yet deaf presidents would not hear this. America was resisting its leaders, as we so wished young Germans had done. We saw our leaders as cruel men crazed by the exciting momentum of their own blood lust. It was one of the few wars in history where women really played a pacific role."

I must have looked puzzled at this, so she went on to explain.

"Ordinarily I don't give females too much moral credit. They seem as bad as anyone else. In fact they are not usually considered independent moral beings, in the sense of having to make choices, except where sexual transgressions are concerned. Perhaps not even then – 'the woman *taken* in adultery.' Hmmn.

And most are not very responsible, we must admit. Though they are made to accept the consequences all the same."

I remarked that it sometimes seemed to me she didn't have a whole lot of respect for women.

"Well," she sighed, "I have sympathy, but that is not the same thing as respect. I understand their historical circumstances. Centuries of oppression create a kind of fog in the brain. Look at – other groups. No one makes women defer to their husbands and refuse to think about world events, just as no one makes an underclass take drugs.

"But it would be a mistake to underestimate the force of female opposition to that war. This time, it wasn't a question of women blubbering on the sidelines as the boys marched off, women were serious objectors. Remember 'girls say yes to boys who say no'? No, you wouldn't remember that, of course. There was a general effort on everybody's part to help people not go into the army. It was not only that you did not want young men to be killed, you wanted your country to stop doing something so wicked. People have forgotten that resistance was not only the sensible but the virtuous course."

Soon after this, Cleve Randolph asked me to sit down, and made me the following little speech: "You wouldn't remember, you are too young, Isabel, but the Communist threat was very real, in the thirties. Many people thought we would go that way. They wanted it. Not the workers, not the real Americans, farmers and honest people, but the intellectuals so-called. It appealed to them, their phony commerce with the proletariat, their self-satisfied sense of fraternity, their – I grant you – idealism, finally their corruption. Their sense of anger at our American values and ideals deepened, they became bitter, they became willing to betray us, America, almost for the pleasure of it. Even after it was clear that Stalin was a monster, even after some of them acknowledged this and went with Trotsky – you are too young to remember all this – even now, they wish America ill."

"My father's mother was a Communist," I volunteered, pointedly. "In Minnesota. She died before I was born, but I've heard the stories. She didn't wish America ill: she wanted to help organize the farmers in Minnesota."

He peered at me with a moment's suspicion, calculated the chronology, and smiled.

"Dear Isabel," he said. "That is history, and it is of history that I am speaking. The need to expunge all that, clarify, wash away the stain of treachery, the uncertainty of who, where, why. Things need to be brought out into the light of day so they can heal, you understand?"

This sounded rather New Age from a man of his years, but these were recognizable tenets, ones that Mrs. Pace herself promulgated.

"So much would be cleared up if we knew, for instance, the real role of Olivia Pace. If not a spy herself, certainly the lover of spies," he went on.

"Mrs. Pace?" I said, beginning to understand the direction of his thoughts and the unconvincing benignity of his air to me.

"Her role in the late thirties through nineteen-forty-five."

"It's inconceivable that she did anything wrong," I insisted.

"Inconceivable. I'm not at all suggesting it. In any case, there would be no consequences now. No one thinks of public accusations or legal actions – though I believe there is no actual statute of limitations on treason, high treason." His voice, on the words High Treason, was unnaturally charged, allowing me to glimpse, beneath the urbane manner and the deliberate lightness of his tone, a fervid preoccupation.

"It has never seemed right to me that men go unpunished for crimes that may have cost lives, that may have jeopardized a whole way of life, and they sit today, some of them right here in perfect comfort. All those Englishmen, and . . ."

He caught himself. "In the interest of history. Inconceivable that Olivia could have done anything purposefully. Unwittingly? One wonders. If you should happen to notice . . . in her files . . ."

There seemed nothing to say. Of course I would not snoop in Mrs. Pace's files and report on them. The melodrama, the cloak and daggerness, appealed to me, however. As he saw, it was impossible for me to sympathize imaginatively with those old passions. But it was sort of amusing, being asked to spy. And I found myself wondering if he were not right to think that old wounds should be healed. I suppose I was thinking of Roxy and Charles-Henri, but what goes for people must go for nations too?

ELEVEN

In my state of vague emotional torment I decided that I wanted to be loved, and looked about me. . . . I studied my own heart and tastes and could not discover any definite preferences.
– Benjamin Constant, Adolphe

THOUGH I HAD REASSURED ROXY THAT I WAS HAVING FUN IN France, mostly I was working or babysitting all the time. But occasionally I went out with either of my two Frenchmen, Yves and Michel, and also a couple of Americans, one a guy I knew from Santa Barbara, Mark Lopez, the other a brother of a friend of Roxy's, Jeff. Both of these men were like brothers; our fellow Americanness neutered us, and our dates were much taken up with cross-cultural notes and survival strategies. Mostly we went to films. Paris is good for film buffs, because anything you might want to see is playing. Sometimes we had dinner.

Scene: Yves and Isabel in a restaurant that reeks of cigarette and cigar smoke; you don't know how they can even taste their food. Yves smoking like the rest.

Me: It's really stupid to smoke. It's the leading cause of death. Do you have to?

Yves: *Bah ouieeagh.* (I can't spell phonetically these strange syllables that mean, Yes, I'm smoking, not smoking is a con. You crazy Americans.)

Me (primly): I'll have the healthy fat-free sole and the steamed vegetable plate, please.

Yves: *Pavé au poivre, saignant* (thick steak, rare, dripping with butter and cream).

Me: Ugh (shudder).

Yves: They do a great *bavette* here, but even better at Balzar, there they use a beef from Normandy raised in a special manner on American *maïs*, you can also find this at L'Ami Louis. They do not import English beef here, on account of the *vache folle* malady, naturally, not allowing it to come to France which I support, but in truth, the English beef, one hates to say so, was very good – the Danes, also, though you would not expect, have an excellent *boeuf*. . ." and he's off discoursing about some esoteric aspect of beef, or it could be mushrooms or anything.

Also, they read comic books, Yves and his friends do, although studying at the university. These are not aspects of French culture they teach in the course I am taking at the *mairie*. I realize there is much I have to learn about France, but so do they have something to learn about America, whereas the only thing in America they care about seeing is *Lazvegaz*.

One night, Roxy and I had dinner at Charlotte and Bob's. Three friends of theirs were there. Here is another, what I consider typical, French dinner conversation:

Marie-Laure: This is good. Where do you get it?

Charlotte: Rue Monge.

Marie-Laure: The Caveau du Fromage?

Charlotte: No, Kramer, opposite.

Jean: This is the original Epoisse. (Turning to me, in English) Try this. In my opinion, the Epoisses are the king of cheeses. The best cheeses of France.

Others: *Non! Oui!* Amis du Chambertin! Livarot! Vacherin!

Marie-Laure: Jean thinks he is original, but Brillat-Savarin also said the Epoisses were the best cheese, and he said it first.

Bertrand: So, you go up to the rue Monge?

Charlotte: Saturdays.

Jean: The orange crust is important. . .

Charlotte (to us): Yes. Did you know that the Camembert

has a white crust because white was considered more refined for women? Although at one period of history, people didn't think women should eat cheese at all. The fermentation could be harmful to their reproductive potential. And it imparted, perhaps, an *odeur*. . . .

Roxy: When was that?

Charlotte: Oh, in the Middle Ages. Around the sixteenth century. Perhaps the Princesse de Clèves would not have eaten cheese.

Roxy (always thoughtful): I suppose that's behind the idea that nice women should only take one cheese. Too much cheese would make them into nymphomaniacs. Are men allowed to take more than one cheese?

(I look down at my plate where I have taken five cheeses, one of each on the cheese plate, and accepted seconds of Epoisse besides. I would have thought it was polite to sample each of their cheeses. But I am constantly making politeness mistakes.)

Jean: The orange crust is from a natural but odd bacteria. When it comes to the organism in Amis du Chambertin, they couldn't get it to grow anywhere but in that particular part of Burgundy. When it became such a success, the *fabricant* tried to move his factory, built a fine new one, but the orange crust wouldn't grow in the new place. He had to enlarge the old one, and each new cellar they dug, it had to communicate with the old one, and remain empty for a while until the *moisissure* had a chance to establish itself.

Bertrand: I still like a *chèvre*.

All: *Oui! Non! Sec! Frais!*

Relations between Roxy and the Persands kept on as before, Sunday lunches, friendly phone calls, and on Tuesdays when I picked up Gennie at the crèche, I would take her to see her grandmother. Suzanne is worried about Gennie not speaking enough French, surrounded as she is by Anglophone aunt and mother, with Charles-Henri so derelict in his duty.

We had begun to garner details about Magda Tellman,

Charles-Henri's new love. Charles-Henri had met her, a Czechoslovakian sociologist married to an American employee of EuroDisney, last year while painting in the Dordogne, where the Tellmans were renting a place on vacation. One can only imagine how their passion came to blaze up. What she looked like we did not know. So far as we had heard, Suzanne had continued to refuse to see her.

About this time I had two strange encounters. The first was with Mr. Tellman, Magda's husband, one day as I was coming home.

To get into Roxy's building, you enter a code on the numbered buttons outside, you hear a click and push open the thick door, which then closes behind you, and a little lighted button shows you where to push to turn on the lights for the hallway and the stairs. You then go down the hallway to the end, where a glass door separates you from the stairs. You unlock this door. The mailboxes are in the hall to the left before you go through the glass door, the garbage cans are in a room inside the glass door on the left. In olden days, and in some buildings still, a concierge instead of the glass door would intercept visitors and accept parcels.

On this particular day, I came in and slammed the street door behind me, groping inside for the light button, for even on the brightest day it's dark in the hall, with its walls of stone and ancient timbers exposed, rather affectedly, to remind you that they have been there since 1680. As I came nearer to the mailboxes, my eyes getting used to the gloom, I saw that a man was sitting on the mail ledge. He got up, slowly, as if he were hurt, or old, though he was perhaps in his forties, dressed in a suit.

"Are you Roxeanne?" he asked, in an American accent. I said nothing, and then as he moved toward me, I hurriedly said, "I'm Isabel." Looking back on it, it was kind of cowardly to disavow being Roxy, diverting some risk to her instead of me. I should have said I was Roxy, standing in for her, for there was something frightening about the man. But I don't think this menace, the slick of some interior spillover blazing in his eyes, was apparent to me in the first moment I saw him. I had simply been surprised to be addressed at all, and was struck silent.

"Why?" I added. I wondered if I should go outside again, he looked so immoderate and somehow dangerous. To get out the door again, you have to push an electrical button on the wall, then, lunging for the door, operate a catch as soon as you hear it click. I have never understood the rationale for this arrangement, common to all doors of all French apartment buildings. I hesitated. He scared me. It came to me the man was probably drunk, some smell of alcohol and anger came off him, and he was American.

He smiled. "You're the sister."

"Are you a friend of Roxy?"

"You could say. You could say we have something in common. I thought I'd like to meet her."

"You haven't met?"

"Haven't met."

"I don't think she's home . . . ."

"I'm the husband."

"Sorry?" I wasn't following. I was thinking about turning flatly around and opening the door. I just wanted to get away from this guy, and I certainly wasn't going to let him meet Roxy.

"I'm the husband of Magda Tellman. 'The husband.' "

Magda Tellman. It just didn't at that instant mean anything to me, though I realized in another split second that Magda was the woman Charles-Henri had fallen in love with.

"Why don't you leave a note?" I said. "I have to go now. Just write her a note and put it in the box, with your phone and stuff."

"Yeah, I'll leave her a note." He smiled at my brilliance. Why did I feel afraid of him? When I turned my back on him, to open the street door, I half dreaded a blow on the back of my head. Then later, when he had gone, I came back in and looked to see if he had written a note. He had, unfolded, on a "From the Desk of" paper. It said "Mrs. Persand, be aware that I'm never going to divorce Magda, if you want to plan accordingly." Roxy never commented on this.

After Roxy had begun to talk more openly about getting a divorce, I went with her to a meeting of American women, where she thought she might get some helpful advice. From the first, it was clear that the agenda of their meeting was just to kick back and complain about the French, especially French mothers-in-law, with their insistence on Sunday lunch, their meddlesome helpfulness, their hostility to Americans and to daughters-in-law in general. Despite these agitations, it was restful, in a way, to be in a gathering of American women. No matter what one thinks of one's compatriots, there is undeniably a rapport that cannot be explained. When you meet another American you exchange a glance of understanding. Who you are, your basic cultural assumptions, are known. If you were speaking French, you would *tutoyer* each other from the first. You wouldn't necessarily like these other Americans, but even the ones you don't like, you always like them better in France than you would like them if you were both back in America.

At the same time, Americans are critical of each other here. They are snobbish about each other's French, for example, much meaner than a French person would be. They laugh at each other's answering-machine pronunciation. The former French teachers are the worst. (Roxy spends hours in Gréyisse's *Bon Usage*. "Maybe I'll just say *'Laissez un message,'*" she finally decides.)

The American women planned programs at which such things as French taxes and French divorce laws were discussed, and the names of helpful *avocats* were shared. From this group I had the strange impression that legal difficulties were universal for Americans here, that we were all prisoners of strange objectionable laws and stranger customs, the first of which was marriage itself.

"Whatever you do," they said, "don't leave the house. That makes you the guilty one. That way, they can get you for desertion – they have some other name for it. It happened to Tammy de Bretteville, and she was left without a dime, just because she went to Nice for the weekend. And she had paid for the apartment!"

"If you did get divorced, would you go back to America?" I asked Roxy on the way home.

"No, of course not," she said vehemently. "Everything makes me happy here. Except, well, you know – the situation. But the buildings. The buses. I even love the pigeons with their little red feet. My heart goes out to the spindly ones. Some pigeons don't thrive as well as others. Sometimes I drop a piece of my croissant for them. I try to give it to the spindly ones before the fat ones see. But people stare at you so outraged. Did you know they have a sports club where they actually catch the pigeons? Tammy de Bretteville told me about it. Then they let them out, old fat street pigeons, and as they flutter lethargically up, the French shoot them for target practice. That's their idea of sport. I was struck dumb when I heard this. It wasn't even for reducing the population of pigeons, which you could possibly understand. It's some deficiency in sensibility."

She must be really depressed, I thought, to be raving on like this about pigeons. "It's better than shooting people, like we do at home," I pointed out.

Roxy had been talking of divorce, but when Charles-Henri wrote her a stiff little note saying that *he* would like a divorce, Roxy replied: "But I can't divorce. I'm Catholic." And there was no good saying, Roxy, don't be like that, because she was like that. I didn't try to argue. No divorce became Roxy's policy as surely as divorce had been her policy last week. Suzanne, who had continued to think that the whole thing would blow over after the baby was born, was relieved at Roxy's position, that there would be no divorce.

Margeeve and Chester, in California, were not so sure.

Because of the strange experience of hearing my name from the beggar of Notre Dame, I had formed the habit of listening and feeling apprehensive when crossing in front of the great cathedral, feeling the eyes of the carven saints on me, and the beggar, always there, turning his blind stone eyes toward me, holding his cup. But he never spoke again. But then one day as I was walking Gennie home, slowly because for some reason I did not have the stroller, Gennie on her little legs, me impatient, I again heard someone say "Isabel." Almost fearfully, I looked around at the beggar, and saw, just near him, coming out of Notre Dame in the horde of tourists, Oncle Edgar, the Persands' uncle, coming toward me, still limping slightly but walking more briskly than he had at the time I had met him. He gave Gennie a kiss and shook my hand. He was dressed rather grandly in a light suit, in his buttonhole some sort of charity flower that I had seen people selling on the quai.

"*La petite Geneviève. Bonjour, mademoiselle.*"

"*Bonjour, Monsieur Cosset,*" I said, startled.

"You should just say, '*Bonjour, monsieur,*'" he said. "I saw you another day, coming this way," he added. This confused me. Had it been he, not the blind man, who spoke? Or had he told the man to speak? Or neither? And why was I not to use his name?

"Unless you are pressed, we have time to offer Geneviève an ice cream." He lifted Gennie up, and carried her as we continued on our way. I had an unaccustomed attack of shyness, maybe from seeing him on television, and couldn't think of anything but to answer his questions like a child, yes I was content with my time in Paris, yes Roxy was doing okay. We installed ourselves at the Vues de Notre Dame, the café where I had met Charles-Henri.

"*Apéritif? Café?*"

We both had coffee. He had an instant of silence, during which it perhaps sank in that he had condemned himself to a half hour with a wiggly three-year-old and a California au pair girl, non-French-speaking.

"I think it's great the way you stick up for the Bosnians," I heard myself say, in the most horrible Valley Girl voice, a voice that fell on my own ears as if I were hearing a skit on *Saturday Night Live.* My remark seemed to startle, then to amuse him.

"Do you? Thank you. Why do you think so?"

This Socratic maneuver struck me silent again. Why did I think so? But I am a good student, and know how to give the professor what he himself has said.

"You'd think people would remember history," I said. "The First World War started like that, with Balkan conflicts." He made no comment.

"And the moral issues. How can we just stand by and permit terror and rape?" This was the argument I really believed.

"You are right." He smiled, perhaps without irony. His views exactly. "Gennie, *mange ta glace comme ça.* And do you think that the Europeans alone, or that the Americans too, should fight the Serb?"

"The Americans too," I said. "But the Europeans have to start, or else the UN, or Americans won't come in like they did in World War One, or Two." Mrs. Pace's good little historian.

"Though it may surprise you, I was not alive during the First War," he began, smiling. "I was born in 1925, and thus was just old enough to have served in the Second War. Later I served in Indochina."

Indochina! Something thrilling in that. Though I am not usually ill at ease with men *(au contraire,* Roxy would say), I was ashamed of how silly I sounded, how impudent to be talking of war and European politics to a man who had stood at the side of the President of France (I had seen them on television, in Lyon for a ceremony).

At this memory, of Oncle Edgar and the President of France, as we were speaking, I felt my palms moisten with deepened self-consciousness. I felt young and absurd, and my heart gave me that unpleasant unease I used to feel hoping a certain guy would talk to me or ask me out. I was aware of a male power over me that I have always resented. This elderly Frenchman, so full of will, experience, moral force, political passion, was affecting me like a man. How totally odd, I thought afterward, walking Gennie home, how almost embarrassing. But of course he couldn't have guessed my inappropriate emotions.

TWELVE

The two wretched creatures who alone in the world knew each other and alone were capable of consoling each other, now seemed to be irreconcilable enemies bent on mutual destruction.
– Benjamin Constant, Adolphe

WHEN CHARLES-HENRI MADE IT KNOWN THAT HE WANTED to divorce, Roxy at first did nothing, took no steps, in no way tried to resolve the issue. I thought it might be a kind of inertia hormone that goes with pregnancy. Except for strange outbursts, about pigeons or a metro strike, she even seemed happy enough most of the time, going to her studio, portfolio in hand, attending her seminar on Thursday nights, having Sunday lunches in the bosom of Charles-Henri's family, for it was she (we) and not Charles-Henri who continued to go to these occasions. "I know Suzanne wishes Charles-Henri would pick up Gennie and come himself, but he hasn't even suggested it," said Roxy. The lunches were civil, and neither divorce nor Charles-Henri were ever discussed. As far as we could learn, Suzanne still had not yet met or even seen the Other Woman, Magda Tellman.

Following Charles-Henri's request for a divorce there had been several weeks of uncertainty and discussion, always initiated by him or his mother. Suzanne would call to talk to Roxy in person, always expressing support, and Charles-Henri would telephone to plead or threaten, conversations that would leave Roxy tearful and furious. "These are your own kids, Charles," she would say, or "Over my dead body!" At last, convinced by Suzanne that she had better find out what her rights were, Roxy did consent at least to go with Charles-Henri to meet with a lawyer suggested by Monsieur de Persand, a Maître Doisneau. I think that is why she consented to go to the lawyer, it was a chance to see her husband. She dithered about what to wear. She wanted to look her best for Charles-Henri. I had not realized that vanity would continue during the misshapen months of pregnancy. If I am ever pregnant, I don't expect to care what I look like.

Maître Doisneau was a darting, slender man behind a large desk, who explained to them what they would have to do. "In general, in a divorce matter, it is in everyone's interest to agree," he said. "If the two of you make a motion together, I can prepare it, and it is all simple. The court follows your wishes as to the distribution of property, you wait several months, we enter a second motion to say that you are still of the same opinion, the court grants a divorce and you are free."

"When – when would remarriage be permitted?" asked Charles-Henri, with fatal insensitivity.

"You could remarry in a week or so. Madame de Persand, of course, could not marry until after the birth of your child."

This shocked Roxy. The unfairness of the female lot, of European sexism, of her particular fate, stabbed at her heart. She said fiercely, "That's unbelievable! You mean that the law is different for men and women?"

"For obvious reasons," said Maître Doisneau, seeming to indicate Roxy's pregnant belly.

"It isn't obvious to me! I could marry as soon as I wanted in California, and France could not stop me!" Roxy snarled, wishing at that moment for a California suitor so she could leave France, marry immediately, and give Charles-Henri's child another man's name. Charles-Henri and Maître Doisneau exchanged glances of masculine commiseration.

"There is no property to speak of," said Charles-Henri, sliding smoothly along. "I would return any gifts given to me, and of course I don't want anything from the apartment. Oh, the things that come from my family, perhaps. I would let my parents decide if there is anything that shouldn't go out of the family."

"Your children are your family," Roxy snapped. "Things going to your children are not going out of your family."

"I was thinking of things going to the U.S.," he apologized.

Roxy was suddenly wary. She sensed the peril of being in a strange language in a strange land. She sensed an alliance between Maître Doisneau and Charles-Henri, the natural sympathy of countrymen, or of males, arising from their similar views on neckties and black socks, from their both knowing the three hundred and sixty cheeses, from their impression of the strange smell of women and their shared hatred of a woman's tendency to cry.

"I'm not going to the U.S.," said Roxy. "I'm staying right here. And I expect you to support me and your children."

"We have talked about divorce by mutual consent. There is also," said Maître Doisneau, discerning trouble, "there is also divorce 'for cause.' In such a case, one of you is the innocent spouse, and must have proof of the other's guilt."

Perceiving from their silence that they had not planned to take this tack, he amended himself. "Excuse me for employing such a term, 'innocent,' I mean only in the legal sense. If you are divorcing by mutual consent, naturally I do not need to know details of the events which have brought you to the law. In such a case no one is guilty or innocent. But when. . . ."

"I am, I suppose," Roxy ventured. "*Innocente.* Not that anyone is ever innocent, it's a very unsophisticated term." She was trying to be equable, but was unable to control a note of self-righteousness that was creeping into her voice. She broke off. Charles-Henri, who had sat stonily, pinched his lips.

"I am no longer living at home," he said.

"Ah," breathed Maître Doisneau, in a tone of relief to have found such a relatively painless breach of marital law. "As you know, madame, that is grounds for an action for cause. The point of an action for cause is that one partner needs to obtain monetary compensation from the other."

"But I don't plan to bring an action," said Roxy. "This is my husband's idea." Audible sigh of vexation from Charles-Henri. Maître Doisneau, failing to follow this turn, proposed another solution.

"If Monsieur de Persand were to bring an action, he would have to identify some cause – violence, cruelty, adultery, or madness – which could apply to Madame."

"He couldn't possibly say any of those things," protested Roxy.

"No, of course not," agreed Charles-Henri. "No, no, the offense is totally mine."

"Monsieur de Persand wishes the divorce, and he has moved out of the house. That was badly advised. Excuse me, but you cannot be both the guilty one and the seeker of the divorce where the innocent party objects, though you could file a motion in which the other party does not oppose. Does not consent but does not oppose. Is that your position, Madame de Persand?"

"I do not wish a divorce," said Roxy. "I oppose divorce."

As Roxy said this, Charles-Henri could see her seizing with force on the sense and implications of staying married. A legal separation would be much better than divorce. That way she could retain at least the perks, the technically consolidated and secure position, of wife. Let Charles-Henri go his own way, she would continue to be Madame de Persand of the Place Maubert, pushing her children in their *poussettes* along to the Ecole Maternelle, buying her *pain* and *légumes* in the market on Saturdays. Her future love life didn't matter. A woman with two kids – what could happen to her, in the romantic way, anyhow? The path of her reasoning showed in the purse of her lips, aging her, allying her with a procession of wronged females down through history who hang on to what they have. I wouldn't have behaved this way, I don't think, but perhaps you feel less reckless when you have kids, more in need of securing your nest, less trusting that life will provide.

"The party who has given cause cannot also be the suing party. It must be the wronged person who asks for the divorce," repeated Maître Doisneau. Here Roxy, suddenly attacked by hot tears, struggled to her feet and prepared to leave. The two men were instantly on their feet, like twin puppets.

"Madame de Persand, where are you going?"

"I must think about all this. I can't say anything now." She stumbled toward the door. Charles-Henri hung back as if it were now Maître Doisneau's part to prevent her or go after her. But Doisneau shuffled the dossiers on his desk, staring down, trying not to catch the expression that passed between the two sundering and angry people who had once lain rapturously each in the bosom of the other.

Scènes, évenéments, rencontres. The days pass as slowly as pregnancy, with little events, meetings, the wonderful sight for me of falling leaves, which I hadn't seen since I was little, in Ohio.

A small bedroom in Suzanne de Persand's apartment on the Avenue Wagram. Little Jean-Claude, aged ten, son of Antoine, is staying with his grandmother while Antoine and Trudi vacation in Miami. He is doing his lessons of French orthography, geography, literature, mathematics, history, and English, all these books weighing, as they come out of his knapsack, five kilos. He writes in little notebooks ruled in squares. He keeps track of what he is to do in another notebook, of which each page is divided into: *devoirs* and *leçons.* Duties and lessons. One could tell him right now that all of life is going to be divided into duties and lessons. Besides these duties, Jean-Claude has household duties such as helping Maria the Portuguese girl fold the giant tablecloths and sheets, plus the Boy Scouts, football, catechism, and piano lessons.

He is thinking that his joke on his parents rather backfired. He had told them he had picked up the phone and heard

Lorraine (detestable babysitter) refer to them as *pauvre cons*. In a rage they had fired her, as he had foreseen, but now here he is at his grandparents' house, overseen with more than desirable vigilance. Gennie and I come and take him out to kick leaves.

I had been at Mrs. Pace's the afternoon Roxy saw Maître Doisneau, had loitered in the Place des Victoires looking at clothes in the Kenzo window, had been slightly late to pick up Gennie. When we came in, Roxy was already home from the lawyer, raving with indignation. That Charles-Henri would expect her to compromise her (newly adopted) religious principles and the inclinations of her heart by divorcing him. That he seemed indifferent to her leaving France, and indifferent to the fate of poor Gennie and the unborn child, content to have them exposed to the dangers and cultural inferiority of America. That he could think of sacrificing the Frenchness of his children – the most priceless thing he could bequeath them – to indulge his crush on a Czechoslovakian slut. That he could turn on her this way, her having no warning or intimation, proving that she herself had no understanding of the human heart and was condemned to blunder to the end of her days, and would never write an enduring poem. "I never guessed, I never realized anything was even wrong . . . ." Etc.

"Let him divorce *me*, I can't stop him. But I'll never divorce *him*," she kept saying.

The things the lawyer had explained were soon explained to her in more detail, by Tammy de Bretteville, about how she could stop him from divorcing her. Unless she agreed to his request for a divorce, or was guilty of something herself, she could stop him for at least six years, at the end of which he could bring an action on the grounds they weren't living together. In this case, he would have to support Roxy and pay all costs.

"Fine," she said. "Fine, fine, six years, that's fine." She said she was prepared to wait until she stood at the doors of hell, to thwart Charles-Henri's lurid, illicit, unforgivable erotic desires.

One day I ran into l'oncle Edgar again, near Notre Dame. He looked imposing and dignified, in a navy blue suit with little ribbons in his lapel and a white handkerchief in the pocket, very like a diplomat. When I said, "*Bonjour,*" he said, "Say '*bonjour, monsieur,*' not just '*bonjour.*'" Another puzzle.

When I remarked on his being there again, he said, "On Wednesdays I often have lunch or a glass of sherry with the Abbé Montlaur." It being hard to imagine the urbane and warriorlike Oncle Edgar consulting a priest, a puzzled expression must have crossed my face, for he went on to explain that Montlaur was an old friend, they had been boys together, reminding me that priests were boys once. This is rather obvious, I know, but in California I had never met any boys who were likely to become priests. I suppose pious boys are common in France, where there must be more priests per capita than in America. I had an image of the two lads, Montlaur and Edgar, saintly but mischievous, swimming in the Seine (where I have never seen anyone swim, it must be dangerous or dirty) and climbing trees, the one boy destined for God and the other for Indochina.

"And how are you liking France?" he asked. "Your life here?"

As he seemed to be asking seriously, I tried to think about the question and give a serious answer. I said there was something to be said for not understanding a lot that goes on. "It keeps you alert. So I have an alert feeling here whereas at home in California I sometimes feel bored."

"Do you sail in the Pacific Ocean? Are you interested in boats?"

"No," I said. "Are you?"

"Yes," he said. "I've done a bit of sailing."

"Near us, the ocean is full of oil rigs. You have to go farther south," I explained, not wishing to seem disdainful of boats, which actually do seem very boring to me, though perhaps they wouldn't be if they were your own.

"I'll take you to lunch one day, Isabel. Say next Thursday. Are you taken that day?"

I recognized these overtures, these attempts at conspiracy from members of the Persand family, occasions contrived behind Roxy's back to discuss The Situation. I was uneasy in them, because they put me in the false position of speaking for Roxy; but I understood that they found it easier to talk to me than to Roxy directly. Since I can arrange my days to suit myself, I said I was not taken.

I had recently seen Charlotte de Persand Saxe on the sly in the same way. She telephoned me one day and suggested we have the coffee we had mentioned having. I spent the afternoon at the Randolphs', then went along to meet her in a café across from Bon Marché. She fished for her cigarettes almost before sitting down, and plunged into the subject not of Charles-Henri and Roxy but of Giles Wheating, the Englishman I'd met. She was madly in love with him.

'It is not at all true, what you hear," she confided, smoking madly. "Englishmen are as – considerate – as Frenchmen."

I have the impression that French people will tell an American things they wouldn't tell each other. Among themselves, a certain set of conventions obtains, a certain competitive mistrust, real-life reticences from which we are exempted by our cheerful barbarousness. On the other hand, there are French things – certain instances of misbehavior, certain sins and breaches, things about sex or money – they wouldn't tell us, but talk about readily among themselves, preferring us to have a better opinion of the French than if we knew. Sometimes these are things that wouldn't bother us at all. For instance, once on a Sunday at Suzanne's house near Chartres the plumbing backed up, and a French lunch guest was allowed to see and advise on this disaster, whereas Roxy and I were forbidden to come near it.

"I've never heard anything – against – about Englishmen," I said to Charlotte.

"You often hear they are rather – selfish – in bed, but it isn't true."

"Well, perhaps some are," I said, thinking it was unlikely you could generalize.

"They are better than French men, in a certain way," she went on, her voice lowered confidentially, and though I longed to say "really? how?" it seemed too prying, even for an American. Janet Hollingsworth would have asked straight out.

"The ones that are interested in women at all," she added.

It is an interesting subject, French men, English men. Actually, from the reputation of Charles Boyer and so on, I had thought there were perhaps unusual things that Frenchmen knew, had expected something unusual and extra, perhaps to do with "The French they are a funny race," as Chester's rhyme went. My actual researches had led me to think, however, that there is a Franco-American norm, or a universal Western norm, to lovemaking. I know nothing of the Orient, or Pacific Islands, though I once read an interesting article about how Samoan men are not up to standard. The article revealed that the female orgasm is unknown in Samoa, that supposed paradise of sexual liberation, and Margaret Mead had not noticed this or she had not thought it important.

Why was I thinking about Samoan men while talking to Charlotte? She was saying something important. "I think Roxeanne ought to divorce Charles-Henri for cause," she confided, coming, perhaps, to the real reason for our visit. "If she doesn't, she'll end up with nothing. The laws here are very severe. I am not the only one to say so. I have been looking into it. She ought to accuse him of adultery and make him pay what he should."

I understood that Charlotte was telling me, perhaps from the whole Persand family, what I should go tell Roxy – that they recognized that Roxy had been wronged; that they would not oppose generous financial arrangments for her and the children. I thought it was nice of Charlotte to tip me off like this, and to feel that way. I wondered what Oncle Edgar's take on it all would turn out to be.

"What does your mother think?" I wondered to Charlotte. I had noticed that Suzanne was helpful and sympathetic to Roxy, but also loyal to her son, and chose her words when talking to Roxy about arrangements.

"Well, of course she still thinks Roxeanne should just be patient and it will all be finished with. Mother expects Charles-Henri to come to his senses."

THIRTEEN

The important thing in the divorce is what follows.

– *Hervé Bazin,* Madame Ex

I DUTIFULLY RELAYED ALL THIS TO ROXY. WHEN SHE HAD GOT over the shock of her first legal consultation, she had begun to see that she should at least discuss divorce with a lawyer of her own. We set about finding one who understood French law but would be sympathetic to Americans. After much consultation among the American community, the choice fell upon Maître Bertram, a French-American with the California firm of Biggs, Rigby, Denby, Fox, with offices tucked into a beautiful *hôtel particulier* in the eighth Arrondissement. Roxy went to consult him. Maître Bertram listened to her gravely. She could not really explain what had gone wrong.

"The reason I ask is that you have a choice, whether to accuse your husband of adultery or cruelty, or whether you wish an amicable divorce. No-fault, I believe they call it in the States. I do not judge. It is not my part, obviously."

"I know I don't want acrimony or anger," Roxy said, feeling her anger swell, the emotion bringing tears that pressed against her eyelids. "I don't even want a divorce. I want to prevent divorce."

"Who wishes to divorce?"

"The divorce is his idea, he wants to remarry," Roxy said.

"Wait until he appreciates the financial implications," predicted Maître Bertram. "I have found that people often change their minds. In the case of a divorce, however, it would be necessary for you to accuse him if you expect to receive a settlement, that is the law. You have to prove fault with his admitting it, or with his lack of contest. You were married in the traditional regime, community property, so in any case, there will arise the matter of distribution of the property."

"Oh, we don't have anything," Roxy assured him. "The apartment, some pots and pans."

"The usual way is to sell assets that cannot be divided. You expect your husband to contest the divorce? Do you plan to sue to retain your name?"

"My maiden name?"

"Your married name, Persand, Madame de Persand. Ordinarily you would have to take again your *nom de jeune fille*. That would be obligatory."

"But my children . . . ?"

"Persand, of course."

"I must have the same name as my children," said Roxy passionately. Maître Bertram was charmed by her beauty, her womanly despair, her fierce resolution on behalf of her children. He imagined the cad Charles-Henri, some kind of madman.

Families, family loyalties. My brother Roger – my natural brother – is a partner (at such a young age!) in Barney, Gehegan, Bryer and Walker, a San Francisco law firm specializing in real estate and taxes. He's married to Jane, a Jungian therapist, and they have a child, Fritz, who in spite of the law that governs the children of psychologists is a nice little kid, about six.

Besides his practice, and obsessive jogging, Roger is active in gun control issues, ever since a lone gunman entered his building at 101 California in San Francisco and gunned down fourteen lawyers and clients only two floors below his. What surprised him, he said, was that when people heard about the massacre, they at first were appalled, but then very quickly, seeking as one does cosmic explanations for tragedy on this scale, explained it to themselves by saying, with the radiance of sudden comprehension, "Ah, but they were lawyers."

"In the same tone as they would say, 'After all, they were only dogs,'" Roger said. He had never thought of himself as a member of an undesirable social category, and he was shocked. "I knew they hated lawyers, but I didn't know how much," he said, a note of self-pity in his voice. I would have thought that besides gun control, it might be appropriate to work, through the bar association or something, to improve the public perception, and maybe even the actual ethics, of lawyers. But that has not occurred to him.

Every few months, Jane and Roger fly down to spend the weekend in Santa Barbara with Margeeve and Chester. Jane and Roger usually stay in the Miramar Hotel nearby, and Fritz stays with his grandparents. Imagine a palm-lined street of adobe houses with rust-colored tile roofs, and the sound of the ocean behind the street noises, and seagulls, and their raucous cries, a smell in the air of flowers and salt and tortilla-frying oil. Santa Barbara is more beautiful than Miami, Ohio, and more dignified than its smoggy neighbor Los Angeles. It likes to think of itself as embodying discretion and old money, in Spanish-style houses, some very beautiful, behind thick adobe walls and fanciful wrought-ironwork. There is, also, a large population of Mexicans who speak no English and are rarely seen on *Santa Barbara*.

When our father and Roger and I moved to Santa Barbara, at the time of his marriage to Margeeve, whom he had met on a Sierra Club hiking trip (much as Roxy would later meet Charles-Henri), I thought it was paradise, the epitome of human privilege and attainment. The tropical charm of the lightly swaying palms, the historical resonance of the Mexican-style architecture (overtones of grandeur and connectedness to human history, reassuringly affirming that there had been a past), culture (an art museum, a preservation committee, a civic symphony, and only two hours on the freeway to the Dorothy Chandler Pavilion in Los Angeles, where plays are performed and visiting opera companies visit). Even the oil platforms offshore had, at night, a certain allure, like distant sin islands. I loved the damp, salty wind. The conventionality of Santa Barbara was reassuring to my midwestern heart. At the same time, I was drawn to the dark maids and gardeners lingering at bus stops, and the boys and drugs in high school. I even loved the orthodontia, so relatively rare in Ohio, so obligatory in California. Paradoxically, where I was wild(ish), my new stepsister, Roxy, having lived her whole life in Santa Barbara, was a perfect midwestern girl, sensible and studious, grounded and sound.

Family dinner at home is easy enough to reconstruct. The discussion would be about Roger's work, Chester's work, and Roxy.

My father, Chester the midwesterner, clings to what he imagines are California ways by barbecuing long after real Californians have given it up because of fears of the stomach cancers that afflict cultures that cook over charcoal fires. Indeed, Californians have pretty much given up meat. The carnivorousness of the French shocked me at first.

"Really too bad about Roxy," says Jane, whose concern about the emotional adjustments and maladjustments of our family is always a little suspect, tinged ever so slightly with self-satisfaction. "Are they getting some help?"

"He says he's incurably in love with someone else," says Margeeve. "He wants a divorce." Her tone held just an edge of mockery, as if she had said "he believes in God," or "goes to church."

"I thought you couldn't get a divorce in France," says Roger.

"That's Ireland," says Chester.

"Oh. How long does it take in France?"

"I have no idea," says Chester. "A year? When's the baby due?"

"Not till December," says Margeeve.

"All that and Isabel on her hands too. Roxy has a lot on her plate," says Roger, who is always sympathetic to his stepsister Roxy and doesn't understand me at all.

"I think it's lucky Isabel is there, in a way. She's bound to be a little moral support," says Margeeve. (Here I can imagine them groaning and rolling their eyes.)

"Roxy needs counsel. She should have an American lawyer, there are some good people in France, I'll get a name."

"Is she seeing somebody?" asks Jane.

"I shouldn't think so, she's six months pregnant, after all," says Margeeve.

"I meant, a therapist. Someone to help her through it." In her métier, Jane naturally believes in human perfectability.

Chester goes outside to bring in the chicken breasts.

"We have a policy or strategy decision to make, in a way," Margeeve goes on. "Or a philosophical decision: how do we actually stand on this?"

"What kind of question is that? What does it have to do with us?" says Roger piously.

"In our hearts, do we hope she stays with Charles-Henri?" It was clear that Margeeve was torn on this question, or she wouldn't have polled the others. Chester, coming in, hears, frowns.

"I don't see anything wrong with Charles-Henri. I don't see a role for our opinions anyhow. Roxy should have the husband she wants. You just wish she lived in California."

"Oh, that's it, I know. Part of me thinks, great, Roxy will be coming back. Gennie. The baby. Part of me thinks it is swell to have grandchildren who live ten thousand miles away and don't even speak English."

"Why don't you spend some time over there? Lots of people would be thrilled to have the excuse of grandchildren in France. Besides, Gennie knows English. Roxy speaks English to her."

"It's too bad not to see more of Gennie, and little X when she arrives," Margeeve persisted.

"Not a good reason to hope Roxy breaks up with their father, though," Chester said. "Besides, we'd probably have to support them."

Margeeve looks sharply at Chester to see if he's kidding. He's not.

"I do think we should offer to pay for counseling," she says. "I suppose they have qualified professionals in France. Do you know anyone, Jane?"

"They're all Lacanians," says Jane, doubtfully.

"Did you realize that Roxy's Saint Ursula might be rather valuable?" says Margeeve, to change the subject. "At least in the immediate context of the show the Getty is organizing, *Source of Light: the School of La Tour*. Paintings from that period where the subject is illuminated by a light source within the picture, rather than – you might think of Vermeer – from a window, or from a light source out of the canvas.

"The Getty wants Saint Ursula?" repeats Roger.

"Just on loan. Isabel could bring it to California when she comes home."

"The Getty could certainly pay to crate it and ship it," Chester said. "And insure it."

"Why do you call it *Roxy's* Saint Ursula?" asks Roger. An ominous question, as it proves.

After dinner, Chester goes out to the patio to clean the barbecue, a ritual he strangely likes. Working without tools as he does in daily life, he likes these, his long tined fork, the heavy workman's leather-palmed gloves, and the wire-bristled brush he uses to scrape the bits of chicken and fish (formerly, steak) off the grill. He likes the smell of charcoal and lighter and grease. He is thinking about Roxy, his stepchild who is closer to him than either Isabel or Roger, his natural children. Some unspoken sympathy has always existed between him and Roxy. Her childhood scrapes had been the kind he got in himself, her reactions and deep seriousness were more like his, while Isabel, so restless and thoughtless, puzzled him. Even her talent for sports puzzled him. And Roger? Roger was like a form of his own worst side, aggressive and insensitive. Both his own children were; it was funny, they must have got it from Andrea, their disaster of a mother, for he himself was thoughtful and calm.

Now he felt uneasy about the future for Roxy. He didn't want her to be defeated by this divorce. Anyone could divorce, most people did, but most people, by the time they did divorce, devoutly wanted to be rid of the other person, the person they cannot imagine having loved and slept with, whose repulsive traits are now an embarrassment, reflecting as they do one's own bad judgment, immaturity, or star-crossed role as one of nature's victims. Roxy, from her tone, was being torn, uprooted, insulted, battered in her heart by the one-sided death of love. She might not recover. He didn't know what to do for her, short of throttling the frog prince.

FOURTEEN

Without being aware of it I nursed in the depths of my being a longing for emotional experience, but as this found no satisfaction it alienated me from all the things which one by one aroused my curiosity.

– *Benjamin Constant,* Adolphe

IN ALL PARIS FAMILY DISCUSSIONS, THE CHARACTER OF Magda Tellman, Charles-Henri's new love, began to take on importance. Charlotte Saxe and I discussed it. Magda was thirty-seven, which would make her a year older than Charles-Henri. I imagined her as dark and glaring, like Maria Callas, with incredible animal magnetism, a steely will, and astonishing sexual tricks. But what she was really like no one as yet knew, either her looks or her mind. Was she urging Charles-Henri to divorce so she could marry him? Was this desperate woman, seeing in him helpmate and salvation, the force behind his great rush to dump Roxy? What did he see in her that he didn't find in beautiful Roxy, mother of his children? I tried to imagine the needs of Charles-Henri's heart, I tried to find some clues to give my sister. But in my own heart I thought, how could she bear to have him back, anyhow, now? I know I have things to learn about patience and forgiveness, but not yet, as Saint Augustine said about wanting to be chaste.

We heard that Suzanne had at first refused to meet Magda. And that then, with maternal pragmatism, she met her. She asked Charles-Henri to bring Magda to lunch at the Dôme, as if they were distant relatives meeting in a strange city, or friends of her children. Charles-Henri was in the restaurant early, solicitous, pushing in his mother's chair, rearranging her napkin. Magda joined them directly from the Gare du Nord. A big-boned, exuberant Slav with long pale hair, pushing forty. Devout, maternal, in every way a surprising version of the femme fatale, a genre whose mannerisms she preserved only in cigarette smoking and drinking vodka as an aperitif at lunch.

In letting Roxy know about this lunch, Suzanne made it clear that she would always love Roxy, and Roxy was not to get upset. "I left no misunderstandings about my views," Suzanne said. "My son knows what my views are about his duty to his children. But I can't say I detested her. A solid bourgeoise. The better classes of Slav are still very nice. They usually speak good French. When I asked, rather pointedly, their plans of marriage, she said they could not marry, she was *croyante,* they would have to have annulments. Astonishing, was it not?"

After she heard this, Roxy very nearly took to her bed, she was so upset that Suzanne could even mention marriage to Magda and Charles-Henri, as if Magda's presence in the ambient world of the Persands was now taken for granted.

It became deeper autumn. There were several notable, strange events in the first weeks of October. In the Luxembourg Gardens the leaves, after a few days of being red and gold, fell quickly in the stiffening fall breezes, turned brown, and rattled along the paths with a particular sound like someone raking leaves in a graveyard. All blue left the sky as completely as if the world had tilted its face in some new direction; it was now the color of basement light. I would have thought this change in seasons would add to Roxy's gloom, but it seemed perversely to please her at first, and I too began to understand why newcomers to California complain that they miss the seasons, for here was a sense that fall was good for the character, and that all afflictions would be recompensed by the coming of spring, eventually.

Indignation and defiance are healthy emotions, I believe. But Roxy couldn't sustain them. She took Gennie to the Luxembourg Gardens and sat transfixed, not brooding about her problems but just immobile there, flattened by inertia and depression, wondering what she did wrong. *Déprimé* is the French word for depressed. Suzanne noticed that Roxy was *déprimée* and I mentioned it to Chester and Margeeve. But none of us understood how depressed she really was, torn by religious principles, spite, injured pride, anxiety, the mysterious toxins of pregnancy.

Sunday afternoon. The Catholic service on Radio France has given way to "Fréquence Protestante," and the stately intonations of the Latin mass are replaced by goofy happiness music, and people are being interviewed about how they feel. Are some American qualities – self-indulgence and optimism are two that I begin to see characterize us – are these somehow connected to Protestantism?

I have lunch with l'oncle Edgar, at Drouant, in the restaurant (as opposed to the café). The restaurant Mrs. Pace tells me, when I mention it casually, has two stars in the Michelin Guide. She is very interested in restaurants. While at lunch, someone he knows sees us, which amuses him.

"He assumes I have a taste for *fruit vert*," he says, a remark I don't understand. (Later I ask Roxy, and it means underage girls. Should I be complimented?) He does not introduce me.

At first I thought that his invitation to lunch, besides its conspiratorial function, might be owing to nostalgia for the company of a young woman, or a liking to be seen with one, an interest in young people and their lively doings, yet it seemed to me that he himself had a more powerful and conspicuous life than most young people do. I would say the same of Mrs. Pace, too. We wrongly tend to think that old people depend on us. Eventually I was to discover that the simplest explanations are the best.

I told him about my life, in response to his questions. It

seemed odd to be confiding in a man, one is so used to men confiding in you. I told him about Mrs. Pace, whom he'd heard of, and whom he said he'd like to meet sometime. I told him about Stuart Barbee and the Randolphs. I did not tell him about life in California, low-riders, greasers, or the two times I got "in trouble" in high school, which was not due to mentally retarded recidivism, just contraceptive bad luck. I did not tell him about dropping out of film school. People talk about knowing who they are: maybe I know who I am and maybe I'm just finding out, but I didn't want Oncle Edgar to find out, for sure. Yet I didn't masquerade as an innocent or try to live up to some conception of charming young womanhood he might have had, dating from vanished times.

We ate: *pied de cochon en salade, salade de crabe, rôti d'agneau* (he had a veal chop), *fromage* (he skipped the fromage), *gâteau aux trois chocolats.* I don't know what it cost, because my menu had no prices on it.

He did, of course, as I expected, bring up the Roxy–Charles-Henri situation, and reported of Magda (for he had been invited to the lunch) that she had an unexpected forlorn quality and thick ankles "like an English girl's," and drank vodka before lunch like a Russian. He explained to me – it was perhaps his mission to explain – that Suzanne would have to stand behind her son, however regretfully, in any instance where you took sides. Of course no such issues would come up, he was sure. It was just that Suzanne would not be prepared to see Charles-Henri ruin his life. I said I would explain this to Roxy.

I supposed it was inevitable that I would come to be used as a go-between, since I did go between, among, these different worlds in Paris – between the French family world of the Persands and those of my two suitors Yves and Michel; the American literary world of Ames Everett and Mrs. Pace, the international art world of Stuart Barbee, the trust fundies and diplomats like the Randolphs. My access to these worlds was lowly – I would carry books back and forth between Mrs. Pace and Ames Everett; I would bring news to Roxy from

Charlotte re The Situation; I even took photos at Mrs. Pace's, at the behest of Stuart Barbee, who somehow had promised her biographer, somebody he knew, to ask her if she would allow it. She was not inclined at first to allow photographs, but there is a side of her that is vain of her beautiful furniture and porcelain and pleased that they should be seen, or that she should be seen in their context. Not that I am much of a photographer, but I used Ames's no-brain camera with an automatic flash.

"Sure, I don't care," Roxy had said, acceding to the request by the Getty Museum to allow one of their experts to photograph her Saint Ursula painting, with a view to borrowing it for their *Source of Light* exhibition. "It's kind of nice to think of her getting her due after living all this time in obscurity at our house." It turned out to be Stuart Barbee who came to look at the painting, photograph it, and determine the amount of insurance that would be necessary in sending it to California. Back to California. He told Roxy it should be insured for forty thousand dollars, which thrilled her. She called Margeeve and Chester, with the glee one feels in hearing that something you have has value you never imagined.

Stuart Barbee also admired Roxy's dishes, "old faience" which had come from the Persands. I wished he hadn't admired them so fervently, for now she would feel worse if she had to give them back. Roxy must have had that on her mind too.

"The Persands have endless old dishes," she said. "She'd let me keep these for Gennie. And the Persand furniture – they have so much great furniture, I know they'd never miss these things I have."

"I admire the French for their cheerful acquisitiveness, their respect for the creations of man's hand," said Ames Everett, who had come in to tea.

"Yes, the French love things more for their beauty or their totemic significance than for their value," Roxy agreed.

"Whereas Americans affect disdain for material objects, as

if it weren't quite nice to collect, or have," Ames Everett said. "Yet they are great consumers. The French are materialists without being consumers. I respect that."

The lawyer, Maître Bertram, told Roxy to begin getting together a dossier of letters and testimonals to her own guiltless excellence and Charles-Henri's wicked faithlessness. She hated to do this, the more so because he told her to get letters from French people, not just Americans, and she found it hard and embarrassing to ask, as if she were asking them to betray their country. One or two actually refused, saying they did not want to take sides. Anne-Chantal Lartigue loyally agreed to write one, to say that Charles-Henri was neglectful and had left the family home, and that Roxy was a devoted mother. "I will say you are a saint," she promised. Mrs. Pace agreed to write one, but this made Roxy and me both a little worried, as Mrs. Pace is so resolutely truthful she would probably say something devastating, for instance about Roxy's cooking, which though not bad is not French, or she might mention that Gennie goes to the crèche. But we should not have worried, because Mrs. Pace is a novelist, too, and in the end her letter made Charles-Henri seem a monster of indifference and cupidity, without the slightest lie.

Another strange event: Roxy also met the husband of Magda Tellman, or I suppose it was he, the same man I had met in the foyer of our building. "Something bizarre happened," she said one day, looking shaken. "I was coming out of the Closerie des Lilas and this man came up to me and asked me if I was Roxeanne de Persand. He was American, and seemed to be drunk, so I guess I shrank from him, and he started to berate me, standing there on the sidewalk."

"Tellman," I said. "Magda's husband."

"So he said. Shouted at me on the sidewalk, outside the Closerie des Lilas, saying I should listen to him and know what side my bread is buttered on. But he didn't explain, he just screamed at me that I should be listening to him, I was just another dumb cunt. I almost felt he was threatening *me,* as if it had been me that wronged him. It was scary, and French people passing by didn't understand what he was saying, so no one offered to help."

Then the most unexpected thing of all. Suzanne telephoned. "I have something to bring up – it is a little delicate," she said, voice dripping with hypocritical tactfulness and false regret (in Roxy's account). "Antoine has surprised us all very much by feeling that it would be improper to send Saint Ursula to that Getty museum. While the lawyers are deciding its ownership."

"Unbelievable," said Roxy.

"I suppose I have no choice but to agree, as Antoine understands legal matters much better than I. But I said I would tell you," Suzanne went on.

Roxy, already so fragile she would go off at the slightest thing, clenched her teeth and twisted up her face while she was talking to Suzanne. "That's astonishing!" was all I heard her say, as meekly as can be, but when she put the phone down, her eyes blazed like a cat's in a headlight.

"Unbelievable," she said. "Unbelievable, that painting belongs to our family, it has nothing to do with the Persands, how dare they tell me where I can send it."

I think of this as Roxy's story, yet my own life picked up momentum right here, with an event, and events bring with them the impulse to testify and crow or cry. Perhaps it isn't Roxy's story so much as the story of an intersection of all our lives – Roxy's and mine, and Mrs. Pace's and so on, where heat and guilt build up. For instance, what if I had not said to Stuart Barbee that Suzanne had beautiful furniture? Or if we had listened to Tellman, really listened. The smallest moment of inattention turns out to be the most disastrous – is that a universal truth? But it is so hard to keep everything in focus all the time.

About a week after this, I went to an art show with Oncle Edgar, and I began to have kind of a crush on him. Even the thought of a little affair with Edgar Cosset was so strangely preoccupying that my interest in daily activities became somehow suspended in a mood of dreamy unease, like a virgin before her honeymoon. I thought of his heavy shoulders and closely clipped white hair, elegantly barbered like a captain of industry's; I kept thinking of the way people looked at him, recognizing him, and of the way the French anchorwomen smiled at him. Thinking about l'oncle Edgar, I even turned down a date with Yves, using Roxy as an excuse. (It actually was hard to get out at night. I did a lot of babysitting.) It was not as if I were running around all the time having fun while the grieving Roxy stayed home. On the contrary, Roxy had lots of friends – American women with whom she went to cultural events and movies, French women, men in the world of poetry. Sometimes if the two of us were invited out, as to Mrs. Pace's, or Ames Everett's, the African lady came down, or the concierge's daughter Gina came up. But this particular night it was actually that I wanted to stay home and watch Oncle Edgar on *Sept sur Sept.*

Toward Roxy I felt a little disloyal, because I was now dreaming of sleeping with a member of the enemy clan, like Juliet, bringing down on us who knew what troubling conflicts and temptations to betrayal. Plus she would think it simply very odd that I would be attracted to a man of seventy (which he must be, by my calculations). Biblical in its oddity. And I pitied her, for if her life was unraveling, I felt mine was knitting into a rich pattern.

Even liking France, I missed California some. It would have been nice to just get down and hear some music. Let's face it, their music is not our music. And I missed the sound of the ocean, and I even missed seagulls, and the California light, driving, and Mexican food – maybe in reverse order. In France, though they think of themselves as having Mexican restaurants, they don't know what Mexican food should be, and they wouldn't like the real thing. They hate spices. On homesick days (PMS) I would wake up staring at the mean little window of Roxy's *chambre de bonne* and feel like the girl in a book I loved as a child who was put up in the attic of her posh school after her father died and she didn't have her school fees. Then I would remember that Rwandans were being chopped and hacked to death by the thousands and the newspapers had not told us the name of a single Rwandan; and mortar shells tore the limbs off little Bosnian kids (whose names were sometimes told, they being European). I would remember that these places were close by. I could be in Bosnia in two hours, and Rwanda by tomorrow morning, but California was a distant island surrounded by water and sand.

Letters come from California in batches, as if they came on a boat or overland bound in a single trunk. I heard all at once from a couple of friends, my ex-boyfriend Hank, and there was a letter from Margeeve, which was a little odd, because it is usually Chester who writes me, Margeeve who writes Roxy. This was however to me on the subject of Roxy:

Iz honey,
This is just to slip you a word apart from Roxy, that you should keep us informed. She sounds so addled on the phone – is she doing what she should re the lawyers and such, or is she drifting, as we all know what she is like. If it's a question of money, we can help to a certain extent, which I've told her, what with credit line etc. but we can't help unless we know what she needs. Would it help if you brought Gennie and came back here? Could she focus better on what she has to do? She says a dossier? Fill us in, Iz, and I hope you are having some fun in spite of all.

xx
Marg.

ps don't let her just give in to everything they suggest if only for her eventual self-esteem. Jane says the same. xx

Needless to say, I showed Roxy this letter, as I thought she would appreciate it.

"I suppose I do sound addled," she admitted. "I haven't told them yet about the Persands objecting to us sending Saint

Ursula. I know Margeeve has been counting on it, she's thrilled, one of our pictures in an exhibition at the Getty. I'm caught between two armies.

"I can't seem to work," she added. "Words turn to mud. Nothing turns out. I feel it's pregnancy, but I didn't have this trouble when I was pregnant with Gennie. Hormones? It's as if it's hard to be creative in two ways at once.

I pointed out that she had a lot on her plate.

One day when Gennie and I got home, Roxy said, with the special look on her face that she gets when she's lying, "There's a box for you." A big orange box, tied in brown ribbon, was set alluringly on the desk, like a cake on an altar. "A messenger brought it," she added, watching me with interest. It's nice to get presents, so I eagerly set about opening it. Roxy lingered in the doorway to the kitchen, trying not to seem too interested, as I pulled out a purse made of leather, caramel-colored, rather pretty, maybe slightly too ladylike, and a pair of black gloves with sheepskin inside. There was a card which, when I glanced at it, I jammed into my pocket like hot money. "I had it delivered," I said, "it was so big, and I was going to the crèche for Gennie," this lie leaping to my lips as if I were in practice at lying, which I wasn't because I don't usually bother.

"Hermès," said Roxy. "It must have been expensive."

"Yes awfully," I said, "but the man said it was last year's model or something," lie upon lie.

"Still," said Roxy, reproachfully. Probably she thought it had come from a man, as it had, from Oncle Edgar. We had noticed it in a window. The card said "Bonjour, mademoiselle" and suggested an *exposition* the next week, rather an educational-sounding one about André Breton. Perhaps I was given it for being a *bonne élève,* for I had remembered to say *"Bonjour, monsieur,"* when greeting him, and not just *"Bonjour"* or even *"Bonjour, Monsieur Cosset."* (No one, not even the magisterial Oncle Edgar, has been able to make me understand the logic of this rule.) On the back of the card was also written, as I saw later, "against the onset of winter," which I took to refer to the gloves, and *"bon anniversaire."* I did not know how he could have known it would soon be my birthday. But I did know, now, that the special interest I felt between us was not just imaginary. I was wildly excited and had to keep my face as blasé as Marlene Dietrich.

FIFTEEN

Won't you change the destiny of my life
And bring good weather to my late winters?
– François Mainard

I THINK NOW THAT IT WAS PECULIAR OF HIM TO HAVE TAKEN me to a boring, improving art exhibition – a bit of supervised culture before the main event – but I recognize that I bring out the didactic in people, that I have, perhaps, an irresistible quality of clay. And Edgar has a streak of the puritan, like many French people, though puritan is what they accuse us of being. Though I don't know why they should be surprised if we are puritans, as we are children of a nation started by puritans. It is more surprising to find in them, the vaunted hedonists, this quality of didacticism and the need to employ their time in improving ways.

We went to dinner at Pierre Traiteur (*foie gras* and *raie aux câpres*), and over dessert he said, "I have long since given up luring young women to my rooms on other pretexts in the hope that things will take their course. We must decide if you will become my mistress."

I suppose the word "mistress" startled me, connoting sex, captivity, dinners at Maxim's, lavish presents – begun I suppose with the handbag – the elaborate set of rules suggested in the opera *La Traviata*, of which I had seen a video, with Maria Callas. An entirely dismal role in life, in which the mistress goes broke, is insulted, is heartbroken, and dies. Also, I am used to sexual advances being more spontaneous, and so I was startled, and temporized, murmuring, "What does that mean?"

"It means we become lovers, and spend a certain amount of time together, like this evening, amusing ourselves. It was your writer Addison, or Sheridan maybe, who deplored the passing of the good old days when amusing a woman was enough to have your way with her. Nowadays it is perhaps not enough, but amusement I suppose is still the point. I know you amuse me, and I think I can amuse you. And there is the fact that I desire you. You are a beautiful young woman."

I thought "amuse" sounded condescending, as in "amusing little trifle," but I had already discovered that words in French have a different intensity, less or more. *Je le déteste*, they say, meaning, I mildly dislike it; *je l'adore* means it's okay. If something is really great you have to say it's not bad, *pas mal*. Also you have to use the words suitable for your station in life. If not, people gasp and laugh.

Amuse, then – what did it mean? Much is spoken of desire, whatever its origin, that odd feeling in the thighs and rush of blood. I felt that too, and understood it. But in my experience, not enough is spoken about curiosity. I was conscious once again of wondering – of wishing to know – how it would be to go to bed with Oncle Edgar. I am often curious about men that way, and I am glad to have been born in a day and age when I can satisfy my curiosity without too much risk of ruined reputation, of pregnancy, or of heartbreak.

In all these months, through all Roxy's trials, adventuring in a strange land, it never occurred to me that it could be my heart that might be broken.

At that moment it was more than curiosity, I was also conscious of Edgar's large male body, and his connection to distant wars in Indochina, his knowledge of erotic murmurings in other languages, his acquaintance with statesmen. These things seemed part of his glamour, which seemed in turn to explain my stir of anticipation, or whatever it is, when you know you want someone, even, surprisingly, an elderly gentleman.

"But I'm having my period," I said. "This isn't a good time to begin." This made him laugh. It did sound crude and lacking in feminine reticence, as I heard when I said it.

"*Comme tu veux, quand tu veux.*" As I wished, when I wished, he said.

When the flower gypsy came in, he bought red rosebuds. "These should be camellias, of course," he said. "Dumas."

Until he suggested I go to bed with him, I do not think I had really been sure this was what he had in mind, though I knew it had crossed my mind, and there was the matter of the handbag. I had sensed his interest but thought it was too weird. Consciously I was surprised, at myself and at the situation. I thought of Maurice Chevalier movies, of *Gigi.*

Now it doesn't seem weird at all. When I say that I love and desire him, I know that other things are involved besides sex. I admire his force and his experience, for instance. He has fought Chinese bandits in the hills of Taiwan, and Russians in Afghanistan. Sex has more to do with it than I could have imagined, but maybe there is also something you could call sexual suggestion, wherein the romantic idea of Chinese bandits operates directly on the nerve endings through the mechanism of the penis. Or maybe it's more direct even than that. There are sensations that one cannot write about or describe, and realms of the imagination whose importance, though dumbly felt, is beyond understanding.

At this particular dinner, nothing was mentioned about the growing tension between our two families, but we agreed that circumspection was required. And that we would not tell our respective families what was to happen. This was my suggestion. It made him laugh merrily. "It would not have occurred to me to mention this to our families, my dear. *Au contraire.*"

He was off to Avignon in the morning, we would meet in a few days. It seems he lives in Avignon and keeps a *pied-à-terre* in Paris. I did not ask, no one had ever told me, whether there was a Madame Cosset in Avignon. It was not that he would not tell me things, it was that I was afraid to ask. When he kissed me in the taxi, I liked it. Which was a great relief, as I had already made up my mind that I was going to bed with him. It was a serious kiss, not the kiss of an uncle. But not a French kiss either.

Roxy did something rather odd, for her, uninterested in material objects as she is. "I went to Hermès," she said. "Well, I happened to be in there. I promise I wasn't snooping, Iz, but anyway, it's called a 'Kelly.' After Grace Kelly, I guess. Your purse."

"It's ladylike, Grace Kelly was ladylike, it's probably that," I agreed.

"Iz, do you know what that purse cost?"

"No, don't tell me," I said. It is much better not to know the value someone sets on you. It could only be too little or too much.

"I know you didn't buy it for yourself," she went on.

As I've said, I don't usually lie. I shrugged instead. "No, someone gave it to me. I did someone a favor." She knew I wasn't going to tell her, so she dropped it, it seemed without rancor. I was sure she had her theories, but I was sure they wouldn't be right.

"Didn't anyone ever tell you not to accept expensive presents from men?" she added after a bit.

I laughed. "Not really. No one ever foresaw that I would get an expensive present from a man."

"Anyway, you should give it back."

"Ha ha. Anyway, he wouldn't take it. Anyway, why shouldn't one take an expensive present from a man, if he wants to give it to you?"

"It puts you in the position of having to do what he wants."

"But if you happen to want to?"

Here she was stymied. "If you both want the same thing, he doesn't need to give you the expensive present," she said.

"But he wants to. It isn't a payment or bribe. I'd sleep with him anyway. The point is, it's a present."

"Then I suppose you can accept it." Her tone was suddenly wistful, as if she was thinking that she was now, with her swollen belly and a reddish rash on her cheeks, beyond the chance of getting expensive presents from someone who just wanted to give them.

For my part, I saw that if Edgar were younger, he wouldn't have the custom of giving expensive presents, that doing so was a relic of a vanished world. Actually, it was Mrs. Pace who pointed this out.

"How delightful," she said, noticing the Kelly. Not that I carried it much, it was kind of ladylike, but in a nice, useful big size. "You must have an admirer. Let me see. And he must be French, and of a certain age. The charming customs of a vanished day." I remembered that she has a closetful of expensive but old purses, in ostrich, alligator, lizard, every kind of endangered creature.

"It takes me back." She smiled. But when they saw I wasn't going to talk about the Kelly, both she and Roxy seemed to lose interest.

If men don't give women this kind of sexual bribe present anymore, the tradition at least persists that they do. When I understood this aspect of it, I was sort of embarrassed. I once tried to discuss it with Edgar himself. Was it a bribe for sex? After all, I would have done it for free, if I wanted to, or not, and it is a rather degrading concept of female autonomy to suppose otherwise.

Edgar laughed. He said that I was the descendent of heavy-handed mercantile American Calvinists who think in terms of payment and bribe. Some things are gifts and ennoble the giver, or are anyway integral to men's sense of their role.

Something disturbing happened shortly after this. One afternoon I had filled in for the aerobics instructor at the American Center, so Roxy had picked up Gennie and was already home when I came in about seven. I heard them in the kitchen, Gennie crying, screaming almost, a terrible wail, and Roxy's voice loud and angry, as if Gennie had scared her by hurting herself. I thought of fire or scalding, and hurried in.

Gennie's face was blazing red and Roxy's wore an expression of uncontrollable rage. I saw then that Roxy must have hit Gennie, and her hand was raised to do it again. The poor little girl ran to me, and Roxy began to sob: she hated Gennie, Charles-Henri, whom this terrible brat exactly resembled, her life, me, the world. This torrent of raving abuse and misery continued as we stood there, me somewhat riveted by Roxy, blaming her not for feeling this way – things can get too much for anybody – but for taking it out on Gennie. I hadn't imagined she could do that.

We went into the living room, Gennie and I. Despite myself, I was thinking of Roxy's entire history of a selfish penchant for misery. She'd always had it, and I'd never understood it. I knew she was more sensitive than I, on thinner ice always, and that I was just not empowered by nature to understand it or be that way myself. Cruder clay. She wept in diminishing fits in the kitchen and banged things around. I comforted Gennie, whispering "sshhh," and we hid out until the storm passed. At home, growing up, Roxy ordinarily apologized after her fits, but this time she didn't. There was the mark of her hand on Gennie's fat, tear-stained little cheek.

SIXTEEN

For the young man is handsome, but the old man is great.

– Victor Hugo

THOSE FEW DAYS BEFORE MY DEFINITIVE ASSIGNATION WITH Edgar, I know I was worried about one thing in particular in my own life. Because I like to look at handsome young men (look at and more), I worried about the body of an old man: How would he look without his clothes? Would this put me off? I so hoped not, I wanted to be in a state of unqualified desire. I guess I was thinking with dread of the pale senior citizens in their black socks on the beach in Santa Barbara, with their thick middles, red forearms, backs covered in white fuzz.

Now I know something about the vanity of French men, especially men who like women, and I know that they keep themselves up. (Quite a few dye their hair, though.) Or perhaps it's not vanity but courtesy that keeps them in shape. Roxy says it's simply the superiority of the French diet, but she thinks everything French is superior. (She may have soured on French husbands.) I think it has something to do with the cooperation of the sexes in France, so unlike the state of war we have at home, where everyone gets fat from despair and hostility, in order to erotically deprive their loved one.

Roxy's fragile temper had a new strain put on it. She had been to see Maître Bertram, her lawyer, about the Saint Ursula situation. Could she send it to the Getty Museum or not? Maître Bertram had agreed with Antoine de Persand, had told her it would be unwise to ship Saint Ursula to the Getty.

"It could seem like a trick to get it out of France, and that would jeopardize the rest of the divorce. It would seem like an act of bad faith, however correctly you intend it. It could even invite charges and imprisonment," he said. He cautioned her against so much as criticizing Charles-Henri. In France, for a statement like "Charles-Henri is a pig and is trying to steal my painting," she could be sentenced to jail for calumnious talk.

Eventually, Charles-Henri, to his credit, called her to say it was all the same to him what she did with Saint Ursula, he wasn't behind this new frustration, it was simply Antoine, trying to be correct, and the lawyers, with their careful ways.

"Tell them, then. You can tell them you don't care," Roxy said. I don't know what he said in reply. Saint Ursula herself seemed newly to wear an expression of combative smugness. But the self-satisfied smile with which she prayed to keep her virginity, and her indifference to those treasures heaped up in her chamber, were those of a natural ascetic to whom, therefore, renunciation cost nothing. I could not help but feel how she would have despised my relatively pragmatic response to the Kelly.

I left it to Roxy to nerve herself up to tell Margeeve and Chester that she couldn't send the painting to the Getty Museum. She knew this would infuriate and disappoint. I hadn't realized how much Margeeve would care. She had never loved Saint Ursula or the Getty; the picture was really Chester's, coming from his side of the family, and she had no hereditary interest in it; and she had only just taken up the study of art, though I could see she might dislike losing face with the Getty if she had been in a long correspondence with them. I was actually ignorant of, or underestimated, the degree to which she had relished the wonderful, status-building grandeur of having a painting you own in a major or even minor museum exhibition. I just wouldn't have thought that Margeeve would have cared about status and grandeur.

Cut to California: Margeeve is talking to Roxy on the telephone, and I can easily infer Margeeve's side of the conversation.

"Of course, Rox, if it would cause legal problems, we shouldn't do it," says Margeeve mildly. "I just hope they haven't printed the catalogue. But they must have legal glitches like this with every exhibition – insurance problems, whatall. Maybe I'll tell the Getty woman that they could directly approach the French lawyers or the French government or something like that, with a guarantee; to return it to France. I'm sure there are legal routes."

This reassured Roxy, who said it was nice of Margeeve to be so calm about it. Margeeve, of course, would have done a slow double burn later, while fixing the salad. French injustice and meddlesome highhandedness came through to her. This was their, her, Roxy's, a Walker family painting and the Walkers wished to lend it to an American museum, period. French strangers were interfering. Not even French strangers with right and good on their side, but relatives of the enemy, people she had never seen, people who were ruining her daughter's life and now hers.

Chester was sympathetic. He would always be indignant on Roxy's behalf, for in his eyes she can do no wrong, unlike me. But he was now also touched to realize how much the museum show meant to Margeeve.

"We'll call Roger. He'll have some advice, I'm sure."

Margeeve thinking: Why am I upset? I can't believe I'm this upset. There ought to be something Roger can do, some legal thing, he must know someone in France that could put up some insurance, we could send an affidavit. Museum to museum something could be done. The Getty could put in the request through the Louvre. She was feeling, she recognized, the sharp hunger-pang of disappointment over something she hadn't known she really wanted, like something half eaten and mislaid. In her mind's eye she had seen Saint Ursula on the white gallery wall, with the words "Private Collection" or maybe even "Collection of Prof. and Mrs. Chester Walker,

Santa Barbara," or at worst, "Collection of M. and Mme. Charles-Henri de Persand, Paris." It was not as if she would boast aloud, it would be a private pleasure, a sense of civic participation. Was she just a vulgar status-seeker? Standing before the painting beside some stranger, would the words "that's my daughter Roxeanne's" escape her lips? Garrulous old women were always telling you something about their children. She was ashamed to see that the temptation would be enormous. In whatever case, she had counted on having a painting in the Getty show, and was now to be disappointed, humiliated really, because she had promised, as if it were hers to promise.

She had hoped for expiation and legitimacy, had never felt quite legitimate since her divorce, since showing the bad judgment to put that extra *e* in Roxeanne's name, since a car accident in 1956 that had been her fault and she had denied it successfully, since not going enough to PTA meetings, since not being loving enough or generous enough. She squelched these habitual themes of self-reproach.

SEVENTEEN

All animals mistrust man, and they are not wrong.

– Jean-Jacques Rousseau, Confessions

ON SUNDAY MORNINGS I SLEEP IN, WAKE ABOUT TEN. A RIFF of church bells is what wakes me, coming from Saint-Nicolas du Chardonnet, whose parishioners are excommunicated Catholic fundamentalists, I think. They are said to stand for everything bad and fascist, but the bells sound holy. I also hear cars and buses, someone playing the recorder, voices in the street. Later, cooking smells will arise, the garlic-parsley smell of snails, and roasting chicken from the couscous restaurant. Across the street, someone in the garret opposite mine opens her tall windows. The sun strikes her windows in the morning, mine in the afternoon, and thus I am in shadow now, while she hitches her chair into the pool of warm light and basks, doing her nails. I wonder what she is thinking of, and what it would be like to live in her pale French body instead of mine, still with its vestiges of California tan.

Roxy and Gennie and I are going later to Chartres to lunch with the Persands. It's civilized, the continuing bond between Roxy and the Persands, their reassurance that to them she continues to be the mother of their grandchild, an immutable relation. Even Antoine continues to be friendly to her, unapologetic for his meddling opinions about Saint Ursula.

Roxy is friendly to them in turn. She has a need to feel that some bonds are indissoluble. So we continue to go to the Persands, either to Chartres or the apartment on the Avenue Wagram, for Sunday lunches, though I have often begged off because (frankly) in the role of supervising Gennie, I was too often relegated to playing games with Charlotte's and Antoine's sets of children too, like a super-nanny or au pair girl, and I would end up feeling mad at Roxy, since she did nothing to correct the situation and let it be thought that I love children and am just a big little girl at heart. I don't actually like children that much, though I like Gennie, of course. At such times I would look at all the Persand family and couldn't help but wonder what they would think if they knew what I was thinking of doing with their uncle Edgar. This delicious reservation added spice to the flat duties of child care, at least.

On this particular Sunday we were at the house near Chartres, arriving to find Suzanne, Antoine and Trudi, and the youngest daughter, Yvonne, in disarray and consternation, talking to a stranger with a notebook who proved to be a policeman. Suzanne, still soberly dressed from the train in her tweed country clothes, distractedly explained that they had been "visited." At first I understood this as "visitation," perhaps a supernatural event, but it emerged that "visit" was a gentle euphemism for being broken into, though nothing had been taken. "One was visited," cried Suzanne, "despite the *blindage* of the *porte,* despite the system of alarm!"

"As soon as I came into the hall, I knew something was wrong," she told the inspector. "I said to myself, what if the visitor is still here?" No one was there, but things had been moved, were different, there was, as Suzanne kept saying, the impression of someone's presence, I could feel it too, the well-known sense of violation. "And then the insult that they found nothing worth taking?" She laughed, reverting to her Frenchwoman's resolute gaiety, taking the policeman by the arm into the salon.

The serious business of getting lunch was settled down to,

nonetheless. As it was now October, and the day too rainy for tennis, I walked with the children and Antoine in the wood, while Roxy, Suzanne, Trudi, and Yvonne toiled in the kitchen. Here was perhaps an adequate trade-off. Getting out of the kitchen, in the beautiful rainy wood, I didn't mind keeping an eye on the children as they ricocheted along the paths, their laughter rippling everywhere, like a sound track of childhood. At first I had thought the French forests were puny, especially now with the leaves falling off, leaving only a dainty pattern of bare branches and the odd trembling yellow leaf attached. In California, we have the redwoods, and stands of pine and Douglas fir, heavy forests of giant fallen logs rotting in soft strata of needles and beetles. These are more like forests in paintings by Corot (as you would expect). Now I have come to feel there is something more welcoming in these. In ours, when you come on beer cans riddled with bullets, it's sort of frightening. You think of crazies lurking with guns or, when you come on patches of clear-cut, you think of the devastation of the planet.

"Their Alps are much more rugged than our Rockies," Roxy had pointed out to me with her reflex Europhilia.

Now, walking single file behind Antoine, Gennie stuck close to me, clinging to my hand, influenced by her recent introduction to Red Riding Hood, as well, perhaps, as by Roxy's violence. I didn't bring up the matter of Saint Ursula to Antoine. I wanted to reproach him for interfering. I wanted to say, "Roxy would return the painting, which after all is hers. What's the problem? Don't you know what it means to Margeeve? Don't you know it really belongs to Chester, it isn't even Roxy's, and it isn't any of your business? Don't you know Charles-Henri doesn't care?" But the convention was, at these lunches, that the problems between Roxy and Charles-Henri belonged to another realm of life and could not be mentioned. Also, I thought of Antoine as an elder, a man approaching fifty, not a confrere to be lashed out at. I didn't know him, I'm trying to say, and now I had come to think of him as a bad person, motivated by greed, out of a story by

Balzac. Yet I said nothing. Was I becoming coopted by my planned liaison with Antoine's uncle?

Resenting my own reticence, I plodded along after him, keeping an eye on Paul-Louis, Jean-Fernand, Marie-Odile, Jean-Claude, Cyrille, Irene, and Gennie. Antoine himself, I noticed, seemed unconcerned about the children, who were safely visible in their plaid shirts and bright dresses, but he was peering intently into the underbrush, and from time to time up a tree, staring at knots or clumps as if expecting them to move. I assumed he was bird-watching, and asked what he thought he saw.

"Nothing," he said at first. Later he sat on a rock in the center of the clearing and stared like a scout for Indians at every break in the vegetation within the semicircle of his view. Only now did I notice that his expression was grim and severe.

"I am looking for the cat of Charlotte," he said.

"Her cat is lost?" I didn't understand, because Charlotte lived in Neuilly, far from the forest of Chartres.

"Mother is upset enough, especially now with this affair of being visited. You have to admire her, she's trying hard to hold things together. The cat is just the last straw."

One disadvantage of not speaking their language is that I miss out on understanding many things as they pass. You are in the position of a child listening to half-understood adult talk, things go by you. I thought this must be one of those situations, because I had not heard anything about a cat.

"Uh, what color cat?" I said.

"It is a little Siamese cat."

I could think of plausible scenarios, cat leaping out of cat carrier and dashing into the woods. And now I could hear that the children were calling "meenou, meenou."

He got to his feet and resumed tramping the path.

"What could a cat eat in the *forêt* here? She might catch a bird," he said.

"Little mice, I suppose. Wood creatures."

"Thousands of cats are released every year, it is criminal. They do not thrive, they starve. Every August, French people leave their animals to fend for themselves in the forest. Dogs, tied to trees, starving. It is horrible, horrible."

"Horrible," I echoed, not understanding.

"Yes, they think a pet is just for a season, then it is expendable like a pair of shoes. But Charlotte knows better."

"In America too, people are often cruel to cats," I assured him, though I had learned that it did not ingratiate you with the French to claim to share their social problems. This challenges either their belief that their problems are worse, or their belief that American ones are so much worse that a comparison is insulting.

"Trudi belongs to a group that rescues them," Antoine said.

I still did not understand what Charlotte's cat was doing here, but was constrained from asking, assuming, however, that it had been left here, which seemed strange.

"The cat knows Paul-Louis, of course, she might come out if she hears him. The other children should stop calling." He spoke to the children, evidently telling them to shut up.

"Minou, Minou," called Paul-Louis.

"We must go back. We'll come out again after lunch," said Antoine. I now perceived his real agitation, or anger, as if a child had been lost.

When we came in, I washed Gennie's hands and walked toward the kitchen. I heard Roxy saying, "Isabel is just like that. She is so competitive, when we were little, we went to a gymnastics class, and then she would go to another gymnastics class at the Y, on another day, for extra practice, so she could be the best in our class."

It hadn't been quite like that. I wanted to rush in to explain. The funny thing was, only later did I realize that Roxy must have said all this in French. Perhaps things said about yourself penetrate the language barrier and burn directly into your brain. Why were they talking about me?

Suzanne served a *ragoût d'homard* from a beautiful tureen. It came to me that, as I admired Mrs. Pace for her brilliance and intellectual assurance, I admired Suzanne for her reflex hospitable vivacity. I was surprised by the realization that until coming here I had not admired any particular women, for though I loved Margeeve I often thought she was silly, and my real mother was a disaster. Perhaps one or two of my teachers, in grade school, that was all, and no one since.

Suzanne a perfect Frenchwoman, overseeing vast family meals, monitoring her investments, paying attention to the *petits soins,* those mysterious details of female upkeep even Janet Hollingsworth could not find out about, and flirting at any age with any male because it is a form of politeness. I began to see how Roxy, from their point of view, might be thought a little casual and uncoiffed. She should be more seductive, not such a straight-shooter. She could lighten her hair, for example, or put nail polish on.

I was wearing nail polish, I don't know why. Well, I knew why. If I were telling an American story, to mention nail polish would be to signal that it was not a serious story, was meant to be read under the hair dryer. But in a French story it is a revealing, spiritual detail. Also, French men think American women are too understated, and ought to be flirtatious. They think we don't try, but they don't realize that in America, if you try flirtatiously, you get blamed for any bad thing that might happen to you.

In fact Roxy tended to bite her nails in secret, though now, in pregnancy, she seemed at her most beautiful, and her nails had grown out some, despite her unhappiness.

The French are odd at the table. Usually they are very elaborate in the way they pass the dishes, the men giving each dish to the lady next to him before he serves himself, and the platter traveling thus twice around the table, to every woman before any man is served. I suppose no man has ever tasted his food hot. Secure in their social privilege, the men are stately in their politeness, seeming to say by their forbearance that they can endure eating cold food.

Also, the dishes seem to start with the oldest lady guest. I can imagine that some women, for instance Mrs. Pace, would not like this designation one bit. And sometimes at table,

French people are infected by mad gaiety. I am never sure what has started this, but suddenly they are throwing pieces of bread to each other up and down the table – polite people who have changed for dinner, throwing bread as in a boarding house.

Inevitably at Suzanne's Sundays there were some of their relatives – schoolboys, grandchildren, nephews or nieces, uniformly polite, each with a few words of English. (Once, though, when Frédéric's father-in-law, a count, stopped by to return a book, I was not presented to him.) Though Edgar had never been present after the first day, today there was a cousin, Pierre, I thought I heard Cosset, a young man in his twenties with clean pink cheeks, a schoolboy look, nice short haircut, good manners. Only halfway through lunch, which had degenerated into one of these bread-throwing occasions, did I realize he could be Edgar's son. Studying him, I thought I could see a resemblance. But there was no fatal attraction, no operatic complication of my feelings. It was still the father I wanted. It came to me that if this Pierre were twenty or so, and his father were, say, seventy, then Madame Cosset must be quite a bit younger than Edgar. This Pierre seemed on good long-term terms with the Persands, had clearly had jolly romps since childhood with the cousins, here at Chartres or at the seaside somewhere. His presence heightened the piquancy of my erotic life, the feeling of delicious secrecy.

At table there was an empty seat, someone expected but not there. I hoped it might be Oncle Edgar, but halfway through the soup, Bob arrived, Charlotte's husband. There was an affectionate flurry of sympathetic greetings as he slipped into his chair, at least the soft sound was affectionate rather than hearty, but it was also inquisitive and urgent. Something had happened which Bob told them about, with much shaking of his head, as if in disbelief, and rueful laughter tempered by a slightly choleric tone to his complexion. A blond man anyway, given to flushes. Of his discourse I understood nothing, of course, except, at one moment:

"Avez-vous trouvez le chat?"

On the way home Roxy interpreted, with a certain malice, the significance of Bob's despair and explained the search for Minou. Charlotte had accepted a job in England, with an English publishing house, a mere pretext in Bob's view to get off with the English man, and had decamped without the children, having first, in an act of supreme emotional sadism, set free Bob's beloved cat.

"Symbolizing that she is another such creature yearning to be free. He would have taken care of the cat, after all. He thinks she did it because she knows he loves the cat. She thinks he loves the cat better than he loves the children, et cetera. What a family!"

Maybe Roxy could marry Bob, was my thought. My mind was on Charlotte and her Englishman, the vagaries of the obdurate human heart, and the strange spectacle of someone else's passionate misery. I could imagine Charlotte at her dressing table, smoking madly, reading the ferry schedule. Roxy, Charlotte, Bob – I wondered what the matter was with Bob, what her objections to him were, and how she could be cruel to a cat.

Roxy said they all had seen it coming. Things other people saw coming were to me out of the blue. All that had gone before, in the family, between Charlotte and Bob, Charlotte and the Englishman, Charlotte and her parents, I could only imagine, though for the others it may have been an ongoing saga. I was excluded by my lack of French from having any sense of the process, the stages, the stepping stones, as over a brook, by which Charlotte and Bob – or Roxy and Charles-Henri – had arrived at this pass, as revealed in passing remarks or discussions at Suzanne's table.

Suzanne, especially, now had a martyred, beleaguered matriarchal air, struggling for gaiety in the teeth of an onslaught. I made a mental note to ask Janet Hollingsworth about this gaiety fetish.

"I don't entirely blame myself," Suzanne sighed at tea on Wednesday. "It is my fault that both Charles-Henri and Charlotte are self-indulgent, perhaps. But the times encourage disruption. Divorce is practically a fashion these days. I blame American films. Women working. Charlotte imagines she can support herself no matter where. She'd have to face reality eventually.

"Something else has happened, too," she continued. "Even more terrible. There is an article in *Le Figaro* mentioning Georges's brother." Georges is Monsieur de Persand.

"How so?" asked Roxy.

"Mentioning a Persand and Pétain in the same sentence. I have called Edgar. He will know what to do."

I asked Edgar later why this was so tormenting to Suzanne. "One does not mention Pétain and one's relatives in the same breath," he explained. "If it were the nineteenth century – or even the nineteen-twenties – I suppose I would have to fight a duel, if Georges wouldn't."

It was the plight of the cat that tormented Roxy. "They die, you know, a housecat can't really get along in the wild," she kept saying. "But how long can they live? We should go look for it, Antoine and the others have to work, but you and I could go tomorrow.

EIGHTEEN

> *Woe to the man who in the first moments of a love-affair does not believe that it will last forever! Woe to him who even in the arms of some mistress who has just yielded to him maintains an awareness of trouble to come and foresees that he may later tear himself away!*
>
> *– Benjamin Constant,* Adolphe

EDGAR AND I HAD DINNER AT LE BELLECOUN THE FOLLOWING Tuesday. *(Ravioli de courgettes,* veal chop, *gratin de fruits rouges.)* Nothing impedes me from eating, but my mind wasn't on it, I just wanted to get the sex over with, to get it behind us, to know the worst or the best.

The first time, though often carried by enthusiasm, is never the best. Yet there has to be a first time. I still had certain fears – would I hate an old man's white fur? An old smell? But Edgar did not smell old, he smelled briskly of bay rum or shaving soap. Impotence? But then presumably this whole matter would not have presented itself. His bearing, his tall soldier's body perfectly erect, his deep-set eyes – these things reassured me.

Edgar himself seemed blithely relaxed, and consumed every smidgin of his sauce *(lotte à la crème de safran)* with that curious instrument they have, half spoon, half fork. (I should explain that from the time of our first lunch, I had taken to noting down the French names of the things we ate. I could not have explained why.)

In the end, it was natural and easy. Though the night was cool, we walked to his *pied-à-terre* on the rue de Bourgogne.

He showed me the kitchen and where the bathroom was. I didn't know if I was supposed to undress, was more used to sort of being undressed by another. When I came out he had taken off his coat and poured us each a cognac. I sat next to him on the sofa. So. He was clumsy with the buttons of my blouse and waited for me to do it. By now I was mad with curiosity and impatience so I kissed him and reached directly for his fly.

"*Attends, attends,*" he said, catching my wrist.

He knew what I wanted, and also, it appeared, what he wanted, for at a certain point his concentration seemed to shift to his own pleasure, and his eyes changed, but not before he knew about me. I think he had been uncertain – he told me this some time later – whether he was taking a worldly mistress or a maiden. His unfamiliarity with Americans, and Californians, of my age, might make that a question, though a question soon answered. A part of my own pleasure, apart from the reliable physiological one, arose from just this difference in our ages and conditions. That which had worried me before now intensified the odd passion I felt. Reassured, I felt that to be made love to by a large, handsome, white-haired man with his large engine (or whatever word Milton would have used in *Paradise Lost,* which I once had to read some of, horrible) and whose speaking might as well have been in tongues – it was like being fucked by God. I was thrilled, my body was made of honey.

Sometimes we had the conversation lovers have: What did he first like about me? How did he decide to make his suggestion? ("At my time of life, one has been in love a few times and knows better than to leave it to its own mysterious and fatal ways – you have to help Love along.")

When I told him I was swayed by his political and military exploits he was amused and remarked that these were the pursuits of a type of belligerent and dominant male he had heard was out of fashion with modern women.

And by his not being American, I said.

"Something that defines a billion people," he said. "On the

other hand I am charmed by your Americanness."

"That is to say bluntness, freshness, and naïveté," I said.

"By no means. Those are not qualities I admire, especially."

One thing I appreciated at first was that he had no wish to tell me his problems, with his wife or whatever, and he appreciated that I had no wish to hear them. Perhaps he didn't have any problems. (Eventually I wanted to hear them.) He said he never permitted himself to accept oral sex. It was a kind of discipline. *Pas de soixante-neuf.* I imagined he could easily change his mind about that.

Even before our affair had officially begun, I had started to struggle through articles in newspapers in which Edgar was mentioned. I wrote out paradigms of the verbs *avoir* and *être* in all the tenses, and just with learning these made some progress. But if we met someone he knew and we had a drink, after the theatre, say, I didn't understand a word they said. This drove me crazy. I've always been an included, insider person, in charge, even, but now I was excluded and probably thought to be backward. *Bonjour, monsieur, bonjour, madame.* I could do these phrases very confidently, and quickly added *au revoir (monsieur, madame)* to my repertoire. But more would not come out of me, except to Edgar, to whom I could muster *je t'aime* in a playful tone.

My slowness with language made me respect Roxy for the seeming ease with which she had changed countries, languages, and religions. When I told her this, she just bitterly said it was a mark of a bad character, a person should rest what she is.

I have noticed she has begun to use French words like "rest" when she speaks English. We would say "stay or remain": people should "stay" as they are. But do we believe that? I don't.

It must have been about now that Stuart Barbee said to his friend, the Louvre art expert Alain Desmond, that he had seen a fine picture at Roxy's, in the process of valuing it for the Getty, the subject a woman praying, the handling of the light reminiscent of the school of La Tour. Would he like to see it?

"By no means, *mon cher,*" said Desmond. "I would then have to say if it was or wasn't. It's better for our institution not to come down on one side or another, in cases of uncertain attribution. In case."

"In case?"

"In case it may come up for sale," said Desmond mischievously. In case it's a *vrai,* he meant. If it's a *vrai,* one would rather pay the price of an *élève* of, *école* of, or *d'après.*

"Quite, I understand," said Stuart.

"You might get me a copy of the photograph, though," Desmond said.

And in fact it was going to come up for sale. This was the newest development in Roxy's divorce. Step by step:

1. Convinced by Charlotte, her friends, and her lawyer that she would get a better settlement if she sued for divorce "for cause," Roxy had accepted the inevitable and decided on doing that.

2. Charles-Henri, faced with the prospect of being divorced for cause, had rescinded his perfect docility and retained the original lawyer, Maître Doisneau, who informed Roxy's lawyer, Maître Bertram, that either Roxy consent to a normal down-the-middle modern divorce, or Charles-Henri would not permit her to use his name and would ask for custody of the children. Since everyone knew that he would have an advantage in a custody hearing in a French court, given the French attitude that children should be the property of the French parent, Roxy had consented to a normal down-the-middle divorce, but now she was bitter at having been outmaneuvered and betrayed. Just as the French ladies in the Place Maubert, and the American wives at the wives' group, had told her she would be.

"It is always like this," observed Maître Bertram, with gloomy satisfaction. "People start out in agreement. Then, the hardening."

L'endurcissement. The hardening. Perhaps that is only

another word for experience or for growing up. An Englishwoman at tea at Mrs. Pace's said to me, "French women are clever, but they're hard. They look hard." I could see how they must seem so; Englishwomen are so much softer and rounder than the trim little Frenchwomen with their perfect makeup. Frenchwomen must seem monsters of calculation to get that scarf on every time. But they had to learn to calculate because of the hardness of the laws.

Down the middle meant that Roxy would have to credit Charles-Henri with half the value of the picture or somehow come up with half its value to give him when they came to calculate the split.

She raged at this, and dreaded having to tell Margeeve and Chester. She thought desperately of plots – false break-ins wherein the painting would be stolen – or of mailing it back to California rolled in a tube. She thought of asking Tammy de Bretteville to take it when she went home to Portland, Oregon, for Christmas.

Or me taking it, saying it was mine. She'd say she couldn't do anything with me (headstrong Isabel), I would just put it in my suitcase and be gone in the night. She went to Bon Marché to look at suitcases it might fit in. But I said I didn't want to go back to California. I didn't tell her why. How I wish now that I had done it. But would that have changed anything?

I didn't go around carrying the Kelly bag, but reserved it for dress-up occasions or when going out with Edgar. For one thing, I now worried about losing it or having it snatched. For another, Roxy. When I would dump my wallet and such into it and prepare to go out, I could see Roxy glare at it, or avert her eyes. It was an irritation to her, it caused distress. For this reason, I tried to conceal it from her notice as much as possible. I knew that it symbolized infidelity, in this case mine to her, by not telling her where I got it. It was as tantalizing as the box to Pandora, and it hurt her, for I had always in the past told her even my most gruesome, frightening, or humiliating adventures. It also, perhaps, symbolized the infidelity of men in general, especially French ones. She knew the donor must be French, for only Frenchmen would know the brand names – Baccarat, Cartier, Hermès. (And maybe a Japanese would.) And it was so clearly the gift of a man to a woman not his wife, it probably made her wonder what Charles-Henri gave Magda (if he gave her anything, being modern.)

Gifts to women – one of those traditional observances that have shrunk down to ceremonial size, the size of a theater ticket or ring. I could see that the Kelly was the artifact of a day when life was different for women, and that in Roxy's mind, formed by the novels of – who? I don't know, Zola? Anita Loos? – it was a better life back then. She saw herself as a victim of new forms of female disadvantage (though I would have argued she was the victim of the old form of disadvantage, hostage as surely as Mrs. Julius Caesar or Mrs. Mark Antony – or Madame Edgar Cosset – to male erotic caprice). There was a Madame Cosset, of course, and two sons, near Avignon.

Roxy hated that she could be expected to fend for herself and her children. Her resentment of her condition seemed to grow each day with the size of her belly and with the size of the dossier she continued to assemble, detailing her own perfections and the failures and faults of Charles-Henri.

We developed something of a routine, Edgar and I. On Tuesday nights, sometimes on Friday if he did not go down to the country, we met in the late afternoon to make love, then went somewhere for dinner or the theatre. In America you would go to the theatre first and then make love (Calvinism?), but this way is better, when your senses are alert and you are not tipsy and sleepy. No theatre in French, though, I drew the line there, because I didn't understand a word, just the ends of the sentences, as in blah-blah-blah-blah *déjà!* blah-blah *n'est-ce pas?,* as though trains were hurtling past drowning out most of the sense.

We might be grandfather and granddaughter, so politely, so gravely does he seat me, help me with my coat, with no gesture of the erotic, nothing but the most decorous intimacy. Of course everyone knows what we are, but no one smirks or winks, we fit an established human paradigm – old, powerful man, young woman. I fancy he can't help but notice certain looks of congratulation directed at him by other men. Sometimes, though, I think I see a flicker of grandfatherly boredom from Edgar and my stomach knots up with the wish to please. Or perhaps I just imagine his instants of inattention. He returns his attention to me with a smile. My stomach knots up because that's where I seem to feel things. As a child I got stomachaches, called by the family "Isabel's stomachaches," and I still do.

Then I exert myself to say something amusing, if I can think of it. Or I ask questions about France. That always seems to please him, he enjoys answering and explaining the meanings of words and how things work in France.

I began to think of buying him a present, to keep things even. I also intensified my efforts to read in French, or sometimes French books translated by Ames.

It was not my fresh youth (the cliché) that stimulated him. For one thing, I was rather experienced, after all, and for another, he was not old, had not entered the psychological space "age" where he would be charmed by the disparity, incongruity, and rejuvenating potential of our relation, or surprised that a pretty young woman would be interested in him. He had not begun to experience what Mrs. Pace says all old people experience, invisibility to the opposite sex. Women look at him. He is an imposing man who has recognition and influence and, apparently, some money, though this I do not know for sure. He had never stopped being attractive to women, so he saw nothing surprising, or nothing too surprising, in my choice. In a way what most charmed me in our affair, what fired my imagination most, was what interested him the least. His history, so ineluctably allied to his smooth good looks and somewhat remote charm, was devastating to me. Nor had he begun to experience any physical diminution, or only what was gradual and imperceptible, nothing pronounced. The slowness of gait had disappeared with the healing of his ankle (though there remained a certain stateliness). Some concerns about the prostate, whatever that is. It's funny to note, in view of what we know about the harmful effects of sunlight, which gives freckles and wrinkles, that what is kept mostly inside the pants shows little effects of aging and looks at seventy what it must have looked at twenty.

I invented a regular job to tell Roxy why I couldn't babysit on Tuesday nights. All through the weekends and Mondays, my mind stayed strangely on the prospect of Tuesday. There is a sense in which intermittent happiness spoils the rest of life, when it ought to spill over into it, igniting it all into a blaze of joy.

NINETEEN

The magic of love – who could ever describe it? Certainty of having found the one being destined for us by nature, sudden light shed upon life itself and apparently explaining its mystery, unsuspected value conferred upon the most trifling circumstances, flying hours whose details elude the memory through their very sweetness . . .
– Benjamin Constant, Adolphe

I WAS CHANGING, IN MY BLOOD AND ENERGY, AND IT HAD TO do with Edgar, though I could not have said how. In part it was the excitement of political consciousness. Perhaps in other circumstances I could have been turned on to something else. Perhaps if Edgar had been a stockbroker, I would have thrilled to the thrum of the ticker tape and learned to read the Dow.

Behind my wish to give Edgar an expensive present was a wish to be thought of as someone sexy and generous, with perfect taste. Someone to be missed, regretted, and never forgotten. I had given the matter a lot of thought, made inquiries, and now had decided to give him a piece of faience, Old Nevers or Rouen or whatever. I had once heard Mrs. Pace and Edgar discuss their collections at one of her parties – of course, I should have guessed that they were old friends. He had admired the handsome soup tureen, which occupies in a queenly way the top of her sideboard.

"This is beautiful, Olivia, what is this?" Edgar had asked.

"Old Nevers. You might think Rouen, from the glaze."

"No, I didn't think Rouen, because of the underglaze," he replied. "But those must be Rouen," he said, indicating a pair of vases.

"Levasseur, Rouen. '*Aux Oiseaux*,'" Mrs. Pace had said happily.

It was clear that I would need advice. I had heard Stuart Barbee admire Roxy's dishes when he came to appraise her painting, so it was Stuart I had asked, about dealers and such, and where I might find something not too expensive. Of course he knew a dealer at the Marché aux Puces who specialized in the kind of thing I had in mind.

I had the address in hand. Stall H. Martin, which had a look of permanence and expertise, was clearly one of the stationary establishments of the flea market which deal in objects of great price. There were beautiful platters and tureens in the window. I had copied the markings on the bottom of Mrs. Pace's tureen, and thrust this at the man – a plump type in his forties, turning bald – and said, "*Je voudrais, je cherche, un cadeau,*" and so on, whereupon he immediately switched to English, as they usually do. He had an English accent, might even have been English, had that raddled, run-down English look too, of people who smoke too much and eat too much sugar and meat.

"It's a present for a friend who has a collection," I said, "I'd like to get him something nice." The man looked at me pityingly, I guess knowing I was in for a shock when he revealed his prices.

"These things are dear," he said. "They don't come cheaply."

"I know," I said. I had realized at least that much from the general reverence surrounding them.

He studied the markings on my piece of paper. "I don't have many pieces of this kind. I have a friend, there are dealers who do. My friend can sometimes lay hands on things like this – he knows the collectors. I could take your name. Are you American?"

"Yes, American. I need – it's for Christmas, I need it soon."

"Why don't you look at these little *assiettes*, they're Quimper, about a hundred years old, anyone would like them, what beauties." He drew me to the window, to a set of small plates arranged like the most charming painting. I could see why people had dishes, so tangible and inviting to the fingertips. These had smiling birds on olive branches tied with bows.

"A pitcher? Or a little vase?" I asked, thinking of something more important, rounder.

"Where in America?"

"Santa Barbara."

"Lucky you. Does your friend like Delft? I also have a charming little cow. Look at this," he said, lifting down a platter. "This is late seventeenth century, one of the earliest pieces I have. Just a little repair here."

"I don't know," I said. "I just know he was swept away by Old Rouen."

"I perhaps could get something," he said. "My friend might. I have some photos, if you'd like to look at those. Mind, these are important objects, big money. Do you know what you'd like to spend?"

"Not exactly," I said. Now, for the first time, it occurred to me that if Roxy's picture sold well, some of the money ought to be mine. Then I could buy anything. I know it sounds goody-goody to say you haven't thought of money, but I hadn't, until then, where the picture was concerned, it had always been so thoroughly Roxy's. Plus it had been hard to think of selling something that had always been on the wall of your house, it was like selling the doorknobs. But now I understood avarice, and my soul burned with the thought that I ought to have some of the picture money, and I relished the idea of buying something hugely expensive for Edgar, something, specifically, that cost as much as a Kelly.

"Sometimes collectors put things on consignment – here are some pictures," he said, bringing out a fat envelope of photographs. "What they are, dates and so on, are on the back."

Since I didn't have much idea of what I wanted, there wasn't much point in looking at them, but I turned them over out of politeness – tureens, platters, vases, little porcelain statues, all most or less important-looking, large and elaborate, and I was pretty sure out of my price range. One thing that struck me was that all these objects were photographed in rooms, on tables or sideboards, shown off to advantage.

It was thus that I recognized Mrs. Pace's tureen, because it sat on her sideboard in the dining room I knew very well. Unbelieving, I turned the photo over. Old Rouen, and all the same markings. It was all I could do to dissemble and pass on to the next photograph. Then I came back to it, as if weighing it, to be sure I wasn't mistaken. How could this be?

"That one? One like that?" the man asked.

"Yes, like this," I said. "This is what I want."

"That is a major piece," he said, taking the photo and studying it. He handed it back. It was now I realized that this could easily be a photograph I myself had taken; I had taken just such views of her rooms, and given the film to Stuart Barbee. One in particular had been just this shot, of her specially prized tureen, the candlestick moved to one side.

"Something of that order," I said.

There are some things that defy explanation, and are too odd, too creepy, to think about directly. I thanked the man and rose, said I would be thinking about what exactly I could pay, what I wanted, I would come back. I must have rushed off in a manner he thought odd. There were lots of explanations, of course, the most obvious being that Mrs. Pace had thought of selling her tureen. Somehow, though, I think I would have known about that.

"Thesis, antithesis, synthesis," says Mrs. Pace. "That is the characteristically French way of thinking about anything." My thesis was that some sort of scam involved Mrs. Pace's tureen. The antithesis was that she planned to sell it, and had somehow entered it into the world list of saleable items through which it had become known to this guy. There was something I was missing, but I never got it. One night I dreamt a synthesis, but it was too odd to survive the morning review.

I decided not to mention any of this to Mrs. Pace for the moment. All the same, a few days later, I called the guy and told him I wanted the tureen in the photo, or one just like it. He said it might take a few weeks.

About Bosnia, there was the difference between Roxy and me that whereas hers was the indignant sympathy of a bleeding heart, mine was an awakened life of the head, if you like, a fascination with the great board game of realpolitik, and my own part in it, humble as it was, setting up chairs for Edgar's meetings. Had I cared about the USC football team? Had I been excited by the slimy creatures in freshman Marine Biology? Possibly. I had a memory of other excitements but they had been paltry compared to this.

Sex was part of it. If desire is electrical energy charging up your cells, which is what it feels like, then not having sex would be to produce something corrosive in you, like what leaks out of old batteries. So whereas our affair was at first, for me, about politics, about the romance of political morality, it became about sex too. Appetite comes with eating, said Rabelais, apparently. A very experienced man knows things I didn't know.

Once, giving in to my demands, Edgar said, "Dear God, think how funny everyone thought the fate of your Nelson Rockefeller." Nelson Rockefeller was a New York governor, apparently, who died at the home of his young mistress, everyone said while doing it.

Perhaps this is just a hot-blooded time in life. Or perhaps I had the extra interest in lovemaking that went with political involvement. But it also went along with the rest of life being a little boring, for I found my walks with Gennie or Scamp or the two of them boring, found helping Stuart Barbee and Con empty their *cave* boring, painting their dining room boring. I had an overqualified feeling, whereas an affair with a sophisticated man of state is a challenge. And Mrs. Pace was a challenge.

But basically, it was the mysteries of heavy Serbian matériel that absorbed me, and also those of *la foufoune* and *la bite* – the pussy and cock – and the dinner that followed the mysteries, with its own elaborate rituals and elaborated refinements, works of genius in cabbage *(Saint Jacques aux choux à l'orange, chou farci)*. And now, my little cabbage . . .

La foufoune, a word I learned from Yves, made Edgar laugh when I used it, though shortly afterward he inquired, peevishly, where I could have heard such words. I could see that his impulse was to make me explain, and that he mastered the impulse.

We had agreed to be discreet, so it surprised me that we went everywhere in public – movies, meetings, restaurants. Perhaps there was a convention by which, if you didn't live in Paris, what you did in Paris was overlooked.

At a certain point, making love, you stop thinking about the other person and think of yourself, or if think is not the right word, feel – but not emotion, I mean sensation – when you want the feeling to go on and on, sensations of the hand, the lips, the cock. I began to want it in the mornings when I woke up, only he was of course not there. I was a cat in heat. I even slept a time or two with Yves, which seemed easier than breaking off with him, and made me feel better, too, which was odd, because you would think that being in love, as I was with Edgar Cosset, would make one less, not more, inclined to do flighty stuff like that.

I knew I was changing. I also began to have vulnerable emotional feelings, like a woman, and could understand Roxy's ravings about destiny and luck. I never used to exert myself with men to be amusing or even nice; being pretty and doing it with them was enough. But now I was really trying. With my dictionary I labored through accounts of the war in *Le Monde Diplomatique*, and love advice in *Frou-Frou* magazine.

Le sexe n'est pas l'unique zone érogène de l'homme. Le plaisir érotique, c'est aussi une question de technique . . . Prenez l'initiative! On peut prendre son pied en s'empalant sur la partie de son anatomie que . . . Goutez chaque centimètre de peau . . . il faut l'étonner . . .

I learned, for instance, that if you drink a little tisane of orange and rosewater or mint, it perfumes your own juices. I feel I never would have found that out in Santa Barbara. I learned this French erotic secret from Janet Hollingsworth, with whom Roxy and I had coffee one afternoon. "I've ferreted out a good one," she said. "Did you know that . . . ?" Quite a lot of tisane, though – a whole teapotful is required, she said.

TWENTY

Paris, city of amusements, pleasures, etc., where four-fifths of the inhabitants are dying of unhappiness.

– Nicolas de Chamfort

UNLIKE MRS. PACE, EDGAR DID NOT BELIEVE IN LIFTING THE arms embargo against the Bosnians, conflicting in this with those French intellectuals who had taken the tack, believed in by Americans too, of letting the Bosnian Muslims defend themselves. Edgar believed in French intervention, through the NATO alliance, though he had begun to think it was too late even for that.

It became known that the Bosnian Serbs, having agreed to withdraw their cannons from around Sarajevo, were now stealing them back and trundling them off to bombard other villages and towns. This treachery affected Roxy as vividly as if these renegade guns were now pointed at the rue Maître-Albert. Her color, already high and flushed with her pregnancy, deepened to a dangerous-looking plum, her eyes shot indignant fire, she tried to pick up conversations in the market, or sitting with Tammy or Anne-Chantal in the Brasserie Espoir.

Since Roxy's troubles began, all the denizens of the Place Maubert have seemed singled out for domestic catastrophe, beginning with the dramatic elopement of Jérôme Lartigue, the theatrical designer, with an American editress, an act of midlife crisis that had struck all the neighborhood as being, at the least, un-French. Anne-Chantal, his wife of thirty years, was so stunned she did not speak for several weeks. The next to break up were Tammy de Bretteville (American like us) and her husband Hugues, and most recently Djuna and Serge, the Serbo-Croatian couple we had long thought riveted by political solidarity against the madness in their country (he had been the Serbian ambassador). They are so poor that they remain together in their same apartment, each shopping in the market at different hours, grim, with separate baskets of turnips and kale.

Both Tammy and Anne-Chantal had written eloquent letters for Roxy's divorce dossier, but these women did not think much about politics.

"Such savagery, how can human beings act like that?" Roxy would moan at each new Serbian incursion, her mind reviewing all human perfidy. These days human perfidy was never far from her mind.

"*Mais*, the Serbs are all right," said Anne-Chantal, "they were abused horribly in the war, *hein*? The Croats murdered millions of them, no wonder they want revenge."

"Everyone's ancestors were murdered by somebody," cried Roxy. "What will happen in the world if people can't forget the past?"

"And the Muslims, what do they want but a foothold for Islam in Europe, that deserves a thought, surely?" Anne-Chantal went on.

"That's not true!" Roxy disagreed. "The Bosnian Muslims are perfectly secular."

"*Alors*, I hope you are prepared to wear the veil?" said Anne-Chantal.

I was not getting along too well with Roxy. She had got very picky about what I was supposed to be doing, or what she supposed I was supposed to be doing, to help her; and in a rather small-minded way, I felt she ought to be grateful, not critical, it being after all not me who made her marry a

Frenchman and launch into a divorce, pregnancies, financial problems, et cetera. I thought I was being nice. I thought I was being a prince to Roxy, actually. It seemed to me that I was the only stable parent poor little Gennie had, and that she shouldn't be put all that time in the crèche, every day, and that with Roxy not working (for she sometimes skipped going to her studio and moped around the house), it wasn't necessary.

"You watch her all day then," snapped Roxy.

Of course, she was depressed, and things were going badly with the divorce. She was now thinking that if she hadn't said anything about sending the painting home, no one would have thought about it. As it was, it had been identified by the lawyers as their only possession, apart from one or two old bureaux and a table from the Persands, that might have value, and thus would have to be divided between them, and thus would have to be sold.

Roxy proclaimed her indignation far and wide. "Outrageous," the American community agreed. "Even in primitive societies the husband's family gives back the dowry if they send the woman back to her own tribe."

"Not always," put in the English anthropologist Rex Rhett-Valy in his reedy Bloomsbury voice. "In India among certain villagers, they keep the cows and burn the spurned bride besides."

We in Paris did not fully appreciate at this time the emotional havoc being created in California by the vagaries of French law. Roxy's picture had already been appraised by Stuart Barbee at forty thousand dollars. Antoine, Charles-Henri's brother, was now suggesting a second valuation. "It is a normal thing, we all know that experts can vary quite widely in their opinions. Just to be sure what is correct."

This had infuriated Roxy, because it implied that the Persands believed it to be worth more, and thought American appraisers were untrustworthy or in our pay, or thought Roxy was keeping the value low so she could more easily buy Charles-Henri out. But even at forty thousand, Roxy had no prospect of twenty thousand dollars to pay Charles-Henri his half, nor did they have enough property between them to count it against the value of the other things. She had telephoned Chester and Margeeve to ask them to help, knowing in advance that they'd say they didn't have twenty thousand to spend on a depressing religious picture that belonged to them anyway.

Roger had gone bananas about this, absolutely ape. Though I doubt he had ever really looked at the picture, he had an active sense of its having come from our side of the family and in a way not being Roxy's at all. Margeeve described it, but anyway I could imagine Roger's particularly overbearing, vulgar way of fuming, egged on by Jane. "It's mine and Isabel's, what the fuck do I care about French law, it's goddamned mine."

Margeeve had half hoped Chester would be struck quixotically by the wish to ransom the picture, and in time for the Getty show, though she perfectly well knew they couldn't spare the money, and if they could they'd spend it on something more sensible.

"Poor Rox," she said, after one of the many phone calls. "She's hoping for a miracle of Saint Ursula."

"What I can't grasp," said Chester, in a tone that revealed his real irritation, "is why he gets anything at all, when he's the guilty party and he doesn't even pretend otherwise."

"I don't understand that either," Margeeve admitted.

"Maybe you should just bring it home with you," Roger said to me in the phone. "How could they stop you?"

Would it have made a difference if I had? It would have been simple enough back then. Would it have averted tragedy? I was too selfish and too indifferent to the situation to think of interrupting my pleasures, my nice life in France.

"I can't come home right now, I'm helping Mrs. Pace with something, I promised, I, obligation, jobs . . ." I was stammering with horror at the idea of going back to California. "Why don't you come get it?"

"Maybe I will," Roger said. His rage was not at me, of course, but there were overtones in the timbre of his bellowing that resurrected childhood quarrels, between us, Roxy and Judith, and the occasions where our parents had taken sides unfairly with their own kids – though they had been scrupulous, usually, about not falling into that trap.

At his offices, Roger was looking into other issues of international law and art property. Roxy and I would hardly know our dear brother Roger in the company of his lawyer colleagues, cupidity sparkling in their talk. Roger's attitude to the painting was as an object of value belonging to our family, but also, in the company of his colleagues, a case, a test of law and cleverness, a patriotic issue and a personal challenge.

"I would say, first of all, not so fast," he advised Roxy. "The jurisdiction is by no means clear. For one thing, a bequest or a gift is not community property. You were married in California, a community-property state, so in principle there's no net gain to a divorce here, but a California court would be more likely to recognize the moral situation. You hear that French courts, when it comes to property, are perfectly indifferent to unwritten understandings and that sort of thing. I think we ought to explore the idea of Roxy coming home, eventually suing for divorce in California. That would render moot the issue of whether she could bring the painting back here, besides. And it could clarify custody issues, since a California court would probably award custody to the American.

"The only trouble with that is that she intends to go on living in France," Chester pointed out.

"Let Roger talk. She thinks that's what she wants right now," said Margeeve, never for one moment doubting that Roxy would ultimately return to America, like a normal person.

Another short scene at about the same time, which we couldn't then have known about, relating to our painting by an *élève de La Tour:*

The sixteenth Arrondissement. A very large room, bookstrewn, a few pieces of inherited Directoire furniture and a splendid *terre cuite* by Clodion of three muses encircled, one missing an arm.

"Have you seen the La Tour?" asks Stuart Barbee of Phil Jacob. They are in Stuart's apartment. Jacob is the elderly American art expert, longtime resident of Paris, who famously had been the friend of Soutine.

"Absolutely not," says Jacob. "It's much better if it has never been looked at by me."

"How so?"

"The Persand family already asked me to value it and I said I was too busy. Just my looking at it drives the price up. I'm sure they realized that. The mere act of my looking at it brings the piece into the realm of the possibly authentic La Tours."

"At whose behest, may I ask, did you turn them down?" Stuart laughs.

"No, you may not ask." Jacob too laughs. "Besides, you know very well. Have you seen our friend Desmond, by the way?"

Things between Roxy and me continued to be not perfect. The handsome leather Kelly continued in some way to come between us, to her symbolizing my disloyalty on my part.

But Roxy was behaving strangely in general. The day before the first terrible event, she had come home excited, odd, flushed, babbling as if on drugs.

"I went to Chartres," she said. "When I went to the Ecole des Beaux-Arts to see the Della Bella drawings, it was closed, so I just thought, *bon*, I'll go to Chartres instead and see if I can't find her. Otherwise it'll be a week before anyone can look for her again. I'm not even sure when Charlotte put her there. She wouldn't have any idea of how to find Suzanne's house, she'd always lived in Neuilly. She'd just wander in the woods, following a bird or hiding from a fox."

Only then did I realize she was talking about Charlotte's cat. "I don't think foxes eat cats," I assured her.

"A cat could climb a tree, it's true. Oh, Iz, I know I'm not going to die, people don't die from childbirth any more, but I feel I'm going to. How long can a cat live in the wild on her own?"

"Well, indefinitely. A resourceful cat," I said.

"Anyway, I didn't find her. I did find a cat. It was dead, I guess struck by a car. It was wearing a collar. Its eyes were bulging out. But it was a ginger cat, not Siamese."

Now she was saying, "I should have talked to that guy, Magda's husband. I should have tried to calm him down and listened to what he had to say. Maybe he knows something, could think of something. I walked on all the paths near where we park, Charlotte would have parked there too. Now look at my ankles. I guess I have to go to the doctor. Ankle swelling can mean a lot of things. Somebody's lovely ginger cat, wearing a collar, some family missing her.

"It can't be good for a pregnant woman to see death. I felt that. It can't be just an old wives' tale that things affect the baby, because I have such a sense of having conveyed something horrible to him. If it's too horrible or he is too frail, he won't want to be born. I feel it as a sort of heaving drilling sensation here." She touched her side, where the distension of her belly began.

"And now look at my ankles, it's a toxin that can kill you, the baby too, I know it."

"Maybe we should call the doctor," I said. "Or Suzanne."

How strange, I thought, that we had to look to Suzanne for mothering, even while she was engaged in trying to take Roxy's things and in feeding her rival. We both needed a mother, but Roxy especially. I had Mrs. Pace.

TWENTY-ONE

Appetite comes with eating.

– Rabelais

ROXY WAS DISTRAUGHT, BUT I WAS HAPPY. I REALIZED IT IN the course of my yearly soul-searching, which for me isn't New Year's but occupies about five minutes on October twenty-third, my birthday. I came home late from hearing Edgar at a meeting in the fourteenth Arrondissement. It was not cold, not particularly, but it was frosty, and the moon was out, silvering the scene with a rimy mist, a glowing, promising light, and there were as many people in the street as at noon, and it made me happy.

If ever you dare say you are happy. Not that you say yes, this is happiness; it is more than looking back on the previous months, I could see I had changed in a way consistent with a person who was happy, thoughts taken up with events and subjects external to myself. Reviewing my character, I was smugly self-congratulatory about my fidelity to my jobs with Ames Everett, the Randolphs, and others, jobs I no longer needed and wanted to dump as they intruded on the afternoons. Especially I wanted to dump my dog-walking of Scamp. Though I had grown fond of Scamp, and Gennie liked Scamp too – so sometimes I would walk him over to the crèche when I picked her up, thus fulfilling two of my routine duties at once – I felt I could do more important things. I only kept on because I had agreed to, and I suspected I was only wanted so Ames could have this guy in in the afternoon, his gym instructor, for sex.

I was happy. I had sex, mystery, romance, and instructional topics. The probably unhappy dénouement of a preoccupying affair – for how could it end otherwise? – was still I hoped far off. I had challenges: the French language, new reading, little nudges of cultural improvement from Mrs. Pace, even my new fondness for little Gennie. I was surrounded by beauty (Paris) and art, and had begun to experience, for the first time in an authorized way, a life of the mind. However rudimentary my life of the mind, it was definitely more evolved than what had been encouraged (or rather, subtly discouraged) in high school in Santa Barbara, and at the University of Southern California, at least in the film school, at least for women.

You can be anything you want to be, Isabel, people had always said to me. Everyone – Chester, Margeeve, my teachers. They were always saying that, and I always knew it wasn't true. It was a conspiracy of delusion. "A healthy, pretty American girl – you can be anything you want to be." But what did I want to be? I didn't want to be anything. That is, each reasonable possibility, given that I was not to be a ballerina, pianist, doctor, or movie star, was too disgusting: personnel manager? psychologist? What horrors were suggested to me.

Roxy always wanted to be a poet, so it was easy for her. But I had never wanted to confine myself to anything. No role was adequate to a big curiosity I had, not about anything in particular, just a huge sense of curiosity. Not that anyone would have believed me if I had tried to describe it. "You could find out about a lot of things if you'd get up before noon," they would have said.

So I am trying to characterize the magic, satisfaction, and slight vainglory of my mood at the time of my birthday. Things were interesting almost for the first time I could remember. I had suddenly come to feel that California was not interesting, not because there were not books and lovers and jobs, concerts and Frederick's of Hollywood, but someone had to show you where to find and how to consume these cultural advantages. If you didn't know where to look, you could pass your whole life with no sense of what you were missing. I was conscious that if I tried to explain this to Chester and Margeeve, they would turn on me in a fury and point out how they had tried to take me since childhood to improving cultural events and I had preferred to sulk at home and smoke dope.

Not that I was not still a loyal Californian, but I knew that in California, though I might have been able to find, say, this book I was reading by a Turk named Bilge Karasu, at home I would not have read a book by someone named Bilge.

I could now say, in a conversation with someone Edgar knew, provided they spoke English, "Well, I'm reading the Turkish modernist Bilge Karasu, Calvino, the Dutchman Cees Nooteboom." And so I was, in translation, of course. Once or twice I detected a faint lift of the eyebrow of l'oncle Edgar, and cooled it on talking like that.

Once or twice Mrs. Pace said, "Isabel, you have good sense about books, would you say the Nooteboom works?" or some other such question, and we would have an interesting literary discussion. She was not patronizing, she seemed to enjoy it, and she would tell me if my ideas were too wide of the mark.

I sensed that my cultural progress, or at least my improved disposition, was being viewed with great relief by Roxy and communicated in furtive asides to Margeeve and Chester. For instance: I am sitting with my friend Yves and a thousand other people in an auditorium in the Centre Pompidou. From audio speakers mounted high on the four walls come a variety of singing children's voices, burbling brook sounds, a cacophony of long organ chords, like the music of the spheres clashing – catastrophic astral sounds. The voices come now from the left, now from the right, now behind me, as if they were popping out from behind trees. The music is in some ways disturbing and reminds me of the lost cat being there stuck inside the speakers. In other ways it is watery, soothing music. I think of Charlotte's cat, of poor Roxy's ankles, of Edgar, of how unlikely I would have been in Santa Barbara to hear the music of Stockhausen. It seems, this scene, to epitomize my new Paris life.

The music of Stockhausen, who is I suppose German, is replaced by that of an Englishman that is much nicer. Yves's eyes have rolled back in his head with the effort of listening to this new music. Yves resembles all the other members of the audience, slightly rumpled, intense – an audience indistinguishable from such an audience at USC, I suppose. The difference is that this audience includes Isabel Walker, who before would never have consented to be seen with the nerds.

I mention Frederick's of Hollywood for I now wear expensive French underwear, the tartiest I could find. Their bras are fine for me because I am not as big on top as Roxy. I toyed with the idea of a garter belt and stockings (framing the V of the crotch, the French expression for setting off being *mettre en valeur*) but thought that might be going too far. I wore *slips brasiliens*, *curaçaos*, *culottes de soie*, *pointus* . . .

I think some people know subliminally about me and Edgar. Mrs. Pace, Roxy, Ames Everett. They know I'm involved with someone, but no one suspects who. I think Ames finds it disgusting. As I leave him, as I move along on my rounds, late for my job at Olivia Pace's, I imagine him thinking: She's not at all virtuous like Roxeanne. Isabel is a little tart, actually, you can smell it sometimes, smell it on her, mindless sex, despite her airs of intellectual precocity.

I imagine this is how he thinks of me, because he seems to know if I've been in bed with someone, and his manner becomes distant, even though he isn't the least interested in women. He might be Herod, I Salome. He seems both repelled by and drawn to what he perceives as my propensity for vice but is really just an afternoon toss with my secret lover.

Edgar was a focused lover, passionate and funny, though it's hard to say why funny. He made me laugh in bed, and gave me pleasure. Neither by itself is enough to make you fall in love. Even together, there must have been something else. It pleased me that he was known, that people spoke to him. France is a small country, and they all watch the same televised roundtable discussions and read the same three newspapers. I know the newspapers had something to do with my eagerness for his arms on Tuesdays. I liked the way he looked at all the parts of me.

Sometimes I was afraid I was too easily pleased in bed to remain interesting to Edgar, assuming men enjoy the challenge of awakening frosty ice princesses, as I have heard they do. Making me come can't be much of a challenge, I am not frosty. I find I can't pretend not to come, though I could, by putting my mind to other things, keep from actually coming. But that is too great a sacrifice, even with the goal of becoming a great courtesan, if frigidity is what is required of them. Am I impeded by my crude, direct sexuality from interesting a sophisticated nuanced lover?

I tried once to discuss this with Edgar, though he was lacking some crucial vocabulary in English. It did at least make him laugh.

It makes me laugh to think of the God's-eye view of us, me with my legs wrapped around the neck of an elderly man, sweaty hair spread on pillow, or, alternatively, me on my elbows and knees, being taken from behind, bracing myself with my forearms, his body covering mine in such a way that he can caress my clit as well as fuck me, a double stimulation, rather like being fucked by two men at once, say two Turkish soldiers, like the ones in the book by Bilge Karasu, the Turkish modernist recommended by Mrs. Pace, where the dark city is a metaphor of the soul.

That book is about torture and political repression, germane to Edgar's interests. I tried to find it for him in French. In it, nameless torturers nightly choose, arbitrarily, a delightful young man in the street, and set upon him to kill him, and when they are finished, he is nothing but a mound of pulverized flesh. Others come and put sawdust over the bloody mess. The sight of his carcass inspires fear, terror, and submission in the people. Of course, Gorazde must be like that, the images Roxy watched mesmerized on the television news. Roxy watched reality on TV, but refused to read a literary account of torture, saying it was "too horrible."

TWENTY-TWO

> *"Yonder," I said to myself, "some poor wretch may be struggling on in grief, or wrestling with death . . . the certain end which brings neither consolation nor peace."*
>
> *– Benjamin Constant,* Adolphe

IT WAS SOON AFTER MY BIRTHDAY THAT I STAYED ONE Thursday night at Edgar's. He had gone on the last train to Avignon, and I was lazing around his apartment, trying to read a book I found on his nightstand. (Tocqueville. "I am ashamed to say I have never read him," he said. "To confess, I was never much interested in the United States, I just thought them a lost cause. But now that I have become the friend of an American, I find it fascinating. He has an enviable gift for aphorism. And what do you make of this, Isabel? 'In France, simple tastes, orderly manners, domestic affections, and the attachment which men feel to the place of their birth, are looked upon as great guarantees of the tranquillity and happiness of the State. But in America nothing seems to be more prejudicial to society than these virtues.'")

We had been talking about whether American movies should be kept out of France. Edgar thought they should.

"If they're so bad, why do people go see them? If you love peace and order so much," I objected.

"This is an essential difference: You Americans think that

if people want something, it must be allowed. Then you punish yourselves with ugliness for indulging what you actually despise. It is that paradox that will destroy you, or so says the philosopher.

"We French know that people want not what is good but what is easy, and to give in to the lazy side of human nature is not so admirable. We give permission to be saved from our worst nature, or to challenge our better selves, to put it that way."

"France is groaning with luxury," I pointed out. "It is much more luxurious and gourmandish than we are."

"Well, and then we reward ourselves for our good character."

Such discussions made me uneasy. Was I a compendium of all American faults and virtues after all? When Edgar had gone, I got to reading Tocqueville myself. Tocqueville says, "The happy and the powerful do not go into exile." Was this true? Applying it to Roxy and me?

Eventually I fell asleep. When I woke up it was morning. I didn't worry about this, as Roxy doesn't expect me to be home nights if we haven't prearranged that I was needed to babysit, and she doesn't check as to whether I am. I sometimes didn't go down to her apartment to have breakfast until after she had left for the crèche with Gennie, so she didn't always expect to see me in the morning.

Paris is clean and wet in the mornings with the ministrations of street sweepers in bright green uniforms who slosh the flooded gutters with their plastic brooms and make little river dams out of pieces of old carpet. As I came up out of the metro at almost exactly eight-thirty, the fat-bristled machines were just swishing by, the Brasserie Espoir had a few people drinking coffee or taking a *coup de rouge*, a man rushed by pulling on his blue work smock. The streets were otherwise deserted. At nine-thirty suddenly people would materialize behind counters and desks, without ever seeming to have got there. It took me a long time to understand that this is because they work near where they live, there's not so much commuting. This morning, a smell of croissants and coffee, a patch of pinkish gold in the sky, an irresistible temptation to hang out a few minutes at the Brasserie Espoir, just thinking about Paris and love. Love is mystery anyway. What makes *that* woman love *that* weedy little male over there? That fat Frenchman is tenderly handing down the bus step that particular little gray-haired oriental woman with duck feet in her flat beige Mary-Jane shoes – how did they meet? The very peculiarness of love elated me on every bus ride, every walk through the Jardin du Luxembourg, instances on every hand of love's blindness and its charm, and my own part in it.

Happy, I bought a *Figaro* – in Roxy's view too conservative, but easiest to read, and struggled with the news. Edgar occasionally writes an article on Thursdays. I found I had actually met in person two of the people mentioned on pages one and two of *Le Figaro*! I exulted in the realization that if only I could speak French (an impossibility), I could in theory remind two important French people that I was Isabel Walker, that we had met when . . . etc., etc. That is, I would have a basis to speak to a former cabinet minister and an archbishop! I found this thrilling, for back in California, Isabel Walker knew no one at all.

Coffee (*café crème*) finished, I went along to the rue Maître-Albert and operated the front door code, trying to remember if Roxy had seen me wearing these clothes yesterday, by which she would know that I had been out all night, and decided: Who cares, I'll go directly to her place rather than to my own room to change.

Otherwise I might have gone straight up to my room.

Instead I went into her apartment and right to the kitchen. Not seeing her, I might have gone upstairs after all, but I didn't, I looked in the fridge, and put the *Figaro* on the table for her to read when she got home. I might have, might have, I say, to frighten myself all over again with the narrowness and fragility of chance.

It was then I heard a thump, the only word I can think of to describe the heavy soft sound of something not brittle being dropped, or of a person falling, as when as children we would hear one of the others fall out of bed.

I wandered back into the living room simultaneously wondering what the noise was and thinking that Roxy must have taken Gennie to the crèche rather early. Looking back, I can't account for the series of deductive thoughts, or the impulse, or the reasons, that impelled me to persist in having a look. I had no particular reason, but I did just knock on Roxy's bedroom door and, hearing nothing, opened the door, glanced inside, and there saw Roxy lying by the side of her bed in a pool of blood. Just as it is always described, a thick, viscous puddle, with her arm and cheek lying in it.

Hemorrhage, I thought, that filmic phrase now all too explicably real. I rushed in and touched her. Her arm was warm and she stirred, her shadowed lids flickered as if she were pretending. I couldn't remember what 911 was in French, but the fire department was marked on the phone, and I dialed that, gasping, "My *soeur*, *sang*, hurry *vite*," and, the best I could do, "*Venez rapidement, s'il vous plaît.*" I gave them the address, and I had the impression they were coming. I tried to lift Roxy up and drag her on to the bed, but I couldn't, it was as if she had been absorbing the pond of blood she was lying in and was weighed down by it, the way a sponge is heavy. A sticky, blood-soaked pillow, lurid as a horror film, lay on the floor under her, ketchupy, almost fake. I expected to see a fetus or something horrible from inside her.

I went into the bathroom for a towel, and only then, coming back, did I realize that the blood was not coming from her vagina, as I had supposed, but from her wrists. She had big slashes in both her wrists, and on the backs of her hands where she may have started too tentatively, forgetting that you have to open the big veins in the front of your wrists. If you really want to die. The blood oozed out of the openings, horrible flaps, and it bubbled like foam. My own hands, wet with Roxy's blood, left fingerprints on her cheek where I touched her, and on her neck where I tried to feel her pulse. One of her wrists was slashed more badly than the other, and this I wrapped tightly with a green wool scarf from her dresser. There was somewhere to press on the human arm, I knew. Tourniquet, that must be a French word, but I couldn't think how to do one.

Thus did my world, outlook, character, and destiny change, all at one moment.

I had, luckily, the impression or illusion of clear thoughts at that moment, was thinking tourniquet, 911, upper arm. I tied the leg of some pantyhose above her elbow and twisted it tight with a pen, wondering whether, if she died, the bleeding would immediately stop. Did the blood gushing out of her wrists mean she was alive? And I was wondering if the baby would die before Roxy or after, or instead of, and how much time did the baby have? And I was thinking that it was odd that Roxy would want to kill her baby after all this time, and also that this was some kind of bizarre accident. But of course you don't slash both wrists by accident, and the backs of the hands.

Blood has a particular, sour and fruity, smell.

I bound up her second wrist with another stocking. Then I remembered that I hadn't given the fireman the building code, and rushed to the window, and there indeed they were, though I hadn't heard any siren. They were staring up at the windows.

I opened the window and screamed out the code. My screaming voice was like the screech of a panicked animal, nothing to do with my slowed-down, deliberate actions. It seemed only seconds until several firemen were looking down at Roxy. When they noticed her belly they were galvanized. *Enceinte*. They began to shout at each other, and to cart her downstairs, not on a stretcher but lumpily by the arms and legs, her body like a large potato between, her hair raking through the mess of her own blood. Blood had now soaked through the scarves and stockings I had wrapped around the wounds.

They had a stretcher at the bottom of the stairs. Here they laid her and began to put better bandages on, and a mask over her mouth and nose with, I guess, oxygen. Some yellowish water in a bottle on a stand was attached to her. Events collapsed into each other, as in a film being run too fast. Relieved of the need to act, I became sick to my stomach, and my ears rang ominously, so that I had to sit down a few seconds on the curb and put my head between my knees until this passed. The skinny, vociferous Madame Florian, on the first floor, came storming out of the building, complaining, I assume about the blood on the stairs. Some time passed, maybe five minutes. I had got up now and was looking at Roxy. Her eyes were still closed, but I could see that she was breathing. They picked her up and loaded her into their ambulance, more like a van. I tried to climb in too, but they pushed me off and said, *"Pas de place."* Stupefied, I watched as they drove off with my dying sister, I had no idea where.

Now I was enveloped by the scrum of passersby – two men in business suits, a child with a school satchel strapped to his back, a green-suited street worker who made me sit back down. The child stared at the blood drying on my dress and arms. *Le sang*. Then Madame Florian stood me up again and drew me inside, talking volubly, waving her arms. I saw she wanted me to change my dress. So fucking French, worrying about what to wear, I wildly thought. In the foyer drops of blood were smeared where we had stepped. I couldn't think at all. Madame Florian marched me up the stairs, me having no volition. She held my hand like a child's, and Roxy's blood came off on her. Blood is unbelievably smeary and sticky, and it was everywhere. If my hands were wet with the blood of a stranger, I would worry about AIDS, but Madame Florian was above that.

"Hospital, I have to go to the hospital," I was saying as she pushed me in at Roxy's door. I rushed to the kitchen to clean my arms, and put the dress in the sink.

"*Oui, oui,* La Salpêtrière," she said, watching me. I found something to wear from Roxy's closet, and took my purse from the living room. Madame Florian came with me to the taxi rank and to my surprise got in with me, saying to the driver things of which I understood only "*centre des urgences.*" In the cab I could think again, over the fast noisy beating of my heart: Roxy tried to kill herself. Or has killed herself.

All this had occupied perhaps fifteen minutes, and the drive only a few minutes more, past the little zoo where I sometimes took Gennie. At the hospital, Madame Florian waved at the driver to stay and walked with me into the foyer, where she spoke on my behalf. I was the sister of Madame de Persand who had just come in? They replied, and I did not hear any words like *morte* or *mourir*.

Madame Florian shrugged away my *merci*s. "*Restez là,*" she said, "and they will talk to you." They did, and I understood enough: Roxy was receiving a blood transfusion, she was alive, I should wait awhile, but she was probably not in danger. Madame Florian hovered, watched me, and moved slowly off.

So I had time, while watching, to try to understand. Roxy had tried to kill herself! Why had I not noticed that she was in such a desperate or deranged frame of mind? How could I have been so wrapped up in my own affairs not to have noticed something like that? I had had no idea.

I had had no idea. Strangely, I heard my own voice saying that aloud, as I was imagining in my mind that I was saying it to Margeeve and Chester. Toward Roxy I felt, or perhaps it was later I felt this, the fury you do feel toward someone who has put you through a scare, but for myself I felt the deepest chagrin and shame, and a sort of seasick disorientation, as if I would never again know whether I was right or wrong side up. How could I have been so happy and oblivious when Roxy was so miserable? A cry for help. A suicide attempt is a cry for help and I hadn't helped.

These were the sorts of reproach and anguish that floated, drifted through my thoughts to avoid directly focusing on what if she died, which was so unthinkable and was what she had been trying for.

Had she? Had she really meant it or was this just a cry for

help? Did she know I would come in and would find her? Thus did I try to belittle or explain away as histrionics what she had done. Then I would reverse myself. Or maybe she had counted on me not coming in and finding her – I couldn't remember what I had said I was doing today. I didn't even know if she was alive.

Also her baby. I remembered how months ago she had said to Suzanne maybe she shouldn't go through with having the baby. These words now took on a different meaning.

Nurses and orderlies looked at me, relative of *la suicidée*. The nurses wore little veils like nuns. They approached me as they would a relative of someone in mortal anguish, or a sinner, with kindness and tact, with soft voices. Danger and death have the power to transcend language. I understood perfectly what they were telling me; Roxy was being prevented they hoped from going into shock. They were considering a caesarean section if certain changes appeared on the fetal monitor. The child was perfectly well. A baby lives longer than the mother, seizing the good of the last molecules of oxygen in the blood until it has no more hope either.

I went on sitting in the waiting room, festering with fear and anger. A young doctor gave a thumbs-up sign that her condition was improving in some way, and this was like setting up a drip flowing into my system, like the bottle over Roxy's bed, of anger and relief.

At first, I planned to call Chester and Margeeve. I wanted them to tell me what to do. I suppose I wanted support. But something held me back, something besides the fact that it was still the middle of the night in California. What held me back was the thought that Roxy might not want me to tell them. I wouldn't have, if I were her. When she came to herself, she might not want to be treated forever like an unstable histrionic depressive whom people were afraid to leave alone.

But maybe that was how she did want to be treated, so as never to be alone. The famous cry for help.

The only help I'd given had been a little babysitting. My anger and relief drained off, leaving a sort of exhausted vacuum into which, very soon, again flowed the bitterest self-reproach. I kept coming back to: how could I have not noticed that Roxy was in a desperate frame of mind, with signs of weird derangement creeping into her thoughts? I had been too wrapped up in my own life.

I thought of calling Suzanne or Charles-Henri. Is that what Roxy wanted? Or had she really wanted out of life? I didn't know, I didn't know, and huddled miserably in the waiting room, peeking in from time to time through the curtains of her bed, third in the semicircle of curtained beds, where she lay, eyes shut and a little frown line between her eyes as if she disapproved of all the ministrations, or had her thoughts fixed beyond, in the abstracted repose of death.

Now I see I was afraid to call Chester and Margeeve, because they would be angry at me. Sent to help Roxy, Isabel never notices her to be on the point of suicide. Another of Isabel's fuckups. Instead she blah blah blah, all the stuff I was doing – sins of self-indulgence, sins of indifference, sins of insensitivity.

Usually I am not prone to feeling guilty. Years of being the bad little sister had made me defensive instead, and perhaps unreasonably emotionally defiant. Margeeve and Chester were not guilt-producing parents, either (though my brother Roger had always been, in my view, a sanctimonious nag, and more attached to our new sisters than to me). Besides, feeling guilty never seems to make you better.

Why was I sitting surrounded by strange magazines (for instance one news magazine devoted to the business and profession of clairvoyance) in the bare, tidy, direct discomfort of this French hospital feeling guilty and sorry for myself? The inappropriateness of my emotions did nothing to make them go away. And why was I thinking about Roger? Because it was too horrible thinking about Roxy. Because some cork had been pulled in my spirit and all this stuff was leaking in. Frantically I rationalized – Roxy had been concealing her state of mind and lying to me. She had not been crying for help, on the contrary had put up an elaborate front of cheerfulness on all those Sundays with the Persands, and going to her studio as if nothing were wrong. How could I have known she was trying to be like Sylvia Plath? When I had this thought, it was the first time I had a corollary, doubting thought: Is Roxy as good a poet as Sylvia Plath? What did I know?

One is never as happy as one thinks, nor as unhappy as one hopes, to reverse the maxim of La Rochefoucauld. They do say that when people decide on suicide, sometimes they cheer up. All the same, there must have been signs and I hadn't seen them. I loved Roxy so much I wanted to kill her, I was so furious at her. How can I express my shame at these self-absorbed thoughts that kept chasing the thoughts of Roxy lying there unconscious on machines, like one of those women in a coma who are kept alive so they can give birth? Is shame the same as guilt?

TWENTY-THREE

In adversity, the worst misfortune is to have been happy.

– Boethius

IT WAS NOW NOON, AN ODD TIME FOR A HOSPITAL VIGIL. I was conscious of being hungry and then suddenly I thought of Gennie, whom Roxy had taken to the crèche and who must be picked up by three-thirty. On the heels of this thought came a new one, so instantly chilling and horrible that I had to stand and pace, shivering, as if I had a cramp, trying to put down, erode, blight the thought: What if she hadn't taken Gennie to the crèche? What if Gennie's little murdered corpse were somewhere in the apartment? I both couldn't and could take this possibility seriously. Roxy would never hurt Gennie, and yet depressed women did horrible things, and I had seen her willingness to hurt her new child and herself.

I knew I had to go to the rue Maître-Albert at once, if only to control this sickening panic, a panic so intense I prayed somehow to lose consciousness until I could be back there, so as not to have to endure the time in between. I tried to think of faster means of reassurance, like calling the crèche, but I had no idea of the number, or how you called directory assistance, or even what the crèche was called. I took a vow to learn French. I tried to think where I had been in the apartment, was there anywhere Gennie could have been without my seeing? I'd been in the bedroom twice, the kitchen, the living room. Only Gennie's room, where she would logically be.

"Infant!" I cried at the nurse, pointing at my watch. "Crèche."

"You can go," she said in English. "Your sister is doing stable, it's okay."

I looked again into Roxy's curtained cubicle, where she was sleeping or expiring, attached to the bottle and machines.

"*Une heure,*" I said, tapping my watch again. She shrugged. I fled.

There was a taxi rank in front of the hospital but no taxis came. I weighed walking, it was not really far, then a taxi did come. I was conscious of my body's adrenalin, like an odd drug – it was like trying to conduct real life when stoned, keeping an elaborate pretence of sobriety, close to passing out but somehow upright, with smiles for the taxi driver, saying the address in a calm voice. It took four minutes to drive to the rue Maître-Albert, during which I suspended my imagination, my power to evoke a scene of Roxy killing Gennie. Where could I have got this power to evoke horrific images? From the movies of course.

Madame Florian must have been watching or listening for me, for she popped out of her apartment on the first landing as I came up the stairs. "*Comment va-t-elle?*"

"Okay," I said. "Blood transfusion."

She nodded. They can all speak more English than they let on. I let her follow me up the stairs, I must have wanted someone behind me, in case I found – something. I both thought I would and thought I wouldn't, expectation and dread exactly suspended in a kind of hum of fear, my head feeling funny with all the blood drained out of it. I marched right into Gennie's bedroom, which was orderly with no sign of Gennie in it. I looked in the closets all the same. I thought I could smell blood everywhere in the house, a close, yeasty odor.

I then taxied to the crèche. I was rapidly spending all my money on taxis. Gennie was there, in the tidy room with blocks and benches, in a remodeled section of an old school building, where a dozen kids of more or less three, Gennie's age, ran around more or less continually or sat to learn songs and drink juice. Gennie had taught me the songs (*"Ainsi font les marionnettes"*). Now she was sitting on the floor facing another little girl, and they were building something in the corral formed by their fat little legs.

"The *mère* is *malade*," I said. "Hospital. *Hôpital*."

"Tout se passe bien? C'est un garçon ou une fille?" asked the crèche woman, beaming.

I shook my head. *"Malade. Malade,"* I said. We established that I could leave Gennie there until six-thirty. Then I got the 67 bus back to the hospital. On the bus I began to cry. It was totally embarrassing.

At the hospital, Roxy had come to, and now was lying tensely, eyes open, looking at the monitors she was attached to. When I poked my head through the green curtains, she saw me and gave a wan smile. But then she closed her eyes as if she didn't want to talk.

"What were you thinking of?" I heard the anger in my screechy tone, a hiss, not the tone I planned to take but evidently the tone she expected.

"I'm sorry, Iz," she said. "I don't know." She sounded so feeble, so baffled and repentant, that I tried to think of how to soothe her. But she closed her eyes again and seemed to drift away.

A doctor stood behind me (fairly young, somewhat attractive). He motioned me back toward the waiting room and said in English, "She will be all right. Her wounds were finally rather superficial. You could say a symbolic rather than a deeply purposeful act, but that does not mean we take this lightly."

"No," I said.

"She will soon put an infant into the world. We are concerned for the state of her pregnancy. You are her only relative?"

"Well, here in Paris."

"What about the husband?"

"Divorce," I said. "There's just me."

"We will decide how long to keep her, to be sure there is no repetition," said the doctor. "Of course we could introduce psychoactive drugs, but that will be a decision later for a psychiatrist. For the moment such medication is *hors de question* because of the child. Anyway, I myself think any temporary psychosis of pre-eclampsia should disappear when the child is born. When is her due date?"

"Not for another month."

"The husband is French?" the doctor asked. "The father of this child? Shouldn't you call him anyway? He should know the pregnancy could be dangerous."

"She was told that. I think she told him."

"Who is her *gynécologue*? We will call him, but you should call the husband."

"Yes, all right," I said. But I hadn't really decided whether to call Charles-Henri, or Suzanne. I was inclined at that point to wait to see if Roxy had gone crazy or maybe this was just some aberration of pregnancy, some destabilizing rush of birth hormones or panic. Instead I would be beside her. But I was scared to learn this way that there were such reserves of rage and desperation in Roxy, and that these are invisible even to a loved one, and especially to a selfish insensitive sister like me.

Of course I would call Margeeve and Chester, though I wasn't sure what to tell them. I could imagine their reproaches. But I *had* noticed. I had noticed she was getting depressed, I just hadn't understood where she was on that scale.

"You, *mademoiselle*, are you all right?" asked the doctor suddenly, taking my elbow and drawing me over to the seats. "I am going to bring you a coffee and a sandwich," he said. Strangely, I felt tears start into my eyes at this kindness.

"I'm okay," I said. "It's just a shock. *Je suis . . .*" I didn't even know a French word for it.

Roxy said nothing more all afternoon, though I sat by her bed asking her questions or just trying to sound there for her.

At six-thirty I went back to get Gennie and took her home to the apartment, and made her supper from stuff in the fridge. There was a black emptiness to the apartment. I tried to clean up the rug in Roxy's room, and the trail of spots where they had carried her out. Gennie kept saying, "Where's Mama?" She says *Mah-maw*, like a French child. I suppose she is a French child.

At about nine, Suzanne de Persand telephoned for Roxy. I could have, perhaps should have, told her Roxy was in the hospital, but instead I just said she'd gone out. Then I sat looking at the telephone for a long time, calculating the time in California (noon) and tempted by the comfort of talking to our parents. But they were not home. I had forgotten. This was their week for a reunion of hikers in Yosemite. Ben, the student that lives with them, answered instead.

"No," I said, "it's not about anything special."

In the end, I told the one person I thought Roxy would most want to know, Charles-Henri. Of course he was aghast, distressed, instantly at my disposal. "*Mon Dieu*, she isn't herself, she was also very emotional during pregnancy with Geneviève. Where is she, I must see her. Would that be good, or would it be worse for her?"

Good, I thought. I hoped his heart would melt when he saw her, and I hoped that was what Roxy wanted. He arrived at the hospital promptly, solicitous and concerned, charming in turtle-neck sweater and jeans, painterly tousled hair. I saw why Roxy loved him.

Did Roxy love him? Or was it, I used to ask myself, something else more territorial, the jealousy of a lioness turned inward on herself? Roxy had never liked to lose things, she would rage, would make us all quail when she mislaid her purse or gym clothes. To see her lying wanly in the Hôpital de la Salpêtrière was not enough to bring him back to her, but I think seeing him reassured Roxy that he was in her life all the same.

As he was leaving, Charles-Henri spoke to me in the hall. His face was drawn and concerned. He sighed. "She telephoned, you know, but I didn't think she'd do it, any more than she has before. I misjudged, I might have prevented this. Of course, it's not going to change anything. You make sure Roxeanne understands that." Under his sweetness, perfect hardness, the absolute security of men that their desires have the right of way. Only later did it register, as Charles-Henri and the doctor both seemed to understand, that if she telephoned him, she must have expected him to find her before she died. A symbolic gesture.

Roxy stayed in the hospital over the weekend, being given hot soup that had potassium and other substances in it. She was morose, or rather pensive, and seemed as shocked as I, or professed to be shocked, by what she had done. "I was just overwhelmed with a crushing sense of futility," she explained. "It wasn't even me so much, it was the world." In a sane tone of wonderment.

I was wary. You hear that seriously suicidal people dissemble. They want to get away to try it again, and they pretend to be well.

"The world, all that horror."

"But why that morning, Roxy?"

"I don't know," she said, her voice trembling with fear, at capricious moods from some unknown place in the personality that could carry you away. "It was a morning like any other. I'd talked to Maître Bertram the night before, and the divorce was on my mind, I'd been thinking how can I go through with all that, and then when I woke up in the morning, it wasn't a frenzy or anything, it was a cold decision that seemed very logical at the time, that I didn't need to go through with it."

She appeared to feel this would reassure me, but of course what I thought was, if she could be seized by a thought like that once, she could again, I'd have to stay with her all the time, she'd have to have psychiatrists, and could she be trusted not to hurt Gennie or the new baby?

Sensing my fright, Roxy tried to reassure me. "I'm fine, really, Iz, I'm fine now."

Though she apologized, at no time did she say, "That was silly, I would never do it again," and in fact she wouldn't discuss it after this one conversation. Once she even said, in a dreamy, mad tone, "I love being pregnant," stroking her by now huge half-round of a belly. "It's funny to have your body change shape this way, it makes you feel like a genie or a shape-shifter." It was weird to hear her say this, as if nothing had happened at all. Yet there remained something strange behind her eyes.

Perhaps she only wanted to be in the hospital, to be taken care of like this, for now she seemed contented. If it weren't for the little bandages on her wrists, smaller each time they were changed, you would not imagine suicide or psychiatric crisis. Over the next two days, I almost began to doubt what had happened, and she began to deny it – that is, to be in denial, pretending it hadn't exactly happened, or had been a kind of accident, as if she had slipped on a rug.

She made me promise not to tell the Persands, and she must have made Charles-Henri promise that too, for they never spoke of it. I think she imagined I would have already called our parents, but I had not. Maybe she was crying out that she just couldn't go through with the divorce-related things right now, and maybe I should have alerted the Persands that the divorce arrangements were too much for her. Maybe they could call them off for a while. I could put the matter in some urgent way – Roxy is in the hospital, ill with stress, I don't think she is strong enough for a court process.

Eventually I decided coldheartedly on the Sylvia Plath explanation. What I didn't fully understand was how much she minded the sale of the painting of Saint Ursula, for it symbolized how she had lost her gamble for adventure in life: she was going out of the marriage with less than she came in with; she was a loser.

TWENTY-FOUR

Suicide is less an act than a tale of the soul.
– *M. Jouhandeau,* Chroniques maritales

THE HOSPITAL BEGAN TO TALK ABOUT LETTING HER GO HOME on Tuesday, but they made me understand they were concerned about two issues, her ongoing psychiatric care and the high-risk pregnancy. In the case of her mental state, the doctors decided it was what they called a "crisis reaction" and would not likely recur. Apparently there are people who have a suicidal impulse once in their lives, when something happens they cannot stand. If they are standing on a bridge just then, they'll likely succeed in killing themselves, but if they have no real means to do it, the impulse passes, and when their lives improve, they soldier on like everybody else. This is why suicide hot lines and so forth are for people with a one-time impulse, while nothing much can be done for the chronically depressed who long for death and save up pills. Or so the handsome doctor explained to me.

It would suffice for Roxy, they thought, to get her through the divorce and the remaining month of her pregnancy, which looked to be still threatened with pre-eclampsia which could even in part explain her behavior. With her physiology back to normal, the doctor predicted, and some counseling, someone to talk to – she must be lonesome, for she was an *étrangère*, after all, though her French was, he allowed, excellent – all would be well.

But when I saw they were going to release her, I was frightened anew. I would tell Edgar, I decided, and Mrs. Pace, either of whom might have a view about what I'd better do. Margeeve and Chester would be gone on their trip another week. Meantime I took Roxy some books from Mrs. Pace's, and coped with Gennie over the weekend.

In the end, I told Mrs. Pace but not Edgar. Some family pride prevented me, some wish to protect Roxy from the faint possibility he would tell the rest of the Persands, or the fear that he, like my parents, would think I had been negligent about noticing Roxy's state of mind. I called him to tell him I couldn't meet him on Tuesday, but I just said Roxy was ill.

"Now that does astonish me," Mrs. Pace said, when I had told her the story. "Roxeanne of all people, so resolutely adjusted and Francophile."

"I know."

"She has been acting a little off balance. But it was obviously something she heard at the lawyer's that threw her."

"The *coup de grâce*," I said, trying a French phrase.

"The last straw, you mean," she said. "It is an entirely different thing. The *coup de grâce* – pronounce the *c* in *grace*, by the way – is not the same thing as the last straw, Isabel. Look it up. But what was it she found out from the lawyer?"

"Nothing new. I talked to her when she got home. They talked about the sale of Saint Ursula, her beloved painting. It has to be sold because it turns out to be worth something, and she can't afford to pay Charles-Henri his half of its value."

"She felt ready to die of bitterness." Her sympathetic tone implied she herself had often been at the brink of suicide for reasons of rage and chagrin. Her view now was that I should stick close to Roxy until she delivered the baby, when her body and psychology would return to normal, and meantime, she, Olivia, would pitch in with invitations and distractions.

On Tuesday night Roxy came home from the hospital. She lay on the sofa, and we watched *L'Opinion* on Canal Sept, just a head shot of Edgar himself for twenty minutes with the interviewer off camera, him telling about adventures in Africa and Mindanao, and his period under Giscard d'Estaing as a subminister of some fiscal department. I understood little of this, but I did understand what he was saying about Bosnia, since I had heard those views numerous times. It crossed my mind to wonder whether he would have had to cancel our Tuesday if I had not, for this program, or whether it was on tape.

"You have to hand it to Uncle Edgar," Roxy said. "The rest of the Persands may be frivolous and lazy, but he really isn't."

"He's not a Persand, he's a Cosset," I pointed out, realizing I should not appear to have thought about it.

"True, but they get their laziness and frivolity from Suzanne, and she is his sister. You tend to forget he has actually been a statesman. Unlike the rest of them he's actually had a public career."

But of course her mind wasn't really on Edgar, or on me. She was dreamily holding Gennie on her knees with her cheek against the child's hair.

"I love being pregnant again," she said. "Iz, put your hand on my belly. I think the new little one needs to know other people want him. Charles-Henri used to do that, pat my belly and speak to Gennie, but now no one speaks to this little one."

This seemed so off the wall, I fell into the mood I had been trying to stave off, of intensifying panic, and not knowing what to do, and wanting to be in the arms of the elderly gentleman I was watching on the TV, and mad at Roxy for being crazy – for grabbing all the craziness just now so that I had to be with her and be stuck with her secret and do the worrying about what would become of her, and of me. I put my hand on her belly, which felt like an overinflated basketball, hard and inorganic. I couldn't feel a baby underneath but spoke to it anyhow, saying, "Not too much longer, little friend, better enjoy it where you are."

Visible signs of the coming holiday season had already

replaced the back-to-school mood of early autumn. Gennie had a little caped coat and knitted hood, like the children in a book I'd had when I was little. The gray light and the gray stones of the Paris buildings gave a monochromatic gloom to the streets, but there was a corollary gaiety to the interiors, the lavish gilt and mirrors of the *pâtisseries*, the array of cakes and *bon-bons*, glazed chestnuts, and chestnuts roasting in braziers at street corners, plucked off the coals by subdued men with asbestos bare fingers. All humanity wore thick coats. I continued to be troubled by my not suffering when Roxy was.

What made me feel most guilty was not the Capulet-Montague feature of my affair with Uncle Edgar, which was continuing even as relations with the Persands worsened (though our ostensible affection remains), nor was it sex itself. For some reason I felt especially guilty about the pleasure and interest I took in the restaurants we went to. This fascination grew in a way I felt could not be quite good, was perhaps a perversion, one I sensed Edgar and I encouraged in each other, a shared secret. Edgar first sensed it in me – an interest beyond the normal – when he realized I had read up on a certain restaurant and knew what the chef's specialties were. This might of course be a good courtesan's normal preparation, finding out what her lover likes and so on, but since he himself is interested in restaurants (but does not always indulge himself, in food), he was not unhappy to patronize ever new, distant and vaunted eating places, now with the excuse of pleasing me. This pursuit also had the merit of getting us out of the center of Paris and farther from the likelihood of him being seen.

Californians are interested in restaurants too, nothing odd about that. Why is it I feel within myself that my interest has exceeded what is quite nice? For instance, I found myself spending 180 hard-earned francs on a new guide to Paris restaurants when Roxy already had *Gault et Millau* and the *Guide Michelin* (last year's) and I should have earmarked the money for relief for Sarajevo. No, there was nothing generically strange about a Californian liking restaurants, but I knew it would be easy for me to go over the top. Just as in bed, we extend the things we do, we go a little further, without discussion, to prolong or repeat the moment of pleasure.

The scar on Roxy's left wrist was visible like a vivid bracelet or mark left by a torturer; that on the right was a pale white line. Both were covered by the long sleeves she kept pulled down. No one else would see them or know, but for me these traces were a continual reproach. I watched her, I stayed home much more now. We watched French television, which is as stupid as American television, *is* in fact American television, most of it, B cop shows and old bad movies.

After a while her bitterness and apathy seemed to lighten. She said it was her biology, the prospect of birth taking her over, with waves of warm nest-building hormones, placid as a cow. "My problems will all come back, I suppose," she said, "but now I can't be bothered to worry. It's strange that I can work now. Usually a little anxiety makes you work better, it's usually necessary, even, but too much wipes you out."

She said she was working well, and she sold a poem to some Midwestern literary magazine, I think Michigan, or Ohio. I have to admit that with Roxy's spirits seeming to lift, or not to descend further, mine sagged a little more, as they had done ever since her suicide attempt. It began to be cold in Paris, and I wasn't used to cold. If it were California I'd be skiing, but this was day after day of rain and darkness, swallowing up the day earlier every afternoon, dark again by four, still dark at eight in the morning, as if you were north of the Arctic Circle. The lofty statues in the Place de la Concorde now loomed like black, menacing shapes wet with the constant rain. You had to remember to wear shoes and coats you didn't mind getting wet. There was a day of beauty in late November when it snowed. I was coming across the Place de la Concorde on the 24 bus, at dusk just when the lanterns went on, and flakes of snow drifted down in this pinkish gray half-light, and it was so beautiful, tears sprang to my eyes. Then I realized they weren't tears for beauty, they were just tears. It was I who was sad, just under the surface, where the sight of something fragile like a snowflake seemed unbearably to predict its loss.

And there was the business of the *bon coup*. It wasn't something that would have bothered me ordinarily. I'm inured to what they think of Americans. Yves introduced me to a friend who smiled in a friendly way and said to Yves, *"Elle, le bon coup américain?"* The phrase stuck in my mind. Maybe it was meant as a compliment, but I didn't take it as a compliment, too puritan for that. I hardly needed a dictionary, the meaning is more or less the same in all languages, something like "the great American piece of ass."

In my low mood I would think of the futility of my life as factotum, girl Friday – dog walker and half-time girlfriend ("mistress") and *bon coup*. I hated the passivity of this life, that I wasn't doing anything about the future. All of Edgar's public harangues about responsibility having finally got my attention, I decided to take a cooking class, and to volunteer for some cause.

Roxy had figured out something to do with Bosnia. She threw herself into organizing, with some other American and some French women, a drive to send Tampax and lipstick to the women of Sarajevo. "Sometimes it's little essentials that really make it possible to survive," she said. "I was getting into such a state of solipsistic misery I was forgetting the people in the world with real problems." In these words I heard the voice of Margeeve, who had said them verbatim over and over in our growing-up years. Roxy composed placards and leaflets, saw to the printing, and joined the corps of women who left them in bookstores and on walls. She spent hours on the phone talking to journalists and getting the announcement put in the papers. I suppose I thought it was slightly ridiculous at first, lipstick and tampons for a place where a mortar might kill you when you went out to pick them up. Eventually I saw that you'd get your period, bombs or not – if you were lucky and got your period. I suggested they send contraceptives instead, but they decided that was too controversial. The idea of the drive, finally, was that the women of France would be asked to buy extra quantities of these essential items and leave them at drop-off points in the streets and pharmacies; then Roxy and benefactor with trucks would come and pick them up.

In the end, I spent two hundred and fifty francs on Tampax and left it at Monoprix. Tons of lipstick to relieve suffering were collected. The rest of my efforts were similarly lowly, like helping to put up chairs at Edgar's meetings, if I got there early enough, in the distant city halls of Ivry or Villemoisson-sur-Orge.

I had various identities when Edgar presented me. At meetings, beforehand, in a city hall or church, "*mon assistante*, Mademoiselle Walker." To someone who knew his family, "You know Mademoiselle Walker? Charles-Henri's sister-in-law?" or "My nephew's sister-in-law, from Santa Barbara, California." I began to feel discontented with these identities, though I suppose I should have been pleased that he did not hide me. What was Mademoiselle Walker doing, really?

His meeting nights were not nights we would make love. He was usually caught up afterward with media people or concerned citizens or cronies who were like-minded, and he would be preoccupied in any case. I would go home alone, or hang around on the fringe to hear him say, "I object to the hypocrisy of our politicians, madame, trying to claim humanitarian heroism with a few ground troops while privately holding that nothing must affect our relations with Germany or the Treaty of Maastricht. In any case, no one talks of the morality of the situation. Not in this country – all is cynicism disguised as pragmatism." Not in my country, either, I guess.

Once Edgar came to Suzanne's on Sunday. As usual I was assigned the duty of walking with the various children, today Frédéric's children as well as Gennie and those of Antoine. Before lunch Edgar sat in the library talking to Suzanne. I could hear their companionable laughter as I got Gennie into her snow boots while the various wives supervised the lunch. No intimate glances passed between us at lunch.

Then, to the table, he said, "I have two extra opera tickets for Tuesday. Poupette is not coming up. What about you, Suzanne? Roxeanne?"

(I knew by now that Edgar's wife was named Amélie but was called Poupette and preferred staying in the country.)

Suzanne said, "No, no, *merci*, I have such a week."

"The American girls, then. Roxeanne and Isabel." Here he did turn and smile at me, a smile so perfect and avuncular I could almost not remember this was the man who so expertly caressed *la foufounette*.

"I'll have to sit at the end of a row, though, no one can get by me." Roxy laughed, patting her belly.

It crossed my mind to wonder how I would have felt if it had been Roxy and Suzanne to go with Edgar to the opera on Tuesday, his and my consecrated night. When I asked him about that later, regretting the jealous tone that crept into my voice, he said Suzanne was well known to hate opera.

I had never been to an opera, though Roxy had, in Paris. They had operas in California, in Los Angeles at the Dorothy Chandler Pavilion, I had just never been taken to one. This was called *Maria Stuarda*, about Mary, Queen of Scots, a great heroine for the French, and was held at the Bastille, which is not the building the populace attacked at the time of the Revolution, since they did succeed in tearing that down; this is a sort of whale-shaped glass modern structure, a huge auditorium for operas and dance.

It was thrilling. Edgar and the other men there wore *le smoking*. It was not the first time I had seen a group of men in evening dress. Proms in high school, for instance; but there the rented suits had looked sort of inappropriately old on boys you saw every day in jeans, their tuxes making them very handsome (I thought at the time) but skinny and sort of geeky too. I was unprepared for the grandeur of grown-up men in evening clothes – jowls, odor of cigar, their portliness, their burliness expressive of their powers, their very presence, their solemn dressed-up attendance at a musical occasion, expressive of their regard for culture and their considerable disposable wealth. Edgar named people we saw: there a socialist presidential candidate, there the current minister of culture, and his predecessor, there a famous dress designer, there the director of the Bastille. It was aphrodisiac to me. Some people (Roxy) are excited by history. For me it was this immediacy of power, this richness not of money but of significance, of opulent testimony to politics. My spine warmed along its length, the music made my throat catch. I even loved the consorts of the famous men, women trim in their pouffy Lacroix lamé dresses, their hair a uniform blonde. I am dark, dark. I thought the most beautiful woman there was Roxy rosy and radiant in a gray silk Mother Hubbard, the only thing she had big enough to wear over her belly. Every man looked at her, I thought envying the man that had got her like that. Perhaps if they didn't know, they thought it was Edgar. She leaned on his arm on the steps.

"*Mes nièces américaines,*" he said to Monsieur le Directeur du Cabinet of the Ministry of Culture. "Madame de Persand, Mademoiselle Walker."

"*Américaines, bravo,*" said le Directeur to us. "*Mes homages, madame,*" making to kiss Roxy's hand. She looked happy.

If I let myself really think about Roxy, my stomach would still roil with fear at how close she had come, at how she had wanted death, at how this meant I could never again understand her. Irremediable strangeness had come down between Roxy and me, or rather between me and every other human being, for I saw I couldn't know them, nor they me, and we were all alone, just as Jean-Paul Sartre seemed to be saying in a book of his I was struggling to read, *La Nausée*, about a man for whom thinking about anything makes him sick.

Edgar shook his head and said, "Read Voltaire, my child, or the maxims of La Rochefoucauld."

Between the acts something really amazing happened, which would not seem to have any significance except to me, an ordinary civil transaction, a conversation, polite and urbane. I mean – the Directeur of the Ministry of Culture talked to me!

"The *mise en scéne* reminds one of Piranesi," Roxy said. Edgar was saying that Marie, Queen of Scots, was surely one of the silliest women in history, he hoped not because of her sojourn in France.

"Are you surprised to find the surtitles in English as well as in French, mademoiselle?" asked the Directeur of me. A well-built, youngish, balding man with a Frenchman's long eyelashes. "What the previous Ministre de la Culture must think of that I cannot imagine," he went on, lowering his voice and indicating a man standing near. "He is the great architect of linguistic purity in France, the great crusader against English."

"He has an expression of pain," I agreed, for the former culture minister had assumed at that instant a look as if he had sat on a pin.

"You must visit the old Palais Garnier while you are here," my minister said. "We still all love it the best. Still in use for dance, if you care for dance, and soon to be a home to opera again."

This conversation was remarkable in at least three ways. I felt a flush rise from the neckline of my rather low dress, of surprise, momentary insecurity, and pleasure. One, it meant I had given responses in French convincing enough to make him suppose I could be talked to. Two, Edgar's friends did not usually speak, beyond *bonjour, mademoiselle*, to someone so young and assistant-like, meaning I must appear more grown-up, more equal tonight. Three, it was supposed I would have an opinion on the opera, therefore I must be wearing a plausible expression of sentience. I did have an opinion, though I did not deliver it. (I loved, loved, loved the opera.) It was enough to be included in the conversation without any airs of remarkable condescension from Monsieur le Directeur. This was an important psychological moment for me, maybe the first in which I knew I would get along in life. The Directeur went on saying things of this idle sort, an attentive man to a woman, an under-minister of the government of France, in the *entracte*, at the Opera, in Paris, to Isabel Walker of Santa Barbara – to me!

As we took our seats again, Edgar touched my elbow with an air of practiced possession. I am sure it was involuntary, this proprietary gesture, this brief impulse to claim and steer me, and he quickly withdrew his hand. Probably no one noticed. Did Roxy notice? I didn't think so. In her happiness – an evening at the opera, ministers, men, enjoying the perquisites of being a de Persand – she had never looked so radiant. You felt that her infant must be benefiting in the womb from some improved condition of her blood, and even, if they can really hear in utero, from the music of Donizetti, confirming human genius and the exuberant promise of life.

TWENTY-FIVE

One is never as unhappy as one thinks, nor as happy as one hopes.

– La Rochefoucauld

THOUGH I WAS HAPPY THAT NIGHT, MY LOW SPIRITS PERsisted. I had begun to mind that this was the longest I had ever been away from my family, perhaps I was actually missing them – hence this sadness and emptiness I was feeling more and more, filled only by Edgar – sex and dinner, the eternal compact by which he offered counsel and reassuring encouragement, he stroking my hair, I parting my legs.

Charles-Henri was coming now on Saturdays to pick up Gennie. He took her to the country, then would deliver her on Sunday to Chartres, where we would pick her up at lunch. Roxy managed never to see him on either day. I would get Gennie ready on Saturdays, he would be gone by the time we got to Chartres. Roxy had seen him only three times since the day he left: when he accidentally came to Sunday lunch on my first day at Chartres, and at the first meeting with the lawyer, and in the hospital. They did speak on the telephone, but in French, things to do with Gennie's schedule. I could always tell by the tight bitterness of Roxy's voice, a slight whine in it, that it was he.

I suppose I'll have a baby someday, but for now it seems like a good way to bring down some man's hate on you. You have done something to him, deprived him of some youthful happiness and autonomy. And of course he has done the same to you. I have noticed no one ever wants to give their babies back, but they aren't so happy afterward, either, like Roxy.

I talked to Charles-Henri several times after our meeting in the Vues de Notre Dame, and he was pleasant, but distant. The drama of his life lay elsewhere for him now, you could tell, with Magda Tellman and his painting. He didn't seem to care about details of the settlement, was leaving it all to Antoine and Maître Doisneau. I suppose that blithe spirits and an indifference to material reality are an irritation in a husband, but they were what was nice about Charles-Henri, and though I officially hated him for being so cruel to Roxy, I liked him actually, and half hoped he would be happy.

The French lawyers did not consider Stuart Barbee's valuation of Saint Ursula reliable, and had agreed that each side should have an independent appraisal of Roxy and Charles-Henri's property. I gathered that if the two appraisals did not agree, the court would look at them, but if they did, the divorce would go ahead with the understanding that the finances had been worked out.

The French appraisers came in mid-November, Antoine de Persand with them. Roxy refused to be there, so I had to let them in and hear their murmurs without understanding much of what they said. Antoine was friendly but didn't translate what the experts were saying. To me, he said, "Isabel, *ça va*? This is a nasty business, isn't it?"

"*Très jolie, superbe,*" said a mustached man of the chest of drawers. This was good, because if he put a high value on it, it could offset the painting; Roxy could just give up the Persand chest and keep the Walker painting. They looked at Roxy's dishes, at the table and ordinary household objects like the television and rugs, including Roxy's bedroom rug where I could discern, though they probably could not, the rusty tinges of rinsed-away blood. Several times they returned to the chest, pulled out the drawers, hunted for a signature.

"*Ce n'est pas signée,*" remarked one. I guessed that was

bad, meant less valuable than if it had been.

Another man altogether came, from the Louvre, to look at the picture, and shook his head. "*Ecole de La Tour*. It is not of interest to us." Hearing him say this, I felt aggrieved in spite of myself, at this denigration of our saint, and because this meant the sale could go ahead at auction. The Louvre did not want it, and so would not impede an export license, opening the way for buyers outside of France – Japanese, for instance, or American.

It was here, on the day the Louvre man came, that I have to admit I spoke up to Antoine, words just blaring out, surprising even me. "It's so tacky, Charles-Henri taking Roxy's picture. She doesn't want anything of his, she wouldn't take something from him that he'd had since he was little."

Antoine was startled, and I judged (with satisfaction) annoyed or stung, and surprised. The Louvre man, a Monsieur Desmond, looked hurriedly away, staring at the picture with the rapt visual attention of a deaf person. I kept on.

"It's not bad enough that he should dump her when she's pregnant, he takes her property too. Also, you would think he would want his children to have the furniture and picture someday, not some stranger buying them. He's just being a terrible shit, or he's getting bad advice."

"Charles-Henri has left this up to me," Antoine said, slowly.

"You, then, are being a terrible shit," I said.

I guess I was as surprised as Antoine that, not counting what Roxy and Charles-Henri might have said to each other, the first words of bitterness between our two families should have come from me, and after all this time. I know it sounds Californian if I say I believed we ought to let them know how we felt. How I felt. Until now they could even have thought we did not mind. Antoine was shamed into silence, I guess.

Nevertheless, the painting, the bureau, the dining-room table and some engravings were taken off to Drouot, the auction house, by a *commissaire-priseur*. Now that there was no chance of Roxy keeping her picture, it was necessary to switch to hoping that everything would sell as well as possible so that there would be as much money as possible to split. Meanwhile Roger had had an idea that might perhaps work: He and I were to sue Roxy and Charles-Henri, who because they were not yet divorced could be sued as a couple, thus encumbering the picture with legal difficulties and enjoining a sale. Roxy was enthusiastic about this idea. It would be a weird situation, me living companionably with Roxy while suing her, and her egging it on.

In the meantime, Drouot would be putting Saint Ursula in a catalogue, and so on, to be sold with other pictures of its genre, when enough had been collected, at a date as yet unscheduled. With an agreement in place about splitting the proceeds of an auction, the divorce could proceed without waiting for the sale.

"Don't sell these little bits of faience," the *commissaire-priseur* had told Roxy, who was there when they came. "You won't get much for them, and they're awfully pretty," he said. "You'd do better to keep them."

"Tell that to my husband," Roxy sniffed.

Drouot, the auction place, feeling that Saint Ursula would slot nicely into a sale already scheduled of northern French painting, which was to take place within the month, decided to prepare a brochure to be sent to those who had already received the finished catalogue. They expected Saint Ursula to sell well, and had stipulated a reserve of eighty thousand dollars. At that figure, Roxy knew she would never be able to buy out Charles-Henri. Roxy called Margeeve and Chester and pleaded with them for a loan of forty thousand, but of course they were just floored.

It was horrible, the gap left by the absent furniture when it was gone, the reproachful bareness, the articulate void telling of failure. I continued to sting and seethe as much or more than Roxy about the total injustice of them taking Saint Ursula. Her enhanced value introduced a new element of cupidity and greed into the normal rancor of divorce. This I could mention to Edgar, though I still had not told him about Roxy slitting her wrists.

"Women are too protected from the consequences of their actions," he said. "It always shocks them when there are consequences." Is this true? He meant, Roxy must have known that by taking a piece of property off to France, she was subjecting it to French law. But this doesn't address the total wickedness of the Persands ignoring that it was in our family, that it belongs to more people than just Roxy, that it means a lot to us and nothing to them, and so on. I said all this. He shrugged. There is a Gallic shrug. There is a French attitude to laws about property.

"You make a moral argument about Bosnia but deny the force of a moral argument in the family."

"What I say about Bosnia is a pragmatic argument from history," he said. "We are not going to quarrel, you and I, *chérie*, about Roxeanne's *canapé* and an ugly saint."

"You'll talk about sex but not about money," I objected.

"Of course – I am French," he said. "You Americans are always getting everything backward."

Edgar would attend a meeting every couple of weeks or so, sometimes more often, gatherings held usually in a city hall or church hall, indistinguishable from the same beige, metal-chaired institutions in America. There were often roundtable discussions, four or five men from the area, Edgar, sometimes a woman, discussing issues of politics and public policy. Of course I didn't understand most of what was said, but the themes began to clarify themselves. These were: the lessons of history, and the role of religious conviction. I gradually came to understand that Edgar was religious, at least officially, believed in God and the Catholic religion, in a not preoccupied but nonetheless sincere way.

At first I was shocked by this. In California, you wouldn't go out with anyone openly religious, because someone who talks about God automatically comes across as a hypocrite. But there was also the French hypocrisy, if that is the word – or inconsistency is a better one – in believing in a religion and conducting this rather unconcerned adultery. I brought up this issue in a general way with Mrs. Pace, without mentioning Edgar and me.

"Well, their piety is more evolved," said Mrs. Pace. "In America we have only two forms, as Matthew Arnold said: the bitter and the smug. In France, it appears, there is a third type, the worldly."

"The genuine?" I wondered.

"I suppose they are all genuine. Bitterness is always genuine. And there is nothing so fervently genuine as the sense of being right. Smugness, *autrement dit*. Why not worldly but genuine?"

(Edgar himself, on this subject, quoted Molière:

God, it is true, doth some delights condemn,
But 'tis not hard to come to terms with Him.)

My soul, just now, was gripped with these very afflictions of bitterness and a sense of being right. I had never felt more American. I had a fight with Yves about it. He had a strange view of American history. He saw it as all controlled by J. Edgar Hoover. "He had something on everyone in Washington, and they had to ask him if it was all right for Kennedy to run," he explained. "He also picked Eisenhower. He was a homosexual, so he was paranoid. He was scared of Bobby Kennedy, though, so he had him executed.

"There are people here who want America to control France," he said. "They want us to watch cartoons and they want to paint Disney things all over, and we're all supposed to drink Coca."

"No one makes you, you just do," I objected. "I wouldn't watch cartoons myself, how come you do?"

"You have an immunity to it, from growing up on it. Here it just sweeps through, like measles through the Amazon." How weird to be culturally menaced by a Disney movie, I thought; I can think of more invidious things than that.

"The French are just cultural pushovers," I said.

"Americans smile too much," he said. "You smile too much." After that I tried to cut down on smiles.

Early in December, about two weeks before Roxy's due date, which was also the scheduled date of the Drouot sale, an irony that Roxy would call attention to, we got a call from Margeeve and Chester. They were making reservations and would be here in a week. Would we arrange a hotel and let them know the address, nothing too dumpy, but not too expensive either; Margeeve suggested the Deux Continents, remembered from a trip years ago.

Our emotions were mixed, Roxy's and mine. Mine at least were mixed with pleasure at the prospect of seeing them (of them seeing me, with my new French phrases, nail polish, demure ballerina hairdo). Are we alone among American daughters in feeling fond of our parents? From my reading, I gather it to be the case. I felt pleasure and dread. I dreaded what they would say when they found out about Roxy's illness (for this is how I had come to think of it), I dreaded their inevitable outrage at her situation, and the hell they would raise about losing the painting. I dreaded an escalation of emotions and conflict. I dreaded what they would say to me. I felt pleasure and dread; Roxy claimed to feel nothing but dread, mostly because of Roger.

They had added that Roger was coming, with Jane, removing any possibility that they saw this trip as a friendly, supportive visit. They were coming to make war, or at least legal trouble, or, as they probably saw it, justice. They would not leave their child to the vagaries of foreign law, or the antique institutions of male privilege.

"Does Gennie have her own passport? An American one, I mean?" Margeeve asked. "She should have that." I considered this an ominous question. Perhaps they planned to kidnap Gennie?

Roxy and I had no need to say anything to each other, though I was aware of certain unsaid misapprehensions I let stand. For instance, I hadn't told Roxy that I hadn't told Margeeve and Chester about her suicide attempt. Perhaps she would be glad, but perhaps she wanted them to know, wanted someone in charge to know.

I don't like to ask favors from people – it never turns out, and they always hate you afterward – but I had always felt Suzanne de Persand's goodwill, and with Roxy's new depression and the ominous arrival of Roger, I could see that the time had come to talk to her. I thought she might help. She liked me well enough. To Roxy her attitude was more complicated, ex-wife of her favourite son, foreigner, etc., even though, given all this, she had been resolutely supportive, no doubt with the aim above all of keeping in touch with Gennie and the new baby no matter what happened.

To me she had been genuinely friendly, and seemed to feel the difficulties of my situation, coming in on this family turmoil, not speaking French, no prospects in life, etc. Like Mrs. Pace she seemed to feel an urge to polish me up, though where Mrs. Pace would directly criticize my clothes or tell me my gloves were dirty, Suzanne employed the powers of praise and encouragement. ("Your hands are so pretty when you wear nail polish, Isabel," or "How amazingly long your legs are in high-heeled shoes, Isabel.") Yes, I had a pair of gloves now, and a pair of fuck-me shoes. On the day I went to see Suzanne, I was wearing all this gear, which I had worn to lunch with Mrs. Pace at a restaurant we had gone to (Pierre Traiteur, where I let her think I'd never been before. I'd ordered *oeufs à la neige*. Mrs. Pace said, "I think you'll find they pronounce it *eugh à la neige*, Isabel.")

After lunch I picked up Gennie and took her to the Avenue Wagram for her weekly visit to her grandmother. This was my chance to explain to Suzanne about Roxy's fragility. I told Suzanne that Roxy was taking the sale of the picture very hard, talked about how it was bad for her condition, and said that I thought the sale should be delayed. Or could I myself undertake a promise to pay for it, over a period of years? Or maybe the two families should get together when Margeeve and Chester got here (I did not mention Roger) and talk the whole matter over?

"You and I should not become involved in these property issues, Isabel," Suzanne said. "The sooner it is over with, the better. The lawyers will work it all out. I'm sure Roxeanne is upset, but it won't affect her pregnancy."

"I'm afraid my brother might get involved," I insisted, wanting to add, you don't know Roger. "My brother the lawyer. It just seems too bad to get everyone hysterical, I've never had the feeling that Charles-Henri would care if things were worked out some other way."

Suzanne shrugged. "Poor Charles. He has a league of troubles. The husband of his *petite amie* is very unpleasant, you know, Roxeanne's lawyers are very determined, and now there is your brother – *alors*. Dare we say these are the wages of sin?"

I longed to tell her the truth: Roxy wanted to die, that has to be thought of. But shame prevented me, and the fear that I would be betraying my sister, and thus my family, by revealing the weakness, the great failure of nerve in Roxy. It was maybe even something that they could use against her, say to take Gennie away.

Suzanne had shown no interest in the legal arrangements between Charles-Henri and Roxy, but I suppose it should not have surprised me that financially prudent French people – Suzanne, even Edgar – would be reluctant to concede something that would lose them money – money for the French side, you could say. Then she said something else. What Suzanne said next opened up everything for me.

"It is a French picture, after all," she said. As if pictures had nationalities! A French picture. I was shocked. I could see that a museum director might have to decide a picture's nationality, in order to put it in one room or another, the Italian or the French room, the sixteenth- or the seventeenth-century room, according to the arbitrary systems of classification museums use. But Suzanne meant that Roxy had no claim to the picture that had scowled down from her girlhood on the gum wrappers and litter of barrettes on her dresser just because, some centuries ago, way before there was an America, the person who painted it had lived, maybe, in the same general region where people from whom Suzanne was descended had also lived, maybe. This terrible idea gave me a glimpse into the stupid Serbs, crazed Irishmen, all those moronic brutes in the Balkans, all those fanatic Arabs in their identical costumes, all deranged by this really limiting idea, the dismal, lazy-minded habit of nationality, and I saw that I would never understand it. Maybe I had some sort of crude New World mentality that prevented me from seeing the charm of belonging to any nation at all. Moreover, in Suzanne's eyes I might as well be a Japanese, carting off her Renoirs and Boulle cabinets to put in my paper house across the sea. ("I have heard the houses in California are made of wood!" Charlotte had once said to me, brightly exclaiming over this curiosity.)

Even Edgar was not above nationality, for though he deplored the divisions of Serb, Croat, and Muslim in the former Yugoslavia, it was to French patriotism or French self-interest he was appealing, in trying to get France to step in and break it up. Later, also, when we discussed the painting, he disagreed with me.

"If places were divested of the qualities that distinguish them, as expressed by the artifacts they produce, there would be no way of telling Dubrovnik from Detroit," he said. So to him it did matter where something came from.

"Besides, Saint Ursula came from Austria or maybe Britain," I said. I resolved then and there with Suzanne that even though I was American, a member of a nation, and thus couldn't help but be afflicted by all those limitations other people saw as "American," I was going to ditch the curse of nationality and not think of myself as anything at all.

Suzanne gave me another cup of tea, in her thin cups with little gold fleurs de lys around the rim. This was the moment when her eye fell upon my Kelly bag, which I had never taken to Chartres on Sundays. Sometimes you see someone see something, see the light of understanding, shock, ripple their lids. What she understood, or saw in the Kelly, I didn't know, but I could tell that my handsome, caramel-colored handbag registered, and that more than raising a question like "What is Isabel doing with an expensive bag like that?" it seemed to explain something for her.

She tightened her mouth into a little precise smile, and when she told me goodbye, I thought her tone had become cold. She was patting the breasts of her pretty navy suit as if she had had some shock and was trying to fan her heart. I supposed she must be thinking the purse must have come from a man, and I was not the nice *jeune fille* she had thought me. Well, that was true. I was used to people realizing that.

"How nice for you to see your parents after all these months," said Suzanne tightly. "They arrive on Wednesday? You must bring them to lunch next Sunday, to Chartres."

TWENTY-SIX

Put none but Americans on guard tonight.
– George Washington

STRANGE TO SAY, I HAD RUN INTO THE HUSBAND OF CHARLES-Henri's *petite amie* again, at the Randolph's. An odd, repellent encounter. I was helping Peg pass the drinks and hors d'oeuvres, and recognized him. This time he was not drunk or in any way belligerent and wore a stylish corporate suit, a regular international lawyer, American like the other guests, who collectively were wearing a lot of aftershave. He didn't recognize me at first, then made the connection.

"Oh, right, you're the little sister. I guess it's true, I've heard about you." He looked me over, then lowered his voice. "Come in the kitchen a sec, I'd like to talk to you." Of course I went, hoping for some tidbit about Charles-Henri.

"You know where they keep things. Just sweeten this Pimm's Cup or whatever it is," he said, handing me his drink.

"In the cupboard over the fridge," I said.

"You're a beautiful girl," he said. "You know, a discreet, good-looking American girl could clean up at our place. We're trying to make it a full-service destination, you follow me? A place say Germans, businessmen, would arrange to have their board meetings. We want to expand our meeting facilities. Maybe you'd come to a party one of these days?"

I was fixed on "clean up," thinking dog-walking was as low as I'd sink, chambermaid was not in my plans.

"We're expecting some German and Danish businessmen, they'll want to come in Paris, see the town, have dinner, they'll especially want someone with them to show them around. American girls titillate them especially, don't ask me why."

"I don't think . . ."

"A kind of private escort venture, pay very, very well. Plus a good dinner, shows, you know. You'd have fun. All you have to do is look good and be sweet. I'm not suggesting anything else."

"I'm kind of busy," I said, shocked by what I thought he was suggesting.

"Here's my card," he said. "Don't get me wrong. You wouldn't be working for EuroDisney. I didn't mean to suggest that. It's a private enterprise. Think about it."

Private enterprises abounded. Behind our backs, in preparation for their voyages, various things had been put in motion in California. Roger had found, in the international section of the library of Barney, Gehegan, Bryer and Walker, seven possible avenues of approach to the problem of the painting, the most promising of which remained to challenge its ownership in an American and then a French court, and to insist that it had never formed a part of Roxy's *dot* or *biens* and was simply something she had taken with her, like her shoes or a valise, without intending to share or give it. There was no gift in writing, and it was an inheritance, therefore not part of community property, at least in California.

He would also have to get an injunction against the sale in a French court, and to this end contacted Duncan, Cribbe and Crutcher, an American firm with offices in Paris, which represented several oil companies, EuroDisney, Warner Brothers, Century 21 Realty, and many other American enterprises, and had French lawyers on its staff. He had several phone conversations with their expert Renée Morgan, a Frenchwoman with American legal training, and would follow up on this when he got to Paris. Meantime, he had got an injunction in the U.S. Federal Court, fourth district, enjoining the sale of the painting at Drouot while its ownership was in dispute.

And this must have been around the time that the Getty woman, Julia Manchevering, collected her colleagues into her office, dimmed the lights, pulled down the projector screen, and showed them the slide of Saint Ursula that Margeeve had sent them months before.

"This is being sold at Drouot," she said. "In a divorce. I think we should look at it."

"Lorraine, around 1620, I should say," said the seventeenth-century expert Rand Carruther.

"Not a La Tour, though, surely," someone said.

"Why not? Nothing wrong with it if you say it was painted before 1641."

"Someone ought to take a look at it."

"What attribution by Drouot? What reserve?"

"École of. They haven't fixed the reserve. It's come up rather suddenly. When Stuart Barbee looked at it for us, to estimate the insurance, he valued it at forty thousand. There must be something wrong with it, it's being sold so modestly, but I still think it wouldn't hurt to look at it."

"No problem about an export license?"

"The Louvre has apparently said it has no interest in it and won't oppose an export license."

Their eyes met. The Louvre not being interested could mean two contradictory things – either that it wasn't any good, or that the Louvre hoped to get it for themselves or another French museum for a low price.

Thus a Getty art expert, as well as Roger and Jane and our parents Chester and Margeeve, would be descending on Paris on Wednesday. We had made a reservation for Chester and Margeeve at the Deux Continents, but Roger was staying at the George V. I was strangely apprehensive, but Roxy's mind seemed suddenly more attuned to her inner state than to issues of art ownership, and she was happy her parents were coming. Her mind was on the baby that would soon be born, she seemed to be listening for its stirring, or for the vestige of a labor cramp, with her mother here.

On Wednesday, which seemed to drag with the suspense of their arrival, we got a call about five from Lille. Their plane had landed there because of a strike at Charles de Gaulle Airport, and they would be coming to Paris by a special Air France bus. We were not to wait up for them if it got late; they would just go to the hotel, dead with jet lag, and call us in the morning. Reprieve.

On Thursday morning I went off early to walk Scamp, with a date to meet Roxy at ten. Usually Ames Everett did not talk to me very long, but today he was interested in the parental visit, and in Roxy's state of mind. Her state of mind was a general preoccupation of the American community now, it seemed to me, as her time approached and her deserted marital state became more poignant, and more emblematic of the risks Americans take getting mixed up with French people here. Many people had been asking about Roxy.

"I suppose she is apprehensive about the sale?" Ames said, and I thought again, as I had thought several times, he is unusually interested in the sale of our picture.

"Is she glad to see your parents?"

"She hasn't seen them yet. They seem to be lost between Lille and the Hôtel des Deux Continents. She's apprehensive, though. She thinks they think she should go back home, to California, right away, just clear out."

"Oh, I hope not," he said. "She wouldn't, would she?"

"She has to do something. Charles-Henri has fallen in love. He wants to remarry."

"What is this fashion for marriage? Marriage is so tacky and unnecessary," Ames complained. "Remarriage seems complete lunacy."

Strange to say, the Thursday of our parents' arrival – in my mind the beginning of the end – was the very same day I understood what people were saying in the metro. It was like the moment in some magic tale, when you find the ring, or swallow the potion, and you can suddenly understand what the birds are saying. I understood French people, and they said:

"I wonder if Gérard will buy a Saab for his next *voiture*?"

"I doubt it, he always buys Peugeot."

All day the magic held. Near me as I drank a cup of coffee in the Brasserie Espoir, two women in their fifties chatted, and their words came as clear to my ears as if they were Americans:

"You never know with Michelle, that's just the way it is, and you have to come down on one side or other, but it isn't easy."

"It's true."

"You could say I've had enough, but what can you do, yet, it's true."

"Her mother, et cetera, isn't it?"

"I told them."

Later, when I had time to think about it, I would wonder if it was worthwhile understanding after all. Maybe it is better to go along in soundproof isolation? It was something of a disappointment to discover that all those words, so alluringly expressed in dramatic, unintelligible, and unreproducible sounds, organized themselves into banalities one might hear on the bus in Santa Barbara (if one took buses there). But the pleasure of being in on it, at last, initiated, thrilled me all the same. From then on I eavesdropped like a spy.

Roxy had been to see Saint Ursula. At the auction house Drouot, they had let her into a salesroom upholstered in faded velvet to stand alone in front of her painting, the symbol of her life in Paris, the symbol of happiness, the symbol of what private passages of love I don't know, just as I didn't know but imagined the pain and rage in her heart at the vanishing of these things.

She had been shocked by the new possibility the painting

could be sold in a few days, *hors catalogue*, as a special latecomer to a long-scheduled sale of important pictures, which Drouot thinks is the proper company for our picture. The sale would be a week from Friday. No, she said, she didn't plan to go, what if Charles-Henri were there? Let the others go, our parents, our brother Roger, her friend Ames Everett. Ames said he would be there to be sure it went correctly. But I knew she would be there in her heart.

Roxy, seeming outwardly to have that cowlike placidity they say comes on in late pregnancy, has observed the gathering forces without outward complaint. For the past few days she has come home, pulled herself up the stairs, let herself in (exact reenactment of the fateful day Charles-Henri left) and rested as instructed by the *sage-femme*. She would sit on a chair and close her eyes. She has read, in the personal column of the *Herald Tribune* want ads, the words.

> *May the Sacred Heart of Jesus be adored, glorified, loved and preserved, throughout the world, now and forever. Sacred Heart of Jesus, pray for us. Saint Jude, worker of miracles, pray for us. Saint Jude, help of the hopeless, pray for us.*
>
> *Say this prayer nine times a day for nine days and your prayers will be answered. This never fails. Publication must be promised.*

She would close her eyes and begin to say, or rather think these words, nine times. When she got to the end, she couldn't be sure what it was she ought to ask for, and so would content herself with a vaguely benign hope that things would work out. She didn't want to confront fate, or Saint Jude or whoever, too directly, by asking anything too hard like that Charles-Henri should see the light. She was not even sure who Saint Jude was, she was only a new Catholic, and what did "publication" mean? But it was soothing to say over, nine times.

Margeeve and Chester, bused in from Lille, had waked in the middle of the night in the Hôtel des Deux Continents, eyes staring open, the curse of jet lag, and then again at ten-thirty, shocked at themselves to have slept so late and stiff from this really uncomfortable bed.

"We have to get another hotel, we're too old for this," said Margeeve.

"That means *me* getting us another hotel, I know," sighed Chester. Margeeve always wanted to change rooms, tables, this was the first time hotels, but he had to agree, little hot room, the radiator sputtering all night, pinging, an odor of benzoin.

"Did you sleep?"

"I woke up at four." The *heure blanche* of jet lag. "I took a Halcion."

"You should have waked me. I'd have given you a jet-lag treatment," said Margeeve.

"We better call Roxy, she'll wonder what's happened to us.

"Much as I'm eager," said Margeeve, "I sort of dread it. What kind of shambles we are going to find."

"The reality of Roxy's housekeeping." Chester laughed. "The reality of Isabel's course of self-improvement. The reality of French legal customs. You never like reality."

"What has reality done for me? Well – everything for me, but not so much for the girls."

"The girls are fine. You know they are. Otherwise we would have heard. We would have sensed it. You'd have been on the first plane."

"I can't wait to see Gennie. Of course, she won't know us," Margeeve said.

It had been six months since we had seen them, so I expected them to look different. In a sense they did, in a sense reassuringly the same, just standing in a new light, reflected as it were from Notre Dame and the rippling Seine. Margeeve's blue suit, a normal California blue, was just a shade too blue, Chester was unfamiliarly dressed in his dark give-a-lecture-at-an-eastern-college suit, which he never wore in Santa Barbara.

He was bearded, something he went back and forth on, so that we the family had ceased to register the alternations, always disappointing him on the mornings he would appear with a newly bare chin. Now I noticed the beard was there – beards are the exception here – making him look foreign, maybe slightly eastern European. Together they looked foreign, but perhaps only to our eyes, and unmistakenly American. We rushed to embrace them at the exit to the metro.

"Well!" they said, beaming, we were all beaming. "Rox, you look like an elephant, it must be triplets."

Her long-sleeved blue blouse had ruffled cuffs covering her wrists.

"Iz, you look great, honey, you look so French!" I didn't ask what that meant.

We proceeded to Roxy's apartment. Of course I had underestimated Margeeve; she didn't hate Roxy's peeling stairwell as much as I had, but exclaimed enthusiastically about its picturesque qualities and great antiquity.

"This is the *salon*," Roxy said. "There was a bureau, you know, in the American sense. A chest, but it's gone to be sold."

"We know what a bureau is," Margeeve said.

The empty place over the fireplace seemed to scream at me, but not at Margeeve and Chester. Now they found everything pretty and seemed amazed at seeing Roxy in this new light – Roxy the competent matron, *maîtresse de maison*, in her own realm. The only other time they had visited, Roxy and Charles-Henri were still living in his student apartment.

"Is Gennie at her play school? I hope you can keep her out one day. We want to take her to Disneyland."

"How much time have you got, Roxy, what does the doctor say?" asked Chester, anxiously regarding Roxy's swollen form.

"We've moved to the Hôtel Saint-Louis, on the Ile Saint-Louis, it's a cute little place," Margeeve said. "That's why we weren't at the Deux Continents."

"I'll make some coffee," Roxy said, seeming happy to slip

into this hostess role, seeming happy to have our parents there at last, seeming happy they could see her in her chosen place, even like this.

"Now start from the beginning," Chester said, "bring us up to date on the legal things. Roger and Jane get here this afternoon."

"Keep Roger out of it!" Roxy suddenly screamed. "I don't want him. Please stop meddling in it, everything is fine."

"Roxy!" cried Margeeve. "Remember it isn't only your picture, it's Chester's, it's Roger's and Isabel's, it isn't for you to say. Roger should do what he can."

"I don't want you to meddle, just bug out," she screamed.

So it hit the fan, and only twenty minutes after they got here. I supposed it was just as well that the acrimony should all come out then and there. Roxy cried and stormed, but we could see it would not prevent Roger's arrival, and the inquiries at law, and a clash with the Persands, and all the other horrors as yet unenumerated. The chasm opened at our feet, then mercifully someone pulled a rug over it.

The rancor, that is, was glossed over quickly by the parents' evident pleasure to be on vacation in Paris, their delight in Gennie, such a beautiful child, they said, beyond the ability of photos to show – even had rotten Roxy taken any photos. We rode together on the 24 bus. "Walking back, we will cross the front of Notre Dame Cathedral," Roxy told them happily, delighted with the role of Paris tour guide, recovering her composure.

With them there, I could feel myself regressing by the minute, saying graceless things like "be careful of the pigeon shit."

"I love it here," Roxy said, on the bus. "It's so civilized. And my children are French, of course. I'll stay; but sometimes I miss California. But then I'm on the bus and I see an old building where d'Artagnan lived. There was really a d'Artagnan and his house is still there! Then I'm so thrilled I don't care what happens to me here. I've loved d'Artagnan since I was eleven."

"Look at those ridiculous hats," said Margeeve of the round-hatted soldiers standing on the corner. "French history seems like a long series of ridiculous hats."

"Who do we have like d'Artagnan? No one," protested Roxy.

When Chester and Margeeve walked back to their hotel to change for dinner, Chester said, "Margeeve, I'm not looking at this as if it were my painting. You're missing the whole point. I don't care about this painting, I wouldn't recognize the damn thing."

We had organized their social schedule so tightly they resisted, assuring us they had things touristic and nostalgic they wanted to do, and by no means required us. All the same, there was to be a dinner at Mrs. Pace's, and Sunday lunch with the Persands, a reading at the Town Crier, a concert at the American church. Tonight we were all to go to dinner with Roger and Jane at their hotel.

There the same effect of strangeness colored Roger and Jane even more highly than it had Margeeve and Chester, perhaps because they were more fixed in my mind as siblings, not grownups, and now were seen to be solemn, prosperous adults, comfortable in hotels, checked in at the George V, a fancy Californiate hotel on the Avenue George V – I say Californiate, for I still have to keep reminding myself that our hotels are copying them, not the other way around.

I wore my high heels and carried the Kelly. The walls of their room were upholstered in turquoise fabric stretched inside ornate frames, and the TV was hidden in an antiqued armoire. Roger and Jane looked worldly in this surrounding, and I suddenly realized my brother is a hotshot lawyer in a suitable dark suit. I saw that Roger must earn a lot of money.

We had drinks, Roxy insisting on Porto, which only someone French would drink before dinner and she was only doing to make an inconvenience and shock them that, as a *française*, she was not forbidden to drink alcohol during pregnancy. "Let me fill you in about the picture," Roger said. "I spent the afternoon at the offices of Duncan, Cribbe and Crutcher, the firm representing us here. They had already filed a petition in the French court to enjoin the sale until the American court can rule on its status as marital property. The French court has not yet ruled. Then the French court will have to agree on the jurisdiction, but at least nothing can happen until then. Curious detail – DCC know the husband of the woman Charles-Henri is mixed up with."

"'Magda,'" said Roxy.

"Something to do with EuroDisney, and apparently pissed off beyond belief, not inclined to give her a divorce, but that's his problem, not ours."

"You mean the sale isn't going to happen? Next Friday?" Margeeve asked.

"It's possible they'll rule by then, with a stipulation pending the outcome. Museums often take things under those conditions."

"Museums?" we said, thunderstruck. This was the first mention of museums, after the dismissive attitude of the Louvre.

"It's not impossible," Roger said. "According to what I am told. That a museum might want this picture." This news seemed especially to thrill Margeeve.

In the dining room, we studied the long and ornate menus.

"Is it okay to drink the tap water here?" asked Jane suddenly.

"Sure, of course, this isn't Istanbul," Roxy said, taking this personally, frowning.

"I'd just as soon not get an upset tummy. You're probably used to it," Jane snapped.

"Really, it's okay."

"Why is everyone drinking bottled water, then?" Jane insisted.

"They think it helps the kidneys or the stomach," Roxy said. "It's a health idea. A status thing."

"Yes? Well, let's have some bottled," Jane said warily.

Looking at this family, my family, set off, to be sure, by their best clothes and the luxurious surrounding of the hotel dining room, they didn't drive me as crazy as they usually did, except for Jane. It was as if the slightly imposing presence of the waiter, the gilded boiseries, the forest of *verres* and *fourchettes* had gilded the family too with a kind of temporary cosmopolitan patina. Even Jane was looking less lady-shrink than usual, in that she usually dresses like Greer Garson as Madame Curie but was now wearing a short-skirted French dress, stockings, hair done, gold necklace – looking French completely. We can't be such total hick idiots if two of our number live in Paris, said our glances. I felt better about us all, though the others glared at me for pointing out that a *tourtière* was not a turtle. Of course they were saying to themselves, how would Isabel know? I didn't point out – how could I – I'd probably been to more fancy French restaurants by now than the rest of them put together.

At the end, Roger, paying the bill, said, "The tip is included."

"You leave something anyhow," I said.

"No. That's the whole point of having the tip included, I think it's a very rational system," Roger said.

"Maybe twenty francs," Roxy agreed with me.

"Fuck it, fifteen percent has already been added," Roger said.

"Maybe in a simple place, you add, Isabel, but here, when you've already paid a fortune for dinner . . ." said Margeeve.

"Nearly seven hundred dollars, if I may say so," Roger said, his voice trembling a little.

"I have some tens." Roxy scrambled in her purse and gave three *dix-franc* coins to me. I put them on the little plate with the bill. Roger's jaw clenched, and Chester looked embarrassed. I knew Edgar would leave about a hundred francs in these circumstances, but who would listen to me?

TWENTY-SEVEN

Whoever you may be, never discuss with another the interests of your own heart; the heart alone can plead its own cause and plumb the depths of its own wounds.

– *Benjamin Constant,* Adolphe

"It is I, the renegade Charlotte," said Charlotte de Persand Saxe over the telephone in tones of great gaiety, late Friday afternoon. Chester and Margeeve had gone with Roxy to the crèche, to be introduced as *responsables* authorized to pick up Gennie.

"Roxy isn't here," I said. "How are you? Are you in Paris?"

"I am calling *you*. I am here, on my way to Lyon. I thought maybe if you had time for a coffee? I thought, you could tell me the family news."

This was surprising, since I would be the least informed of anyone in the family, the most unable to distinguish discord from lively discourse, say, in discussions at the table. For instance, I still did not really understand how things stood with Charlotte and her husband Bob. What had been, surely, a sexual scandal – her "liaison," as Suzanne had put it, with an Englishman – had now subsided to some mythology about "Charlotte's job in London." Bob appeared from time to time at Sunday lunch, and the children were often there. I had even stopped holding anything against Charlotte about the cat (Roxy had not), because I assumed I had somehow missed the explanation. In a way, I was getting used to being slightly out of it, and it was restful, I suppose like being deaf, where the wits can wander in inner reflection.

We met in the Vues de Notre Dame. "It is difficult being in London," she sighed, lighting another cigarette seconds after stubbing out the first, and pouting flirtatiously at the waiter. It seemed to me her hair was paler, and she had gained a pound or two. "The English have so little sense of *plaisir*, and it is so gray there. But the work is interesting. I miss the children, but they are coming on their holidays. How is your French getting along?"

She had heard that our parents had arrived. She had heard about developments concerning Saint Ursula. She too deplored Antoine's interference, and she worried about Charles-Henri.

Then, abruptly, she said, her eyes on me, "My aunt is coming to lunch on Sunday." At first I didn't understand, and my blankness must have showed, for she leaned forward.

"My uncle Edgar's wife, my aunt Amélie. The family is in an uproar, you know."

Had she been sent to tell me that her family knew about me and Edgar? What was I supposed to do? Blood drained from my head, so that at first I blurted, "Do you think – do you think they'll say anything to my parents?" It was just something to say. I didn't care what they said to my parents, I couldn't shock my parents. It was I who was shocked.

Here I had been thinking about her, and about Roxy and Charles-Henri. Now I had a sensation that was like the moment in the surf when you have been borne to shore, the wave behind you lifting and buoying you up, when all at once the sea withdraws, the sand beneath you changes direction, water sucks you back, scrapes you over the sharp backs of shells, the firm bottom is gone. At this moment, the rich warm tide of French life turned, or, to change the metaphor, like a film running backward, I suddenly saw a jumble of images, of foie gras and buses, musical concerts in medieval churches, the windows of chocolate shops like museums, lacy G-string bikinis – all these things running backward pulling me back toward the beach-bunny movie that had been my life in the Santa Barbara reel.

All would be lost. The scenes I had been dreading – Margeeve and Chester finding out about how ill Roxy had been – were not the scenes I should have been dreading. My own life was to be ruined.

Was it Edgar I regretted? It seemed so, the man himself, whom I loved and who loved me as long as it didn't get too disruptive and attract the scrutiny (amused? irate?) of his sister and wife and nieces and nephews . . . Even in a panic I did not think, I did not make the mistake of thinking later, when I went over and over this conversation in my mind, that Edgar would fight for me or disrupt his life. No, I knew my place. I was a simple one-celled animal, the au pair girl, the junior player, without protection. I would be discarded. I knew that.

I hoped otherwise, of course.

"At first I thought, very strange, then I thought, not so strange," Charlotte continued, lowering her voice still further. "My uncle has a bad reputation, you know. I suppose he is attractive, but very old, surely?"

Scenes flashed before me. The elderly man and young woman in a restaurant. He is handsome, well tailored, slightly florid, distinguished silver hair, perhaps slightly stout, hands lightly raddled. He is known, people look toward him trying to remember where they have seen him. Young smiling woman with him, neat in dark suit, hair knotted like a ballerina's on the nape of her neck. Long neck, good nose, good profile, ladylike. Expensive bag. Up close, they would be heard discussing Prokofiev. They have been to the ballet. People looking couldn't know that she is wearing stockings instead of pantyhose, held up with frilly black ribbon garters, and blue lace underwear, the *artillerie de nuit* he will help her wriggle out of later, when he will kiss, caress *la foufoune*, she will kiss, caress *la bite*, they will pass a sweaty, satisfying hour, but they will not skip dessert now; he is having *salade d'agrumes*, she is having *clafoutis*.

Are they in love? No one would think anything of the kind

in any case, from their airy laughter. Perhaps each has a different definition. The young woman believes him wise, witty, paternal, worldly, cultivated, and a great lover. She believes he is the key to her future, though how this mechanism of fate might operate, she could not say. His power over her is not why she loves him. She usually dislikes people with power over her, even sexual power. She wants to be the one to have it. But he has sexual power too. It is not that she is passive, but that he has the ideas and dictates the rhythm. He is a sensualist and can teach that. She was always kind of grab-it-and-go, before. He has focus. For instance, when he focuses on the area of thigh between the top of the stocking and *la foufoune* itself, on that little crease at the top of the leg, it is as if he had never touched, kissed, admired that particular landscape before, never seen something so alluring.

Is he in love with her? She doesn't know. He says it is a pleasure of his time of life to be attentive to the things he has always valued but not had the leisure to take slowly. These intense treats following upon *quenelles de brochet*, *sauce Nantua* and *nougatine glacée*, *coulis de framboise*, the music of Prokofiev, the thrilling bodies of the dancers, become inseparable, dance a kind of orgasm, dinner a forepleasure, the whole a kind of addiction. Did you have a good time in Paris, Isabel? Yes, I had a great, great time in Paris.

I realized I could still fail to understand the words "my aunt is coming to lunch." I could stonewall this. But I wanted to tell Charlotte, I love him! Feeling the words rise to my teeth was for me almost the first time I had thought them even to myself. Charlotte's perfume and cigarette smoke dizzied me. I might, right there, have cast myself on Charlotte and said, What shall I do? If I did that, I might have had one ally at least, though a weak one, Charlotte herself the flake in her family. But I didn't have the presence of mind, all was blotted out with dread of that lunch on Sunday, and, as I say, with the sensation of horrified loss, like watching your diamond ring go down the sink and nothing to be done.

When, later, I thought about what we did, how we laughed,

those dinners, those discussions of Joubert, I could see that our love had a tangible, precious history of its own, and was part of his history too, like a piece of valuable family silver – and hope crept back.

But at this moment, with Charlotte, another part of me defiantly thought, Am I not a fighter? Isn't that the American way? Am I just supposed to be terrified by Suzanne, and Edgar's wife, and meekly go away? And at the same time I thought, I must be crazy, nothing has even happened yet, just calm down.

So I changed my tack. "I think Monsieur Cosset is a great man," I admitted. "You know I go to a lot of his meetings? I hope no one thinks there's anything wrong with that? I totally believe he is the only person doing anything about Bosnia. He thinks that France should intervene and so should the U.S. . . ."

This threw Charlotte a little, I could see her reviewing her English. What was I saying here? There was a silence.

"We haven't met Madame Cosset, or maybe Roxy has," I went on. "I do admire Monsieur Cosset your uncle."

"She will be there on Sunday," Charlotte repeated. "*Moi*, I go to Lyon, I am sorry not to meet your parents."

In my mind I was screaming, "I love him. I will not give him up." To Charlotte I said, "It'll be nice to meet your aunt."

TWENTY-EIGHT

The next day was Saturday, and Roxy and I had suggested an expedition to the Marché aux Puces, the flea market, for Chester and Margeeve. Roxy loves to browse in the Puces, and I had an errand I did not discuss. I still hoped to buy a piece of faience for Edgar's Christmas present, a plan that now had a bitter poignancy, for I imagined fatalistically that I would present it after he had told me we would not see each other anymore, as my parting gift and eternal reminder.

Margeeve, it turned out, also had a long list of things she had promised to find for people in Santa Barbara, and the flea market was high on her agenda. Chester, officially hating shopping, went along with good enough grace. We took the bus, easier than the metro with Gennie and her stroller, in the mood of high optimism that always goes along with expeditions to this curious world where everything can be found, or sold – drums, jewelry, jeans, African curios, porcelain, entire rooms of woodwork peeled off the walls of castles.

Roxy believes the 24 bus is the best in the world. From the Place de la Concorde, it turns east, passing between the Seine and the Louvre. On the walls of the Louvre are the crests of monarchs – all the Louis, Napoleon, and Napoleon III. It stops at the Samaritaine department store, then goes across the Pont Neuf by the Place Dauphine, where you can glimpse the peculiar little pie-shaped park with old gentlemen playing *boules*, then along the *quai* past the prefecture of police, where Inspector Maigret had his office, and across the river again in view of Notre Dame, and along the Boulevard Saint-Germain to her stop, in the Place Maubert.

When people come to visit, her family or people she went to school with, she always takes them on the 24 bus, and though they always seem to like it, none have appeared to feel the way she always feels riding it, almost overcome with delight that her own bus could run by the side of a place where Pierre Curie was killed by a carriage; in sight of the very place Marie-Antoinette awaited her execution, and where Romans had marched before that. Or that she could live where Abélard walked, in the time of Chaucer, when nothing at all was happening in Santa Barbara, California, where history had not even begun.

It was sort of interesting to see Paris through the eyes of Chester and Margeeve. They seemed prepared to like the city, but to disapprove of the French, especially Margeeve.

"What's appalling is the way the beggars have to assume a kneeling position that way, kneeling in Christian supplication, hands prayerfully folded. It's horrible. Evidently you have to express your pitiful, abject condition before they will give you money."

"Ours just say fuck you, give me money," said Chester.

"Ours have dignity, put it that way," Margeeve said.

"We like ours to be belligerent so we can hate them and not blame ourselves for their plight," Chester disagreed.

"I think it's sanctimonious for a society to demand abjection," Margeeve said.

"They have very few homeless here," Roxy put in sharply. "It is a benevolent society and they have a big social safety net."

"Those beggar women with small children on their laps, it's appalling," Margeeve said, "immobilizing small children for hours on end like that."

Being with them made me realize how many things I had come to understand and take for granted, things that must have seemed strange to me too, at first. For instance, going to the flea market on the bus, Chester suddenly said, "Doesn't it bother you? Just sitting here?" And it was true, the bus was standing stock still in the street, unable to pass a van parked on the side. Roxy and I hadn't even noticed. Roxy was talking to Margeeve, my mind was focused on the prospect of Sunday lunch at Suzanne's tomorrow. Buses never moved very fast.

It was not that I minded meeting Edgar's wife Amélie, I had no problems with that. A wife of thirty years, a woman between fifty and sixty, by my calculation, represents – what? Nothing I could horn in on, and no threat to me either. But I was imagining the assembly at the table as a tribunal of censorious judges denouncing me in their foreign tongue, Jezebel/Isabel. Edgar probably wouldn't even be there. I had been lost in thinking about this, while my father was fretfully squirming around.

"We've been stuck here for ten minutes," he said. We saw he was right. Behind us a string of cars was forming, exasperated people leaning out of their windows, horns tooting. A man in some sort of military uniform spoke in at the bus driver's window, expostulating, with gestures, and the bus driver reacted angrily. "*Passer? Peux pas,*" he said belligerently. "*Demandez mon nom.*" Roxy translated the altercation for Chester and Margeeve. Chester fidgeted and grumbled about the stupidity of the van driver. Roxy laughed happily to hear Chester be typical of himself, and said, "I'm so glad you guys are here." But what struck me was how Roxy and I had got used to buses being stopped, and hadn't even noticed.

Our parents kept calling our attention to how we had changed, for instance then, and they kept remarking on my clothes, which, though it was true I now had some dresses, really hadn't changed that much, allowing for the differences in climate and so on, or so it seemed to me. From what they said to me, I could imagine the conversation behind my back:

"It's funny, Roxy is the same, but Iz has changed a lot," Chester would say.

"Well, Iz had farther to go. Roxy was always kind of herself, however pregnant and forlorn now."

"She looks so . . . Iz, I mean."

"*Soignée* is the French word," Jane would say. Jane knows French.

"I was completely unprepared for it. What is the explanation?"

"She has always liked to be in the swim, and here the swim is *soignée*." (Margeeve.)

"She looks like the star of a British porn film, you know, the beautiful cruel nanny, with her hair up like that, sober little dark dress," Roger would say. (This had actually been an observation of Yves's.)

"Well, I wouldn't know. I have never seen a British porn film." (Chester.)

At least I felt, from the way they looked at me, as if they thought I might be doing something like porn films on the side. They had a quizzical, suspicious and hopeful look when they looked at me, as if all this grooming and the odd French phrase were too good to be true and thus probably to be deplored.

Roxy is scornful of the flea market, evidence of human materialism on a scale unimaginable to either of us before coming to France. I suppose it could be that America just hasn't had a long enough history to accumulate all those objects. And so many of them ugly! Though I have to admit, my eye had begun to be accustomed to bronze panthers, plaster cupids, infinitely mended plates, hinges, mattresses, jeans, mirrors in their hundreds torn from the chimney breasts of all Paris, marble busts, torn canvases, chandeliers, medalions, seventeenth-century prints (a specialty of Ames Everett), deco lamps, things that cost thousands of dollars, and nothing that didn't cost at least thirty francs. I had long since begun to think in francs.

Chester and Margeeve hardly knew whether to react with aversion or delight, or that combination of the two by which they would enjoy it thoroughly because they knew it couldn't happen in California, just as the French react to Las Vegas – affecting to love it, they still wouldn't want it in France. We could observe their astonishment as we wandered in the acres of alleys of carvings, old clothes, a million vases and statues. I guess I like the idea that things don't die but go on living, recycled, and have a kind of immortality, but Roxy hates it that the human owners die, and she says that objects living on beyond their owners depress her.

"Objects should commit suttee," she said.

"I agree," said Margeeve, but Chester objected that objects have a talismanic and memorial quality that keeps their owners alive. I liked it when our parents went on like this, rapping about nothing. It was a nice afternoon for all of us, strolling in the flea market like a family of regular American tourists, dread of tomorrow forgotten, no painful agenda of international legal dispute, no disappointments looming for Roxy, no tragedy and death.

"You can understand them collecting all this junk," Margeeve said, "they've had so many wars. When people lose everything, the smallest things become important." This made Roxy laugh, though somewhat bitterly. In the end, it was Margeeve who made the first purchase, a little brooch with a picture of Charles de Gaulle on it. It seemed like a funny thing for her to want.

While the others had lunch, I went to find the tureen man in Stall H. Martin, in the Marché Paul Bert. I was glad to get away from them for a while, with my own thoughts about meeting Edgar's wife tomorrow. I knew I was overdramatizing my situation, imagining a heavy scene of public denunciation, then renunciation, reproaches by an angry wife, and the sordid shock of Edgar pretending there had been nothing between us. The sting of anticipated anguish is almost worse than the real. I was imagining the embarrassment of my parents, Roxy's derision, Suzanne's disappointment. At the center of these imaginings was always Edgar's detachment. The new idea that he didn't love me as much as I loved him intensified my passion, making more poignant the certainty of its end, tomorrow, or soon.

On the heels of such thoughts, my more combative side would assert itself, the side that resolved, as I wandered in the *allées* of the Puces while Roxy, Jane, and our parents took the menu at sixty-eight francs at the Resto Péricole, exclaiming over the excellence of the lamb, the succulence of the white beans, the modest price, the surprising geniality of the waiter no matter what you had heard, while Jane, an ovo-vegan, ate Margeeve's *tourte à Maroilles* and everybody's *crudités* – my combative side resolved that I wasn't going to just give up.

"Of course I remember you, dear," the dealer said. "I think I am close to laying my hands on that tureen. Very pricey, be prepared. I'll call you in a couple of days."

"I think I might be getting some money," I explained. The whole intricate scam was not clear to me then, or of course I would have alerted Mrs. Pace.

On the way home, the whole family fell into a lively quarrel in loud voices on the public bus. Perhaps Chester and Margeeve, having spent their lives saying "shhhh" to us, now had a sense they couldn't be understood because they were speaking English.

"I think we should withdraw the painting from the sale, roll it up, put it in a suitcase and take it with us," Margeeve began by saying. I heard a quaver of emotion in her voice. Perhaps something in the flea market had upset and moved her. Even Chester was looking at her with some puzzlement.

"How could they stop us? It's ours. We'd just go into the auction house and get it," she went on. (I had actually thought of doing that, of rescuing it for Roxy.)

Chester was looking uneasy, and Roxy sullen.

"It's my life," she said. "I'm not going to become a criminal here. I have to live here."

"La France is not going to come chasing after it, after all," Margeeve said. "Isabel could just bring it."

"I'm not coming home," I said.

Now everyone jumped on me. "And when your money runs out? Work permit? Green card?" And above all, "Why not?" Roxy looked as if she appreciated me drawing their fire.

"I'm starting to like it here," I said. "I came to learn something about Europe and to learn French, and that's what I'm doing."

"Oh, honey," Margeeve said, oddly dabbing at her eyes.

"I can do things that I can't do at home," I added.

"Like what?" they asked, truly baffled, though you would have thought it was evident.

"Music," I said. "Art exhibits."

"We have music and art exhibits, maybe on a smaller scale, okay," Chester objected.

"For example, I recently went to a Stockhausen concert in the IRCAM center, part of the Centre Pompidou," I said.

"Stockhausen! Stockhausen!" It was a red-flag word for Chester, apparently. "You think there has never been the music of Stockhausen in Santa Barbara, California, is that what you think? Could it be that we could never drag you to anything like that?"

"You who went all the time to Stockhausen concerts," I snapped.

"Stockhausen, Beethoven, I didn't see you there. The mall and the Planned Parenthood clinic."

"That's uncalled for," said Margeeve.

We had dinner at Roxy's, except for Roger and Jane, who were going to Taillevent with some lawyers they knew. I went up to bed rather early, needing to escape. It was Saturday night. I often stayed in on Saturday nights now, babysitting. Roxy was often invited out, and Edgar went to the country. I read a little and did my nails. I thought about the painting, and whether, as Margeeve had suggested this afternoon, one could not just take it. In an address, I had once heard Edgar say, "*Joubert disait, 'C'est la force et le droit qui règlent toutes choses dans le monde; la force en attendant le droit.'*"

I had noted these words in the idiotic phonetic way I hear

the French language, and asked about them later. Had I understood? Force and Rightness control the world? Force while waiting for Right, he translated.

"That worries you, *chérie*? It sounds like fascism?"

About eleven, as soon as I had got into bed, victim of a strange agitation and the dread of the lunch at Chartres tomorrow, I got hungry again, and thought of apples on Roxy's sideboard. I thought about taking the picture. I thought about apples. Since my room is on the fifth floor, under the eaves, and Roxy's is on the second, you think twice before creeping down the narrow staircase. I tossed, turned, worked on my French lesson:

Est-ce que vous travaillez à San Francisco? Oui, j'y travaille.

Est-ce que vous cherchez un menuisier? Oui, j'en cherche.

Est-ce que vous donnez les clés à la dame? Oui, je les lui donne.

Either hunger or ambivalence kept me awake, lying there weighing whether it was worth it to get up and go down just for an apple, even though you know once the idea is planted, you might as well get up at once. Eventually I got up.

I now own a satin nightgown and a negligee – a lace-trimmed flowered silk kimono – but it was not suitable for going out on the stairs in. I had been reading whatever books I could find about the lives of kept women, *Gigi*, *Nana*, *The Splendors and Miseries of Courtesans*, *Camille*. Not that I was kept, exactly, but we did not go Dutch at dinner either. One of the books I had read – none of them, I must say, would encourage a person to lead that headlong, precarious sort of life – had actually given advice about lingerie, which is where I saw it called "the artillery of night." Not that I had ever spent the whole night with Edgar.

Anyway, I put on my coat over my artillery of the night and went out on the stairs. It was midnight. Below in the street I could hear some merry voices somewhere. Mademoiselle Lavois, on the third floor, leads a *"vie irrégulière,"* according to Madame Florian. I had a powerful feeling of wanting to be somewhere else, preferably California, instead of hungry, staying at home on Saturday night, climbing down some cold Parisian staircase in the middle of the night for a pitiful smidgen of food.

I was not wearing shoes, so I suppose I did not make any noise on the stairs – the famous stairs where the *pompiers* had dragged Roxy, and where it seemed to me I could still see spots darkened by blood. My key was in my hand, but the door to Roxy's apartment was open below me. Roxy stood in it, talking to a man whose back was to me, at first I supposed Chester, or Roger, even Charles-Henri. They became aware of me at the same moment, the man turning. I had not seen him before. I hung back.

"*Allez, donc, bonsoir,*" he said to Roxy, and kissed her, three cheek kisses, sign of extra affection, and went on down the stairs.

"Iz!" said Roxy. "I thought I heard someone."

"Starved," I said. "I came for an apple. Who was that?"

"Maître Bertram, my *avocat*," she said, in a tone of feigned lightness, no invitation to discuss it. It was a funny hour for a lawyer to turn up. "That was fun today," Roxy said. "I think they had a good time. It's nice having them here after all."

"I thought it would be, sort of," I said.

"I just don't want them, you know, stirring things up, tomorrow at lunch, for instance. Just don't let them get on the subject, of the painting, or the divorce or anything."

"I'm always such a leader of the conversation." I laughed.

"If it should come up."

I like it in *The Sun Also Rises* when Jake Barnes says of life, "I did not care what it was all about. All I wanted to know was how to live in it." That was how I felt, there were so many puzzles. I guess I could count on one hand the number of sleepless nights I have had in my life, usually with stomachaches, but this was one, a sleepless night when all passed in review – Roxy and Maître Bertram on that kind of terms, our parents in Paris, the photograph of Mrs. Pace's tureen in the flea market, and Sunday lunch tomorrow when I would somehow be exposed. As what? As a silly young woman, a troublemaker, as foolish and deluded, exploitative (the Kelly), gullible, unscrupulous . . . Of these characterizations, or self-characterizations, which did I most mind? To be thought, to have been, foolish, undoubtedly. But how had I been, how was I being, foolish? Falling in love with a man, however unsuitable or unlikely, is not entirely within one's conscious control. Was I in love with Edgar? I always came back to that, because although I thought so, I did not know. The distance in age, in culture, in worldly situation, was too great for that to be an entirely appropriate designation.

And the photograph, the photograph of the tureen was back on my mind.

The French are always saying "that is true" (*c'est vrai*) or "that is not true." It is a simple way of looking at things. But what they don't explain is how to behave in the face of truth. Must one bow to it, or resist it? And does it account for all the aspects of everything? For instance, Charles-Henri no longer loves Roxy, *c'est vrai*, but what about Maître Bertram?

TWENTY-NINE

May the Sacred Heart of Jesus be adored, glorified, loved and preserved, throughout the world, now and forever. Sacred Heart of Jesus, pray for us. Saint Jude, worker of miracles, pray for us. Saint Jude, help of the hopeless, pray for us.

Say this prayer nine times a day for nine days and your prayers will be answered. This never fails. Publication must be promised.

WE HADN'T SEEN MUCH OF ROGER SINCE HIS ARRIVAL. He had been busy all day Friday with French lawyers, and American lawyers in France, and he went to the Louvre on Saturday instead of coming to the flea market with us; but he had announced he wanted to talk to us all on Sunday before we went to Chartres for lunch. He and Jane came to Roxy's at ten on Sunday morning. Margeeve and Chester walked over from their hotel on the Ile Saint-Louis, looking happy as honeymooners. Roxy made coffee, and we assembled in the living room, with its conspicuously bare mantel.

"Let me put you in the picture," Roger said. "It looks likely we can enjoin the Friday sale. It's not that unusual to intervene at the last minute, the auction people simply announce at the auction that the picture's been withdrawn. I don't know if they alert major clients who would be coming from abroad. That's issue number one, enjoining the sale. Number two, the issue of ownership, based on Isabel's and my challenge, and Dad's naturally, has yet to be ruled on. Is that picture Roxy's, was it not just a loan to her from us? The de Persands have kind of steamrolled this settlement business, just assuming the picture belonged to Roxy, thus to Roxy and Charles-Henri.

But it's not a settled issue, not even in French law. In California, it would most definitely not be community property.

"But meantime, they may have in fact done us a service, in that the picture is out there, getting known in the art market, and there seems to be buyer interest from museums and dealers. We've already learned that it's worth more than we thought. These things have a way of escalating. The thing may turn out to be worth a lot more than we thought. Apparently Antoine de Persand got somebody from the Louvre to look at it. Isabel, you were there, right?"

"Actually, Roger," said Margeeve, who had appeared to be thinking of something else, and whose tone was strangely remote, "since California, as you point out, is a community property state, that picture would be half mine before it was yours and Isabel's."

A beat, while Roger assessed the meaning and, above all, the tone of this, deciding whether it revealed some unsuspected avarice on the part of Margeeve. But it seemed she was only defending Roxy's moral right to have taken the picture. She waved her hands dismissively, indicating she had no more to say, and sat back.

Roger answered her objection. "Even if Chester inherits the picture after his marriage, you are not entitled to half as community property, because it's an inheritance. Anyway, you don't want to be suing Roxy, even technically, so I would not advise you to be a party to the suit."

"Of course, how ridiculous," said Margeeve. "I'm not suing any of you." She sat back again. Was she disappointed? Roger went on.

"The Louvre. Apparently if the Louvre had wanted the picture, they could ask the Ministry of Culture to refuse to issue an export license. French pictures in some categories cannot leave the country. National treasures. Not the case here, though – luckily for us, for that would limit the number of buyers, would rule out Americans, Japanese."

"Well, it's unbelievable, our own picture we sent to France

and . . ." began Margeeve. "How can they tell us we can't take it home again?"

"What I'm working up to, is that I think we should go ahead and sell the picture in any case. Possibly in London. I've done a little homework. There's interest, there's been exposure, the market is good right now. There are certain advantages about London – taxes, notably. So I've been in touch with Christie's, you know, as in Sotheby's and Christie's? Tomorrow we're having lunch with the Christie's guy, or I am at least, and you should come too, Dad and Margeeve. The actual sale would have to wait until the ownership issue is settled, but meantime the picture would be out of France, which I think wise, in case they change their mind about our right to export it."

"What if you can't enjoin the sale here?" asked Chester.

"We can challenge the sale. We could also challenge the de Persands after the sale, if we can't stop the sale itself. I'm not sure how fast the courts can act here, they've had the issue for two weeks. We're at a disadvantage, I don't need to tell you, as foreigners, even with a French lawyer."

Here Margeeve directed an imploring look at Roxy, as if hoping she would come to her senses and abandon her ill-advised admiration of foreign lands and people, degenerate predilections that had brought all this down on us. This would never have happened, she seemed to be saying, if . . .

"Oh, God, let's just sell it and get it over with," Roxy said, abruptly. "What's the difference? I can accept that, by coming to France, I signed on to these French rules, and I'm willing to abide by them and take the consequences."

An eruption of irritation in the room at Roxy's obtuseness.

"Is it that you don't get it, Roxy, or are you just pretending not to? It isn't just your money going down the drain here, we all have a stake," Roger said. "The picture belongs to all of us. Us more than you."

"None of you had any problems with my taking ugly old Saint Ursula until there was money involved," said Roxy. I noticed that her cheeks had lately developed a pattern of redness, I think called the mask of pregnancy, which flared now, giving her a piratical, desperado look.

"Yeah," Roger said, "but now there is and we do."

"If you were going to make all this fuss, why didn't you do it before this?" Roxy complained.

A confusion of acrimony and opinion ensued, from which I could sort out only that Roger wanted to wrest the picture from the French and sell it at Christie's, Margeeve was apologetic at Roxy's seemingly willful refusal to think justly and financially about the rest of us, Chester evinced mild discomfort, however he might feel privately, I nursed my hope for the ten thousand dollars I might reasonably expect, a part of which would be spent on faience, and Jane backed Roger.

"The de Persands are not missing any bets here," Roger observed. "The brother's fine hand – he's Antoine? – is everywhere, even more so than Charles-Henri's lawyers. Antoine's taking quite an active role. I'm quite sure they all know what's going on and what the stakes are."

"We should get the eleven-forty train," I pointed out. "We're invited for one o'clock."

I think my parents were vaguely pleased when Gennie, usually a good, perhaps too docile, little girl, pitched a fit and said she hated Sundays. I thought she had sensed the irritability that was overtaking the conversation, but my parents took it to mean she hated the Sunday visits to Suzanne, and I noticed Roxy didn't correct this impression.

THIRTY

Le scandale du monde est ce qui fait l'offense,
Et ce n'est pas pécher que pécher en silence.
– *Molière*

THOUGH THE PERSANDS WERE, DESPITE OUR APPARENT GOOD relations, the enemy, we exulted in the grandeur of their Chartres house. That is, we exulted in how it would astonish Jane. The idea persisted with her that Europeans lived in post-war privation in bombed-out buildings, even though she could see that was far from the case, just as she was charmed by the market in the Place Maubert but seemed to regard it as a thing for peasants to bring their wares to, rather than as a resource for Roxy's bourgeois neighbors. "Those poor women lugging their groceries through the streets," she would say, brow knitted with sympathy for prosperous matrons in Max Mara suits, their shopping caddies loaded with champagne and pâté. "Women's lives are always the hardest in any society." I wondered if I had been like that when I first came, making erroneous judgments based on innocent American notions. Roxy exulted a little, too, to think how the Chartres château would impress Chester and Margeeve, who had been intimating that Roxy had fallen into the hands of impoverished European fortune hunters, like a victim out of Henry James.

The Persands have gates, a wall, and a paved forecourt

where the family parks. There is a half acre or so in back, where the tennis court is. The taxi from the station let us off in the street to walk through the door in the wall and up a path at the side. The house is two stories high, a simple rectangle of pale stone, with regularly spaced French doors on the ground floor, long windows above, and a mansard roof with third-floor rooms in it, with ivy climbing on the shutters. It is imposing, undeniably. In Santa Barbara, we did not have a tennis court or pool, we did not have ancestral faience, we did not have a country château at all.

As we drove up, I could see we had slightly misjudged. The château did not daunt, it infuriated Margeeve and Chester, whose sense of injury was heightened by the idea, seeing their house, that the Persands must be unbelievably rich. Roxy quickly observed that you can never tell with the French, because of the way things come down to them. Of course it was never just plain folks who lived in the Persands' château in the seventeenth century, but neither are the Persands as rich as movie directors or the lords of Beverly Hills, they just bought it at a good real estate moment long ago. Americans, me at first anyway, find European grandeur confusing, because it doesn't necessarily mean people are rich. Certain kinds of fancy French *hôtels particuliers*, which would only be imitated in the U.S. in theme parks, are for the French regular family homes, dating from days when all houses were big, and stone was the only thing to build with, and mirrors were put in because there weren't electric lights. Inside, things are run down in a way I like, the marquetry peeling, the old damasks a little faded, lots of antique stuff around, much shabbier than Montecito.

Now I was idly considering how Margeeve and Chester would react to the Persands themselves trying not to think about what unpleasantness might develop, beautiful surroundings or not. On the train my stomach had hurt in fear of meeting Amélie Cosset, but also I feared – though ashamed of this, I had to admit to myself that I feared – being embarrassed by my family. I had thought I was too old for that particular, humiliating form of disloyalty I used to feel all the time, but no, it flooded in on me – a too lively sense of Margeeve's royal blue suit, Chester's unfashionable beard. I knew what a bad person I was for feeling this, a bad, ungrateful, immature person with shameful values, and to make it worse, Margeeve slipped her hand through my arm as we walked over the cobbles and said, "I am so proud of you, Iz."

It was instantly apparent to Roxy and me that the Persands must have had one of those family meetings we had just had, and had agreed that they would all behave with unimaginable perfection, warmth, charm, robust cheer, manifest affection for Roxy and me. Antoine and Trudi were there, Suzanne of course, Charlotte, though she had said she wasn't coming, and Edgar's wife, Aunt Amélie – Madame Cosset. All were smiling, ironed, correct.

"Welcome, welcome," Suzanne said, full of warmth and smiles, kissing my parents on both of their cheeks. "How nice to see you after all this time, aren't you thrilled with Gennie, don't we have an adorable child here of whom to be the grandparents?" Of course, resolutely blithe as she always was, she made no reference to the family problems, the divorce, or them ripping off Roxy's picture.

"Isn't Roxeanne a wonderful mother?" she said to Margeeve. "Geneviève is an absolute dream." I could see that Margeeve was not impervious to this. Gennie herself was not impervious and danced around us shouting *"moi-moi-moi"* or something in her hard-to-understand baby-talk French.

Madame Cosset was not what I had imagined. I had expected someone small, faded, and well dressed. Aunt Amélie instead was large, bony, rambunctious, and, in gabardine pants and a mannish purple alligator polo shirt, the most underdressed person at lunch. She had short, smartly cut gray hair, was said to play tennis, though she didn't today, and had gardener's hands. I tried to imagine her and Edgar in bed together – rather, I tried to avoid imagining it. It was hard either way.

Suzanne was obviously fond of her. They chattered

together in animated French, pulling their spectacles off and on as they peered at culinary details in the kitchen, and switched to English in the living room with my parents. Madame Cosset brought a pan of string beans in and strung them, holding them on her lap. Edgar did not come.

When I did not look at her, she looked at me, or so I felt, though not with bitter looks. I might even have been imagining her interest. It might have been that she did not look at me at all. But no, the two of them, Suzanne and Amélie, were looking at me together after Chester and I had absolutely beat the pants off Antoine and his wife, Trudi, on the dampish clay court, on the miraculously warm day. My stomach was starting to feel better. It seemed I would be looked at but that nothing would be said.

The day, warm enough to play tennis, was cool if you were sitting still, so Margeeve stayed with Suzanne, Madame Cosset, and Charlotte in the glass room that looked out into the garden. Margeeve later told me, but not Roxy, that Suzanne said to her, "I am sorry about all this, the dispute between the children. Believe me, I do not like it." That was the only specific allusion to the divorce, in the whole day.

I had not seen Antoine, my opponent at tennis, since the day I spoke out about my belief that the Persands were ripping off Roxy and the rest of us. Now we faced each other over the net with, on my part, the wish to drive a tennis ball down his throat, and I couldn't tell what he wished, for he smiled as usual, and is actually rather handsome, though he smokes nearly as much as Charlotte. But he hit his serves to me as hard as he could, and never hit to Chester, from some macho, sexist assumption that my father, though in his late fifties, would be a better player than I. Chester and I beat them handily, though Antoine would beat Chester in singles, I think. Chester lost his serve once, and I never did.

Suzanne served champagne or Lillet for aperitifs. There was considerable directing of meaningful looks, looks whizzing around the room on all sorts of subjects. "You have a lovely home here," said Margeeve, and Roxy darted her the look of shame I felt too. Presently Nathalie, the girl from the village hired to serve the lunch, came in and said, *"Madame est servie,"* a formula which had never, ever, been uttered before at these lunches and which I judged to be a subtly intimidating bit of pretension on Suzanne's part to French formality. I saw Margeeve's eyes go instinctively to Roxy, as if to follow her moves. Though Margeeve is a perfectly middle-class person, you could see she felt like she'd been a cocktail waitress or something.

The menu was also designed to be impressive. Or was I being harsh here? Perhaps Suzanne was genuinely trying to give our parents a nice lunch? I could not say it had ever before been less than nice, but today the food, though served simply, was superbly delicious, beginning with foie gras of a good quality. I was getting to know something about foie gras, which Edgar especially liked. Perhaps his liking for it was in Aunt Amélie's mind too, for the subject turned to Edgar, causing a churn in my stomach. I wish I could understand why simple spoken words have this power over my insides, as if they are tied to a string I have swallowed.

"Where is Edgar, Amélie?" asked Suzanne.

"Oh, *Bruxelles. On dit.* Presumably. *On ne sait jamais,*" said Madame Cosset with great insouciance. "I never any more ask."

To my parents she explained, "My husband is in Brussels. He is sorry not to be here." Was this meant for me, was it loaded with some kind of irony? I could not tell.

"My brother occupies himself with politics," Suzanne explained to my father. Antoine said something in French I didn't understand, and the Persands laughed, quickly checking their laughter, as if it had been rude of them. Madame Cosset had shared the joke, whatever it was.

"No, really, my uncle has done remarkable things," said Antoine.

"Well, we are so happy to receive you here, we are so desolate about – you know," said Suzanne, raising her glass slightly to Margeeve.

"So nice of you to have us," said Chester. "And to meet Gennie's aunts and uncles we hadn't met. We are also sorry about . . ."

They must have simultaneously realized that Roxy might in some way be affected by these remarks about her marital situation, as though they were criticizing her looks or wits in front of her.

I noticed that Margeeve, though rather younger than Madame Cosset or Suzanne, was being handed the dishes first, as the oldest woman. It has always seemed tactless to me to allude to a woman's age this way, but perhaps the dubious honor came from her status as guest? Was she irritated or pleased? And after the foie gras a new cultural misunderstanding loomed, for the main dish was a pair of roasted chickens, which smelled delicious and shone with brown glazing like a magazine photo and were of course, in my parents' minds, just chickens, a rather cheap food in Santa Barbara.

Roxy, usually so unperceptive, also saw how Chester and Margeeve would misunderstand chickens and hastened to praise these birds (which are indeed different from ours; theirs are expensive, tasty, and allowed to spend their lives running around in a barnyard). "Oh, what heaven, Suzanne," she said. "Did you get these *poulets* from around here? I wish I had a good poulterer. Half the art of cooking in Paris consists in knowing where to go to get things, doesn't it?

Poulterer? In this archaic word I saw the depth of Roxy's tenseness, perhaps even matching my own. To me what was plain was that Roxy, having been wronged by the Persands, was all the more determined to be loved by them, and to behave wonderfully. Having wronged her, they were all the more determined to have her good opinion. Love reigned, much to the confusion of Margeeve and Chester. They must be seeing that they'd never get Roxy away, but if they did, they hadn't given up. Since their arrival they'd kept bringing up the beauty of Yosemite or the beach, telling how Margeeve had found a float, like a giant bubble, washed up right in front of the Miramar, things like that, in hopes of making

California sound magical. But now Roxy was determined that the Persands and our parents must love each other too.

Here came a peculiar interruption. Nathalie appeared at the door of the dining room with a sweating, apologetic, smiling man who proffered a bottle of wine. Antoine rose, the man stepped into the room.

"Monsieur, excuse me for deranging you but I wanted to bring you this in thanks for saving my *panier*," said the visitor, though of course in French.

"Ah, the *panier*," said Antoine. "Not at all."

"The *panier* and all the *couverts* and *assiettes* and a *bonne terrine de lapin*," the man said. "They told me at the station where you could be found."

"*De rien, de rien*, but it is nice of you to think of us," said Antoine. There was more conversation, but in faster French.

". . . be off, *bonjour, mesdames, messieurs, excusez-moi* . . ." After a few more words, he retreated with Nathalie and would not be dissuaded, would not sit down.

"I found his picnic basket on the train," Antoine explained to my parents. "We left it with the stationmaster, it was nothing at all."

"It's correct of him to bring a bottle, how nice, how unnecessary, *c'est gentil*," they said over and over. Their asperity, any incipient disagreement or squabbles, and the subject of chickens, now vanished before this reassuring evidence that there was still correct behavior in the world, selfless goodwill – theirs in saving his picnic basket, his in rewarding them.

"It isn't bad at all," said Antoine, reading the label on the bottle. "I'll open it, we had better leave it for the cheese."

"Roxeanne is a perfect *française*. Do you know?" said Suzanne presently to Margeeve. Here she lowered her voice and adopted a tone of special gaiety, as if to signal that one was not to mind too much what she was going to say. "If I had been shown a catalogue from which to choose daughters-in-law – here is Roxeanne, an American, here is Trudi, a German girl, here is *une française* – I have to admit I would have chosen the French girl, naturally, Edwige, my eldest son

Frédéric's wife. I would have not thought of a German girl or an American." Here she looked with deliberate fondness at Trudi and Roxy. "But they are so much more *françaises* than Edwige, she can't make a *croque-monsieur*. Frankly she is completely *nulle* at housekeeping, she is a professor in Montpellier." I was wondering, of course, what she would think of a Czech daughter-in-law, should Charles-Henri marry Magda. Perhaps everyone was wondering, for there was an anxious stir as one could hear the real anxieties in Suzanne's voice, a kind of quiver of intensity.

Suzanne turned to the kitchen door, caught the eye of Nathalie, and Nathalie brought in the cheese. "Gennie, darling, no cheese for you, just run into the garden," said Suzanne to Gennie. "Your girls are so different," she continued, looking now at me. "Isabel from Roxy." Now I saw what was on the agenda. Me.

"It is Isabel *l'américaine, maman*," Antoine said with a laugh. I didn't know what that was supposed to mean.

"Oh, shush, Antoine," Trudi said.

"Both so charming in different ways," said Suzanne.

It crossed my mind they might not actually know that Roxy and I are stepsisters with not a drop of blood between us. Perhaps Roxy had never explained it.

"Yes, quite different," Margeeve said.

"Isabel is so enterprising," Antoine went on.

"Antoine," said Trudi.

"Americans are enterprising in general, I believe," remarked Madame Cosset. "Enterprising and practical."

I resented this. Practical, we try to slit our wrists, we wander the earth, we die for love. I wondered what practical means in French, maybe something quite different. What about *enterprising*?

"Americans think of French people as rational," said Chester, rather uncomfortably. "Rationality, the Age of Enlightenment. Thermidor."

"Of course she is very strong, Isabel. It is strong to be practical," said Antoine. Trudi said something to him in French.

"The American girl is a famous type, of fearless ingenuity," said Madame Cosset. "I have a friend – the Countess Cortenoux, you know her, Suzanne – who clings to the belief they are all heiresses out to claim French husbands, but in my opinion those days are finished."

"I think of the French as very practical," put in Margeeve. "I suppose *rational* is the same thing."

"Mother, I don't think one can generalize at all about national characteristics," said Roxy. "Really." Imploringly.

Margeeve stared into the carcass of the chicken with an expression of aggrieved innocence, for it had not been she who started this train of talk.

"Je chasse," said Antoine, gallantly changing the subject. "I hunt. Do you hunt?"

"Well, no – what do you hunt?" asked Chester.

"The deer."

"Shoot them, I suppose?" Chester agreed, gloomily.

"*Mais non*, the birds are shot, the stag we hunt with dogs. It is very beautiful – the horses, the dogs, the scent, the hunters in their coats. The *curé* comes to bless the dogs. You run the noble stag to ground, that is the idea. He becomes exhausted and can no longer run."

We, the Americans, were struck into silence, an embarrassing instant too long, wondering if we understood.

"What happens then?" asked Margeeve.

"Then the dogs kill the stag. You have the expression 'in at the kill,' that is what that refers to."

Further silence, during which we were collectively appalled, and they had an intimation that we were appalled, though they cannot have known how much.

"Do people ever get killed, you know, fall off a horse or anything?" asked Margeeve.

"*Non*, not usually, though, regrettably, sometimes."

"Oh, good," said Margeeve, "that makes it a little more even then."

"Are you planning to go to Roland Garros?" asked Chester hurriedly of Antoine.

"They are certainly being 'practical' about Roxy's picture," went on Margeeve, returning to the subject of the French character.

"Difficult to get tickets! Terribly difficult to get them!" cried Antoine.

"They were offering them in California, through the American Tennis Federation. Roland Garros–Queen's–Wimbledon tour, you have to sign up this far in advance, though," Chester said. "Three weeks, I forget the cost, it wasn't cheap."

"Roxy will have noticed already, she is a perfect *française*, so developed in her instincts . . ." began Suzanne. "While Isabel . . ."

"We are thinking of going sea-kayaking in Patagonia," cried Chester.

Isabel, Isabel. Why was my name suddenly so current? Several people spoke at once, in French, protesting, a snort of laughter from Antoine, I could not hear what Madame Cosset had said. I was distracted just then with an insight I am not sure I had had before. I imagined the company as the octet of the opera I had seen, where everyone steps forward and sings about his own concerns, for instance Roxy would be singing, "Charles-Henri, *l'amour*, despair," and Antoine would be singing a duet with Madame Cosset, "Isabel, home-wrecking little slut," and Charlotte would be singing, "Poor me, why did I go to London, it is so cold there." Suzanne, "What shall I do to keep this scene from deteriorating? Do not take my grandchildren away." My parents: "Why can't we just take our daughters and our picture and get out of here?" Trudi? Well, I don't know what she'd be singing. The point was that no one was sharing his or her feelings in the encouraged California way, and this was called "politeness" or "civilization." Everyone knew what everyone was thinking all the same, or I thought I did. I learned something from this, about keeping one's counsel, about smiling, about civilization, indeed.

During the second of my inattention, the conversation had

evidently taken a turn, a dread topic, an idea had briefly boiled up, Roxy's voice suddenly stood out saying, "I suppose the moment has come to say . . ." But now a horrible, burning silence seemed to strike dumb everyone at the table. The moment had evidently come but in French, and passed, and I had missed it. Now they were staring in stricken silence. I tried to guess from Margeeve's expression what had been said, or from Roxy's stricken frown. I knew it had been about me, though it hadn't.

Finally Madame Cosset spoke, in husky tones of shock. "This Beaufort is not right!"

"No, it has a peculiar, smoky taste," Suzanne gasped.

"Yes, it's not right," they shouted together. Antoine took some from the plate and tasted it.

"No, it's not good," agreed Trudi in an anxious whisper. Perhaps she, who was not a *française*, had been charged with bringing it.

"Supposedly a very good Beaufort," said Suzanne crossly. "I shall certainly speak to Monsieur Compans myself. But all is not lost, for the Reblochon is good. *Servez-vous.*"

The meal ended (*glace vanille, sauce caramel*), Suzanne led us from the table for coffee in the salon. Roger, Antoine, and Chester installed themselves on the sofas. Jane asked for the bathroom. (Terrible *faux pas.* The French appear never to pee. Roxy rolled her eyes at me.) Since I had to too, I went to show Jane. "A very nice lunch," she whispered. "I think they're quite nice." Typical of a shrink to be impervious to tension and angst. Nor did she notice the beautiful old bedroom wallpaper of birds and vines, and she took offense at the bidet, which she at first took to exemplify French sexism by being a toilet without a seat, just for men.

As we came downstairs, through the glass doors I saw Suzanne and Margeeve talking on the terrace. Trudi had vanished to the kitchen, and Antoine was coming out with the coffee on a little tray. Margeeve turned around as she heard us come down, and looked at me. Her expression was worried and tense.

"We should be going," Roger said presently. "Jane and I, anyhow. We're going to hear vespers at Notre Dame."

"We should be going," everyone cried. We assembled our jackets and purses.

Nothing had happened, really. Madame Cosset shook my hand. Did I imagine her little smirk, her knowing smile? She shook the hands of all the Americans, and Suzanne kissed us.

THIRTY-ONE

On the train, free of the strains, we all relaxed a little, like actors on a set between takes.

"A very nice lunch," said Margeeve noncommittally. She appeared abstracted. "They really don't seem mercenary in the ordinary sense."

"I would never suggest to a client they have lunch with the adversary," Roger observed. "The danger is not so much that fighting will break out, it's that harmony will break out. People never like to believe the worst."

Is that true? I had a lot to think about.

Roxy, for her part, seemed relieved and even ebullient to have the afternoon over with. Harmony, as she deeply desired, had broken out. But her happiness was short-lived, because Margeeve had not finished.

"Roxeanne, I think you should come back to California immediately," she said.

"We've been over that," Roxy protested.

"As soon as you can travel. I know the airlines would never take you now. It's just ridiculous to think of staying, this is not your culture, these are not your relatives, I don't think you can count on them. Of course they love Gennie, they'll love the baby, but how are you going to support your children? What kind of life would you have here, the divorced wife hanging around like a kind of fifth thumb?"

"I've thought about it and thought about it. I'm not coming home," Roxy said. And so on. I am abridging the conversation. This quarrel about Roxy's future took up the forty-five-minute journey from Chartres to the Gare Montparnasse. Of course, we were none of us saying what was in our hearts except Roxy, who kept repeating her objections to going home, saying, "What would I do there?" and "My children are French."

Then, virtually as the train moved into the station, Margeeve turned to me and said directly, "Iz, I understand you've gotten mixed up with an old uncle of the Persand family?" Here she seemed to strive for a glare of maternal concern and disapproval, but something behind her expression did not seem that outraged. Of course, they no longer wrung their hands over my morals, so perhaps it hadn't shocked them.

But I was shocked. "Who told you that?" I looked over at Roxy, who also had a shocked look on her face.

"Suzanne talked to me. Mother to mother. I just throw this into the hopper of our French experience," said Margeeve. "Iz, she was very apologetic for mentioning it. On the terrace, just as we were leaving."

Margeeve recounted the scene. She and Suzanne were sitting in the little glass room that adjoins the terrace, filled with ferns and aspidistra, lined with photographs and little drawings by various Persands. Suzanne busying herself pouring them another coffee and passing the sugar (in cubes). "There is something a little delicate I would like to mention," she had said to Margeeve. "With the others not here." She sighed. "We are so fond of both Roxeanne and now of Isabel too, it has been lovely to have her here these months and so wonderful for Roxeanne, especially – how do you say – *pendant* the pregnancy and the problems. She is a lovely girl."

"Thank you, we think so," said Margeeve. "Of course."

"Yes, so willing and so cheerful. She is amazing with all the little children, she is delightful, on Sundays, she takes them for walks and is so good with them."

"Really? I mean, I'm happy to hear it."

"How to explain. I feel you and I can talk. The two *grand-mères*. You have not met my brother, I believe, Monsieur Cosset, but he is a person quite well known in France for his political comments, a *personnage*. He is actually quite eminent. I am afraid, though, that he has something of a reputation as a *tombeur*."

Margeeve did not immediately follow this apparent non sequitur, but sensed Suzanne's confidential mood, and there was something she herself had wanted to bring up – the picture. Listening for an opening interfered with her ability to pick up on Suzanne's hints.

"We have a situation in our family, which I hope you'll understand. It concerns the painting, it isn't really Roxeanne's," said Margeeve.

"Oh?" Suzanne in her turn disconcerted by what appeared to be a change of subject.

"That's why my son has started the lawsuit, it's really a matter that concerns our family, did Roxy have a right to bring it to France? You see?"

Suzanne did not. "I know the French have a reputation for understanding these things, but let me assure you my brother's philandering over the years has far exceeded the normal, and has caused much pain to poor Amélie, though I think she is perfectly resigned to it by now." Here she must have perceived that Margeeve had not understood.

"We are afraid my brother has taken advantage of Isabel. I would be so sorry if Isabel might be hurt by someone much older, and more experienced, and I'm afraid a little unscrupulous where young women are concerned."

Margeeve was bound to attend to the idea of Isabel being hurt. Suzanne continued.

"Of course when she goes back home it will seem less painful," continued Suzanne, "assuming it is painful at all, but Isabel has such an open, helpful nature, we all love her and would not want her to be wounded by someone who, in all candor, has not always been very nice to women."

"Oh, dear," said Margeeve vaguely.

"I would think if she were to return to America . . . after Roxeanne's delivery, of course. We will see that Roxeanne gets the help she will need . . . If Isabel went back to California, I have no doubts the whole thing would fade from her mind, she is bound to have many admirers in California . . . Perhaps in time she will understand . . ."

Now, in the train, my humiliation was total. I had a vision of Suzanne saying to Antoine or Charlotte, "Did you see Isabel's *sac*? *Mon Dieu*, is it possible, Edgar up to his old tricks?" And I understood Margeeve's expression, which was disapproval mixed with amusement. My father, who had looked up from reading the *Pariscope*, had a more ambiguous scowl of attention. Roger and Jane were politely silent. Roger I suppose was wondering how this new news would help our case. "Well, are you asking me to explain it, or what?" I said, crossly. I was imagining their dismay.

But Margeeve was laughing! "Madame de Persand apologizing that her horrible roué of a brother had seduced our young flower Isabel. They are very consternated and concerned." Margeeve went on. Roxy too began to laugh. Chester's face darkened slightly. I found it irritating that my virtue or lack of it should be a matter of family levity, and said so.

"'We would so hate it if poor Isabel as well as Roxy should be made unhappy by someone in our family.' She wanted us to speak to you, of course. To save you, I guess." Her smile, her light tone – I quickly understood that Margeeve was happy for me to be the instrument of discomfiting the Persands. She seemed to have no curiosity about Edgar himself, or what I might be feeling. She was treating the whole thing as a joke because the Persands were treating it seriously, thinking I was the victim of their most disreputable relative. I found it a bit disquieting, in truth, to think that he was disreputable, because Edgar, though he had never concealed his past, had not stressed, either, that it was anything but the normal past of a Frenchman, eyes on duty, church and government, family, and dinner. Perhaps it was not.

What I minded more, though, I have to admit, was this laugh my family was now having, about me as an instrument of their revenge. There was something coarse about it. I had never seen them before in that light, and perhaps it was unfair to see them that way now, indulging in a little laugh at the people who were after all taking them for a lot of money, for thinking that their Isabel could not take care of herself. A small triumph, after all, but I did not like it to be at my expense. I knew what I felt and knew, and could not explain any of it to them, about Edgar, about my heart. I knew what they would say if I told them I was in love and meant to have my way. They would say I had said all that before.

"He's seventy at least!" Roxy was exclaiming to Margeeve and Chester. "I had no idea! How could I? She" – meaning me, as if I weren't there – "has never said a word. He sends expensive presents, of course. I've seen those." Roxy looked distressed and defensive, as if she had been caught lying down on the job, the job of looking after the unreliable Isabel. I could tell them something about her.

"Well, it's true," I snapped, "but it's none of their business, or yours, for that matter." Then their eyes changed. I could see that they were saying something to themselves to the effect that it had never been any good trying to reason with Isabel.

"You've been trying to make it hard for me the whole time you've been here," cried Roxy, turning savagely to me. "How could you do something like that? No wonder the Persands are being so difficult." And she went on, much raving of this kind, about the effect of my affair on her; and she was comforted by Margeeve and even Chester for this shock to her delicate poet's system.

"You girls are both coming home," Chester said.

THIRTY-TWO

THROUGH SOME ASSOCIATION OF IDEAS, I HAD SUGGESTED WE meet the man from Christie's at Pile ou Face, a little restaurant not too far from the Hôtel Drouot, the auction house. The Christie's man was Piers Janely, large, plump, and affable. I immediately saw he was a shade too large for Pile ou Face, taking up too much space in a discreet little room. He had a high-colored English face, and his voice had a range between upper-class loudness and the dealer's smooth, confidential croon. I had forgotten or never had noticed the almost affected inflections of English English, which sounded odd and stagey against our own flat California accents. Hearing French around you all the time makes you more conscious of the accents of English. Like Piers, Roger and I are tall. The three of us moved, stooping, up the circular stairway.

Chester was going to the Louvre with Margeeve, said he would come for dessert if he could but not to count on it. He said he trusted us. Neither he nor I was sure why we were meeting this Christie's guy anyhow, but Roger had been corresponding with him.

"Let me say at once that your picture is fabulous, marvelously beautiful," said Piers Janely. "What would an *oeuf fermier* be? Just a boiled egg? Only in France could they serve you a boiled egg with such panache. Such effrontery, one might say. And the price! I think I'll try the egg, to start." All this said in a voice perfectly audible downstairs, I was sure.

"I've explained the legal situation," Roger said to me.

"Knotty, but by no means the worst we've had to deal with," Janely remarked. "Of course things are always worse when the French are involved."

"They're not involved, in the largest sense," said Roger. "As I wrote you, the Louvre is not interested, which clears the way for export."

"Then the *foie de veau, pommes mousseline*," said Janely.

"Oh, you should have something more *cuisinée*," I suggested. "How often do you come to Paris? What they do wonderfully here is *pintade au cerfeuil*, with some chestnuts." I felt Roger studying me oddly.

"Let me look at the wine list," Janely said. "I used to do a bit of wine, before moving into Old Masters."

"They say the real wine experts are all English," Roger said.

"Undoubtedly, it's absolutely true. The French have very faddish notions and often overlook some quite amazing vintages." He studied the wine list and waited for us to order. I had the eggs myself, being fond of the purée of *morilles* that comes with them, and the *croustade de poulet*, reflecting that I might be eating another big meal that night with Edgar. When Roger had ordered, Janely asked the waiter to bring us a red Trévallon, which I thought was an interesting choice.

"Your picture, I must say, from La Tour's best period, in my mind, though by no means the period he is best known for," Janely said presently. "In my opinion, La Tour."

He waited for us to absorb this astonishing news.

"That doesn't seem to be the general opinion," said Roger presently, his voice husky, as a man's becomes when he is torn with desire. "The school of La Tour, or a follower of La Tour is the most anyone will say."

"Of course," said Janely. "What do you expect? If they tell

you it's a La Tour, the price will go out of sight and they'll have to pay more for it. It's that simple, frankly."

"But the Louvre?"

"Suppose you were a museum," Janely said. "You wanted to acquire, say, a Renoir some local people had found in their attic. I don't say the Louvre would mislead in any way, I would never suggest – I mention the psychology of the situation. Before you proposed a price, would you go round first to tell them how valuable their Renoir was? Hardly."

The simplicity, the obviousness of all this, struck me and Roger both.

"If they wondered whether it were really a Renoir at all, would you assure them it was? No, you would not. To preserve your own integrity, you might tell them you couldn't be sure."

"I see," said Roger after a moment. "What do you think?"

"I think it is a very fine La Tour which in competitive bidding will achieve a very fine price. More than one person will know its value. Our catalog would state the case correctly."

"What price range?" Roger asked, his voice husky with avarice.

"Perhaps a million pounds. We would advise a reserve of nearly that. That would mean it would not be sold under that sum.

Roger and I both calculated the difference between a million pounds, even as split with the Persands, and the forty thousand dollars of Stuart Barbee's first estimate. I felt funny – the mere process of thinking about a huge sum of money introduces a kind of unpleasant excitement, a feeling of hectic interest, a hum in the brain. Tureens and beautiful clothes floated through unbidden. I tried to think of something more worthy, I imagined two million dollars, split with the Persands leaving a million, split with Roxy and Judith – it would still come to five hundred thousand for Roger and me. A dizzying, empowering sum. It was to become Isabel the heiress instead of Isabel the dog-walker. I am detaching these thoughts from each other in order to put them down, but they occurred simultaneously, with the force of electric shock.

Either Roger was making the same calculations, or he was struck dumb by the mendacity of great institutions.

"Barbee, the guy who came for the Getty – wasn't he an independent appraiser? He had nothing to gain or lose, that was just insurance."

"Hmmm, rather," said Janely.

"Who do we get to tell us, then?" Roger asked.

"We have, obviously, a point of view opposite to the museums and dealers. Like you, we want to sell at the maximum price. We don't serve our own interests by overestimating, however, and most of the time we are close to predicting the actual sales price. Sometimes sales disappoint, sometimes they exceed our estimate – that is what happens most often. We are accurate because we are confident about our attributions and we know the market. We have to. There is no doubt in my mind that you have a good early La Tour and it could be worth as much as a million pounds."

"Drouot would have more experience, surely, with French painting?"

Janely raised a brow. "I don't pretend to know what liaisons might prevail among French institutions. It's safe to say Drouot is playing it safe."

"I would feel more comfortable at Christie's," Roger admitted.

"This is extraordinary," said Janely of his soufflé. "The French really are matchless."

Chester climbed the stairs just as we were finishing, so we had another coffee with him. Mr. Janely paid the bill.

"A million, Dad," Roger told Chester. "Mr. Janely is sure it's a La Tour." At this, Chester just looked uncomfortable.

We were rocked, thrown, Roger and I, by this lunch, and didn't have much to say to each other walking back toward the Place Maubert, each lost in thought, counting our riches, plotting our actions, trying to stifle those improper hopes now springing up that had so carefully been bred out of us by our parents and their strictures against greed. (Well, I never noticed that these had weighed much with Roger anyhow.) We didn't at all disagree that Saint Ursula ought to be sold at Christie's. After a discreet interval following its withdrawal from the sale at Drouot, it would come blazing out as a La Tour and the Louvre would have already signed off on it. We were each thinking of what the money would mean to us, and Roger was probably thinking of how we could get out of having to split it with the Persands. I agreed they had no right to it really.

THIRTY-THREE

I do thank you for your efforts, which have done me good, and all the more so because they will not cost you any sacrifice, I hope. But don't let us talk about the future, I beg of you.
– *Benjamin Constant*, Adolphe

I WAS LOOKING FORWARD TO SEEING EDGAR THAT NIGHT ON his return from Brussels – just for a drink, not a proper assignation, because I had a lot to tell him – all this, and the news that both our families knew about our affair. If he didn't know that already. I was scared of this conversation, because it would be a moment when he might say we had better not go on.

We met about six in the bar at the Lutétia.

"I had coffee with Charlotte," I said directly. "She says the Persands and everyone knows about us and are in an uproar. My parents also – Suzanne told them."

Edgar appeared startled. He tasted his scotch. "Well, does that spoil it for you, *chérie*?"

"Not for me. I was thinking of you. Of your wife." His wife was not a forbidden topic, yet we had never talked of her. That was a point of pride with me.

He shrugged. "Inhibiting but not absolutely fatal." There did seem a glint of irritation, though, at the prospect. Discussions, perhaps ultimatums. Perhaps he knew exactly what to expect. "How did they know, I wonder?"

"She didn't say. I was too stunned to ask. I can't imagine."

"Never mind, Isabel. *Pas de problème*. We will ignore what Charlotte told you, as if she had not told it you."

Could we? I wondered. Can you unknow something? Would we ever get them out of the bedroom with us? Or would we always feel their eyes, their irritation, even their laughter? (I had not forgotten the malicious amusement of my parents.) They had all intruded on the perfect private intimacy of our world.

"Or will it be more amusing, the better to *épater* the respectable?" Edgar went on. Amusing was the word we had started out with. In the semidarkness of the bar, his magisterial presence reassured me, but the shadow across his face did not. "Is it sweet to shock? Don't worry, little one, what we have cannot be taken away." He meant this to be reassuring, but I was not reassured.

"Tomorrow night we're invited to Mrs. Pace, me and my family, I mean," I said. Tomorrow, Tuesday, was the night we usually met. Edgar looked at his watch.

"Let's go to my rooms for an hour, *chérie*. I have to go out later, but not until nine."

This was what I wanted, to be in his arms, yet this break with our Tuesday tradition made me feel more at sea than I had been feeing.

As Edgar went to get his coat, I heard (understood) an elegant Frenchwoman say to her companion at the table behind us, "It isn't true that the American girls who come here are all heiresses, *riche et bien placée* the way it was even in the fifties. Today you don't know who they are, they come from states you never heard of. It isn't true, either, that Americans don't speak French. My dear, they *all* speak it, *exécrablement*."

There was something elegiac about *les galipettes*, too, and at the climax I sobbed, from the anguishing keenness of my sense of impediment and release, but also because at that moment I was sure it was the last time. "*Bonjour tristesse*/You are written in the lines of the ceiling." He stayed inside me a long time when it was over, holding me tenderly.

Then he got up and poured himself a cognac, and said,

"Isabel, I'll be going to Zagreb for a couple of months, to help with the negotiations there." After a moment of chill, I wasn't surprised. I ought to feel that it was good – I was happy he was being useful to his country as he should be, where he could help. It was a tribute to the potency of his thought, and validated my admiration once again. Yet I was being abandoned, and it was as I expected, and it made me angry and scared.

"What will *I* do?" I said. "Will you want me when you come back?"

He appeared to think about this, though I have no doubt he had thought about it already. "You will not always want me, my dearest Isabel. We must think of that. Perhaps this is the natural time to part."

I heard this with the sinking of heart that comes when you are told something you were afraid of, the test you know you flubbed and now must see the low mark, written in your record for all time.

"No, I don't think that at all. I'll wait, I'll come with you . . . ."

"Of course we will always love each other. But you will not always want me. I know, if you do not," he said. "It was your Emerson, I think, who said, 'every hero becomes a bore at last."

"I don't want to talk about this," I said.

Edgar has the idea of, uses the word, destiny. Applies it to himself. "I'm afraid this useless preaching is my destiny," he said once of his television appearances and town meetings. "At one time I thought my destiny would be as a statesman." Now his destiny was coming to pass.

Destiny seems a grandiose word for "future," though. Maybe you have to be religious to use it, or a statesman, as he said. Maybe you have to be as old as he, when the idea of "future" is not so comfortable. The words stayed in my mind, because I had never thought of myself as having a destiny, though of course I had a future, anyone does except the immediately doomed. Roxy was destined to live in France, a destiny conferred upon her, inadvertently, with her French first name. Hers a manifest destiny. Mine? Whatever mine was, I couldn't be sorry Edgar was going to Zagreb, for his sake. He wanted it so much, and he might really help there. Yet it fit in too well with the dignified slow-motion collapse of my French world, and the death of my hopes. At first I had no words of protest or reproach. Maybe I was too stunned. I was immediately doomed.

"You are young, beautiful, and wise," he continued. "You will not always want me, Isabel." Of course the words shot to my lips: And you are an ugly old fool. But I didn't say them. We talked brightly of the relations of the Bosnian Muslims with the Croatians.

So. On with the *soutien-gorge*, the *combi satinée*, *slip dentelle*, *bas-collant*, fuck-me shoes, and out into the night.

Fighting tears of chagrin, I walked home alone along the Boulevard Saint-Germain. It was clear that he was saying more than just that he would be away in Zagreb; he was saying goodbye. He was dumping me. That accounted for his extra tenderness and somewhat portentous manner, accounted for certain things he had said I had not understood. I had been thick, as usual. I had resisted knowing. Goodbye forever, he was saying. Being dumped and being blamed for it: "You will not always want me, Isabel."

It was windy and cold now in Paris, December, the weather too ominous a metaphor for May-December lovers, and it was black as midnight by seven-thirty – *dix-neuf heures trente*, but I would never learn to think of time that way. My spirits chafed at the flatness of the world. I had on my old down coat which Margeeve had brought over for me, but I shivered, becoming angry where I should have been reassured by Edgar's lovemaking. He was vain of his lovemaking because it denied age; he had just wanted to prove his vigor, and now it would be proved in Yugoslavia, which was what really counted for him, his patriotism was really narcissism – I was having that sort of thought.

The headlights flashed reflections in black puddles of cold

rain. Usually, miserable weather in Paris makes you think of human courage – defiant umbrellas, resourceful buses – and for that it is cheering. But tonight the rain described my solitude (*"il pleut dans ma chambre, il pleut dans mon coeur"*, I thought). From the street, looking up, I could see only the ceilings of the lighted apartments above, but even the ceilings, ornate with plaster fruit, lighted by fairy chandeliers, suggested opulent contentment from which I was excluded. I imagined the truffled chickens, the families at table, laughter, all the young women who could play the piano. Even Charlotte could truffle a chicken and play "Für Elise."

I could do nothing and had lost everything: Edgar, my family, and France (for I saw too clearly how the boat was nearing the shore, the gangplank would soon be let down, my trunks stowed for the voyage back). Back to my family – but they were all strangers after all; I had not got over my pique at them for their reaction to hearing about Edgar and me, for making fun of my love and my fears, for taking me so lightly. If they loved me, or even knew me, they could not have said, "Their roué of an uncle has seduced our flower Isabel," and laughed. Were not all their thoughts about me revealed in that sarcastic remark of Margeeve's? (Had my father at least protested in his heart, thinking how could she say that to Isabel?) As if they were still focused on my sexual behavior in high school, or on some definition of me that didn't take into account my qualities of . . .

Of what? When it came to an answer, my mind was a blank. I knew myself to have qualities, but was made to face, in the solitude of icy rain on the Boulevard Saint-Germain, just crossing the rue Saint-Jacques, that they were not apparent to anyone else. Could everyone in the world be wrong and I right? What had I done or not done in my life, to have them take me so lightly when they took Roger and Roxy and even Judith so heavily? What do you have to do in the world to break through to seriousness? These useless questions seemed of cosmic importance to me.

To me and perhaps to the roué uncle, of whom his family

thought I was the victim, while my family thought he was mine. There was something funny in that, if I'd been inclined to laugh. My spirits one minute would lift to magnanimity. If I was only his victim, last fling, expedient mistress of the moment. I didn't care. The heart has its own imperatives, Edgar's as much as mine. A stab of gratitude to Edgar brought tears to my eyes. Why? Because he thought me worth telling things to, about Clausewitz and Marshal Ney. Because I sensed that our conversations were over. They would not survive the stares and whispers of our families, nor the distance between Paris and Zagreb. Yet – some Frenchman wrote – "absence diminishes commonplace passions and enhances great ones." Thus I wavered between anger and understanding, and between despair and hope. After all, he had not positively said it was over, only that maybe it should be.

Hope took various forms. Maybe – for I had always been able to construct a better scenario – maybe I had underestimated the extreme urbanity and tolerance of the French (think of Charlotte's marital sabbatical, for example)? Maybe they would learn to take us for granted. A vision came to my mind of years from now, on the lawn at Chartres, Sunday lunch, Isabel and Edgar a settled couple, Isabel tucking a lap robe over his knees as he sits in his wheelchair, Suzanne calling them in to lunch. Amélie has gone on a cruise to Egypt.

But, a future pushing an elderly gentleman in a *fauteuil roulant*, would that be enough for me? Somebody else said, "He who lives upon hope will die fasting." What would become of me? That was really the gist of my self-indulgent misery – pity for Isabel *seule*. A saying of Sartre's had powerfully struck me, if only because it seemed to have so much more force in French than when I had heard it in Sunday school in Miami, Ohio: *"L'important n'est pas ce qu'on fait de nous, mais ce que nous faisons nous-même de ce qu'on a fait de nous."*

Was it possible I had begun to think in French?

I was disconcerted by the way events, instead of coming to a head as they would in a film, seemed to recede like the Sea of Faith in Matthew Arnold's poem. I could hear the long, withdrawing roar. Perhaps Edgar and I would never say goodbye; the days between our meetings would simply drag out, he would spend more time in Brussels, or Bosnia, and I – where? My future had not announced itself. I seemed condemned just to blunder along, nauseated like Sartre's hero by the flatness of the world. The Persands would never confront me, no voice would be raised at me ever, there would be no climaxes, courtroom or salesroom dramas, no acrimony would ever find expression – the world as flat beneath my feet as the moving sidewalk in the Châtelet metro, which seeming to take me somewhere, would only take me to the next station. This flatness was called civilization. In France, even the frisky American spelling of civilization with a *z* had been softened to Civilisation.

Maybe I should go to EuroDisney and fuck German businessmen for money as Mr. Tellman had suggested.

Just kidding.

I tried to tell myself there were things to look forward to: Roxy's baby and maybe some money from Saint Ursula. But these thoughts were not enough to dispel my misery.

Roxy's blood on the stairs at 12 rue Maître-Albert would always catch me up, if I was thinking of myself, dark reproachful spots saying it's Roxy who must be watched over and guarded, she is the flower. You Isabel are a tree, sturdy and rooted, whatever they think. (La Fontaine has a saying, though, that the rose – or is it a reed? – bends in storms but trees are blown over.) Roxy is brave really, just that one lapse or outburst, now she is soldiering on, to have her new child alone, for in the end no one is going to help her – not Margeeve and Chester at their breakfast with their papers and tea, they aren't going to be making all the formula and putting on the little shoes and worrying, and neither am I, however much I might intend to, and neither is Charles-Henri on his weekend visits, nor Suzanne . . . . At thoughts like this I would remember the picture. What if we really got a million dollars?

That would save Roxy. Say what you like about money, that it's disgusting or a taint, it would make all the difference for Roxy between grimness and a life of art. Elated with selflessness, I climbed the stairs sincerely thinking I would give Roxy my share of Saint Ursula. "Have no truck with first impulses," said, I think, Talleyrand, quoted by Edgar in one of his speeches: "for they are likely to be Good."

Then, outside Roxy's apartment, I heard a chaos of raised voices. The mood of family acrimony, which had erupted several times before, was fully upon them. Inside, it was explained to me: Charles-Henri had appeared not an hour since to tell Roxy he had agreed that Saint Ursula should not be sold, should instead be settled on Gennie and the baby to come, thus effectively removing it from the realm of the divorce.

Roxy had just told the others. "It's what I wanted all along! That solves everything! I knew he'd do the right thing when he really focused on it," she said, her face radiant. All was right with the world. The picture could be withdrawn from Drouot, could hang in its accustomed place over the mantel, all could be as before except for the cost of insuring it for eighty thousand dollars. That would be expensive but she'd manage. I could imagine her feeling of reprieve, her sense of being smiled on by fortune again.

Then Roger had said, "Roxy, no way."

No way are you going to appropriate property worth several million dollars belonging to Chester, Isabel, and me for the use of you and your children.

They all began to talk at once.

Roxy: That picture was given to me when Uncle William died and we all chose pictures.

Roger: What bullshit, you can never get away with saying that. He wasn't even your uncle.

Margeeve: Roger, if you take that attitude I will remind you that half that picture belongs to me because I am married to Chester, you said so yourself. It was Chester who inherited the picture. So it's half mine.

Roger: No way, Margeeve, I explained that to you.

Jane: What about Fritz, after all? Why should Roxy's children and not Fritz . . . ?

Me: (timidly) Let Roger tell you about our lunch with the Christie's guy . . . .

Chester: (in defense of Roxy) I'm not so sure Uncle William's will didn't stipulate that everyone could pick out something he or she liked.

Roger: Not children by marriage, I hardly think. People not even related to him.

Me: Roxy! It's worth millions of dollars. Come on!

Margeeve: I'm not so sure I would want to sell it. We could loan it to a museum for safekeeping. What good is money, really, and it would just go to taxes, isn't it better to have an art treasure and do good with it?

Chester: How ridiculous. This is ridiculous.

And much, much more. What was new, a note we had never heard before, was the note of asperity between Chester and Margeeve, but I couldn't guess who blamed whom.

"I can't believe this, we are bickering about the birthright of an unborn child," Roxy cried, amid the chorus of our shouts, mine as loud and greedy as anyone else's. So much for my handsome resolution as I mounted the stairs.

I never would have guessed how they felt, all the odd ways they felt. I guess it doesn't say much for me and Roger that we were holding out for money but, caught up in it, I certainly didn't think that Roxy could hog the painting for her children and said so, over and over, with increasing bitterness, all of us bitter where we had been a happy family (and would be again, no doubt). Thus I learned something about the position of money. In the end, the collective weight of our indignation convinced Roxy she would have to refuse Charles-Henri's offer, and the sale, whether at Drouot or Christie's, would proceed.

"We should weigh withdrawing the picture from the sale at Drouot," Roger decided. "On the grounds we are considering that offer. While we wait on a ruling about whether it belongs to the *biens*, as they call it, of the marriage."

"I thought you might leave me at least one thing I loved," Roxy cried.

Alone, in my room, I swung from despair to rage, thinking about Edgar and my own docility. Had he admired my docility, the absence of reproaches, the dearth of tears? Could I just be dismissed like that, with a casual announcement that we were no longer anything to each other? Were my compliance and good sense so perfectly to be relied upon? I who had given up almost all other social life, who had sacrificed . . . It was self-pity in the most extreme degree. The berating speeches I composed in my mind sank into speeches of entreaty, speeches and then letters. All night I wrote angry and imploring letters in my head, about how I wanted to be with him always.

The trouble was that the word *always* immediately suggested its opposite, finite mortality – probably to be encountered sooner by him than by me. It was a reminder of his age and my youth, and of me having to minister to infirmities he'd rather not think about. I tried to say: I want to be with you under any conditions, or let me just be your secretary and aide-de-camp. But all remonstrances came out wrong, with the suspicion that Edgar was right that sooner or later we would part. He had told me to read a French novel called *Adolphe*, and in it Adolphe says, "Woe to the man who in the first moments of a love-affair does not believe that it will last for ever!" I tried to remember what I had thought from the first, and, it was true, from the first I had always had the intimation of troubles to come. What a curse it was to have a critical and objective nature, how I envied Roxy her unreflective passions, her life of an artist, authorized to rearrange reality.

The idea of life without Edgar put me at sea again after months of life harmoniously arranged. It made me have a bout of nausea, horribly barfing in the little WC outside the door of the African family's room. My problems seemed worse for having known happiness. I had learned one lesson from Mrs. Pace, though, a real American lesson: Whatever happened, I would smile.

Early the next morning, Tuesday, Roxy came up to my room. It was hard for her to climb stairs now, she had gained nearly forty pounds. Standing in my doorway, for a second it didn't seem to be Roxy, just a heavy female figure, Woman, it could be from Rumania or Split, fleeing from mortar. It was her shapeless brown cloak that made her look like an unfamiliar Slav, and her slightly swollen face, become round and puff-eyed.

"Mrs. Pace wants you to call," she said. "Also – Iz, I don't think it's as strange as the others do, I wanted to say before they came over. About Uncle Edgar. They haven't met him, they just hear 'seventy.'"

"I suppose," I said. "I don't care anyway."

"I didn't realize you needed a father figure that much. Probably you think Chester paid more attention to me than to you." (I did think that, but I didn't care.)

"I am interested in his politics," I said.

"I envy you, actually. Not Uncle Edgar, but, I don't know, I envy you a passion."

"Rox, you'll be thin again," I said. I wondered about Maître Bertram, and that strange little moment on the stairs.

"Oh, I know," she said. Her sighs lacked conviction. People say that at the end of pregnancy you don't think you ever will be as you were.

I went down to Roxy's apartment and called Mrs. Pace. She told me they'd been burgled, and she wanted me to come over quickly. I rushed to her apartment to find a scene strangely reminiscent of the day at Chartres when the Persands had been "visited." Mrs. Pace had been both visited and burgled. A policeman dusted for fingerprints and Robert Pace, in his dressing gown, was already on the phone to the insurance. They had been out late the night before and had not looked around when they got in. Then at seven this morning they had noticed that things were gone from the sideboard. Of course I knew the tureen would be gone. I should have spoken up.

Mrs. Pace (carefully dressed, stockings, suit, pin in the lapel) said, "I need you, Isabel, just to take a calm look around and help me compile a list of the things that are gone. They say you always fail to notice things yourself, you are too distraught and angry. I've noticed the obvious things, of course. All the things on the sideboard – tureen, silver teapot, Bow platter. Then the VCR, and the little table in the hall. What's very strange is my files, which couldn't possibly interest a French burglar.

"Burgling seems such a French crime," she added, her detachment never deserting her. "Domestic, focused on material objects, requiring a certain power of discrimination, and non-violent. But the interest in my files does elude me."

"They were probably just looking for hidden jewelry," I suggested, dismayed at my own role.

Table, tureen, Bow platter. Almost nothing else was gone, though eventually we noticed the absence of a good little Claude drawing that hung in the powder room. The years 1940–1952 had been pulled from her files and lay on the desk. As I was putting them back, I saw that 1950 was gone.

"What happened in 1950?" I asked, for we hadn't got to the definitive stage of our sorting.

"Old Communist Party stuff. That was the year I was treasurer – Oh, I do mind about my faience, Robert," she cried. "I mind terribly about that."

It was funny that I minded too, as if it had been us who had been burgled. I felt the same indignation and sense of violation. I saw it all as a part of a pattern of loss that had begun to form out of the indistinct materials of life and impose itself on me.

I remembered all at once that Cleve Randolph had wanted to look in Mrs. Pace's files, though of course there could be no connection. What did all this mean?

I rushed home to get ready for our expedition to EuroDisney. As I was putting Gennie's coat on, I got a call from the antique dealer at the flea market. He had a tureen. It was rather, though perhaps not exactly, like the one I wanted, and perhaps I'd like to make a date to come and see it? I said I'd come soon, I'd call him.

THIRTY-FOUR

> *But whoever it is who has thus determined the course of our life has, in so doing, excluded all the lives we might have led instead of our actual life.*
> – *Marcel Proust,* Time Regained

NOW I MUST PICK MY WAY CAREFULLY AMONG THE EVENTS of the next few days, which would further change our world and change us. Of course, I know that each event in life changes the next, so that you can say this of any sequence of things that happen. But "catastrophes have a somber way of sorting things out," said Victor Hugo. Could we have avoided this one, if we had listened?

The expedition had been planned to EuroDisney. Margeeve and I were bringing Gennie, and Suzanne de Persand was also bringing two of Charlotte's children – Paul-Louis and Marie-Odile. Roxy had planned to come along, but at the last minute she said she didn't feel well enough.

We were all solicitude. "Do you think it could be the baby coming?"

No, Roxy said, discouraged, it didn't feel like labor coming on; but all the same, it seemed too hard to trudge over the acres and acres of some amusement park in the cold weather: We thought, and said to each other once we got on the RER train, that she probably just wanted a day to herself without us and without Gennie.

I had been feeling a snobbish disapproval of going to EuroDisney. I couldn't imagine Europeans going there, let alone us, with such a place of our own in California, if we had happened to want to go to it, which we didn't. Oh, Chester and Margeeve had taken us when we were kids, of course, and of course we had loved it, then.

To get to EuroDisney takes about forty minutes on the train, to the east of Paris. Since Gennie didn't have a hereditary knowledge of Mickey Mouse and Donald, she wasn't too excited. She was much more a French than an American child. I supposed they said things like ooh-la-la to her at the crèche, for she says ooh-la-la, and she obviously doesn't get these French phrases from Roxy, who speaks to her only in English. But today she knew we were going on an outing and it was special because her other grandmother and little cousins were there too.

"How pretty it is!" said Suzanne politely as we approached a set of pink buildings through a park of rhododendrons already in bloom, and poinsettias for the approaching holidays, and artfully sprayed snow at the corners of the windows. I had expected that EuroDisney would be an embarrassing, envious, derivative collection of cardboard castles, an American dream of old-world splendor, so I was surprised that it was so pretty, with a wedding-cake pink hotel that somehow looked familiar, Victorian turnings and Tiffany glass. It was American. I had expected to feel a rush of cultural indignation, a sort of humiliated, apologetic feeling that America had put over anything this dumb on Europeans. But it was hard to object to.

"It looks like the Del Coronado, that hotel in San Diego?" Margeeve said. "It looks like it's modeled on one of our California hotels," she explained to Suzanne.

"California, yes, I imagine California to be like this, I saw only Santa Barbara, you know," Suzanne agreed. "This is actually very charming, this hotel here, though one hears the food is not good."

Now I try to remember what we did the hour or so before

the strange event. I believe we had a nice time, it was all so decorative and sweet, an idealized America, and I had to admit it was nice to be back in America, especially America refined to its ideal essence of gingerbread porches and Tiffany glass, and harmless anthropomorphic bunnies and mice, amiable dwarves, optimistic fables, Santas and handsome cowboys, choo-choos, hitching posts. I know we are supposed to mind that, but it's hard not to appreciate, while you're there, the absence of gum wrappers and assault weapons. Or so I imagined.

We went on the little Western train that took us into the Sierra Nevada and through scenery that looked like Tahoe – none of it seemed exotic to us, but Suzanne often said "very pretty" and Gennie laughed to see dance-hall girls and villains. We went into the castle of Sleeping Beauty. "La Belle au Bois Dormant," Suzanne explained to the children. We took pictures of each other and went on the Pirates ride.

My French world had fallen with a crash, like the lurches of my stomach on this stupid ride, clinging to Gennie, who screamed at the glaring faces of the cutthroats and the realistic crocodiles.

Now I saw that my love for Edgar had been just like this, a kind of insulated make-believe. Yet while, when we came out of EuroDisney, we would be the same as before, I was not the same for my time with Edgar in the make-believe world of France. I had changed beyond reclaim, though I could not say how. I mourned over our last conversation, then I rallied and groped for rays of hope that we might go on somehow. His announcement had come too hard on the heels of my telling him we were discovered for there to be any connection; he was going to Zagreb, that was all. Then I plunged. He had been going to tell me for a long time that things were at an end, and it was coincidence that our families had found out now. How had they found out? Was it the Kelly? How much was our picture worth? Was the man in the flea market planning to sell me Mrs. Pace's tureen? These questions consequential and inconsequential swirled around in my head with the dizzying progress of the little barque that bore us across the Spanish main.

It was just then, standing among the pirates of the Caribbean, looking at the rocking of the little distant ships on the blue main, that one of the pirates came up to us and spoke. His eye was deep and baleful, his grinning, piratical mouth like the mouth of a shark. Despite myself, when he laid his hand on my arm, I jumped. You don't expect the scenery to accost you, it was like the moment in a horror movie when the eyes of the portrait move.

"Little sister, isn't it? This is a break." Long John Silver, the Jolly Roger – after a second his features became those of Magda Tellman's husband. He smiled, and smiled at Margeeve and Suzanne.

"This is my mother, and . . ." I hesitated, remembering his drunken violence. Now he seemed calm, but I wondered if it was wise to mention Suzanne's name, or Gennie's and the other children. It wasn't a full-fledged thought, something just stopped me from introducing them. It seemed strange that he could be here, dressed in a loose white shirt, tucked out, like a pirate's blouse, but of course he had some connection with this place.

"I'm glad to see her," he said, almost jovially, to Suzanne and Margeeve. "I need her to help me with something. While she's gone, I'll show you ladies around a bit."

They appeared startled, looked at me for confirmation that I knew this guy.

"That's okay," I began to say, "we were just going to the Futureland, or whatever it's called."

"Listen," he said, taking my arm too firmly and leading me a step or two away, "I want you to go get my car for me. There's a reason I can't go myself right now. I'll tell you right where it is. This would help me out a lot."

I was so used to all the stuff I did for people as factotum and gofer, I was ready promptly to say "sure," but instead something made me hesitate, and I said sorry, I couldn't. He tightened his grasp on my arm. I began to see he was nervous; he was sweating, though it was cold and he had no coat on. With the hand that wasn't holding me, he fished in his pants pocket and got his wallet out. He let go of me and pulled something out of it, a picture of himself encased in plastic, with writing – some kind of badge, which he pressed into my hand.

"When you've done it, you can take the ladies to the Disneyland Hotel for a sumptuous lunch, on me, all the comps. Look, take this, this entitles you to all the comps in the park.

When I didn't say anything, he grabbed me again. "It's a white Opel, rented, and it's parked against the west fence in Frontierland. I don't remember the license, if there are more than one, you'll have to try the key. Just get on the train right here, at Fantasyland – no, it'd be faster to walk. Walk that way, following the tracks, till you get to Frontierland. Here are the keys."

"Look . . ." I said.

"Do it," he said, and there was something in his tone that compelled me. Perhaps there was something threatening in his voice, perhaps it was the intensity of the pressure of his fingers, or the way he looked at Gennie. In a foreign land, Americans oblige each other more freely than we might perhaps do at home. I told myself it was not so strange to be helping him out. But I'm sorry to say it was the complimentary pass that convinced me.

"Drive it along the service road to where we can see you from the Sleeping Beauty tower, that's where we'll be. It'll only take you fifteen minutes and it will help me a lot. Meantime I'll show them some interesting insider stuff."

"Isabel?" cried Margeeve.

"I'll be back in a few minutes. This is Mr. Tellman," I said. I walked, though irritated and uneasy, in the direction he had shown me, at the perimeter of the park.

It seemed to take longer than fifteen minutes. I walked through a landscape of pines and scrub sage, as if I were in California. As if I were in California wearing seven-league boots, traversing huge tracts of landscape in a stride. An old jeep rusted in a gully, there were cactus and longhorns. Over a rise I saw the silvery bleached timber of a redwood bunkhouse. I might be in Tahoe. Presently, distantly, behind the little rustic railroad station, through the mountainous thickets, I could discern a parking lot. I had walked perhaps twenty minutes. I took a path, the wrong path, then another which crossed under the tracks of the miniature railroad. Then I was among parked service vehicles, little trucks and electric trolleys, some oil drums, some large trash receptacles. A white Opel sat, almost alone, at one side against the fence. It was unlocked. There was the service road along which I was to drive. I found I was apprehensive, as if I were stealing this car. It was too strange to feel right. Yet what could be wrong, in full daylight in EuroDisney amid thousands of people? Rangers in cowboy hats watched me open the car. I knew they were French – French people worked here – but they looked American in their Stetsons and boots. As I pulled around toward the service road, a Sheriff's car, a Plymouth car that said "Sheriff," pulled across the exit and men got out carrying guns, but these were French policemen, and the guns were pointed at me.

I got out of the car with my hands up. What American moviegoer wouldn't know to do that? People watched from above, from the trestle of the miniature train, watching this typical American tableau. Maybe they thought we were part of the living diorama of American life.

The gendarmes made me sit in their car while they parked the Opel again. They asked questions. What was I doing? Whose car was the Opel? Where was the man who had rented it? What connection to me? I could speak French better now than when Roxy had slashed her wrists. I could say a few words, anyhow. I could make them understand about the guy, how I knew him, that he was with my mother and my little niece, and a small, blonde Frenchwoman and two of her other grandchildren.

The trouble was, I wasn't sure they believed me. In any case, they made me sit with them.

THIRTY-FIVE

O bizarre suite d'événements! Comment cela est-il arrivé? Pourquoi ces choses et non pas d'autres?
– Beaumarchais, Le Mariage de Figaro

LIKE A BADLY EDITED FILM, THE MONTAGE OF ENSUING events was hard to follow, so rapidly and incoherently did it unfold, so badly did I understand the muttered French, the air of urgency and importance with which the men climbed out, and got back in the cars, unlocked and prepared their guns, spoke over their radios. We drove along the service road where Tellman had told me to take the Opel. Two other cars crawled slowly behind us, and two were waiting at the rear of a different landscape, trees fancifully pruned, delineating arrival in Fantasyland. The sugary, pointed pink and blue towers of the castle projected above the trees. Most of the visitors to Fantasyland had now donned yellow slickers with pictures of Mickey Mouse on them, bought from the souvenir store in expectation of the rain that had been threatening. A few drops fell. I didn't see Margeeve or Gennie, or Tellman. "I think they are in the tower," I told the gendarmes. "When I left, they were going there."

"Does he still have the gun?"

"Gun? I didn't see a gun," I said. "*je n'ai pas vu* – a gun." What was the word?

I hoped he didn't have one. I knew he was volatile. The fact of his craziness came over me in hindsight – his grip on my arm, the sweat on his forehead. And now he had Gennie. How had I gone off like that, with such docility, leaving her there? Margeeve, Suzanne, left with a crazy person. The gendarmes frowned, they were grim.

I began to understand the story from what they told each other. He was an American, he had tried to kill his wife but had not succeeded. She had managed to crawl to a neighbor, she had managed to tell them he was crazy and that he had a gun. She might die, was expected to die. Thus he was a murderer. They looked at me, as if watching for my reaction. Was I his girlfriend, in on the plot? American, they said. Gun-crazy, he had shot her, but she didn't die. Not yet. "You are the *petite amie*?"

"Your boyfriend," they said to me. "You are going to call out to him." But they wouldn't let me get out of the car. From there, I thought I saw Tellman's malevolent eye looking out of the window of the tower, but it could have been a cardboard pirate too. The police surrounded the tower and herded the people in yellow slickers away, families and mothers with strollers, herded them towards Peter Pan's Flight, saying that the Pirates were closed now, shooing them all away.

"Dumbo, Dumbo est ouvert!" someone cried. *"Dumbo est ouvert!"* The tourists rushed off toward the Dumbo ride.

"He is American? He speaks English? Does he speak French? Do the ladies speak French?" One of the policemen asked me this, in heavily accented English. I explained again who they were. I didn't even try to explain who he was: my sister's former husband's lover's former husband. Had he really tried to kill Magda?

I told them about my mother, my sister's mother-in-law, my three-year-old niece being in there, two other little kids. I wondered if they were scared, I wondered if they really were even in there, and whether he would hurt them. Even if he had hurt Magda, why would he hurt them?

Once I thought I heard a wailing far off that could be

Gennie. I tried to be a blank, I tried not to think, but I also had to think what to do. I had to pee horribly. Maybe that is an effect of fear. Fear plus a powerful and inappropriate ennui. It seemed we had been sitting there for hours. I almost wished something would happen but nothing did.

"Let me call to my mother," I said.

"Allez-y," said the gendarme, pushing me out of the car. "Stand here, no closer, I am going to give you a microphone."

They fussed with a large megaphone on a cord, then held it in front of me. When I cleared my voice, a great cough ricocheted among the towers of the Château de la Belle au Bois Dormant.

"Margeeve," I called, my voice booming back at my ears. Nobody answered. Maybe she wasn't there. *"Encore,"* somebody said. I called again, but when no one answered they put me back in the car.

I am sitting in this police Renault at the opening of the service road. A young gendarme waits with me. I am rigid with unanswered questions: Are they waiting to know if I can be a help some way? Do they think I am involved? Why can't I go up closer, where the others, men wearing helmets and bulletproof vests, have assembled? This is not per se terrifying, since the French police often dress that way for very casual riots along the Boulevard Saint-Germain. But the air now is of a situation, of a crisis, of grave crime. Other men in ordinary suits arrive, I take them to be Americans, who stand unarmed and unprotected and shout up at the teeny mullioned fairy-tale windows: "Yo, Doug. Doug, it's all right, man. Talk to these people." I am sure I hear a distant wailing that could be Gennie.

The yellow slickers have drifted back from Dumbo and form an outer circle beyond the reach of the police. Dogs are brought. Two German shepherds. The crowd parts respectfully to let them and their handlers through. The dogs watch the tower too. Why?

"Yo, Doug, this isn't the way, man. Come on out. No one will shoot."

"Send out the little girl, Doug. You don't need more trouble. And the women."

And one of them said, "We've got the young woman, Doug." Was that me?

Knots of French police conferred with new Americans in EuroDisney security cars. I looked at my watch: eleven in the morning.

Noon. One. At one-thirty, in acutest misery, I explained that I had to use the toilet. The young man got out of the car and came back with a policewoman. From this I figured that I was somehow in custody and not to go anywhere alone. I wasn't worried, I was innocent of everything and had friends – did I not? – in high places. But it was odd and confers a queer sense of importance to be in custody. I could not see that any sign had been seen of Doug Tellman. There was much milling around. For some reason I wasn't really scared about Margeeve and the others; it was too unlikely, too unbelievable, too like a fantasy drama enacted to suit the place. It was as if, when you are involved in a drama of the heart, real events have no significance.

The policewoman, with no more idea than I about where we would find the toilets, led me off toward a promising low building at the edge of the service road behind us. "Do you speak English?" I asked her.

"Very leetle," she said.

"Do you really think they are in danger? My mother and Gennie? He has no reason to hurt them. He doesn't even know them." As I said this, it crossed my mind that it was Suzanne he might hurt, if he realized who she was, mother of his hated rival. She shrugged.

There were rest rooms. We took a pee, the policewoman too. It seemed unprofessional somehow. *"Comment tu t'appelles, toi?"* I asked her. These were the first words Yves had spoken to me, and a phrase I had mastered. I knew you could not ask Monsieur le Ministre in that familiar tone, but maybe a fellow woman? Even she looked a little startled, then amused.

"*Je m'appelle Huguette, moi,*" she said, "*Toi?*" We walked back outside to the unchanged scene, through the crowd of yellow-slickered bystanders. An American said, "Hostage situation."

"*Moi, je suis Isabel.*"

She led me toward the car. "Can't I just stand here?" I pleaded. But she made me get in again. Some sort of odd vehicle, looking like one of those machines that toss tennis balls, was being wheeled into place. Another hour passed. I didn't know if they had any idea whether he was really in there, but they continued to focus on this tower of the Château de la Belle au Bois Dormant. We waited and sat, with nothing happening to clarify my situation. Eventually, to pass the time, I told Huguette the story of the flea market, the tureen photo, and the theft of Mrs. Pace's tureen; to my surprise she wrote some of it down.

At last an older policeman came and put his head in the car. With him was one of the Americans in suits.

"What can you tell us, mademoiselle?" asked the American. It was the first time in these several hours that anyone had asked me what I might know about what was going on. I told them my story in English, the EuroDisney man translating for the brisk French gendarmes. I explained how Mr. Tellman had asked me to get his car, and then when I got it, how the police stopped me, the part they knew.

"He's in there," the Disney guy said. "He was spotted. Unknown whether anyone else is in there with him. He hasn't made any demands, he hasn't responded."

"My mother and another woman and a bunch of kids are with him," I said.

"Hostages, presumably."

"Am I under arrest or anything?" I asked.

"Not for the moment. We will need to understand your role," said the older gendarme, in perfect English.

"I don't have a role," I insisted. "Can't you see that?"

"*Mais non*, Americans are totally inscrutable," says Huguette to me. "Their smiles. They mask themselves with smiles. And they will not tell you their family name. 'Just call me Marilyn,' they say. It is very sinister." But to me it was they, and the situation, that were inscrutable. For the first time, I began actually to worry.

In the fog of concern and interest, in the suspended space capsule of the police car, while I was left to wonder what would happen, I thought of something Edgar once said: "You Americans imagine everything will work out for the best." Is that true?

"I used to ask myself why you believe that," he had said. "It is not the message of Protestantism, or of history either." The French are very hung up about Protestantism. They imagine it forms a whole world view, whereas to me it doesn't seem like anything. Who is right?

"Your founding fathers expressed a hope for the future and a commitment to preparing the conditions that would make possible the best outcomes. But somewhere along the way, hope was transubstantiated into belief incarnate. I believe you call it the Power of Positive Thinking," he had said. "Of course French people have no such delusions that things will work out for the best."

Would things work out for the best? Or would a maniac whose wife had left him harm my mother, Suzanne, and three little children? Since I was an American, I naturally believed he would harm them, exactly the opposite of what Edgar had said I would believe. All the hostage dramas I had seen on the evening news, every bit of footage of drive-by shooters and 7-Eleven busts, came to me, and they all turned out badly, with the miscreants and sometimes the hostages shot by police or burned alive. It was the French who seemed insouciant. Fascinated, cramped, and beginning to be wretched, it seemed to me that the French police were almost casual, almost unconcerned. They seemed prepared to camp under the windows of the tower forever.

Minutes, hours, slowed interminably. Eventually my mind drifted above the incoherent scene to the future, where a number of things became clear. I would go to Bosnia, or at least Zagreb. Why not? Either with Edgar or with a relief organization. I could drive a truck, I could be Edgar's assistant, or secretary to a delegation, I could be a reporter, I could make documentary films. In this way doing something worthwhile to make things come out for the best. It seemed beautifully clear, and it eased my mind to have at least one thing beautifully clear. The projection was as actual as a memory, me detached from my family and what used to be my country in a no-man's-land of turmoil and adventure which was beginning here, today, at EuroDisney. I would sleep with Doctors without Borders, and Bosnian Muslim diplomats. I would take dictation and write up my observations. I would help those poor women in kerchiefs. I would find homes for the rape babies no one wants. Edgar was right about responsibility and courage, that they are the things you have to have. I hoped I would turn out to have them.

It was another forty-five minutes before anything noticeable happened. Without warning, something was tossed out the window and landed heavily at the feet of a police inspector. Experts approached it gingerly, dogs sniffed it. It was Margeeve's purse. "It's my mother's purse!" I told the policewoman, Huguette, who had stayed with me in the car, and she quickly went off to tell the others. Now the somber men were looking inside it, and smirking at Margeeve's hankie and roll of Clorets.

Inside the purse a note in Margeeve's handwriting: "The children are coming out – don't shoot." The forces shouted the news down the ranks. The tourist crowd, a shifting population at the periphery of a cordoned-off area, heard and picked up the cry: the children are coming out. The women he was keeping to ensure his own safe passage somewhere. Where did they suggest? The experts exchanged looks of relief and satisfaction. One danger averted, the children unharmed, and a dialogue begun, always the finest of signs.

The sight of Margeeve's purse made real to me her plight in a way I had not really been able to feel before. I could imagine her fingers being wrested from it, or her proffering it, suggesting he put the note inside. She is clear headed, I couldn't imagine her going to pieces, she would be calm, Suzanne too, they would occupy themselves with the children. I was sure they were all right. Yet, were they?

"There is no course of action to suggest," said the gendarme to the Disney representatives. "He must come out. We make him understand he will not be harmed. Make him understand he must send the women out."

"He could go to Algeria, or Iraq," someone said.

"We are ready for the children," said the megaphone.

Presently, at the foot of the tower of Sleeping Beauty a little crooked door opened and, to my relief, Paul-Louis came out, gravely leading Marie-Odile and Gennie by their hands. The police trained drawn guns on them nonetheless. Paul-Louis blinked at the array of police and cordons and film equipment, and drew himself up slightly taller, a brave little boy. Marie-Odile and Gennie looked relatively unconcerned and certainly unhurt. They were enveloped by officials, and I then couldn't see them from where I sat captive in the police car.

"Don't you want me to talk to my niece?" I asked Huguette, my keeper. "I'm her aunt, I take care of her, she'll be glad to see someone she knows."

"Yes, a good idea," she agreed. "Come along." She opened the car door for me, as if she were a man.

When she saw me, little Gennie ran to me, saying something over and over in her hard-to-understand baby-talk French.

"What does she say?" asked the policemen, and I had to explain I couldn't understand her.

"The boy says they've not had lunch," put in Huguette. I hadn't either, it occurred to me. I offered to take the children and feed them.

"Yes, get them out of range," said the American man who evidently spoke for the group of American Disney people who were taking part, chiefly by shouting "Yo, Doug" at intervals toward the windows of the tower.

This is how we're having Mickeyburgers and chocolate shakes when, after an hour, Margeeve and Suzanne come out, almost without announcement, shaken but composed. They confirm my story, that I was not an accomplice, I was simply persuaded by Tellman to go get his car. A new shift of police come on, and the old ones come into the restaurant where the children, the policewoman, and I are sitting, and everyone sits down together and orders Mickeyburgers.

"He never told us why he was holding us. We got the idea he had committed a crime," Margeeve was explaining volubly to the police. "He tried to get Suzanne to think of someplace he could hide. He didn't hurt us." She was very up, thrilled by her adventures. "He had a gun, that's how he kept us there."

They were appalled to hear what he had done to Magda. I watched Suzanne, to see if I could guess her deepest feelings, but amazement was all I could read.

I wanted badly to hang around at this point, to see the drama played out, but it was clear someone needed to take the children home. Luckily (it seemed) Suzanne and Margeeve, energized by their ordeal, seemed up to getting back to Paris on their own with the children. How strange it is that the privileges conferred by being at the center of a drama are so fleeting. No Disney limousine to drive them back to Paris, no police car for them, but only a journey on the little perimeter train, then a taxi at the main gate, hailed by a policeman, the single concession to their brief star status as hostages. Life is capricious, proffering an instant of importance, then turning its back. Warhol's proverbial fifteen minutes. I walked with them to the taxi stand, and then back to the scene with the policeman. Of course I wanted to see the dénouement. Lights had begun to come on in the park, the festive air of night mounted, bands began strolling, people began going into the restaurants for snacks and wine.

When the police and I arrived back at the Château de la Belle au Bois Dormant, it appeared that Tellman had surrendered. He was sitting on the ground outside the tower, surrounded by police and the Disney officials. He seemed smaller, his spine sagged, his beard had sprouted, giving a gray cast to his skin, something was spilled down his shirt, and it appeared he was sobbing. He didn't look at me. Someone put something over his shoulders. There seemed to be a disagreement between the Disney men and the police, something that caused the Disney men to back off, shouting angrily. After a while, Tellman was put into the little Renault where I had been made to sit, and driven off. The police had lost interest in me. I watched for a while and then went on foot toward the entrance, amid the roving bands and cavorting men in lion costumes. In Paris, by now or soon, Suzanne would be learning about the death of her youngest son, but I did not know, as yet.

THIRTY-SIX

WE HAD LEFT ABOUT EIGHT-THIRTY IN THE MORNING. ROXY relishing the quiet day, had taken her time getting dressed. Having concluded she was not going into labor, and with a cheerful sense of relief to be rid of the rest of us, she decided to treat herself to hot chocolate at the Brasserie Espoir. She put on her coat and went downstairs. On the stairs she could hear a murmur of voices below her, and when she came into the front hall, she found it crowded with gendarmes, and little, violet-clad Madame Florian, hysterical, being seen to by a strange nurselike policewoman. Drawn to the drama, Roxy peered where the others were looking. The door to the *poubelles* in the utility room under the stairs was braced open with a trash can, and she could vaguely make out the inert legs of an apparently lifeless corpse visible behind or perhaps in the trash bins.

For a second her head rang with horror and excitement. She had heard the sirens but had not imagined them coming to this quiet building, where the only noise is the occasional shouting of Mr. Moabi, an Algerian oil dealer on the fourth floor who screams at business associates over the phone. Then came the odd idea that the lifeless body was Charles-Henri, struck down by divine justice. She was both afraid and certain that this was so. A new throng of gendarmes packed into the dim hallway. Madame Florian, wearing her coat, was sitting on the steps recounting the discovery in her high, childlike cadences to a person with a notebook. She had seen only the legs, she had been afraid to go in.

Roxy too was afraid to look again into the gloom of the utility room, but could not avoid seeing the form being covered with a cloth, some centimeters of a denim leg and foot protruding from the bin. Now she was filled with the opposing certitude that one is never to be delivered by magic from the untenable or unbearable but must go through it to the end. Charles-Henri would not be struck by death in order to deliver Roxy from the moral disadvantages of being a deserted wife in a strange land, no. And she loved Charles-Henri and did not really want him dead. All the same, a scary feeling, almost of happiness, gnawed in her, not that it was Charles-Henri, for of course it couldn't be, but she was somehow happy that at least this bolt from God, a body in the *poubelles*, would divert all attention, especially her own, bringing days and days of animated inquiry and gossip and the exchange of rumor in the Place Maubert, and she would not be able to think about Charles-Henri all the time.

Next, with sickened certitude, it came to her that the body must be Tommy Smithers, an American boy who had lived in my room in the garret before me, always drunk and waiting for money from home, perhaps slightly schizophrenic, somebody's unbearable son out of sight out of mind, pathetic Tommy who tried to borrow money from her again last week and whom she heard weeping on the stairs.

She had believed there were such things as murder mainly in America, or so they were always saying here: it is so violent, your country – people carrying guns as in a cowboy movie, the streets clotted with *foux*, with madmen, as in *Taxi Driver* or with gangsters as in *Bonnie and Clyde* – these were historical personages, no?

It was like the American procedure, she supposed, watching

a policeman who took fingerprints from the trash door and the front door. Another policeman stood at attention outside while it was going on, as bland and friendly as the young men who guard President Mitterrand, in the next street.

When she told the police her name they looked at her long and speculatively: *une américaine*. Did she know the dead individual? Had she heard nothing? What had she been doing last night around eleven? But they did not make her feel that they suspected her, they were courteous and dispassionate, nor did they tell her who he was, how old, how he had died. To their questions, she recited the names of the others in the building – her sister Isabel, the African family, Mademoiselle Lavois on the third floor, Mr. Moabi, and Madame Florian, whom they had met. Isabel, her sister, lived in the attic room, and an American, Tommy Smithers, had lived there before that. The officers nodded and wrote these things down. Then she wondered if the dead man could be Mr. Moabi, always so combative and apoplectic on the phone, surely inciting people to kill him.

"The body must have been left there by someone who knew the code to the street door, and who had a key to the trash room," said the detective.

"Not necessarily, sometimes we leave the little door open at the side," Roxy said. "The men can then take the *poubelles* directly out into the street without entering the building."

"Ah," he said, writing this down.

"Are you sure it isn't Mr. Smithers? He lived in the *chambre d'étudiant*."

"Excuse us now, madame, we will call on you a little later."

"I will go to the Brasserie Espoir," Roxy said.

Outside in the Place Maubert, all was normality. Still stunned and excited, she went to sit at one of the little terrace tables at the Brasserie Espoir, the brasserie dog underfoot, the waiters in clean morning aprons, a smell of coffee, of croissants, an aroma of the smug consensus that this was a morning arranged as mornings should be arranged, in a society that has grasped the meaning of morning, watching the mothers in their sensible shoes pushing the strollers, trailing dachshunds.

"Bonjour," said Anne-Chantal Lartigue, kissing her quickly and sitting down beside her. "I am glad to see you. The men are repairing the electrical *minuterie*, so the code to my building will not operate, and I am not allowed to enter for another half hour. Isn't that stupid?"

"Someone was found dead in our building, disposed of in the trash," Roxy told her in a wondering voice.

"Really? Who on earth?"

"They didn't tell. Madame Florian found him."

Anne-Chantal laughed merrily to think of Madame Florian and a corpse. Only then did Roxy begin to feel how unnatural was this gaiety that seemed to attend the death of a stranger, or perhaps even someone known to them, in her own hallway. But it is a way that the French have, too, of dealing with grave things, the way the Chinese are said to laugh when you fall down in an embarrassing way and may have hurt yourself.

"I must smoke," said Anne-Chantal. "You don't mind? I received the most terrible news this morning, that Jérôme – this is unbelievable – plans to spend the summer in Paris! At first I was hysterical, now I am calm. How can the man dare?"

No good pointing out that the man was a Parisian, after all, and could not leave that fact behind when he ran off.

"Seriously, though, how awful for you, a dead man, did you see him?" Anne-Chantal went on.

"I saw his foot," Roxy said, trying still to bring herself to a sense of this event and knowing that she could not, for her heart was still numb, something she felt no power over at this moment.

"How did he die?"

"I have no idea, actually."

She had been bad to Tommy Smithers. She had refused finally to lend him money, he was so exasperating, so pathetic, so continuously in turmoil, you couldn't help him out every time. Her imaginings became dreadful. Tommy had gone hustling somewhere, pickpocketing or picking up men, had been murdered by a vengeful client who knew where he once lived. Or drug overdose, that was possible too. Or suicide.

They looked over at the police inspector hurrying toward them.

"We'll be interviewed," Roxy said.

The policeman took off his hat. "Madame de Persand," he said, "we are sorry to tell you, it is grave news, it is your husband."

Roxy simply stared.

"So Madame Florian has attested. I am sorry, Madame. Could you perhaps? Could we ask you . . . ?

Roxy felt as if she had had a spinal, a cool sensation of numbness proceeding down from her neck. Now she felt nothing. She blinked at the policeman, who blinked at her. He had small round glasses. He was wearing his hat. She rose.

"That's impossible, my husband is gone," she said.

"Yes, so Madame Florian has attested. That he no longer lives with the family."

"It can't be. I don't think I should look," Roxy said. "The baby. No, I cannot look."

"Madame."

"There is a mistake."

"We understand. We are sorry. Perhaps you should not look."

"*I* will look," said Anne-Chantal. The officer seemed to be reassured by the presence of a native Frenchwoman. "I am sure it cannot be Monsieur de Persand. Madame de Persand should not look."

"If you would, Madame. You are . . . ?"

"Lartigue, Anne-Chantal. Madame. Sixty-eight Boulevard Saint-Germain. Take me to see the body."

"We are obliged to ask Madame de Persand to come also," said the policeman to Anne-Chantal, as if Roxy were not there. "But we are agreed she does not look." They crossed the rue Lagrange. All was as usual. The retarded boy who always sat on the bench was this morning bundled warmly into a coat by his mother. He groaned and barked, and the

Brasserie Metro dog barked back. The officer gallantly took Roxy's arm.

Now police cars had blocked the rue Maître-Albert. There would be sun today despite the rime of early morning frost on the bedraggled chrysanthemums in the garden of the Place Maubert. People in fur coats hurried by without looking at the commotion of police and men in plain clothes. Others stared at Roxy and Anne-Chantal as if to ask what they had done. Roxy was conscious that the policeman (strong pink face, still smelling of his shave, for it was early) slowed his steps for her sake. His touch, light on her elbow, could instantly tighten to catch her if in her unwieldy bulk she should slip. Surely they were wrong, it could not be Charles-Henri, that idea she did not take seriously.

"Madame was *à côté*," said her policeman to another who was waiting. From the hall, as they entered, Roxy could see the bizarre sight unchanged, human leg in blue jeans protruding from the trash bins, an arm illumined by the flashes of men inside photographing the scene in the dark space below the stairs.

"Madame de Persand is advised not to look," cried her policeman to the others. "She will stand here. Madame Lartigue will identify monsieur."

Roxy, feeling nothing, stood in the hall while Anne-Chantal went a few steps into the utility room. Feeling nothing, she could not even summon a feeling of surprise at Anne-Chantal's little cry, her little choked trill of dismay, or horror. "Oh *mon Dieu*, it is he."

Abruptly Anne-Chantal, shaken-looking and pale, pushed her way out of the utility room and embraced Roxy. "Oh, my poor dear, it is he."

Her policeman tightened his grip on Roxy's arm in case she should fall, as if expecting her to fall, but Roxy felt nothing. Then a slight leak began from her deadened spine into her brain, a drop of understanding, Charles-Henri in there, inexplicably dead, his legs sticking out.

"But how?" she managed finally. It made no sense at all,

thus was probably not true, yet you were to proceed as if it were true, policemen expecting you to faint or cry. She looked around, confused, to read the countenances of others. Anne-Chantal took her other arm and, to the policeman, gestured with her head toward the staircase. Roxy thought of Charles-Henri smiling, his scarf blowing, standing by a cliff they had once climbed up to, and she had been afraid the wind whipping his scarf would pull him off.

Now she felt that same crawling fear. It was too late to save him. He had fallen. His body lay broken. A sob escaped when she tried to speak, like the groan of a hinge, a sound squeezed out of her by a sudden thrash of the child inside her.

"Yes," said the inspector. "There are things we must ask madame. His whereabouts, his residence, where he was last night? But perhaps we could conduct the interview at the Commissariat de Police, it is just nearby? Madame? That will be easier?"

"Yes, just as you like," Roxy agreed.

"Are you able to walk, madame? It is just *à côté*."

This was Wednesday, not a market morning, and Roxy and the policemen walking together attracted no attention. Crossing at the light toward the rue Monge, her policeman exchanged nods with the guards at the rue de Bièvre, where President Mitterrand might be sleeping at this very moment, unaware of the shattered decorum of his neighborhood. Roxy had been inside the police station before, making an attestation when her purse was stolen. Only now did she put it to herself that her husband was dead and she was going to the police station to make an attestation, as if for some old purse.

"How did he die? Oh, tell me?" she cried.

"Can't you tell us, madame?" said the policeman. He held her elbow really very tightly. Looking sideways, she could see that his face was not friendly, not sympathetic as she had thought, she had mistaken his tone. He must think I have killed Charles-Henri, came her thought. To her horror, she heard herself giggle, like a child in school.

She thought for the millionth time, as every time she saw it, how ugly the police station was, monolith of concrete looming over the Place Maubert; goodness knew how many lovely old buildings they had pulled down, nearly a square block to build its horrible cement piers, the blind windows. They climbed the steps. Considerately slowly. Frenchmen (except for Charles-Henri) had a reverence for pregnancy, *mamans*, *bébés*. Charles-Henri was no more. Her head felt lighter and more peculiar as more of this idea dripped into it.

Inside the station, men appeared to be waiting for her.

"Madame de Persand?" said a higher official (she supposed from his more numerous buttons). They went into his office. She was sat upon a chair. Somewhere behind her she heard whispering, as the higher official settled himself into his chair, behind his desk, offices alike the world around, desk, metal bookcase, little flag on a stand, seals on the wall, wastebasket – "Madame de Persand?" Yes, Anne-Chantal was still with her, standing protectively against the wall just inside the door.

"*Crime passionnel,*" said a whisper behind her. "*L'américaine*. A gun was used. They all have guns. *Bien sûr, il s'agissait d'un coup de fusil. Elle est américaine.*"

"Your name, madame, *prénom*, *nom de jeune fille*?"

Roxy barely heard herself answer these questions, easy questions about her name, her life, her marriage. The higher official, she was thinking, looked something like her own father, same high bridge of the nose, same rusty hair. Was that not strange? Was it not strange that Charles-Henri should be dead? Later she would cry, she promised herself. She would feel, deeply feel to her heart, the pain, the poignancy, the loss of her handsome young husband. The horror of it would overcome her, she promised herself. It just had not struck her yet.

"Would you mind, madame, we will do a certain test concerning your hands," said the higher official. Anne-Chantal appeared to be smiling at her, making a little thumbs-up sign. Courage, she seemed to be saying. Good for you, she seemed to be saying. But good for you for what?

Roxy in the police station also felt a need to pee. Alert to any change within her, she asked herself was it the baby coming, but no, it was just pressure on her bladder as she got up to follow where they told her, into another room, to put her hands into soft wax or whatever it was, just routine they said again and again, they had to do it. They did not let Anne-Chantal come with her, but Anne-Chantal was hovering there supportively in the hallway, chatting with the policewoman who had welcomed them. The reality of things began to weigh more heavily on Roxy now, Charles-Henri dead, policemen asking serious questions, though she knew she was herself in no danger, she gave no thought to herself, concentrated all her power on feeling the horror, and indeed the mystery, for how did he happen to be dead? They had not said how.

She thought of her fatherless children. She thought of poor Suzanne, and the rest of the family, of how they all had loved this blithe, talented person, so lighthearted, so winsome. She thought of how the baby would never know him, Gennie not remember him, just a stupefying tragedy that had not yet burned into her own breast the way it would soon, she knew it would, but was beginning to sink in all the same.

"You may return home," they were saying, "but do not leave the area. We will escort you."

"I will stay with her, she must not be alone, we will call her mother," cried Anne-Chantal. "We must call the Persands. Have you notified the Persands?" Roxy's head spun with a sort of exhaustion in advance, thinking of all the notifying, all the pain in store. It was strange that a policeman was coming with her and Anne-Chantal.

He said he would stay downstairs, in the foyer of her building. The utility room was sealed with yellow tape.

It was only noon. Was that possible? She thought she should call Roger. She thought she should lie down, and Anne-Chantal agreed. Anne-Chantal took Roxy's telephone book and sat in the salon to make the calls.

Through the long afternoon, into the early twilight, Roxy keeps asking Anne-Chantal if Suzanne is back from Disneyland, and Anne-Chantal keeps calling the number and shaking her head. Eventually she reaches Antoine. Antoine arrives at the rue Maître-Albert. He spends a long time in the corridor with the police and then comes up to Roxy's, face, pinched, tearful and grim. He embraces Roxy and drinks a cognac. Then he calls Frédéric and Charlotte. Roxy can hear Charlotte's screams through the telephone. Antoine's voice is husky but controlled, in charge.

"Roxeanne is under arrest, I think," says Antoine to Charlotte. "Her status is unclear."

"Trudi is in the country, she's coming," he says to Roxeanne. His staunch, loyal demeanor makes it clear that he does not for a moment believe that poor Roxy had anything to do with this shocking tragedy. The Persands are coming to her side. All agree it is strange that Isabel and her mother and Suzanne and the children are not yet back from EuroDisney. There is such pain at the prospect of having to tell Suzanne the horrible news about her son. It is beyond horrible to think of her blithely unaware, yet, with it so likely they will return soon, *inutile* to go searching. It occurs to Roxy again to wonder how he died, and by whose hand? Could it have been by his own? They never said.

Anne-Chantal, hearing her moan of distress, rushes in to feel her forehead.

"Is it the baby?" she asks. "Oh, how beautiful if the baby would come soon, to lift our hearts with a new life."

"I must go see him," she cries. "Is he – still down there?"

"No, no, definitely not, you must not look. Later, at the interment."

THIRTY-SEVEN

AT EURODISNEY, I KNEW NOTHING OF ANY OF THIS, FOR NO one revealed it. I wanted to try to understand the strange day by myself, and so I decided, with Tellman's complimentary pass, to try the food at the Disneyland Hotel. In the somewhat heavy-handed charm of the Victorian dining room, I ordered dinner and thought about things. It was a wide-ranging reverie about making love to Edgar in Zagreb, getting rich from Saint Ursula, and wondering what would happen if Magda Tellman died. If she died, I supposed Charles-Henri would come back to Roxy, and that would set me free.

Looking back, this seems rather callous, but I just wasn't ready to go home to the others yet. Thus, eating *blanquette de veau* and drinking a half bottle of Côtes du Rhône at the Disneyland, I missed the distressing scene when Suzanne and Margeeve brought Gennie back to the rue Maître-Albert and learned from Anne-Chantal the news about Charles-Henri, only hearing it myself about ten when I came home. The police at EuroDisney had not known about the death at 12 rue Maître-Albert.

When I got to the rue Maître-Albert, Roxy's lights were dark. I climbed the stairs to the garret without stopping.

There was a note on my door to say they had all gone to the Avenue Wagram. This was puzzling, but not necessarily ominous. Perhaps, I thought, Suzanne had proposed dinner for her heroic band of erstwhile hostages. I went down to Roxy's and called my parents' hotel, though, to make sure they weren't there, and they were not. Then I decided to telephone Edgar – it was he I wanted to talk to anyway, so I went back down to Roxy's apartment and sat in the dark living room.

"Ah, Isabel, how are you?" he said.

"I'm okay. Has anyone told you about today?"

"Which part of the day? The Serbs have resumed shelling Sarajevo. My sister was held hostage for seven hours by a crazed American in the Disney theme park, then there is the matter of the murder of my nephew."

"Who?" I cried with sudden horror, seeing that it would be Charles-Henri, of course.

"Charles-Henri. Shot three times in the chest and left to die in the *poubelles* at Maître-Albert.

I don't know what I said. It was clear enough. Tellman had killed Charles-Henri, and tried to kill Magda.

"At first, naturally," continued Edgar, in the same dry, almost angry tone, "the police suspected Roxeanne. I spoke to the Commissaire. But the injured Magda had crawled from her cottage to the Spectorama warehouse by the motorway and found help. She told her story. Her husband had shot her."

"My God," I said, thinking, poor Roxy, poor Charles-Henri, how stupid. Tellman a murderer, he might have killed the children after all. I even thought, poor Magda, maybe Charles-Henri was the love of her life, does anyone care about poor Magda? Does anyone believe in love? I felt like crying, but it was all too strange for tears.

"*Mon Dieu,*" Edgar said. "What a world!" he cried in the bitterest tone. "The red and the black – who would have thought the black would so quickly supplant the red?"

I think he may have been talking about Bosnia. "May I come over?" For I wanted to be in his arms.

"*Non*, *chérie*, I am just going to the Avenue Wagram.

Suzanne is very distraught. Your parents are there, I think."

"I'll see you there, then, I guess."

I heard a noise and turned around in the dark living room, startled to find Roxy had been standing in the doorway of her bedroom.

"They're over at Suzanne's," she said.

"Roxy, how horrible, I didn't hear, I didn't realize you were here. I just got here, I . . ." I began. "I'll stay with you."

"I made them go. I wanted to be alone," she said. "They took Gennie over there. I've taken some sleeping stuff. Supposedly not harmful to fetuses. I'm going to sleep."

"Roxy, my God," I tried to say again, but of course there was nothing to say: sorrow, pity, shock. The way life can turn around in a minute, you never know. "It was the husband, that guy Tellman . . ."

"I know, I heard. I think they thought it was me," she said. Her voice was drugged, bemused and sad.

"You can't be alone! I'll stay here."

"I'll go to sleep in a minute. I couldn't go with them. I made them go. Iz, there's something – I feel as though I killed Charles-Henri. But I can't ever tell them." From her face, I saw that she did think that. Her eyes were the strange sleepless eyes of Lady Macbeth.

I didn't know what idea had gotten into her drugged brain. Of course she hadn't killed him; Roxy could not be blamed for this. Think of her unwavering loyalty to Charles-Henri, her resistance to divorce, the little pledge of his love so soon to be born – not even the Persands could blame her. I made her go back to bed. I felt tender toward her, and full of pity.

When she was lying down, she grabbed my arm and hissed at me, "I wish I was a hard-hearted, cold person like you, Isabel. You always have everything the way you want it. Maybe someday you'll suffer too, but I doubt it. But I don't hate you. I used to, I think, but . . ." Whereupon her eyelids fluttered closed, and she had drifted off into some kind of stoned sleep.

I was shocked, but part of me was not surprised she

thought these things. I wondered if they were the bitter reflections of the sad moment or the secrets of her unconscious.

Of course I couldn't leave her alone. I thought it was strange that the others had left her. I sat on the sofa in the dark, burning to go to Edgar.

It was only a few minutes before someone rang the doorbell.

"Ames," he said, and I buzzed him in.

"How is she?" he asked, his usually smirky face transformed by love and concern. All at once I saw the nice side of Ames, like a mirror reflecting backward on a hundred other instants, things he had told me and guided me. His excellent cooking and his responsible dog ownership and reputation for charity.

"I talked to her a half hour ago, and she told me she was alone. How could they have left her alone?"

"She probably made them. People don't cross Roxy."

"I'm staying with her. I came over to stay with her."

"Could you, Ames?" I said. The limitations of my judgments about people became clearer all the time. "I'd like to go be with my mother and Suzanne. Did you hear about what happened to them?"

I had plenty of time on the metro to the Avenue Wagram (two changes) to wonder what Roxy had meant when she said she used to hate me, but I didn't take it seriously and put it out of my mind. I was too stunned in myself.

In Suzanne's big Haussmannian apartment, Suzanne, her tear-stained face resolutely smiling, seated, surrounded by her eldest son, Frédéric, Antoine and Trudi, Charlotte and Bob, Chester and Margeeve, an unexplained man perhaps from the police, Roger and Jane, a doctor called Monsieur Quelquechose, Roxy's lawyer Maître Bertram, and another man, talking to him, who could have been the Persands' lawyer. And Edgar. I saw my father looking covertly at him as Edgar bent over Suzanne's chair to talk to her. Altogether a scene of great animation. An atmosphere of resolution and courage, Gennie in bed already, a discussion with Jane of sleeping pills for Suzanne, Antoine trying to get Monsieur de Persand on the telephone somewhere in Poland, Paul-Louis and Marie-Odile huddled on cushions on the floor. Edgar turned to look at me when I came in, it seemed with a more acknowledged familiarity, or maybe I was imagining that.

Later, when I went into the kitchen to make tea, he came in. His voice was low.

"I am leaving on Sunday. I'm sorry to leave my sister at such a time. I am sorry to leave you."

"It wasn't Roxy's fault," I said. "Roxy loved him."

"A timely death, from Roxeanne's point of view," he said, watching me. "A widow's halo instead of the scarlet compromises of the divorcée. Her children safely to inherit. A seamless bond with Suzanne, and so on. Suzanne. It is a hard thing to see your child die, the hardest thing, I imagine."

They do believe it's Roxy's fault, I thought. They think if she had been a better wife, and used cube sugar and done her nails, he wouldn't have taken up with Magda.

"I had not thought of the *crime passionnel* as a particularly American form. This Tellman. American violence you read is usually related to drugs or robbery."

"Oh, what shall I do?" I cried. "Will you want me when you come back?"

But he had no opportunity to answer, as Antoine came in at that moment.

Of course I was as crushed and miserable as the others, and sat with them as the hours wore on, all the hours that had to be got through until things could be done, tomorrow, to ease the thinking about it. Was I surprised? Not entirely. From what we knew had happened to Magda, it seemed obvious that Tellman had killed Charles-Henri. I supposed it was obvious to everyone else. The man was in custody. I hadn't minded about him shooting Magda, it was no more than fascinating, for I had never seen her. But I minded about Charles-Henri. It was my first death.

"*Oh, oh, mon petit,*" moaned Suzanne, dry-eyed and tiny, sitting on the *canapé*. "*Je ne peux pas le croire.*"

THIRTY-EIGHT

GOING HOME, GENNIE AND I SHARED A TAXI WITH MY parents, the first moments we had been alone. They were shocked, of course, but mostly were concerned for Roxy and, it seemed to me, not above feeling at some level that Charles-Henri had brought down righteous vengeance on himself for his treatment of their daughter. There was a note of that, though they would have denied it. "It's amazing, the workings of fate," Margeeve sighed. Fate being, as I knew, a sometime code for divine judgment, which of course she didn't usually believe in.

"This was a day I won't soon forget," Margeeve kept saying.

That night I slept on Roxy's sofa, in case she should call out in the night, but she didn't. I rose early, before she was up, and fed Gennie. When Margeeve and Chester got there, I said I had an errand, and went to the flea market to look at the stolen tureen. It was a way of keeping my mind off things. There is nothing your mind can do with a fact as immutable and unacceptable as death anyway, and I was denied the distraction of doing the busy work of death, Antoine and Roxy herself did all that, calling people, and giving statements. In

Libération, which I read on the 85 bus, I found an account of a gunshot murder by an irate American employed by EuroDisney, of his wife's lover (name not mentioned) and the attempted murder of his wife. He had been arrested after a hostage drama at the park itself, according to this account, and was being held.

It was Mrs. Pace's tureen, as I had known it would be. Stolen for a client (me) by thieves (who?) unaware of the coincidence that I myself had taken their photograph of it. But who had given them the picture, and the orders?

I asked to see more photographs. He had thirty or so in an envelope and laid them out before me. It wasn't long before I found what I was looking for, as detectives say in books: photos of Suzanne's living room at Chartres, featuring a nice array of faience plates that hang on the wall. "The Persands have wonderful old dishes," I had said to Stuart Barbee. Stuart had seen the things they had given Roxy. They – someone Stuart knew – had "visited" and taken photos.

That Stuart Barbee could be involved in a ring of porcelain thieves seemed a bit far fetched, and so did the apparent fact that the porcelain thieves had been interested in the very files of Mrs. Pace that I had been asked to spy into, which would have to mean that Cleve Randolph was involved – even more far fetched. It would have to mean that the CIA was running a French porcelain thievery ring. To puzzle over this funny idea provided a certain amount of distraction I was grateful for, though I didn't get far with a solution. But I did call the number of Huguette, the policewoman, at her bureau and leave a message, as I'd promised I would.

I was stupefied at the price of the tureen, twenty thousand francs, around four thousand dollars. I thought I had better leave its recovery to the police. I temporized by telling the dealer I'd have to see if I could get enough money together.

I have to admit I was thinking of maybe some slightly less expensive tureen, in view of the way things were turning out with Edgar. On the other hand, maybe the right existential *geste* would be to buy a really ruinous one for him. There were lots of tureens in the world, also pitchers and plates. I would just have to see.

Then I went back to Maître-Albert, to the muted closeness of a morning after death. I was glad Charles-Henri had already removed his own things from Roxy's apartment so we didn't have to look at his shoes and his hairbrush.

Roxy so brave, being beautifully brave. Admired by all for her grave dignity, the way she was bearing up, the imminence of her confinement. Her friends from around the Place Maubert brought *tartes* and pâtés. The day was flat, odd, long. Charles-Henri lay in a police morgue somewhere. They told us it might be a long time before the police would give him up for burial. Edgar brought the Abbé Montlaur to visit Roxy.

Roger reported in the afternoon that his employers were attempting to get Doug Tellman released on bail with a writ of habeas corpus.

"Yes, Isabel, habeas corpus exists in France," said Edgar ironically when I exclaimed on the impossibility of that. "You Americans seem to believe that only Americans are unequivocally blessed. That all other nations on earth are constrained by the feebleness of their moral energy or the benightedness of their institutions." Like last night, his tone was angry at me, as if he regretted knowing Americans. His tone burned deeper into the hollow burn in my stomach the death had brought on.

"I do?" I said.

"You Americans have the conviction – perhaps because you have been endlessly told it – that you are the freest nation in the world, which is hardly true. If one mentions, say, your murder rate, you say, 'That is the price we pay for freedom,' but one might like to ask, freedom for what? Freedom to walk safely down the street is not a freedom you have."

I had not deserved this lecture, particularly. "I don't think those things." I perceived that I was being held responsible for all the deficiencies of my tribe. Even the Abbé Montlaur had a frosty expression of assent to Edgar's words. "You mean

Americans, you don't mean me," I protested.

"You are very American, Isabel," Edgar said.

"Since France is so obsessed with *liberté*, no doubt they'll let him out," I said.

"I killed him," shouted Roxy histrionically. We saw she had been dozing and had come awake these words as if from a dream. "He was coming back to me. I know it. Why else was he there, in the building, last night?"

If she thought he was coming back to her, so much the better, though that made for an unbearable irony too, that he should have been struck down just then. Maybe he was. I was relieved Roxy had not really killed him. That was part of the moral strength of her position. Even the Persands knew that she had not killed him, his own erotic caprice had led him into death. It was an American who had killed him, though. An American with a handgun. We were all aware of that.

May the Sacred Heart of Jesus be adored, glorified, loved, and preserved, throughout the world, now and forever. Sacred Heart of Jesus, pray for us. Saint Jude, worker of miracles, pray for us. Saint Jude, help of the hopeless, pray for us.

Say this prayer nine times a day for nine days and your prayers will be answered. This never fails. Publication must be promised.

Lying in her drugged half-sleep, it had come to Roxy that she had killed him with this prayer. She had said it nine times a day for nine days and God had looked into her heart, divined the unspoken, completely unconscious wish there, and answered it.

It had not escaped me that when they all spoke of what had happened – to the press, to their friends, to the anxious, the shocked, the religious, the merely curious – they said *l'américain*. They did not say that Charles-Henri had been killed by his mistress's husband. No, they always said he had been killed by *un américain*. Edgar put it that way, so did Anne-

Chantal, so did Suzanne, so did the official spokesman Antoine, and so did the newspaper.

Roxy in her heart thinking about the efficacy of prayer and about how God works in mysterious ways. She wished to discuss a certain issue with a priest. Telling Margeeve she wanted to be alone, in the late afternoon she walked across the Pont de l'Archevêché and through the gardens of Notre Dame and into the vast, somewhat dank interior.

There, to Roxy too was given a glimpse into the future. Only slowly it began to dawn on her that she was a widow and that a widow was something different from a divorcée. That she could have her chest of drawers back from Drouot, and Saint Ursula, there wasn't going to be any divorce.

How she fought the inexorable warm feeling of relief that flooded over her, for it meant she must be a monster. She analyzed, took the temperature of this emotion, to make sure she wasn't in any sense happy or glad Charles-Henri was dead. She thought about what black clothing she had in her closet.

Relief different from gladness. Of course, she told herself, she was not glad, she was devastated. She fled to church, unable to bear the undistracted access that repose afforded to the turmoil of her wicked thoughts of relief, as one by one the real advantages of this lucky tragedy sank in upon her.

When she came back again from Notre Dame, a walk of a few minutes, she looked excited, even radiant. Not because she had seen a priest, she said, but because her waters had broken, on the ancient pavings of the cathedral, and she was bound to go into labor soon. The drama of this coming event, its risky testimony to the future, the noble effort required of her now, the putting forth of another hostage to fortune, reassured her, reassured all of us. The delicate perfume of high excitement overpowered the heavy odors of the floral tributes and ritual pâtés and cheeses that suffused the apartment. Margeeve telephoned Suzanne. We inquired after Roxy's contractions, and spoke to shocked mourners on the telephone, balancing the emotional expenditures appropriate to life and death.

About midnight that night, when she had had a few definitive twinges, Chester and Margeeve took Roxy to the *clinique maternelle*.

I washed up the coffee cups and wine glasses that littered the tables, and slept another night on Roxy's sofa, manning the phone. Nothing woke me but my own troubled dreams. I dreamt of Santa Barbara, the corner of Morales and Tenth Street, a certain gas station there. My car had run out of gas, and I was walking to this gas station when another car passed me, almost grazing me, coming up on me from behind, frightening me. I was wondering if the driver meant to kill me or if it had been an accident. Then the gas station man came out and said, "You don't know who that was, do you?" This dream was so vivid, the pale, bright light of Santa Barbara so vivid, and the sea smell, that I was really there, and for an instant, waking up on a sofa in Paris, I was disoriented and panicky. The phone was ringing.

THIRTY-NINE

Dawn was at hand, and I could already make out objects in the landscape.
– Benjamin Constant, Adolphe

It was Friday and it was Roger on the phone, his voice suavely businesslike, as if one down day for a death was the limit and now we must be up to speed. "Today's the sale. Are you coming?"

In the confusion and anguish of the past days, I would have forgotten the picture, Drouot, the money, but Roger had whispered to me the night before, "Isabel, I think we go through with the sale, before any new legal conditions obtain. This way it can be argued that selling it was Charles-Henri's intention as well as Roxy's, because God knows what complications if the Persands get the idea it's part of Charles-Henri's estate. This way there's no question of us appearing to do anything he hadn't sanctioned beforehand. In the circumstances, I think we just get it sold now, whatever Roxy says, before whatever new conditions of her legal life set in, *fait accompli*, as the locals say."

What had gone on behind the scenes we had no way of knowing, but at Drouot, officials had assured him that with major picture dealers and museum curators already on their way to attend, the sale would be brilliant. Perhaps whiffs of museum gossip, hints of the presence of a Christie's man speaking to Roger – for whatever reason, they had also now proposed a much higher reserve than the eighty thousand dollars they had originally set. The alluring promise of money has tangible effects, even on auctioneers, and they had clearly been influenced by Christie's confident attribution (as revealed to them by Roger).

"If nothing is happening with Roxy, I'll come with you," I said.

There was no word from or of Roxy, but Chester, at their hotel, said she had been put to bed with indolent cramps and had not been in vigorous labor when they left at three. He sounded sleepy and slightly cross to have been waked up.

"Aren't you coming to the sale?" I asked.

"I don't know. I'll see what Margeeve wants to do. She'll probably want to stay with Roxy."

"I'll go on with Roger," I said.

"We don't need to be there," Chester said. "It isn't as if we were going to bid on it."

I needed to be there. I had a sort of superstitious feeling that I needed to be everywhere, to control everything, it was all getting out of control, or would, if I didn't watch it and note it; I had to be everywhere at once.

We could hardly get into the room where the paintings would be sold. In the atmosphere of commerce and luck, in the poker-playing deadpan gambling atmosphere of an auction house, mere humanity seemed to play only a minor role. Inanimate things reigned, money ruled, competition festered, elation soured. A hundred objects were being carted away or carted in, throngs of people buzzing in French jammed doorways to the various salons, people gazed at rings in glass case, and battered harpsichords.

Ours was a hot-ticket sale, it seemed, attracting a graver and more barbered crowd than those who had gathered to buy the attic odd-lots in the *salle* opposite, but who jostled each other viciously all the same. Pushing my way into the room, I became aware that here and there were familiar faces I had not noticed at first. Stuart Barbee and Ames Everett were there, talking to a heavy well-tailored gray man and – something a little surprising – Antoine and Charlotte de Persand, with Charles-Henri's lawyer Maître Doisneau. Here also was Maître Bertram. There was Monsieur Desmond, the man who had appraised Saint Ursula for the Louvre, and there were a group of men in bow ties and tweed sport coats that could be (for all I knew) from Santa Barbara. Perhaps from the Getty. There was even – it took me a minute to remember who that youngish, balding, familiar man with the long eyelashes was – Monsieur le Directeur du Cabinet, whom I had met at the opera, the Under-Minister of Culture. Now that did astonish me, as Mrs. Pace would say. In a dark suit, double vents, standing to one side in voluble conversation with two other dark-suited men, who had both put their briefcases on the floor, making me think of spy films where they are going to switch the cases. Monsieur Desmond went over to them.

I waved over someone's shoulder to Antoine de Persand and Charlotte. "I didn't realize you'd be coming."

Antoine frowned a little, as if he were surprised to see me, and weighed his answer for what seemed a long moment.

"I suppose it is up to me now, to see that Roxeanne's *affaires* are conducted correctly and to look after the interests of my niece and the baby," he said, shrugging unhappily. "What is correct, of course, that is not so easy to say." He jostled his way closer to me.

"The baby is on the way!" I whispered. "Maybe here by now!"

"Yes, your mother called. Suzanne has gone to the *clinique*. A baby will ease her heart a little."

"Maître Bertram is here, Roxy's lawyer," I observed.

"Yes, I spoke to him. He says there is an important Poussin being sold here today as well." That was probably why the Under-Minister of Culture was here, looking after the patrimony of France.

Behind rows of chairs where privileged bidders were sitting, standees closely thronged. I am tall, and yet, stuck in the back as we were, I could hardly see the podium. Roger, who is taller, was better positioned too, but neither of us could understand what was going on anyway. An auctioneer at a raised dais stood indicating a painting on an easel behind him. His explanations, in rapid French, would excite murmurs or silence, then people would mention sums of francs, inaudibly, several people, then at the end only two, and it would be abruptly over, with the sharp crack of the gavel and a rustle of comment from the audience. In this fashion, several paintings were whisked in and out and away before our eyes: a Watteau, an *Inconnu*, a Lapautre, a Bouguereau, a Rosa Bonheur.

A groundling undertone of excitement mounted with each successive exchange, affecting me, perhaps Roger too, with an anxious wish it could be over. As so often, I had too much the feeling of being a powerless spectator caught up in an unwanted event. Could it be true that Saint Ursula would come in, meet her fate, and be gone in this summary way, even as Roxy lay groaning, unaware, in some clinic somewhere? The treachery of our action in letting the sale go on struck me only now.

When a large mythological scene – hunters in togas chasing a deer – was brought in and placed reverently on the easel, the room became hushed. The important people were evidently not gathered as I had thought for our Saint Ursula, but for this Poussin. The auctioneer discussed it a moment in a somber, portentous tone: "A company of the followers of Diana – Regard the coloration . . .

"Am I bid a million to start?" he asked. A man two rows ahead of me made a tiny gesture that I could see from where I stood, but I could not see other bidders who nonetheless were there, driving up the price, up, up, up, to forty million francs. When this price had been achieved, with no change of expression, when a long and even agonizing pause announced the end and the collapse of the rest, and the bang of the gavel completed the sale, the Poussin was carted from the room as unceremoniously as the painting of *inconnu*. The auctioneer permitted a sigh, a stretch, a pause. Ames Everett, seeing me, winked. The Under-Minister of Culture nodded with a half smile, wondering, I was sure, where he had seen me.

Other pictures, and finally Saint Ursula. My heart pounded to see her amused and slightly repelled expression. I tried to see Roger's face but could not. I sensed his excitement all the same. We stood trembling in the crowd. "La Tour," I heard the auctioneer say, but not *école* and not *élève*, though he could have, the words spun in my ears. "Do I hear two hundred thousand?" he said.

It seemed no more than forty seconds before Saint Ursula was knocked down at six million francs, a struggle between two bidders principally. One was the man standing with Ames and Stuart, the other, in his tweed sport coat and bow tie, an American, I was sure. I had no idea which had bought our painting. For a second I even had trouble calculating the amount in dollars. My heart was thundering. More than a million dollars!

It was only at this very minute that I realized we wouldn't have to split it with the Persands, either. I wonder if Antoine realized that. I could see his expression of glassy shock, muttering to Frédéric. I calculated further. Let's say split four ways – me, Roxy, Roger, Judith – there would ultimately if not immediately be for me two hundred and fifty thousand dollars! Surely Chester would advance me the price of a tureen – not Mrs. Pace's, of course. I thought of all the other things I could do with a quarter of a million dollars. I wondered if this could do anything to make Roxy less unhappy. Probably it would make her feel worse, to profit somehow from the death of her beloved. I tried to leave the room, to breathe luxuriously in the hall, but I was packed too closely in. There were another ten pictures to sell, then it was over.

"Isabel!" said Stuart Barbee, coming up to me when the crowd began to drift out. He was trying to smile, but his face was distorted with a misery I had seen earlier when he stood talking to Ames. "Isabel, I'm so happy for Roxeanne. She needs some luck, poor girl . . ."

"What's the matter, Stuart?" I asked.

"Conrad has been arrested," he whispered. Conrad his friend the English hairdresser.

"What for?"

"For burglary."

How it worked I figured perfectly: Stuart gave Conrad photos and tips. Unknowingly? Conrad gave the photos to a dealer friend who showed them to clients. Then Conrad went and burgled the things that clients asked for. I wondered, had it been Conrad who had "visited" Suzanne after we told Stuart about all her beautiful stuff?

I considered extorting from Stuart at least Mrs. Pace's tureen. I could say, get it back or I will tell you everything. I'll describe how I took the photo, gave it to you, then triggered its theft by promising to buy it from the dealer. Get it back or I will involve you. But then I thought it might be better not to let him know my role; we would get it back through the police anyway. But what was Stuart's role? And the connection with Mrs. Pace's files? It still seemed funny to imagine the CIA running a porcelain burglary ring.

"He was just standing there, outside a house in Chartres, and the *flics* came up and grabbed him," Stuart went on.

"*Bonjour, mademoiselle,*" interrupted the Under-Minister of Culture in the rustle of the crowd. "Miss Walker, am I right? So you interest yourself in the art treasures of France?"

I guess I don't believe in God, at least not as much as Roxy does; all the same, it is hard not to believe this little consolation was sent by some benign cosmic intent. The Under-Minister was talking to me! And that was not all. I was glad I had dressed up, and was carrying the Kelly.

"I had to see the fate of my little La Tour," I said with what I hoped was immense composure.

"Indeed! Your La Tour? I came because I was interested to see what would happen with the great Poussin. As to the La Tour, we had hoped . . . yours, you say?" Smooth diplomat's charming smile, concealing concern.

"It belonged to my family." I was conscious of Stuart's ironic look. Well, didn't it?

"Indeed! Extraordinary. Do you know who the buyer was?"

"No, not yet. Have you met my brother and sister-in-law?" For the jubilant Roger, Jane at his elbow, had made his way to my side. They and the Under-Minister (Monsieur LeLay) exchanged *bonjours.*

"I wonder about the export situation? Obviously it is a national treasure. It appears there was a moment of inattention at the Louvre. We must look into it – the Louvre will review it," Monsieur le Directeur went on. "I wonder that they didn't review it before this. I will look into it." I felt myself grow wary. Could they bring up the export license thing again?

"Perhaps – I hope you are not pressed, mademoiselle? Would you consider having lunch with me, for I would very much like – in my role at the ministry – to hear the history of this lovely French picture, how it came to be in your family and so on. Today, or some other time soon, what do you say?"

Covertly, I studied him. It seemed to me this was not the diplomat but the man talking. I accepted, of course, though not for today. I explained that my sister was having a baby.

"Give me your *numéro de téléphone, mademoiselle,*" he said, pulling out his elegant little *carnet* from Hermès.

Baby Charles-Luc was born that afternoon, weighing three and a half kilos – the phone was ringing as the ecstatic Roger, Jane, and I arrived at Roxy's. An easy delivery, mother and baby doing well. We headed for the clinic to meet the baby, and tell Roxy the news.

At the burial on Monday, a cold, funereal day, Roxy was very beautiful in a black suit I hadn't seen before, which must from the way it fit her slightly stouter figure have been new. She carried the baby, little Charles-Luc, wrapped in dimity and lace, as if this were a christening rather than a funeral. At one point she handed him (a minute, wizened, red creature) to Chester, who gazed at him proudly, and Roxy occupied herself with Gennie, who fidgeted in her little fur-trimmed blue coat, overawed by the collection of relatives and mourners gathered in the cold winter morning among the imposing granite-winged monuments of the Cimetière du Montparnasse.

Of course Magda would not come to the *obsèques*, we had heard she was still in the hospital. Nonetheless I looked for a mysterious person in a black veil lingering on the fringes behind the willow shrubs. The scene made me think of the funeral of John F. Kennedy, which I had seen a newsreel of. I think Roxy was remembering it too, though neither of us was born then, for she seemed to borrow her demeanor of dignified, grieving widow from the performance of Jackie O. She knelt at the grave. Behind her, standing a little apart from the Persands, was Maître Bertram. There were Madame Cosset with Antoine and Trudi, Yvonne, Charlotte and Bob, Frédéric but not his wife, Suzanne also in black, and – I was most curious – Monsieur de Persand, a tall, thin man with a white mustache and a restless, angry expression when he glanced at us and at our uninhibited New World sobbing. How correct they were in their mourning garments. How correct they had been all the way through.

It was an American who had killed him. I knew they were not forgetting that. Nor had his American wife been able to prevent it, with her inadequate arts. Members of a childish nation – I knew what they thought – cradle of killers and art thieves. (And of porcelain thieves, they would have said, had they known.) How much better, they must have been thinking, if the Marquis de Lafayette had never gone over there.

How beautiful Roxy was, Roxy who was now theirs forever, widow of their son, mother of their grandchildren – the widow a hallowed person in France, I gathered, emblem of fidelity and patient grief. She stood a little apart from the Persands and also from our parents, solitary in her sorrow except for the attentive Maître Bertram.

"'*Je suis la ténébreuse, la veuve, l'inconsolée,*'" she whispered, kneeling by the grave, paraphrasing (she told me later) some lines of Nerval. "'*Pleurez! Enfants, vous n'avez plus de père.*'"

Maître Bertram assisted her to rise with a light, solicitous grasp of her elbow. Her expression of grief contained inner serenity, a luminous certitude. Perhaps she had everything she wanted. I was given a glimpse of Roxy, just then, as someone who always will get what she wants.

"Oh, Iz," whispered Margeeve when the clods began to fall, "now Roxy can come home." Maybe she would, maybe she wouldn't.

She had no need to choose. She had everything she wanted. *L'américaine*. She could have everything. She had helped herself. She had borne and survived, and would continue, no doubt. She could choose among continents, languages, religions, and roles.

Not to speak of myself, but I was thinking how perfect Roxy was, a lily of the field, and of how she had what she wanted. I thought of Mary and Martha. In our days of going to Sunday school (we had to when we were your age, Margeeve and Chester had explained when we asked them why they didn't go) the story of Mary and Martha was one of the many Biblical stories from which I had drawn a moral the opposite of the one intended, and was on the wrong side, as in the novels of Henry James, which Mrs. Pace had suggested I read. I knew you were supposed to be Mary; but Roxy was Mary.

FORTY

One should always have one's boots on and be ready to leave.

– Montaigne

CONFINED, IMMURED BY GRIEF, THE CONVENTIONS OF bereavement and the new baby, we became aware only slowly, through Roger via his fellow lawyer contacts, that the situation of Tellman, arrested by the French police, had drawn the sympathy and indignation of the American community. Mrs. Pace confirmed that this was so. And I thought from her tone that she shared in part the general view that Tellman, a disturbed person, was being treated more harshly in French law than an enraged French lover would be treated – say, a fiery Corsican or a North African or an African, beings whose murderous rages would be taken for granted and responded to, if not with forgiveness, at least with a touch of condescending leniency congruent with the less civilized mores of their respective countries. A rich American lawyer excited unspoken enmities, implacable agendas of retribution.

The indignation of the American community on Tellman's behalf was fueled mainly by his lawyer colleagues, who recited the humiliations the poor guy had been made to suffer by his tarty Czechoslovakian wife and her insolent Frenchman lover – indignities greater than anyone could bear, let alone a fragile person like Doug, with his valiant struggle against some substance abuse problems he'd been able to handle until all this struck.

We had heard that there would be a meeting of interested Americans to consider organizing a protest on Tellman's behalf: letters to the newspapers, delegations to the Minister of Foreign Affairs, perhaps intervention at the ambassadorial level. I did not expect when I went for my regular afternoon at the Cleve Randolphs to find a foregathering of concerned Americans there – some of the same EuroDisney people who had been there during their cocktail party, a dozen lawyers, Stuart Barbee and Ames Everett, Mrs. Pace, and even the American ambassador, Leo Burleigh, whom I had seen only from afar. It was for these that Peg Randolph had asked me to pick up some party food at the *traiteur*.

I came in as diffidently as a maid, carrying the pink boxes, and sidled toward the kitchen.

"We mustn't lose sight of the fact that this is an *American citizen*," Cleve Randolph was saying. "They are presuming him guilty until he can prove his innocence, which is totally un-American to begin with. *Guilty until proven innocent* – that's what's so intolerable about the Napoleonic code."

When people saw me, the room fell as silent as a library. Faces turned to look at me; I could almost hear knuckles crack. Peg Randolph came toward me, wearing an expression suitable to be seen by the grieving, as I must be supposed to be doing, sister-in-law of the victim, and the heroine in her own right of, or at least participant in, the drama of the Tower.

"The man needs psychiatric help," she said.

"I know," I said, sidling nearer to the kitchen door so I could get on with putting little slices of smoked eel pâté on a platter and black olives in her Limoges bowls.

"Crime of passion," the others went on.

"What would you do if someone was shtupping your wife?" said someone.

"And there's another principle involved: Can foreign governments just do what they want with an American citizen?"

"I'm afraid they can," interjected the American ambassador, vainly trying to calm them. "Think of the boy who was caned in Singapore. The president pleaded for clemency, and even that did not avail."

"Just shows the contempt our president is held in," said Cleve Randolph. "And you can see why."

"American nationals are bound by the laws of the country they are in," repeated the ambassador. "The issue is that we are dealing with a disturbed individual here, and he needs psychiatric help. He wasn't really responsible for this admittedly horrible crime."

"Stuart Barbee's friend Conrad has been arrested too," whispered Peg into the kitchen.

"Basic human rights," I heard Ames Everett say, heard everyone saying much, much more, voices raised, faces indignant. I thought of a discussion I had had with Edgar about basic human rights. ("People who believe in Human Rights today are the same people who twenty years ago – longer ago than that, now – believed in Workers. Then Workers moved to the right, as they got a little money, and it was necessary to put the matter more broadly.") Of course, I had never met a Worker.

Now I noticed that people wore their names on paper stick-on badges, evidently distributed by the EuroDisney people, and the badges also bore the likeness of Mickey Mouse.

There was another hush of embarrassed silence when I – sister to the widow of the victim, etc. – came in with the brie and pâté of smoked eel. They imagined that of course I would want him executed. Of course I didn't want him set free; but the thing was, I could see that they were right, he was a disturbed person. Child of my parents, of California, of America, I could see they were right that he needed help. Was this goodness or apathy? I wondered what Roxy felt.

I liked the bland and benevolent faces of my countrymen, handsome as pilots or the men in jewelry ads. The accent of one's birthplace lingers in the mind and in the heart as it does in one's speech, said La Rochefoucauld.

It seems we all try to get beyond America – but something keeps pulling us back. Will I escape the magnetism, the undertow? I thought so, for a while at least, but I wasn't so sure about Roxy.

I had the thought that none of us would be eating pâté of smoked eel if we were in Santa Barbara. By now I had eaten eels, and snails, and tripe, and brains, and winkles and cockles, and oysters, and salsify, and cèpes, and little teeny birds plunged whole into pots of foie gras that you ate head and all. What was Tellman eating in his jail cell? What did people get to eat in Sarajevo?

In any case, I couldn't stay for the discussion, as I had promised to pick up new cases of donated Tampax and lipstick for Sarajevo, and then I was meeting Chester and Margeeve and the others for dinner. They were leaving tomorrow. Edgar had been in Zagreb since Sunday. I hoped my heart would not ache forever. I am not sure.

All of these Americans transplanted to France, they too probably had eaten those poor little birds – are they called greves? grebes? merles? What do the animal rights people say about them? The animal rights people disapprove of foie gras. Of the way the goose is forced to swallow grain, how it is stuffed down his gullet through a funnel, engorging his liver. What did I feel about *foie gras*? Are Americans still Americans when they are transplanted, or do they become something else, like, say, Lieutenant Calley, or like me, for that matter, a person without a country, planning to go to Zagreb, planning to lunch with an Under-Minister of Culture, planning to drink a lot of orange tisane, planning to really buckle down to studying French.